Traci Douglass is a *USA TODAY* bestselling romance author for Mills & Boon, Entangled Publishing and Tule Publishing. She writes sometimes funny, usually awkward, always emotional stories, about strong, quirky, wounded characters overcoming past adversity to find their Happily Ever After. She believes Love is Love is Love, and is grateful for every thread in her intricate brocade of happiness—though she rarely remembers everything. Imperfect Characters = Perfect HEAs. Connect with her through her website: tracidouglass.net.

Also by Traci Douglass

Finding Her Forever Family
A Mistletoe Kiss for the Single Dad
A Weekend with Her Fake Fiancé
Their Hot Hawaiian Fling
Neurosurgeon's Christmas to Remember

First Response in Florida miniseries

The Vet's Unexpected Hero
Her One-Night Secret

Available now

Discover more at millsandboon.co.uk.

THE VET'S UNEXPECTED HERO

TRACI DOUGLASS

HER ONE-NIGHT SECRET

TRACI DOUGLASS

MILLS & BOON

First Published in Great Britain 2021
by Mills & Boon, an imprint of HarperCollins*Publishers* Ltd,
1 London Bridge Street, London, SE1 9GF

www.harpercollins.co.uk

HarperCollins*Publishers*
1st Floor, Watermarque Building,
Ringsend Road, Dublin 4, Ireland

The Vet's Unexpected Hero © 2021 by Traci Douglass

Her One-Night Secret © 2021 by Traci Douglass

ISBN: 978-0-263-29764-5

05/21

MIX
Paper from
responsible sources
FSC™ C007454

Printed and bound in Spain
by CPI, Barcelona

THE VET'S
UNEXPECTED HERO

TRACI DOUGLASS

MILLS & BOON

To Charlotte, my editor extraordinaire,
who always has my back and helps make my stories
into something worth reading.
Thank you!

CHAPTER ONE

DISASTERS USUALLY HAD most people running away from danger. EMT Jackson Durand wasn't most people.

His rig stopped outside the ambulance bay doors at Key West General ER and Jackson hopped out the back, followed closely by his EMT partner, Ned. Jackson's adopted brother, Dr. Luis Durand, met them at the entrance ready to take on the case.

"Forty-one-year-old firefighter with Key West FD," Jackson said as he and Ned lowered the gurney from the back of the rig down to the ground. "Riding his motorcycle and thrown from the bike, no loss of consciousness on scene. Obvious open left femur fracture."

The patient on the gurney moaned loudly and tried to get up, but Jackson held him in place with a hand on his chest as they wheeled him into the ER and down a brightly lit hall to an available trauma bay, picking up nurses and techs as they went.

"Sir," Luis said, stepping in beside Jackson. "Can you tell me your name?"

The patient bucked as they transferred him from the gurney to the hospital bed and one of the nurses lifted the sheet covering his lower body to look at the wound. "Reed," the man on the gurney said. "What's wrong with my leg? It hurts so bad."

"Your leg is broken, sir." Luis placed his stethoscope on the man's chest and listened before continuing. "Pretty badly, I'm afraid. But we're going to take good care of you." He nodded to Jackson then took over his brother's position at the patient's bedside. "Okay, we've got a good airway here. Good breath sounds bilaterally. Sir, can you open your eyes again for me? Looks like you're getting drowsy. Reed, can you wiggle your left toes for me?"

The patient screamed then, writhing on the bed. "Argh! It hurts…it hurts. I can't… I can't. My leg hurts so bad."

"Blood pressure?" Luis asked the nurse across the table.

"Seventy over forty, Doc."

Jackson hid his wince, barely. He felt for the guy. With an open compound fracture of the femur like that, it had to be sheer agony, but they couldn't risk giving him any pain meds for fear of his blood pressure dropping even lower, which would cause even more problems, including death if he stopped breathing.

"Right," Luis said. "Let's give him six units of blood, stat."

Jackson and Ned cleared the room to allow the staff more room to work. While Ned took the gurney back to the rig, Jackson headed down the hall to the supply room to stock up on supplies before his shift ended. Along the way, he greeted staff as they passed by. He knew just about everyone here and had a well-earned reputation as the go-to guy when it came to EMT services in the Keys. He liked being the man with the plan and the popularity that went with it. Mainly, though, he liked the control. Hopefully his rep would earn him a coveted promotion soon; he just needed a chance to prove himself.

He entered the supply room and began to fill his kit with fresh gauze packs, elastic bandages, syringes, gloves, and Steri-Strips. The neatly ordered shelves were a perfect reflection on his brother, Luis, who was the head of this department. Thoughtful, quiet, efficient. Everything in its place and a place for everything. All equal. Yep. That all fit Luis Durand to a tee. The complete opposite of Jackson, who thrived on chaos, quick decisions and excitement. Always better to keep moving, keep going, because those who fell behind got left behind.

He'd learned that lesson the hard way.

"Hey," a nurse said, coming around the corner of the aisle where he stood. She was dressed in pink scrubs with a jacket covered in cartoon babies. OB floor. Jackson's gaze flicked to her face then back to the supplies he was sorting through. She was cute, maybe late twenties, Asian. He didn't remember her name, but from the expectant smile on her face, she obviously remembered his. Probably because they'd gone out, had a good time, maybe more. He had a reputation outside the medical field, too.

"Hey," he said, not meeting her gaze. He wasn't embarrassed about his flings. He only slept with women who knew the score. No strings, no complications. If they'd been together, then she'd gone into it with her eyes open, too. He grabbed a handful of alcohol wipes and shoved them into the outer pocket of his pack, ignoring the hot prickle of her stare on the side of his face.

When he didn't say anything more, she stepped closer and smiled, shaking her head. "You don't remember me, do you?"

"Of course I do," he said, concentrating on the zipper of his pack and thinking maybe it was time to get out of the game. Not settle down, because he didn't do relationships—get in too deep and all you ended up with was heartbreak and disappointment—but his thirtieth birthday was coming up soon, and frankly he was getting too old for this crap. Maybe he'd get a dog or something to live on the houseboat with him. He hazarded a side glance at the name tag on her jacket. "How could I forget you, Susie?"

Her snort rang loud in the quiet supply room. "And that proves my point. I'm Amy. Borrowed this jacket earlier because I was cold." Heat crept up his neck as he straightened, hiding his wince. "But don't worry. I'm not offended," she said, jovially. "We hooked up at the St. Patrick's Day party at Durand's earlier this year. The night's pretty blurry for me, too, since we'd both had way too much to drink. It's all good."

Right.

His adoptive parents owned one of the most popular bars in the touristy section of Key West, Durand's Duck Bill Pub. He'd had a lot of good times at that bar—a lot of forgotten nights, too. He flashed her a slow smile, hoping his charm might get him out of another sticky situation. "Ah. Yes, right. I do remember you now, Amy. You won the green beer contest and hung a T-shirt from the rafters."

She shook her head and laughed. "I lost the whiskey

duel and ended up having to kiss that gross leprechaun statue near the entrance. Nice try, though."

"Thanks." He winked and sidled past her. "Gotta go."

"Of course you do," she called as he walked out of the supply room fast. "Thanks for the memories."

"'Bye, Amy," he called back, glad to be out of the firing line. By the time he returned to the bustle of the ER, his brother was at the nurses' station barking orders into the phone to what Jackson assumed was the OR.

"Yes. Fireman thrown from his motorcycle with a known bad femur fracture. Suspected pelvic fracture. I'm also worried he may have an as-yet undiagnosed solid organ injury, perhaps liver or spleen, that's adding to the loss of blood. We'll need ortho to assist for the leg, but my primary concern right now is saving his life. Okay. Yes. I'll be up ASAP. Thank you."

"Another busy day in the neighborhood, huh?" Jackson moved in beside him at the counter and placed his refilled equipment pack at his feet. "You think he's going to make it?"

"I'm going to do everything I can to make sure he does," Luis said, heading toward the stairwell up to the third floor, only to be cut off by the man's family and fire crew. Jackson concentrated on filling out the requisition forms for his supplies while his brother did his best to put the new arrivals at ease. "Yes. Reed has got a bad leg fracture from the accident, and we're taking him to surgery now to repair it and also to make sure there's not more bleeding internally. If you have a seat in the waiting room, I'll be down as soon as I can with an update. I…"

His brother's voice trailed off and Jackson glanced up to see what had cause the rare occurrence. Luis was always well-spoken, always prepared, always on top of things. He had a mild case of Asperger's, so that kept him constantly thinking, constantly working through problems in his head that usually spilled out of his mouth as well. So, him going speechless was quite an event. But all Jackson saw were the same people as before. A middle-aged woman sobbing on the shoulder of a teenaged boy and girl, who he assumed were the patient's wife and kids. Behind them was Reed's fire crew in their uniforms, their fire truck parked outside the doors beside the ambulance, lights still blazing. Jackson recognized the firefighters, as they often went on the same runs as EMS, since many of them were trained as first responders as well. Bud Landry, John Cheeves and Stacy Williams. Luis definitely wasn't gay, so the guys were out as the source of Luis's sudden silence. Which left Stacy.

Blonde, twenty-seven or twenty-eight maybe. Pretty, in a natural, wholesome, beach bunny sort of way. Curvy and cute, but more than capable in the field and courageous as hell. Looks could definitely be deceiving in her case. Luis was staring at her like he'd seen a ghost.

Huh. Interesting. Maybe he'd been bitten by the love bug at last.

An overachiever in nearly every facet of his life except the personal, Luis pushed himself hard. Always working, always helping, always growing. He'd told Jackson once it was because his parents had died bringing him to the US from Cuba, sacrificed everything to give their son a better life. Luis felt obligated to live up to the legacy they'd given him, one of bravery and self-lessness, even if doing so was to his own detriment. It was the one area he and Jackson had in common, but for very different reasons.

Luis's past was rooted in affirmation and acceptance. Jackson's in abandonment.

His mother had left him behind at four years old with no explanation and no word since.

He had no idea why she'd given him up, just that she had left him, and deep down he knew he probably deserved it.

The nearby elevators dinged and broke Jackson out of his thoughts. Seemed to break Luis out of whatever spell he'd fallen under, too. He excused himself and shoved into the stairwell like his butt was on fire. Jackson went back to finishing up his blasted paperwork, pushing the painful past away.

Of all the aspects of his job, the bureaucracy was his least favorite. He much preferred being out on runs, saving lives, helping others, protecting those who needed it. In fact, protection was his calling, his reason for being. Plus, being an EMT meant he got in, got out, got on with the next patient, never getting too attached to any one person or case. Attachment—that's where you really got in trouble.

Because everyone left, sooner or later, once they saw the real, unworthy you.

"Dude, I'm going to take off," Ned said, clapping him on the shoulder as he walked by, jarring Jackson out of his thoughts. "You need anything from the rig before I go?"

"Nah, man. Thanks." Jackson planned to use the staff locker room downstairs to shower and change after his shift before heading to the latest meeting of the local emergency response team in the hospital conference room. He was incident commander for this one, and if things went well, it could lead to him landing the recently vacated regional director spot for the local ambulance authority.

"Oh, wait," Jackson said, initialing and signing on the dotted lines. "You can take this full pack back with you if want."

"Will do. I'm going to run down to the cafeteria and get a soda real quick first, then I'll be back to get it. Sure you don't want anything?" Ned asked as he walked over to the elevators.

"No. Thanks, man. Have a good rest of your shift." Jackson smiled over at his partner. If he got in and out of the showers fast enough, he'd grab a bite himself before the meeting. Coming off a twelve-hour rotation, he needed time to wind down, though, before thinking about a meal. "Take your time."

Jackson flipped to yet another sheet on his clipboard and started on the next form, only half listening to the drone of the TV in the waiting room behind him.

"Tropical Storm Mathilda is expected to strengthen into a major hurricane by the time it reaches the Gulf early next week. As of right now, projections are still vague as to exactly where the eyewall will make landfall, but we do expect it to at least brush the Keys on its way toward mainland USA."

Jackson sighed. Another early August day in southern Florida. They'd been having meetings off and on since the start of the hurricane season in May. Each week a few new faces appeared in the conference room, and the team was rounded out as conditions changed.

The incident commander's job was to coordinate all the different team members into a cohesive whole and direct their resources to the areas that needed them most during the crisis. Considering he'd worked as an EMT in Key West since leaving the coast guard four years ago, and had pretty much seen and heard it all, it was a task he was well prepared for. Plus, he loved what he did. But he also had more to contribute, and being named regional director would give him that opportunity.

Jackson dotted the last i and crossed the last t on his paperwork, then handed it back to the nurse behind the desk, just as a female voice behind him asked, "Excuse me. Can you tell me where the conference room is, please? I'm here for the ERT meeting."

He turned to see a petite, dark-haired woman with a huge, panting golden retriever at her side. The dog was almost as big as she was, with a goofy doggo grin on its face, tongue lolling, and a red therapy vest on its back. Jackson couldn't resist crouching to scratch the pup behind the ears. "Who's a good boy, huh?"

"His name is Sam, and he's working," the woman said, her tone edged with annoyance this time. "Directions, please? I don't want to be late."

Jackson glanced back up into her anxious dark eyes. He straightened and gave her a polite smile. "Sorry. I should've asked to pet him first. Come on. I'll show you the way." He stowed the pack for Ned with the nurse behind the desk then gestured for the woman to follow him. "You're way too early, though. Meeting doesn't start until three. It's only two now."

"I know." She moved around him, and the dog trotted obediently at her side. "I'd rather be early. I always like to be prepared."

They walked out of the ER and into a quiet corridor leading to the administrative wing. He gave her a side glance, their shoes squeaking on the shiny linoleum and the dog's leash jangling in time to the clatter of its nails on the floor. Trying to ease the awkward with humor, he joked, "Isn't that the Boy Scout motto? Always be prepared."

"Could be. I really wouldn't know." She stared straight ahead, her steps evenly measured to avoid all the cracks between tiles. Hmm. Her cheeks were pink, too, and he couldn't tell if it was because it was hot outside—almost ninety today—or if she was still mad he'd petted her dog. Either way, it was clear she wanted nothing to do with him.

At the end of the hall, they reached a doorway marked with a gold plaque that read Conference Room A. She gave a curt nod and finally faced him, though she kept her gaze fixed on the dog. "Thank you."

"Uh, sure." He slowly backed away, more intrigued than he cared to admit. People liked him. Women liked him a lot. Except for this one. She posed a puzzling challenge, and he did love a challenge. The list of new team members ran through his head as he tried to pinpoint her identity. "I'll see you later, then."

Confusion flickered across her pretty features, and she frowned. "Why?"

"I'll be in the ERT meeting, too. Jackson Durand, by the way. That's my name."

He waited for her to tell him hers, but she didn't. Just led her big old dog into the conference room, then closed the door behind her.

* * *

Lucy Miller took a seat on the far side of the large, empty table in the conference room and released her pent-up breath. Eyes closed, she repeated her mantra, the words her therapist had given her a few months earlier to lower her anxiety.

You can do this. You're in control.

Near her feet, Sam curled into a big ball and went to sleep, sighing deeply. She was exactly fifty-nine minutes early, and that was fine by her. Of course, a nice round number would've been better. Two hours. That had been her goal, but then she'd gotten way-laid by people in the ER and had to ask for directions and…ugh.

Her shoulders slumped, and her tote bag slipped down her arm into her lap.

No. It was fine. Everything was fine. She fought back against the voice in her head that whispered that without her routines, without her counting and control, everything would slip into chaos. That she was broken. That she wasn't capable of handling life or even the simplest tasks by herself. Those were lies. Fed to her by the people closest to her, the ones she should've been able to trust.

Her family and her fiancé. Well, ex-fiancé now.

Stupid Robert.

But she was capable. She was strong. She was self-reliant. That's what her therapist had said, and that's what she tried to believe.

Even if some days were harder than others.

Of course, being in an unfamiliar place made her issues worse, as did stressful situations and strange people. Normally, she tried to avoid all of it by staying safe and happy in her private animal sanctuary on Big Pine Key. Her medication helped, too, especially on days like today, when she forced herself to go out and meet her obligations, like volunteering with her therapy animals in the children's ward of Key West General. Today it was with Sam, but she also had a cockatoo named Bubba she brought along too sometimes. Bubba was molting at the moment, however, so not looking his best.

The blast of cold air from the vent above her head felt good on her heated cheeks, and she put her head back to enjoy it a bit. Getting here early, finding the seat she wanted—not too close to anyone else, and with a clear path to the exit—helped. As did the silence, the stillness. It was like having her own little nook where no one would bother her. Nice. She tipped her head forward again and looked down the table toward the front of the room. There was a window. And a plant. A whiteboard and a podium for the speakers.

She wouldn't be speaking, thank goodness. Honestly, she was only here as a favor to a friend at the local animal shelter. Her friend had said that during evacuations due to hurricanes, the local animal shelters often became overrun with pets left behind, and they needed her sanctuary to take in additional animals after the latest storm, Mathilda, blew through. They'd asked her about search and rescue, too, but she didn't have any trained dogs at the moment, only Sam. Her good buddy. The bestest boy.

Jackson Durand had been right about that, at least.

His handsome face flashed into her mind again. Strong, compelling, his smile warm and inviting.

Stay away, the alarm bells blared in her head.

No. Lucy wasn't looking for love or any other kind of relationship, not after Robert and his betrayal. Since breaking off her toxic engagement, she'd sworn off men—sworn off new connections of any kind, really—after escaping the controlling, manipulative clutches of those she'd left behind in Charleston.

Lucy took a deep breath to ease the coiling anxiety inside her those memories always brought, ready to strike at any moment. She'd trusted them to have her best interests at heart, only to find they wanted to keep her basically locked inside a cage, locked inside her disabilities, until she doubted everything, including her own ability to survive. Her chest squeezed with hurt, and her breath caught.

Focus on the numbers. The numbers make you feel better.

There'd been forty-seven steps from the time they'd left the ER to this conference room. She'd not stepped on one crack. That was good. A new record. Her OCD had her counting like that a lot. How many steps from one place to another, how many hairbrush strokes to untangle her hair each morning, how many keystrokes to fill up one new patient intake form for her animal clinic.

She'd gotten her doctorate in veterinary medicine just to prove her family and Robert wrong.

Well, that and she loved animals. They never lied. Never betrayed you. You could trust animals.

A few more people arrived, none of whom were Stacy Williams, the only other person she knew on the team. Lucy sat forward to fiddle in her tote bag, setting out her legal pad and pens just so. Then, restless and overstimulated, she pulled out a mirror to check her face. Still there. Still the same. Still "just so."

Honestly, living a life of "just so" was exhausting.

If she could've stopped, she would have, but the idea of not counting, not arranging, not giving in to her tics only made her anxiety worse, so...

No. It had been a hard-fought battle the last two years, first leaving Charleston, then moving to Key West, but she'd finally come to accept who she was, painful as it had been. She didn't need other people. She didn't need romance. She didn't need affection. All she needed was peace and quiet and space to live the life that was best for her. Alone. Because alone didn't hurt you or smother you or make you feel broken.

Being on her compound, with her animals, gave her a level of peace she'd never known before. And if she still got lonely some nights, well, that was a small price to pay for peace of mind.

Up until today, she'd hoped that peace of mind would stay forever, but then she'd heard the weather reports and— *Oh, boy.*

Any thought of the approaching tropical storm had those knots of tension inside her tightening. Which was silly. Storms and hurricanes were a part of life in this area of the world. She'd been warned about that when she'd bought her property. The previous owners had taken good precautions to prevent property damage as well, including storm shutters and structural reinforcements. But still...

Her throat constricted, and her pulse tripped.

If she lost her sanctuary, she wasn't sure what she'd do. She had to make sure it was safe, no matter what. So, she planned to stay there and ride out the storm. Didn't matter what the experts recommended or what Stacy thought she should do. She'd grown up in Charleston and they'd had plenty of hurricanes, even if her family's home there had been far from the coast. She could handle it. She wasn't going to budge. She'd protect the house, board up the windows, secure the pens, batten down the hatches. She'd moved down here to be brave, and that's what she was going to do.

You can do this. You're in control.

"There you are. Sorry I'm late," Stacy said, sitting down next to her at the table. "I saw you in the ER before with Jackson, then you disappeared on me. I thought maybe he'd worked his magic on you and stolen your heart. He's got a reputation as a player, you know?"

Lucy frowned, remembering the man who'd walked her here. He was gorgeous, she supposed, if you went for that whole tall and muscled type, with his smooth mocha skin and soulful green-gold eyes. Not that she'd noticed. Nope. The player part she could totally see, too. He'd been far too charming for his own good.

Stacy laughed as Sam turned excited circles in front of her. Everyone loved her dog, and the feeling was mutual. He was friendly and outgoing and gregarious. Basically, everything his owner wasn't. Lucy tugged once gently on the dog's leash to get him to sit, an odd ache in the pit of her stomach.

"How many people will be in this meeting?" Lucy asked as more and more arrivals filled the room. She resisted the urge to fiddle with her pens once again, and her lungs ached slightly as her anxiety spiked once more. Having Stacy there helped. Her best friend was one of the kindest, most generous, most loyal people

Lucy knew. She was beautiful, inside and out, and her son, Miguel was an angel, too. They visited her at the sanctuary on the weekends sometimes. Miguel was mildly autistic, and being with the animals helped him developmentally. In fact, Lucy was helping Stacy acquire a therapy dog for him from a trainer in Miami.

"Twenty, maybe thirty people," Stacy said, tucking a piece of sun-streaked blond hair that had come loose from her ponytail behind her ear. "I know busy places can be hard for you sometimes. They're hard for Miguel as well." She pulled out her phone and scowled down at the screen. "Sorry. They brought in one of the guys from my crew earlier to the ER."

"Oh gosh." Lucy's anxiety was tempered with concern. That explained the slight gray tinge to her friend's tanned complexion. "Is it serious?"

"Badly fractured leg, possibly some internal bleeding as well. He's in surgery now."

"What happened? Was it a fire?"

"No. This was Reed's day off. He was riding his motorcycle and went off the road." Stacy set her phone on the table, screen down. "They'll know more once he wakes up. If he wakes up."

"I'm so sorry."

Lucy had never been on a motorcycle. She never took unnecessary risks. They scared her too badly.

"Thanks." Stacy nodded, frowning. "His family is here now, waiting. Funny, isn't it? How one moment can change everything."

For some odd reason, she got the feeling her friend was talking about more than just a motorcycle accident. Lucy placed her hand on Stacy's atop the table. "Everything okay?"

"Yes. No. I don't know. Something else happened in the ER. I saw someone I didn't think I'd ever see again and now—"

"Hello, hello," a now-familiar voice said from the front of the room.

Lucy looked up to find Jackson Durand, freshly showered and changed, and her pulse tripped despite her wishes. She swallowed hard and grabbed the pen closest to her, tapping it on the table with relief.

Hurricane Mathilda might be on the way, but something told her this man was far more dangerous.

CHAPTER TWO

"RIGHT, SO, AS your incident commander, I'm officially calling this meeting of the Lower Keys Community Emergency Response Team for Tropical Storm Mathilda to order," Jackson said from behind the podium. "Let's start with Assistant Fire Chief Stacy Williams with an update on the training program for posthurricane cleanup volunteers in the area."

As Stacy moved to take over, Jackson refocused his attention on the woman he'd escorted here earlier. She was sitting in her seat, still tapping that pen, her big dog at her feet like a shield. She'd pushed her chair back slightly now, he noticed, and turned it to face the front of the room, giving him a view of her feet bouncing on the floor like she was excited or nervous. And sure, the impending storm got everyone's adrenaline pumping, but this situation was nothing out of the ordinary for this part of the world.

Jackson frowned. He'd been through countless storms growing up. It was part of being a Conch—the nickname people affectionately gave native Key Westerners. Watching his intriguing new stranger, though, had him thinking her fidgeting was something more. Given the way she always seemed to be fiddling with her pens or papers or whatever, he wondered if she had some kind of disorder—anxiety, OCD maybe, or both...

Luis sneaked in silently through the door then leaned against the wall beside Jackson. It wasn't like his brother to be late, but with the surgery on that motorcycle accident patient, it wasn't unexpected. He gave his brother a side glance, noticing again how he seemed transfixed by Stacy at the front of the room.

Concerned, Jackson whispered, "Everything okay?"

"What?" Luis started, then blinked several times, as if just then remembering where he was. He glanced over at Jackson, scowling before his usual professional mask slid back into place. "Fine. Just tired. And preoccupied by my case. What did I miss?"

"Nothing much. We just started," Jackson said, still not convinced there wasn't more going on.

Exhaustion went with being in the medical profession. In fact, Jackson was pretty sure it was at the top of the job description for both of them. Paramedics and doctors and nurses, especially those on the front lines in the emergency department, worked crazy shifts. And both Durand brothers pushed themselves to the limits every day. Jackson striving to prove himself worthy and Luis because he was basically superhuman. Okay, maybe that was exaggerating, but it certainly felt that way to Jackson sometimes. Two years older, Luis had been pushing himself for as long as Jackson had known him. Growing up together in their adopted household, having Luis to look up to was both a blessing and a curse. His older brother's lofty goals and selfless work gave Jackson an ever-shifting finish line to try to reach that kept him working harder, longer, faster, better—even if he'd never get to Luis's pinnacle. It was fine. Jackson strove to meet his own high standards and surpass the expectations of those around him, because maybe then he wouldn't get left behind.

And speaking of left behind...

"Who's the new person over there?" Jackson asked, hiking his chin toward the woman who'd been invading his thoughts for the past hour or so. "Do you know her?"

Before Luis could answer, Stacy said from the podium, "And I'd like to welcome my friend veterinarian Lucy Miller here today. She runs an animal sanctuary on Big Pine Key and will be assisting the local animal shelter in housing displaced animals after the storm. Everyone, say hello to Lucy."

Jackson watched as Lucy visibly withdrew into herself under the scrutiny, and he cringed inwardly for her. Stacy meant well, he was sure, but man, all that attention had to be excruciating for such an obvious introvert.

"You didn't tell me she would be here," Luis whispered.

Jackson was confused by the vehemence in his brother's voice. "Who? Stacy?"

He hadn't mentioned it because he didn't think it mattered. As far as he knew, Luis didn't know Stacy, but it was clear from his brother's expression he'd been wrong. Normally, he'd prod for more information about that, since any crack in his brother's perfect armor was a rare and powerful thing, but before he could do so, Stacy wrapped up her presentation.

"And with that, I'll turn things back over to IC Jackson Durand, who will update us on the EMS response plans for Hurricane Mathilda," she said.

Right. Time to get back to work.

Jackson jogged back up to the podium. "Thanks, Stacy. As you all know, EMTs are likely to be the first on the scene of a disaster. As per our usual protocol, we take charge of the incident and remain so until it's resolved or others who have legal authority assume responsibility. This won't change with Hurricane Mathilda. When EMTs arrive at the scene of an emergency related to this storm, we'll implement the incident command system listed in the binders before you. As incident commander, I've established our command post here at Key West General and will receive updates from all quadrants of our combined efforts and will then provide an assessment of the overall situation to local officials and media, identify response resources required and direct the on-scene response from here at our central ICP."

He'd served as a member of these teams for years now and knew the speech backward and forward, though this was the first time he was giving it as IC. It felt both surreal and super special. His chest swelled with pride and a pinch of hurt. Briefly, he wondered what his birth mom might think of him now, being in charge of such an important event. But then he shoved that thought aside quickly. She wouldn't know or care about his accomplishments, because she'd refused to have any contact with him for the last twenty-five-plus years. He finished his report, then turned the podium over to the chief of police to discuss law enforcement's preparations for the storm.

Good thing, too, since his attention kept returning

to Lucy Miller. The name suited her. Short, sweet and no-nonsense. She stared back at him, her dark eyes wide, her long hair tied back into a neat ponytail at the base of her neck with a light green scrunchie the exact same color as the top she was wearing. Her cheeks were flushed, and dark brows knit. She crossed her arms, fingers tapping on her skin, three times. Stop. Three more times.

Yep. Definitely something going on there.

"That's right isn't it, IC?" the police chief asked, and Jackson found himself at a loss.

Crap. He cleared his throat and stared down at the notes in front of him, trying to get his head back in the game. This wasn't like him. He was Mr. Efficiency. Mr. Two Steps Ahead of Everyone Else, because he had to be. Mr. Get the Job Done. This was ridiculous. He had important things to do here. Way more important than watching some woman he'd just met, no matter how attractive.

"Weather," Luis whispered helpfully from where he'd taken a seat at the table.

"Right. Current reports have Mathilda veering west of the Keys with only the possibility of some minor outer band involvement as she passes. Therefore, our current readiness level is staying at three. If the path of the storm changes however, we will update the status appropriately. Please keep your phones on and be ready to respond to any alerts. Also, remember that if the readiness level reaches one, all team members are required to shelter in place within the city limits of Key West for the duration, so prepare accordingly for that as well. Might not come to that, God willing, but better safe than sorry."

Jackson shuffled his notes, his gaze flicking back to Lucy again. She was chatting quietly with Stacy now, who'd taken a seat beside her at the table again, and Lucy smiled at something Stacy said. And man, what a smile that was. Like a sunbeam breaking through the clouds above. A good smile.

A beautiful smile.

His gut clenched, and he looked away fast. Nope. He frowned then shifted his attention to the cop's presentation. Jackson had no time for this. He was busy building his career. If he did well as IC, it could land him the regional director position, which would lead to more money, more prestige, better benefits and a bigger home, instead of the tiny houseboat he currently resided in. Not that his life was bad. It was fine. Good. But he'd never been one to settle for good, and Jackson wasn't about to start now, because the idea of staying put and committing to one person, heart and soul, scared the bejesus out of him. Besides, he'd been burning the candle at both ends for years for this opportunity. He was not about to blow it now over a woman.

He checked his watch. After the current speaker, there were closing remarks, then the meeting would be over and he could get back to work, back to life, back to not thinking about Lucy Miller with her dark eyes and sweet smile and distracting, irritating, intriguing issues.

Lucy sat through the meeting, taking notes as appropriate and doing her best not to think about the man watching her across the table like she was his new favorite science experiment. Dammit. She still couldn't believe Stacy had introduced her to the whole group like that without warning. She avoided the spotlight like most people avoided wasps' nests.

At least the meeting was over now, and people were clearing out. Sam whined from near her ankle, his tail thumping against her chair a mile a minute as passersby stopped to give him a pat on the head. Extrovert that he was, Sam loved it. And it helped divert attention from Lucy, so win-win.

Or most attention, she should say, as the man she'd done her best to ignore for the last hour slid into the seat beside her that Stacy had recently vacated.

"Nice to meet you, Lucy Miller," Jackson said, watching her with his mesmerizing gold-green gaze.

Heat prickled her cheeks, and she avoided looking at him. The fact he could sit there all composed and grinning after not telling her up front he was head of this whole thing made her want to kick him in the shin. Unfortunately, Sam was all over the guy, blocking her target.

Instead, she tried to kill him with kindness, keeping her voice polite and pleasant. "Did you need something?"

He didn't answer right away, and she finally gave in and looked at him. Big mistake. The glimmer of interest in his eyes, coupled with a hint of irritation, rattled her completely. Fresh anxiety bubbled inside her like lava, and to ease it, she picked up her purple pen and squeezed it tight.

Except disturbing the specific order she'd laid her items out in on the table always triggered her compulsions and…whoops. Here it came. Unable to stop herself, she glanced at the rest of her pens still lined up in a neat little row. Red, blue, black, green. Red goes first. Always, always, always. She used red the most. It made sense. If she used it the most, then it had to come first. Somewhere in her mind, she knew the voice in her head telling her this had nothing to do with reality and everything to do with her OCD, but she couldn't stop.

You can do this. You're in control.

Yes. She was in control of her condition. Not the other way around. If she wanted to move the stupid red pen, then she could. She had the power to move it...

"You all right, Lucy?" Jackson asked, his eyes narrowing. "You seem flustered."

She looked over at him, helplessness choking her throat. Because once her anxiety set in, her sole focus was on her pens. She'd taken her meds before coming here today, but then getting lost in the ER and the stress of the meeting had made her symptoms worse. She should've doubled up on her dose like her therapist had said. Next time she would.

Stupid Lucy. Poor, weak, broken Lucy.

"Hey..." Jackson leaned forward in his seat, uncrossing his long legs to rest his forearms on his knees. Sam took that as an invitation and immediately launched himself into the guy's lap, all sixty pounds of him. Soon, his face was covered with wet doggy kisses as he tried to see past the mass of fur in front of him.

"Oh God." The shock of it jarred Lucy out of her anxiety spiral at last, and she scrambled to get her errant pet off his lap. "I'm so sorry. He's usually much better behaved than this."

Jackson chuckled and shrugged, wiping the sleeve of his blue T-shirt over his face. "It's fine. I tend to have that effect on people, though usually it's women."

Lucy snorted, more as a stress reliever than anything. "Overconfident much?"

"Always," he countered, grinning. Then he leaned an elbow on the table, bumping her pens and scattering them.

He didn't do it on purpose. Lucy knew that, but it was still a battle for her not to freak out. Her first instinct was to straighten them out again, reorder them. Except she couldn't do so without touching him, because his elbow was right there. She took a deep breath.

"Okay?" he asked.

"Sure," she said, with far more enthusiasm than required.

Perfect.

If he noticed, at least he didn't say anything, thank goodness.

"I wanted to stop by and introduce myself properly, since we didn't get a chance to before the meeting." He held out his hand over her messy pens. "Jackson. Jackson Durand."

I don't care, I don't care, I don't care. My pens are out of order...

"Nice to meet you," she said.

Then it became too much and Lucy swiped her hand as quickly as possible over the pens, sorting them, straightening them, grazing his elbow in the process. She ignored his hand completely.

Jackson blinked then sat back, watching her closely. "So, you're a vet?"

"That's right." Lucy concentrated on the pens and not him, afraid of what she'd see in his eyes. "Why?"

"No reason." He shrugged. "I could've handed those to you."

"Handed me what?" Her mind whirled with competing demands. First, her OCD wanted her to line up those damned pens again. Second, her reasonable side told her to let it go and talk to the handsome man beside her. Unfortunately, her OCD won, so she placed her pens back on the table again, lining them each up a second time with the edge. Red, blue, black, green, purple. Evenly spaced. Just so.

She kept her eyes glued to her task, particularly the red pen screaming at her to get the heck out of there and get back to her sanctuary. This whole meeting had messed with her schedule, big-time. Lucy lived by her schedule. Each day, she wrote out a list and crossed every item off before she was done. Today had included cleaning out Bubba's cage, then there was checking on Mitzi's egg mound and, as always, feeding and walking Sam. Now she'd have to add making sure she had enough supplies to last for a few days in case the storm was worse than predicted, because she sure as heck wasn't leaving her compound, rules or not and...

Speaking of Sam... She looked up at Jackson. "He's trained to be a therapy dog. He knows better than to jump up on people like that."

"Really. It's okay. I'm used to it. Like I said, some people find me irresistible." Jackson gave her a charmingly crooked, wry smile she felt all the way to her toes.

Oh boy. Not good. Not good at all.

Lucy needed something, anything, to distract herself from her unwanted awareness of this man. "Fine. Whatever. Good for you if people find you irresistible. I don't. I mean, there's nothing wrong with you, but—"

He crossed his arms, his smile widening as she babbled away like an idiot.

Her cheeks felt hotter than Hades now, and the more he teased her, the more frazzled she got. "What I'm trying to say is you are who you are, and I am who I am, and people don't change who they are."

God, where had *that* come from?

Jackson studied her, his expression serious. "Okay. But what if they're a jerk?"

"Oh, well…" Flustered, Lucy forgot to be nervous and just laughed, easing some of her inner tension. She shrugged and stared down at her toes. "Point taken."

"Well, it was nice to meet you, Lucy Miller," he said, clasping his hands atop the table. Those were nice hands. Long, tapered fingers, well-kept nails. Strong hands. Capable hands. He was a paramedic, after all. He saved people. A small spark of warmth burst inside her. He'd certainly saved her just now, from dying from terminal embarrassment. "I wish I'd known earlier you were going to be here. I'd have brought a copy of the required binder with the emergency response team plan for you. I don't have a spare with me now, but if you give me your address, I'm happy to run one by your place on Big Pine Key tomorrow. It's my day off."

"Oh…uh…" Sitting beside him in the conference room was disturbing enough to her equilibrium. The thought of him at her compound had her quaking in her tennis shoes. "That's okay. Give it to Stacy and she can bring it to me. Or I can swing by the hospital and pick it up." She pulled a clean sheet of paper from her legal pad and picked up her red pen. "Just tell me what time would be best."

Jackson frowned. "It's really no problem, and it would be more convenient for me to drop it off. I'll be in your area, anyway. Unless there's some reason you don't want me there?"

An awkward silence fell between them as they studied each other.

She couldn't help wondering what it might feel like to slide her fingers through his short black hair, learning its texture and temperament. The fluorescent overhead lights gleamed off his high cheekbones and there was a hint of dark stubble on his firm jaw. His lips were full and firm, with a slight tip to the outer corners that gave him a perpetual smirk, like everything amused him. Maybe it did.

"Don't worry, I won't overstay my welcome. Promise. I'll google your address," he said at last. Jackson stood and picked up his papers but didn't hold out his hand this time. The smile was there again, though, still charming, too. "See you tomorrow, Lucy Miller."

Her heart stumbled a bit before racing forward.

"Uh, yeah." Lucy pushed to her feet as well, staring at his retreating back. Wide shoulders, narrow waist, trim hips. She forced her attention back to gathering her own supplies as Sam whined at her feet, panting up at her with his lopsided doggy grin as if telling her to get a move on already. "All right, mister. We're going."

CHAPTER THREE

THE NEXT AFTERNOON, Lucy stood in the small clinic building on her compound in Big Key Pine, tending to Bubba the cockatoo. He was approximately fifteen years old and nearly bald at the moment, except for the still magnificent crown atop his head. His previous owner had died shortly after Lucy had opened her sanctuary, and her good friend and fellow vet on the island, Dr. Dave, had felt she and Bubba might be a good fit.

Said owner had also loved music, apparently, since Bubba had a tendency to quote lyrics at the most inappropriate times. "Come on, Bubba. Take your medicine. There you go. There's a pretty boy, yes. Eat that orange wedge. Yes. Good birdie."

Sam sat near her feet, whining, and Lucy rolled her eyes. "You don't get oranges. And you just had a treat, anyway."

Bubba eyed her warily but continued munching on the orange wedge clutched in his foot with the pill tucked safely inside, bobbing his head as the door to her clinic banged opened and Jackson backed in.

Usually her work focused her and cleared her head, keeping her anxiety at bay like nothing else. But one look at Jackson and her nerves went haywire again.

Bubba seemed to sense her disquiet, because he began dancing back and forth on his perch, what was left of the orange slice stuck to the side of his beak, crooning, "Swee-ee-ee-t emo-o-o-o-tion…"

"It's okay," she said to soothe the bird as much as herself as her trusty canine companion trotted across the room to greet the new arrivals enthusiastically. "It's going to be okay."

She did not have emotions for Jackson Durand, sweet or otherwise, because she never let anyone that close. Not anymore. Lucy raised her chin and snapped her fingers, bringing Sam back to her side. "You're late."

"Sorry. I know." He turned then, the binder he'd promised tucked under one arm and a squirming, mewling bundle wrapped in a beach towel filling his hands. "But I ran into a bit of a problem."

Lucy frowned. "What's going on? What is that?"

He rushed over and set the bundle carefully on her exam table. "I was on my way back here from Miami and found this little guy on the side of the highway."

Her veterinary training took over, immediately drowning out everything else, including her thundering pulse from Jackson's closeness. "Right." She gestured for him to stay put, then pulled on a pair of gloves. "Any idea what happened?"

"Not sure. Like I said, I was coming back from the mainland and spotted something squirming out of the corner of my eye near the median. When I realized what it was, I had to stop. I was on my way here, so figured you might be able to help."

"I'm glad you did." Carefully, she unwrapped the towel from around her new arrival and took stock of the situation. Small Bengal kitten. Male. Eyes barely open. Lethargic. Underweight. Five, maybe six weeks old. Trembling. Back left leg severed below the knee. Wound clotting and not actively bleeding.

"He must've got caught in traffic." Or been thrown out by careless owners. Biting the inside of her cheek, Lucy forced her anger down. "Stand here with him while I get my supplies, please."

"Sure thing," Jackson said, stroking the kitten's matted fur with a finger as he crooned softly to him.

Lucy grabbed a saline IV bag and popped it into the microwave nearby she'd installed for this purpose. While the saline solution heated, she pulled out a warming blanket and plugged it in before sliding it under, then wrapping it around, the tiny feline. Finally, she snatched an otoscope from the front pocket of her denim overalls and leaned over to look in the kitten's ears. Next she checked its mouth. The gums were pale, but its teeth looked fine. Checked its temperature, too. Low, but not nearly as down as she'd hoped.

The way some people treated animals was reprehensible. By the look of that leg, the poor thing had probably been crushed by a tire, or perhaps caught in a trap. Wouldn't be the first time she'd seen that around here. Unfortunately, it was an all-too-common occurrence in these parts, with alligators everywhere. In fact, the sanctuary's longest resident had been the victim of the same kind of trap. It was inhumane.

Lucy put the used thermometer in the sink for sterilizing, then rolled her tense shoulders to relax them. Mistreatment of any kind made her furious.

Maybe that was why she'd built such a strong barrier around her heart. Robert might not have hurt her physically, but he'd abused her heart and her trust, and for that, she couldn't forgive him. It was because of him she wouldn't let anyone else near again. Opening up her emotions meant letting the good in with the bad, so it was better just to not care at all. At least where humans were concerned. With animals, it was a whole different ball game.

She shoved the buds of her stethoscope in her ears and listened to the kitten's heart, lungs and abdomen. Nothing worrisome. BP was good, too. The little guy lifted his head and whimpered when Lucy tried to better examine the leg.

"I know, sweetie. It hurts, huh? I'll get you something for that in a moment, I promise. I'll make it all better." She could feel Jackson's stare on her, hot and heavy on her prickling skin, but she ignored him as best she could. She wasn't sure why she was so aware of him, but she didn't like it one bit.

Lucy focused on her patient instead. The wound had clotted, and though it didn't look infected, the kitten would need surgery to amputate the rest of the leg at the hip joint. First, though, she had to make sure the animal stayed stable enough to get an IV into him for fluids and antibiotics.

Straightening, Lucy met Jackson's gaze. "He's in decent condition for now, which is shocking given what you told me. If you hadn't come along when you did, I doubt the kitten would have survived much longer. His vitals are a little low, but good. If he's doing this well in a couple of hours, my colleague, Dr. Dave, whose office is just down the road, can do surgery to remove the rest of the leg. The kitten will then need to stay with me for a few more nights for monitoring."

Jackson frowned. "Why can't you do the surgery here?"

"Normally, I would, but with the hurricane coming, my supply shipment is delayed and I don't have some of the things I need." Lucy sighed. "Dr. Dave is very good. He was my mentor. He'll take good care of the kitten for you. And we have an agreement on the prices, because of the sanctuary."

"I don't care about the cost." Jackson rubbed his hand over the top of his short hair. "Do whatever you need to do to save him. I'll make it work."

The fact he cared so much about a creature he'd just found made Lucy's chest squeeze with something far too close to affection toward him. No. No, no, no. She didn't want to care about Jackson Durand. Been there. Done that. Had the emotional scars to prove it.

He shuffled his feet then shoved his hands into the pockets of his jeans. "He'll be okay with three legs, right? I mean, humans do fine getting around, but I don't know much about—"

Lucy nodded. "He's young. He'll adapt. There'll be a healing period and adjustment involved, of course."

"Well, little guy. Looks like you're in the best possible hands. Yes, you are." Jackson stroked the kitten's head, and the little guy sure liked what he was doing. His tail limply thumped the table, and he watched Jackson with trusting eyes. A bond seemed to have formed already. Lucy had learned to trust her animals' intuition when it came to people, but there was still something about Jackson Durand that made her nervous. She didn't want to think too hard about why.

"Do you want to keep him afterward?" she asked him.

"Oh." Jackson looked up, seemingly startled by her question. "I don't… I'm not sure I should…" He took a

deep breath. "With my work hours, I'm not home a lot."
He frowned down at the kitten again. "I've never had a
cat before, either. But I guess if no one else wants him,
I could take him for a while. Like a foster situation."

"Do you want to name him then?"

"Oh. Um…"

She sighed. "You don't have to."

That line between his dark brows deepened for a
second, then he tilted his head and smiled. "How about
King? You know, because he has those stripes like a
tiger?"

"Sure." Lucy got busy inserting an IV filled with
warm saline to bring the kitten's temperature up
slightly and started antibiotics. Then she drew some
blood and ran a CBC to check platelets before checking her new patient's vitals again. The little guy took it
in stride. Pleased the kitten was doing well, she pulled
out her cell phone to call the neighboring clinic.

While Jackson looked around, she spoke with Dr.
Dave.

"Hi. Yeah, I've got a surgical case for you. Kitten
requiring an amputation. Can you work him in before
the storm hits? Yes, he's stable. Okay. Great. I'll have
him there in a bit. Thanks. 'Bye."

She tracked Jackson around the small space as she
spoke to her colleague, unable to keep from taking
in his tall, muscled form. He really was handsome. If
you went for that type. Then again, Robert had been
handsome, too, and look where that had gotten her.
Trapped in a relationship where her fiancé, the man
who was supposed to have her best interests at heart,
had only loved her when she was totally dependent on
him. Nope. Lucy had learned not to fall for pretty. No

matter how charming and kind that package might be. To distract herself, she turned away to check on her new patient again, giving the kitten a scratch behind the ears and earning a mewl of happiness.

"King, are you ready to go see Dr. Dave? He'll take good care of you."

Two more mewls.

Lucy looked over at Jackson next, locking gazes with those mesmerizing eyes again. Her pulse tripped, and she swallowed hard. Seriously, she needed to get over that and quick. "My colleague can take him now if we can get King there soon." She stroked the kitten's back. "If you drive, I'll hold him and give you directions."

"Okay." Jackson smiled, and Lucy forgot to breathe. Dammit. Not good. Not good at all.

While Lucy went into the back with Dr. Dave, Jackson stood in the vet clinic trying to figure out exactly what the hell had possessed him to agree to foster a kitten—let alone one that would soon have three legs. He didn't know much about it but was pretty sure nursing King back to health would take a while, and he wasn't sure he'd have the time to commit to it, what with the current IC job and the cleanup efforts after Mathilda moved through. Then there was the regional director position. If he got the promotion, it would mean even more time away from home. And if he didn't get it, well…he didn't want to think about that. It was too important to him to fail. End of story.

Chest itching inside, he turned to inspect a rack full of dog toys and leashes, none of which would apply to his situation. Honestly, he was restless. Had been since he'd left the courthouse in Miami-Dade County, where he'd gone to pick up the results of his DNA testing. Not for a disease or anything like that. It was just one more effort to try to figure out who he really was and the identity of his birth mother. There was a woman there who specialized in tracking down hard-to-find people, so he thought he'd give it a try. After all these years, he probably should just leave it, not care anymore. His birth mom obviously hadn't, seeing as how she'd never tried to contact him in all this time.

Still, there was a hole inside him that nothing seemed to be able to fill, a gaping pit that he'd tried to patch on his own by always staying busy, always doing for others, like maybe that might improve his worthiness somehow. Prove he was worth keeping, worth staying around for…

Stupid, Jackson. So damned stupid.

He moved on down the wall to the cat toys. Brightly colored things with feathers and bells and squeakers. He picked up what looked like a stuffed mouse and jingled it near his ear. Silly thing.

Jackson placed it in a basket to buy then kept looking. He hadn't lied to Lucy. He worked a lot. Took on extra shifts. Not just for the overtime but for the experience. More hours logged looked good on his record and, hopefully, gave him a leg up when it came to promotion time.

Not an overachiever by nature, like Luis, Jackson still had ambitions—and that hole inside to fill—and at the moment he couldn't square a new pet with all that. Same way he couldn't quite square the calm, collected, curious Lucy he'd seen in her clinic just now with the fidgeting, flustered woman from the day before.

Sighing, Jackson moved on to the food. Wet, dry, mixed. He had no idea what a kitten that little would eat. Formula, maybe? He should probably ask Lucy. And yeah, he was going to keep it, at least for a while, because that's what he'd said he would do. And because he knew the pain of being left behind. Besides, Jackson Durand never went back on his word.

Just then, an exam room door opened in the back and voices drifted out. Lucy and Dr. Dave, he assumed. The guy had seemed nice enough when she'd introduced them, his handshake solid and strong. He was maybe late fifties with the tanned, sun-weathered face of a true Conch.

Turning around, he spotted Lucy walking with Dr. Dave from the exam room, deep in conversation.

The first words that had popped into his mind yesterday when he'd met her had been *buttoned-up*, *locked down* and *repressed*. All sharp edges and nervous tics. Now, though, seeing her laughing and talking with Dr. Dave, the same way she'd been with her friend Stacy during the ERT meeting, had him shaking off an unwanted shock of awareness.

Or maybe that was exhaustion. Yesterday had ended three back-to-back twelve-hour shifts, and after today he was staring down another long run of another twenty-four hours on call, and that was even before Hurricane Mathilda arrived. Afterward there would be cleanup and rebuilding and...

Because, oh yeah, the National Weather Service had upgraded the tropical storm to hurricane status the night before. Which meant he'd then upgraded the readiness level of the ERT to two, with the trajectory of the storm altering slightly overnight and bringing it within closer range of the Keys. He needed to tell Lucy that as well.

His inner tension notched higher as she pointed toward him then smiled.

No. Stop it. He didn't want to be interested in Lucy Miller that way. Didn't want to think about her cute grin or how he'd gotten a whiff of her flowery, clean scent back at the clinic when they'd stood side by side at that exam table. And he especially didn't want to feel that warm, fuzzy feeling inside because she gave shelter to animals no one else wanted, like bald parrots or orphaned kittens.

She walked out now to join him at the counter. "Dr. Dave is going to start working on King now."

"Good." He paid the receptionist for the stuff in his basket then walked back out to his truck with Lucy. "How long will it take?"

"An hour, maybe two," she said as she opened the passenger side door of his old truck and climbed in. He walked around the front and got in behind the wheel then started the engine while she buckled her seat belt. "Dr. Dave will text me when it's over. And I'll pick him up for you tomorrow."

"Or," Jackson said, backing out of his spot, his arm across the seats as he peered over his shoulder. He did his best not to notice the fact his fingers had brushed against her bare shoulder when he'd done so, or how she'd shivered and pulled away from his touch. Lord, he needed to get his head in the game and out of fantasyland already. "We could grab a bite to eat while he's in surgery and I can see for myself how he does when it's over. You know, in case anything goes wrong."

He signaled then turned out of the lot back onto Palmetto Avenue, still berating himself for asking. God, what was up with him? The sooner he got out of here, the sooner he could get back to his houseboat and get some sleep. But there he was, asking her to lunch while heading south back to her place.

"Um…no. I'm not hungry." She frowned as she picked through the bag of things he'd bought for King. Her stomach rumbled loudly, and her scowl darkened.

Jackson gave her a side glance and a grin. "Liar."

"I can eat back at home."

"Or you could eat with me." He wasn't even sure why he was being so persistent about this, just that he wasn't ready to leave here yet. Because of the kitten. That's the excuse he was going with, anyway. "Come on. One meal. My treat."

Lucy looked like she wanted to argue, but he turned into the parking lot of a local beachside pub and cut the engine before she could stop him.

"Just lunch. That's all." He got out and walked around to open her door for her. "Please. It would make me feel better to see for myself King made it through the surgery all right. Then I'll go home."

She opened her mouth, closed it, then opened it again. Unbuckled her seat belt and finally got out, not looking at him. She was still dressed in baggy denim overalls, but she could've been wearing the crown jewels, given her queenly posture and rigid attitude. "Fine. One meal. And I can pay for myself."

"I'm sure you can." He closed the truck door after her and bit back a smile. "But I'm a gentleman and I invited you, so I'll pay."

"Really?" She gave him a quick side glance. "Stacy said you were a player."

Stunned, Jackson stood there blinking for a moment as Lucy walked away.

He needed to have a talk with Stacy, apparently.

Once they got inside, the hostess seated them at a table on the outside deck overlooking the marina. The air smelled of sea and deep-fried food with a touch of alcohol from the bar inside. The call of seagulls filled the air, and the silly birds landed on the railings and strutted on the deck, no qualms about begging for food. It was an atmosphere Jackson was familiar with, having grown up working in and around his parents' pub in Key West.

A server came by and took their drink order—iced tea for him and water with lemon for Lucy—then gave them menus before departing. He hid a smile as Lucy pulled a disinfectant wipe from her bag and wiped down her side of the table and her seat before thoroughly cleaning her menu. Then she rearranged the silverware and napkin before finally looking at the specials for the day.

"Know what you're going to have?" he asked, having decided on a grilled chicken salad himself.

Usually these oceanfront places were known for their seafood, but he'd been spoiled by his parents' Cuban recipes and had never found any others that compared, so he stuck with greens. He needed to eat something healthy anyway, after all the vending machine and cafeteria food he'd grabbed between runs.

Lucy frowned over at him from atop her menu. "I don't know. I've never been here before."

"Seriously? You live in Big Pine Key and you've never eaten at this place?"

"No." She shook her head and set the menu aside.

"I usually cook at home. Or sometimes I order out and have food delivered, but always from the same place close to my house."

"Hmm." He was going to ask more, but the server arrived with their drinks and took their orders, interrupting him. Lucy ended up getting the same salad he did, minus the chicken and with the dressing and most of the toppings on the side. Basically, a bowl of plain lettuce with things she could put on herself. A mini salad bar. He waited while she fiddled with her glass and carefully removed the lemon wedge from the side, squeezing it into her water before placing it in her napkin and rolling it up into a tiny sealed packet then setting it in the far corner of the table. It was quite a production.

"So…" he said at last, breaking the awkward silence.

"So." Lucy blinked down at her hands in her lap. Finally, she sighed and looked up at him, her expression serious. "I have a condition."

"Sorry?" He sipped his tea and frowned, trying to catch up with her mind. He suspected he already knew what she was going to say but was surprised she'd just come out with it like that. Then again, bluntness could be a symptom of certain disorders like autism or OCD. Impulsivity, too. He tried to make light of it, as humor was always his fallback when things got too heavy. "Nothing fatal, I hope."

His joke fell flatter than her stare. "Obsessive-compulsive disorder."

"Oh. Okay." He sat back as the waitress delivered their salads. Nothing fancy, just a classic grilled chicken salad. Hard to go wrong there. He poured on his dressing while Lucy arranged her silverware yet again then set about picking through her food, removing anything that looked suspicious. Luis used to sort his candy by color because some of them were better than others, he said, but he'd gradually grown out of it as he'd gotten older, finding other, more socially acceptable outlets for that energy. Things like traveling abroad on mission trips to help the underprivileged.

Jackson started eating while she was still futzing with her lettuce. "That must be tough."

"It's fine. I've always been this way, so I've nothing to compare it to."

"I guess that's true." Jackson hailed the server for an extra napkin, waiting until they were alone again before continuing. "I noticed some tics at the meeting yesterday."

She froze. "What?"

"With your pens. Needing them in the right order. And when you walked down the hall, you didn't step on any cracks." He smiled. "Oh, and the tapping, with your fingers or your pen. Always in threes."

Her cheeks pinkened, and she swallowed hard. "How do you know about that?"

"I observe people. It's what I do. Plus, my brother has a mild case of Asperger's."

"Your brother?"

"Yeah. Dr. Luis Durand? I think you might know him from the hospital, or the meeting yesterday. Runs the ER at Key West General."

"Oh. Right. Yes, I know him," she said, glancing up at him. "You don't look anything like him."

"I'm handsomer." At his teasing, her cheeks got even redder if that were possible, and he quickly added, "I'm joking. Sorry. We're both adopted."

"Oh." Lucy took a small bite of salad, chewing slowly before swallowing. "You're a paramedic."

"Yep."

"And watching people is important in your job?" Her dubious tone made him chuckle.

"Of course." He ate another bite of salad, realizing it was actually better than he'd imagined. The creamy ranch dressing was homemade and garlicky without being overpowering. And the grilled chicken had a spicy coating, not quite Cajun, but close. The cool, crisp romaine was its perfect complement. "You can't properly treat a patient without understanding them. Medicine is about more than just diagnosing an illness."

She took that in a moment before going back to her salad sorting. "I suppose it is."

"Take your vet work, for example," Jackson went on. He probably should've just shut up, but for some reason he couldn't. Now that he had Lucy here and talking, he wanted to know more about her. Like a puzzle he needed to figure out. "When I brought King in today, you could've just stuck in an IV and taken him off to surgery, but you spent time comforting the little guy and getting to know him first. You established a connection."

Lucy gave a small flinch at that last word. Intrigued, he followed that trail farther.

"Must be hard, running a sanctuary. You must see all kinds of horrible things."

"Sometimes. But caring for those others have cast aside is also the most rewarding thing I've ever done. Those animals need me, and I won't let them down.

I provide them with a better life, for whatever time they have left."

"Admirable. Really." He wiped his mouth then pushed his empty bowl aside, ignoring the zing of warmth her words had caused inside him. She was talking about animals, not people, being cast aside. *It's not about you, dude.* Considering their brisk interactions yesterday and today, she wouldn't care if Jackson got cast off a pier, let alone left behind by his birth mother. Not that he'd be telling her about that. He didn't share that with anyone.

"Must give you a sense of control, too," he said, desperate to get his errant thought back on track. "Running your own little universe on that compound."

Her astonished expression made him laugh, breaking his inner tension. His shoulders relaxed and he could breathe again. Jackson shrugged. "Like I said, I'm familiar with OCD and its side effects."

"Right." She ate a few more bites before speaking again. "The few times I've encountered Dr. Durand when I'm at the hospital visiting the children's ward, he always seems friendly and supportive of me and my therapy animals. He's a good man."

"The best I've ever met," Jackson said with confidence. "And not just because he's my brother."

"Why?"

"Why what?"

"Why do you think he's the best man?" Lucy sipped of her water, narrowing her pretty brown eyes on him. "And you said you're adopted. What about your birth parents? Are they dead?"

"Wow." His brows rose. "Okay."

She blushed harder and lowered her gaze. "Sorry. I don't mean to blurt things out like that."

He chuckled. "It's…interesting. Nothing wrong with being blunt."

Lucy's frowned deepened. "Most people don't like it. Robert always used to keep me at home, away from people most times, because of it."

"Hmm." Jackson narrowed his gaze. "Well, I don't know this Robert guy, but he sounds terrible. And it's your lucky day, because I'm not most people." Jackson winked, enjoying how she got all flustered way more than he should.

What the hell am I doing? He had no business flirting with Lucy Miller. She obviously had a lot of stuff of her own to work through, and he wasn't looking to get involved with anyone, anyway. Flings, that's all he did these days. And from what he'd seen of her so far, Lucy was not the one-night-stand kind of gal.

He'd invited her to lunch because he'd needed to eat and to be polite. He should leave it at that.

Except something about her kept reeling him in closer, like a marlin on a hook. Kept drawing him deeper into curiosity about who she was and why she was the way she was, beyond her condition. Lucy Miller had walked into his life, quite literally, the day before, and that had to mean something. He didn't believe in coincidence. And he wasn't sure why exactly, but he felt compelled to find out.

"We should go," she said, pushing her half-finished plate away abruptly.

"You're not done eating yet." He sat back and

crossed his arms. "And King's still got a ways to go before he's out of surgery. Plus, I'm your ride. I'll wait."

"Then I'll walk." She picked up a breadstick and bit off the end. "I assure you, I'm used to being on my own."

"I'm sure you are." She'd mentioned this Robert guy, who'd kept her at home. He wasn't sure who the guy was or what his deal had been, but he didn't like him already. And as a man who kept his own distance from people, at least emotionally, he knew there was a story there, but he didn't want to push too hard. After all, this was one lunch, between people who'd go back to being strangers soon enough. Honestly, he should already be on his way back to Key West to wait on a text from her about the kitten. He could've used his day off to relax, catching up on some reading, maybe clean his houseboat.

None of that moved his butt out of the chair, though. "It's fine. I've got nowhere else to be."

Lucy kept chewing her breadstick, her sigh full of reluctant acceptance. "It doesn't bother you?"

"What?"

"My OCD?"

"Should it?" He'd grown up around Luis and worked around people with mental disorders all the time— nothing new there.

She shrugged. "Most people run the other way when they learn about my issues. Or else they feel like they need to take care of me. I'm not broken. I don't need to be fixed. I'm not an invalid."

"Understood." He snorted. "But did you ever consider that maybe they just want to help?"

"I don't need help, either." She gave him a steely look. "And I don't need your pity."

"I don't pity you."

"Good." She placed her napkin on the table then stood. "I'd like to go back to my compound now."

"Sure." Jackson paid the server then walked with her back out to his truck. The breeze had picked up, but it was still sunny and humid. More seagulls cried and swooped through the sky, looking for trash people had dropped. Another perfect day in paradise. Hard to believe this could all change soon when the storm moved in.

The short drive back to her place was quiet, until he pulled up at the rear of her compound, instead of the main gate. It was the way he'd come in earlier, too.

"Thank you for lunch," Lucy said, clambering out of the truck. "I'll text you with an update as soon as King comes out of surgery." She pulled out her phone. "What's your number?"

"My number's listed on the team contact page of the binder I dropped off earlier."

"Got it." Lucy started to close the door, but Jackson stopped her.

"Hey. I need to let you know, we moved to readiness level two today."

"And that means what?" she asked, peeking back into the truck at him.

"Read the binder," he said, grinning. "If we get to level one, you'll need to come into Key West for the duration. I don't expect things to get that bad, though. All the forecasts are currently taking Mathilda well past the Keys, so we should just get a brush of the outer bands at the most. Rain and a bit of wind. That's about it." He hiked his chin. "And thanks for taking care of King. I'll wait for your text."

CHAPTER FOUR

"HEY, CAROL. HOW are you doing? You look great," Jackson said the following Friday. The retirement village where the woman and her husband lived on Key West was a frequent stop for the EMTs. He set his med pack on the floor of their small, tidy condo and crouched by the lady's bedside. "Why are we here today?"

"She ate kung pao something or other," her husband, Vic, said from his rocking chair in the corner. "Told her not to touch that stuff."

"Eh…" Carol waved dismissively at her husband. "Get outta here."

Her Bronx accent was strong today, and Jackson bit back a grin. "You know all that salt will get you every time with your high blood pressure, Carol."

She gave him a pouty look. "I didn't have that much."

"Well, in your case, with your heart problems, any amount is too much," Ned chimed in from the other side of the bed, where he was getting out a cuff and stethoscope to check her vitals. He gave Jackson a side look then grinned. "I think you just wanted to see us again."

"You're not wrong." The older lady shot Jackson a sly smile. "Why aren't you guys married yet? Are you and he a couple?"

"What?" Jackson shook his head. "No. I'm not gay. Neither is Ned, that I know of. Not that there's anything wrong with that."

"Of course there's not," Vic said, his chair squeaking as he rocked slowly. "Our son's gay."

"Pressure's high. One eighty over one hundred," Ned said, pulling out his earpieces, then pressed a finger to each of her swollen ankles. "Two-plus pitting edema bilateral lower extremities." He looked up at Carol. "You're going to need a shot of Lasix, honey. Same as before. You're retaining fluids again because of all the salt in that food."

She sighed. "Fine. I know what that medication is. You don't have to tell me."

"Don't get mad at us," Jackson said, drawing up the injection. The diuretic would help flush out her system. Her attitude, however, was here to stay. He hoped that if he was blessed enough to reach the ripe old age of eighty-eight, like Carol, he'd be that feisty, too. He glanced over at her husband, Vic, as he tapped the syringe to get the air bubbles out. "Whose idea was it to get the food?"

Vic shrugged. "Hers, but I don't blame her. I mean, you have to indulge once in a while, right? Life's too short."

"True." Jackson finished drawing up her meds then grabbed an alcohol pad to clean Carol's arm before giving her the injection. When he was done, he shoved the used needle into a portable red biohazard container then stripped off his gloves before putting a bandage on her arm. "How long have you guys been married again?"

"Fifty-nine years," Carol said.

"Seems twice as long," Vic said.

"Shut up, you." Carol rolled slightly to give him a look over her shoulder, but her smile was indulgent. She turned back to Jackson again.

"Well, it's good this happened now and not tomorrow," Jackson said. "You guys ready for the hurricane?"

"We are." Vic stood and walked over to his wife's bedside and took her hand. "They're moving us all into the clubhouse later today for safety reasons."

"Good." He finished shoving his equipment back into his pack then joined Ned at the end of Carol's bed. "Make sure you take all those warnings seriously, okay? This storm is nothing to play around with, understand?"

"Yes, sir," Carol said, winking at him. "You're sexy when you take control."

Jackson chuckled and shook his head. "You just don't quit, do you?"

"No, sir." She squeezed Vic's hand. "That's the secret to our longevity."

He and Ned let themselves out, then headed back to Key West General. By the time they got there, it was early afternoon. Jackson found Luis in the ER, staring at some CT images on a computer screen at the nurses' station.

"Those of the motorcycle accident victim we brought in last week?" Jackson asked, checking out the scans of a badly fractured pelvis.

"Yes." Luis scrolled through several more images then clicked off the computer. "He's doing much better, according to the last report I got from the ortho surgeon. Took four hours of surgery to repair all the damage. They're going to evaluate his leg today."

"That's tough, man. I know when we picked him up from the scene, there was a lot of gravel and denim and bits of bone we had to debride from the wound. I hope they can save it." Jackson followed his brother out of the ER and down the hall toward the conference room, where an emergency ERT meeting had been called. In true hurricane form, Mathilda wasn't playing by the rules and had adjusted course yet again. Jackson had spent his time between runs deciding whether or not to raise the readiness level to one and had just come to a conclusion about five minutes prior.

"Me too." Luis held the door for him as they walked into the already-full conference room. "They applied a fixation device yesterday to Reed's leg, but he still has no pulse in his left foot, so there's been some compromised blood flow and possible nerve damage. His life's more secure at this point, but the future of that leg is in doubt. As soon as this meeting's over, I'm going upstairs for another update."

He nodded then walked up to the podium while Luis searched the room for an empty seat. Jackson kept his gaze straight ahead, determined not to seek out Lucy. Nope. He'd spent more than enough time texting back and forth with her over the last week about King. Not to mention how his thoughts kept returning to her during the night, too. She was interesting and she was taking care of King, that was all. And maybe if he told himself that enough times, he'd believe it.

Luis took a seat next to Stacy Williams and looked about as comfortable as a turkey on Thanksgiving, but Jackson didn't have time to think about why that was. Today was all about the coming storm and making sure they were ready.

"Right. Let's get started, then," he said. "Thanks, everyone, for coming on such short notice. We've got a lot of new information to cover today, so best get to it."

Jackson waited for the hushed murmurs to die down then jumped right in. "Unfortunately, the news I have today isn't good. Based on the latest forecast models from the National Weather Service, Mathilda is expected to strengthen to a category four storm by tomorrow morning, and though it won't make direct landfall in the Keys, we are expecting the outer bands to cause significant storm surge and wind damage throughout the area as it passes by. Therefore, I'm raising our readiness level to one, effective midnight tonight. You all know how this goes and should have been expecting it."

"Tomorrow morning?" Luis said, scowling. "That's much sooner than originally expected. I thought it wouldn't hit until tomorrow evening at the soonest."

"Like I said, things have changed fast." He took a deep breath. "And given the hurricane's current speed and trajectory, once it hits the Gulf of Mexico and the warmer waters there, it's going to be a monster. So, I've already put out bulletins to the local media, per our ERT protocol, and everyone on the team quarantines in Key West until after Mathilda passes. All top-level protocols are now in place and emergency services mobilized. We are warning residents in the Keys to evacuate to the mainland now or find lodging within Key West proper for the duration of the event. Any questions?"

A flurry of hands went into the air, and Jackson patiently answered them all until everyone was satisfied. Surprisingly, there were no objections. He'd thought for sure Lucy, at least, would have protested. Finally, after the meeting was adjourned and all the team members went off to brief their respective groups, Jackson made his way over to where Luis sat beside Stacy. Neither of them looked happy.

"Everything okay?" he asked, coming up to them.

"Not really," Stacy said, rubbing her crossed arms. "Lucy isn't here today. I even said I'd pick her up and drive her in, but she refuses to leave her compound."

Jackson's stomach plummeted to his toes. Guess that explained her lack of protest. "I'll call her and talk to her about it."

"I don't think it will do any good," Stacy said, her expression concerned. "She's determined to stay there and ride this thing out, but I think this one's going to be bad, Jackson. She's tough, but not that tough."

"No. You're right. She can't stay there by herself." Jackson scowled. "It's too dangerous."

"Well, good luck getting her to budge, brother," Luis said, scrubbing a hand over his face. "All she has to do is not answer her phone. People do what they want and what they think is best, no matter the danger or whom they hurt in the process, even themselves."

At that last part Stacy gave a pained gasp, and Jackson's instincts went on high alert. Yeah, there was definitely something going on there. But he didn't have time to ask about it. Not with Lucy's life on the line. Instead, he took out his phone and tried to call. No answer. He fired off a quick text next then waited. No reply.

Previously, she'd always answered right away, even if it was just a curt, one-word response.

Dammit.

Luis was right. She was avoiding him, and now was definitely not the time to do that. Not with preparations for the incoming Mathilda barreling down on them at warp speed and people's lives and his future at stake. But more than anything he was worried about Lucy, picturing her stranded all alone out there on Big Pine Key, possibly hurt or worse.

Then his phone buzzed, and hope flared to life.

Only to be quickly doused. It wasn't Lucy. It was Ned letting him know another call had come in. He was on duty until nine o'clock tonight. The muscles between his shoulder blades knotted tighter. "Stacy, go ahead and brief your departments. I'll handle Lucy. Don't worry."

Jackson waited until she was gone, then turned to his brother. "Can you take over IC for me tonight after my shift ends?"

"What? Why?" Luis frowned. "You aren't going to do anything reckless, are you?"

"No." *Yes.* Maybe. They made their way back toward the ER and the ambulance bay. "I can't leave Lucy out there by herself." He stopped and rubbed his hand over the top of his short hair. "Look, the level one doesn't go into effect until midnight. If I drive out to Big Pine Key after my shift at nine, I'm sure I can get her and get back to Key West in plenty of time."

Luis gave him a look. "That's cutting it awfully close. No. I don't like it, Jackson."

"Well, good thing it's not up to you, then." He dug in his heels. The brothers rarely fought, but when they did, it was usually over a matter of principle. "Look, I'm the one taking the risk here, okay? And I'm fine doing it." At his brother's dubious stare, Jackson's anger spiked, more at himself than anyone. *Fine. Whatever.* "Stop glaring at me like that. Really, it's fine. And this has nothing to do with sex, if that's what you're thinking. Lucy barely tolerates me. But as IC, I can't just leave her out there to die, can I? Besides, she's disobeying my orders already by not being at the meeting. If I let her continue to do that, I won't be seen as an effective leader, will I? So yeah. I'm going out there to get her."

"So, this is about the promotion then?" Luis asked, sounding thoroughly unconvinced.

"Of course it is," Jackson said, throwing up his hands. "What else would it be about?"

Luis gave him a too-perceptive stare for a moment, then sighed. "I just hope you know what you're doing, brother."

Me too. "Keep an eye on your phone tonight. I'll text you if there are any problems."

With that he turned and walked out of Key West General ER and headed toward the waiting ambulance, wondering himself just exactly what the hell he was doing, but knowing it was already too late to change his mind. The decision had been made for him anyway, the second Lucy had chosen to stay home rather than attend the meeting this afternoon.

He'd rescue her come hell or high water. And given the severity of the storm approaching, it would most likely be both.

One of the reasons Lucy had bought the compound was its isolation. She liked her solitude. And if she got lonely, she had her animals to keep her company. Usually. Now, she'd had Dr. Dave take them all to Miami with him and his partner for the duration of the storm. Well, most of them, anyway. The only ones left were Sam, who never left her side, Bubba, King and Mitzi.

Mitzi Gator never left. Just like Lucy.

She parked her car outside the front gate and let herself into the yard where the pregnant three-legged alligator lived in the pond on the far corner of the property. She was currently feasting on what looked like a seagull she must've caught. Normally, Lucy would've moved the reptile to a specialized place for her kind, but Mitzi had been a resident here since Lucy had moved in, and she didn't want to send the grumpy gal away until after her eggs had hatched, which, according to the calendar in the clinic, wouldn't be until after the storm. Not great timing, but nothing to do about it.

One more reason why Lucy couldn't leave. Mitzi might need help, and she refused to abandon her.

She locked the gate behind her then walked the far perimeter toward the front door of her vintage two-story house. The place had been built sixty years ago and needed some repairs, but overall it was cozy and livable and inviting. Just what she wanted in a home.

Sam met her at the door, tail wagging and tongue lolling. She crouched to give him a good scratch behind the ears. "There's my baby," she cooed, kissing his furry snout. "How's my handsome boy doing, huh? Are you a good boy? Yes, you are. Sammy's such a good boy."

The skies had grown darker by the hour and the palm trees stood out in stark contrast, sending a blot of alarm through her gut. But Lucy had worked hard to get here. She'd be damned if she'd let a storm chase her out of it now, even one as fierce as Mathilda was predicted to be. She tossed her keys on a side table in the living room then headed for the kitchen, where she sat at the table to make a list of everything she needed to do by nightfall, while Sam curled up at her feet with his favorite squeaky toy.

First there was installing the metal shutters over the wind-resistant windows. Then there was barring the fiberglass exterior doors and the heavy-duty metal door on the garage and the clinic supply area out back. All of it should keep her property protected against up to 140-mile-per-hour winds. According to the last weather report she'd heard on the way back here from the big box supply store, Mathilda's maximum sustained winds weren't expected to exceed 130, so she should be fine.

Plus, she had the basement. Which was where she headed next, to check her supplies. A planner by nature, Lucy kept well stocked on items she might need for both herself and any of her patients. But her OCD added another layer so, in addition to the usual water and canned goods, she also had plenty of other things, too, like a large cooler and lots of battery-powered lanterns, along with boxes of nonperishable foods she'd ordered in case of an emergency. She wasn't a prepper but could probably give one a run for their money.

She rearranged things by pushing the supplies against one wall to clear space for King's and Bubba's cages. Sam's, too. Mitzi would have to make it on her own for now, since there definitely wasn't enough room for her down here, not that Lucy would even try.

"What do you think, Sammy?" she asked the dog, who was sniffing everything in sight. "We'll bring your bed down here, too. And your food and your water. We'll be just fine, won't we?"

The dog looked up at her and whined, his ears back like he was worried.

Or hungry. Lucy checked her watch. Damn. It was after six now and way past Sammy's dinnertime. "Come on, boy. Let's get you something to eat, huh?"

They went back upstairs, and she filled his bowl before checking her phone for messages. Lucy frowned, seeing three from Jackson, which she quickly scrolled past, and one from Dr. Dave.

She hit redial on the vet's number then leaned her hips against the edge of the counter, waiting for him to pick up.

"Hey, Lucy," Dr. Dave said over the sound of a radio in the background. "Thanks for calling me back."

"Sure. Where are you?"

"Todd and I are getting ready to head to the mainland. When are you leaving?"

"I'm not." Lucy frowned. "Mathilda's supposed to brush past us. I'm staying here, in the basement."

"I don't think that's a good idea, Lucy," Dr. Dave warned. "I've been down here through a lot of hurricanes, and I don't like the track of this one. With the speed constantly changing, it could get rough. We're leaving in about an hour to drive north. You're free to go with us if you want. We've got room."

"No," she said, firmly. She loved her mentor, but she wasn't about to budge. She couldn't. If she lost this place, she wasn't sure what she'd do. "I've got provisions, and I'm prepared to ride it out."

"Are you sure?"

"I am." She straightened and bent to pick up Sam's now empty food bowl. "Be safe."

"You too," Dr. Dave said. "And if you change your mind, Lucy, the news said Key residents could hunker down in Key West. Go sooner rather than later."

After letting Sam out to go potty and cleaning his dishes, she went back outside to make sure the clinic was secure and bring in the last of the supplies she'd bought today from her car. The sky had turned a weird greenish-gray color, whether from the approaching storm or from evening setting in, she didn't know. Either way, her adrenaline spiked, and her sense of urgency notched higher. Once she'd finished at the clinic, she battened down anything that might blow away in the storm then went to pull out the metal shutters from the storage shed in back to start fixing them into place on the windows. She set the ladder up to start on the upper floors first. An hour later, those were done and Lucy started on the lower level just as the first raindrops fell.

Huh… According to her watch, it wasn't quite 9:00 p.m. yet, but given how the winds had picked up, Mathilda's outer bands might arrive earlier than expected. She worked methodically around the house until she reached the last window, this one on her office. Sam alternated between circling her ankles nervously and barking at the leaves rustling in the wind. Hot and thirsty, she went inside for a drink and had just gotten a bottled water out of the fridge when her cell phone rang, the perky tune at direct odds with the ominous weather outside.

She gulped her water and frowned at the caller ID. Jackson. Again.

Part of her said to ignore it. Let it go to voice mail again. Except he'd left six messages already. Dammit. She answered bluntly. "I'm not leaving."

"I'm on my way to get you," he said, ignoring her statement.

"Like hell you are." Sam barked, and she gave the dog a stern *Be quiet* look. "Stay where you are, Jackson. I'm fine. We're going to hunker down in the basement. There's food and water, and I've already moved the animals down there, including King. He's doing fine, by the way."

"I'm glad to hear the kitten's good, but the storm's getting stronger, Lucy." The alarm in his voice ratcheted her own anxiety higher, but she tamped it down as best she could. "I'm not leaving you there alone."

"It's not your choice to make." She'd been down that road of people thinking she couldn't do for herself. She refused to go back to being powerless again. "I'm fine. Seriously. And what about your team? You need to stay in Key West to oversee everything. Stay there. I'm not your problem."

"You've been nothing but my problem since the day we met." His voice sounded exasperated. "You disobeyed orders by not showing up at the meeting today, and you're disobeying now. I'll be there shortly. This isn't up for debate, Lucy."

"You're right. It isn't." She ended the call before he could respond. God. She might sound crazy, but she needed to do this. Why couldn't anyone understand that? She needed to stand on her own, prove she could handle this. For herself and for anyone else who'd ever doubted her abilities. She wasn't helpless. She could do this. She would do this.

Then a gust of wind howled around the corner of the house, and the ladder outside her office window teetered precariously before settling back into place. Sam barked, running to the basement door then back to the kitchen as if urging her to go. Now.

Fight or flight pounded through her system, causing her anxiety and OCD to flare supernova bright, but Lucy refused to be scared off. She bent to reassure Sam, who seemed less certain about their predicament. "We can do this, boy. Yes, we can."

There was one more shutter to install, then she'd head to the basement with Sam. She stared out through the screened-in porch only to stop and stare at the mess of leaves covering the floor. She'd swept the whole place up earlier. Cursing under her breath, she grabbed the broom and pushed them all into the corner. Then she headed outside and around the corner, only to get distracted by Mitzi at the pond. She should make one more check of the egg mound before hunkering down for the night. Oh, and the garage. Better move her car in there and lock it up tight. She turned to do that, then halted. Did she lock the front door? She couldn't remember now...

Focus, Lucy. Focus.

Right. The last storm shutter. She headed in that direction. Except when she got there, the force of the gusts made picking up the heavy piece of sheet metal harder than she'd expected. Then the stupid ladder blew over and smashed one of her planters, scattering ceramic shards and potting soil everywhere. Now she needed to clean that up, too.

You can do this. You're in control.

But her usual mantra only went so far as conditions worsened and things spiraled more and more out of control…

"Go inside," she said to Sam who'd remained steadfastly by her side through it all. When it became obvious that he wouldn't budge without her, she finally relented. "Okay. Come on."

She'd worry about getting that last shutter on later. For now, she needed to take her meds and hope for a good dose of luck.

CHAPTER FIVE

"DAMMIT!" JACKSON SHOUTED as wind screamed in his ears and a burning pain sliced across his thigh.

The moment he'd caught sight of the dark shape hurtling toward him, he'd acted on instinct and leaped into a diving roll. But the fierce gales blowing in off the ocean slowed his movements enough to allow the claw of the large alligator to snag the leg of his paramedic uniform pants…and his flesh. He came swiftly to his feet, ignoring the heat shooting up his thigh from the wound. Eyes trained on the animal, he dropped into a crouch. It looked huge, easily ninety to a hundred pounds, but Jackson had a hard time getting past its mouth—wide-open and lined with vicious teeth.

"Why couldn't you stick to puppies and kittens, Lucy?" he muttered as he took a slow step back. The gator remained still, but that open mouth and the speed with which the thing had overtaken him earlier made him more than a little wary.

When he was a good twenty feet away, he carefully straightened, keeping his gaze steady on his target. "There's a good alligator."

After that last phone call, Lucy's obstinate refusal to leave had blared through his head like a clarion call.

Of all the stubborn, stupid decisions to make... No. Issues or not, he was taking control. She had no idea what they might be up against, but he'd been through enough hurricanes to know never to underestimate one. She might not want to go, but he intended to cart her out of there by any means necessary. Or, at least he had, until the gator showed up.

He straightened a bit more and took another step back. The gator across from him maintained its aggressive stance. A true standoff. Well, if he was going down, it would be fighting.

Then, out of nowhere, a heavy weight blindsided him and dropped him to the ground.

Jackson hit hard on his chest, but quickly regained his senses. His first thought was another gator had nailed him from behind, but no. Those were human hands gripping his shoulders. A quick glance across the yard showed the gator had backed away, as if unsure what to make of this new intruder. He flipped over fast and pinned his assailant beneath him, only to realize it was Lucy.

"What the hell are you doing?" he yelled, partly to be heard over the howling wind and partly out of sheer frustration. She peered up at him, eyes dark and wide through the wet hair covering her face. Gradually, he also became aware of her petite frame and the press of her breasts against his chest, his senses heightened because of the storm raging around them.

She shoved hard at him, but he didn't budge. At least not until her fist hit the wound in his thigh where the gator had scratched him, then he cursed loudly. Hot, searing pain bolted straight to his brain, and Jackson pinned her hands above her head, the move bringing their faces inches apart.

"Answer me, Lucy! What the hell are you doing out here?"

She stared up at him, her gaze sparkling with defiance, and for a second he got lost.

"I could ask you the same thing," she growled, struggling under him. "I told you not to come."

That stubborn, tenacious tilt to her jaw was back, along with the sense he got of her vulnerability underlying it all. The enduring essence of battles fought. Some won. Too many lost. He recognized her grit, because he saw the same thing when he stared in the mirror every day.

Jackson lifted his weight off her and stood, pulling her up with him as he went. He paused to glance over at the alligator, but the darkness and the storm made it difficult to see.

"Did you hurt Mitzi?" she yelled over the wind.

"Who?"

"Mitzi, the alligator. Is she hurt?" She yanked free and raced across the yard toward the pond.

"The thing could've killed me," he roared, chasing after her. His words were swallowed by the wind. They kept running. Swearing under his breath, Jackson ignored the daggers in his thigh as he closed the distance. Finally, she slowed near a thicket of palm trees. Through the waving fronds, he made out the hulking shape of the beast as it cowered near a huge pile of earth, leaves and twigs.

"Lucy!"

She spun around, her expression a mix of concern and anger. "What?"

His patience unraveled, mainly because she seemed more concerned about that alligator than her own well-being. That was the last straw. "We need to go now before conditions get worse."

"I told you I'm not leaving." She looked away, squinting into the thicket.

"I don't have time for this," Jackson shouted.

"Neither do I. Go. Don't let me stop you. You shouldn't have come to begin with. I told you that."

Yep. She had. And if he'd been a different person, he might've listened. But as it was, Jackson couldn't leave. His honor and instincts wouldn't let him. She might not care about herself, but he did. It was his job to care.

Determined to end this, he closed the short space between them and grabbed her arm, thinking he'd pick her up and toss her over his shoulder to cart her away. Except no sooner had he reached her than Sam ran up to them, wet and bedraggled and barking like crazy. One more thing to worry about. Fine. Instead of the truck, Jackson pulled Lucy toward the house, the dog nipping at his heels as fresh jolts of pain shot from his injured leg. "We're leaving. Now. Grab the animals and anything else you need and let's go."

He was used to taking charge often enough in his job as an EMT—surely he could handle one pissed-off woman. At least that's what he'd thought, until Lucy dug in her heels and tugged hard, making him stumble and sending a fresh zing of agony up his leg. "Lucy, stop—"

"No! You stop!" she yelled. "This is my property and you're trespassing."

"I'm trying to help you," he yelled back, wondering how his efforts had gone so horribly awry.

"I told you I don't need your help!"

Any other time he'd have said fine. Let her do what she wanted. But now there was a hurricane about to slam into this place, and he'd sworn an oath to save and protect, and dammit.

He couldn't leave her here alone. He knew all too well what that was like.

"Can we at least go inside and discuss this?" he shouted back, and turned toward the front door.

She stayed put, making him drag her awkwardly for several feet. "I don't want you here." When he didn't slow down, she tugged again and yelled even louder. "Go away! I don't need you! I don't need anybody!"

The fraying tether on his patience snapped and Jackson whirled around fast and she smacked into his chest. He bent and shouted right near her ear so there was no doubt she heard him. "Too bad. I'm here and I'm not going anywhere until you're in the truck with me. Now, we can do this easy or hard, but either way, you and your animals are coming to Key West. Which will it be?"

She glared at him, not the least bit intimidated. Under different circumstances, he'd have admired that. "Last time I checked, this was still a free country."

"There's a difference between freedom and stupidity. Now move it." He dragged her toward the porch, not realizing until he was halfway up the stoop that the front door had been blocked off with a galvanized steel sheet. Cursing, he backtracked to the gravel pathway around the side of the house and noticed the same measures had been taken with the windows.

Good for her. Bad for him.

Dammit. There had to be a way in, since she'd gotten out.

"Let. Me. Go!" Lucy tried again.

He spotted a small screened-in porch and headed that way, going straight through and not stopping until they were standing in her kitchen. Then he slammed the door shut behind them, muting the howling wind. His ears rang with the sudden lack of noise. "You have five minutes to grab your things while I get the animals. Where are they?" He let go of her at last. "I'll turn off your utilities on the way, too, if you tell me where the fuse box and valves are."

When she didn't move right away, he thought maybe she was in shock. He'd seen it happen under far less stressful conditions. But a quick visual assessment of her showed no signs. No rapid breathing. No dilated pupils. No pale skin. In fact, her cheeks were pink, and her eyes sparkled with rage.

"I told you, I'm not—" she started.

Jackson looked at his watch, a muscle ticking near his jaw. "Four minutes, thirty seconds."

"Leaving," she finished, tapping the toe of her sneaker against the tile floor.

Lord Almighty, why was she making this so difficult? He knew her OCD probably had something to do with it, but he was one of the good guys, or at least he tried to be. So why then, as he stood there, leg throbbing and pride hurt, did he feel like *he* should apologize?

That was stupid. He had nothing to apologize for. This was a matter of life or death. He couldn't leave her here. End of story.

They stared at each other, at an impasse, just like

before with the gator. Except Jackson feared Lucy could be just as dangerous to him in a different way. Yes, she was six inches shorter than his six-two height and barely a hundred and thirty pounds soaking wet. Physically, it should've been an easy fight for him to win. Mentally and emotionally? Well, the more time he spent with her, the more difficult it proved to be.

"I appreciate you coming all this way. I do. But I'm not leaving, Jackson. I can't." Her quiet response caught him off guard.

"Why? Why can't you leave? Are you agoraphobic, too?" It made sense, as the anxiety and phobias went hand in hand with her OCD. But property could be replaced. Lives couldn't.

"Why do you care?" she countered, then held up her hand before he could answer. "Never mind. Look, I get that you think you need to swoop in here like some superhero and save the day. But your time would be better spent as IC, with your team helping people in Key West who need to be rescued."

Her voice had taken on a slow, soothing quality, the same one she'd used with the injured kitten he'd brought into the clinic. The same one he used with patients in emergencies. King had responded well and done what she'd wanted. Too bad it wouldn't work on him.

"Time's up." He showed her the glowing dial of his smart watch then sidled past her down the hall to what he assumed was the basement door, based on the meows and squawks echoing from below. "I'm going to get those cages and load them in my truck." He grabbed a plastic bag off the counter and thrust it into her hands. "Pack up what you want of your stuff. Last chance."

"You can't just come in here and take over," Lucy yelled from behind him.

"Already did," Jackson called back as he descended the wooden stairs to the basement. At the bottom, he stopped and scanned the space. King's cage was in the corner. The kitten meowed loudly when it saw him and licked his finger through the bars. Jackson smiled despite the situation. "Hey, little man."

The kitten's back area where they'd removed the leg was still wrapped in thick bandages, and an IV tube ran from his front leg to a bag hung up on one side of the cage. Getting all this upstairs alone was going to more difficult than he'd first imagined. In the opposite corner was Bubba, dancing furiously back and forth across his perch, screeching song lyrics and tossing food out of his bowl all over the floor with his beak.

Yeah. Maybe too difficult.

With a sigh, Jackson straightened and made his way back up to find Lucy. It was harder to see now, since the sun was hidden by thick storm clouds and steel shutters covered the windows, so he flipped on the lights. The living room at one end of the hall was neat and tidy, as expected, but impersonal. No pictures or personal touches at all. Same with the kitchen.

He checked another open doorway across the corridor and found her office. Again, clean and impersonal. Hardwood floors, minimal furniture. The only splashes of color were a watercolor painting of a sunset hanging on the wall and a stained-glass lamp on the desk. With her OCD, he shouldn't have expected a bunch of knickknacks, but still it felt odd. No connections, no memories, no ties to her past.

Jackson started to walk to the hall again and bumped

into a file cabinet. Something tumbled off the top and hit the floor. He picked it up, hissing slightly as his injured thigh protested. A picture frame. Huh... He turned it over to reveal a photo of a younger Lucy with a man holding her from behind, his arms wrapped around her middle and his chin resting on her shoulder. They were both grinning and Lucy had on an engagement ring. *Hello, Robert.*

Bang!

The wind snapped a tree branch against the side of the house, jarring him back to reality. That was the strongest gust yet. And now hard rain pelted the house. Yep. The outer bands were getting close. Too close.

Time to go. Now.

He tucked the frame under his arm and hobbled for the stairs up to the second floor.

"Hey, Lucy?" he called up. "I need your help with—"

Booming thunder and cracking lightning cut him off.

Dammit.

They could make a run for it on the Overseas Highway. It was only thirty miles back to Key West, but man, he really didn't want to get caught out there in the middle of the hurricane. No way they'd survive. Which meant staying put was the best bet. Except hunkering down here meant he had to let Luis know he had to continue as IC until the storm passed. It was the last thing he wanted to do, but the only choice he had for now.

He pulled out his phone and texted Luis then shoved the device back in his pocket with a decisive nod and went to find Lucy. "Looks like neither one of us is going anywhere for a while."

CHAPTER SIX

"What?" Anxiety knotted tighter in Lucy's gut. He couldn't mean... The thought of being stuck with Jackson Durand for the duration of the storm was almost enough to make her wish she'd evacuated.

Almost.

She raised her chin and crossed her arms to hide the trembling in her limbs.

You can do this. You're in control.

Except the harder she fought her OCD urges, the more they wanted to come out until she couldn't stop herself from tapping her foot on the floor.

One, two, three. One, two, three. One, two, three.

The fact he stood there watching her didn't help. Honestly, his too-perceptive gaze unnerved her more than the hurricane outside. Another loud crack outside the still-uncovered office window had her running to see huge limbs from an oak tree across the compound snap off like dry twigs and made her throat dry. "We need to get in the basement. Now."

"Agreed. But we need to cut the utilities first. And get that last shutter on the window there."

Right. Tasks were good. Tasks kept her focused.

"I'll get the shutter." Lucy rushed toward the kitchen door. "It can be tricky getting them into the tracks."

He stopped her, the air between them crackling with tension. "I'll get the shutter. You stay inside and cut the utilities. Where's the metal sheet?"

Rather than waste any more valuable time, she pointed toward the kitchen. "Near the back porch."

"Flashlight?"

"In the box on the counter. There's also battery-operated lanterns, extra batteries and some small propane tanks."

He headed down the hall to the kitchen, and she stared after him, the reflective letters on the back of his EMT shirt highlighting the V between his broad shoulders and narrow waist. For reasons she didn't want to think about too much at present, Jackson seemed even rougher, tougher, more masculine than usual, and deep in her core there was a fluttering response.

"Lucy," he called, dragging her out of her inappropriate thoughts. "Come take one of these lanterns to use after you shut off the power."

She did as he asked, the heavy silence between them filled by her pulse pounding loud in her ears.

"Be sure to fill the tubs and sinks before you shut off the water," he said before heading out the back door.

"Already done," she said to no one but herself. Her stomach went into free fall at the thought of being stuck together with him through the hurricane. Memories of being trapped in a home with Robert, him not allowing her to do anything for herself, him always telling her he knew best, him smothering her with his good intentions until she'd been all but unable to do for herself.

She couldn't go back there. Couldn't let that happen again. Couldn't depend on Jackson, no matter how much her aching heart might want to. Down that path was insanity.

The loud thwack of the screen door slamming against its frame startled her out of her paralysis.

Utilities. Right. She headed to the closet, lantern in hand, to shut off the power and water.

By the time she got back to the kitchen, Jackson had returned, his body silhouetted in the doorway by the black skies behind him. A muscle ticked near his tense jaw, and his high cheekbones stood out in sharp relief, making him look almost feral.

He gripped either side of the door frame, as if he might be sucked back out into the storm, and mumbled something she couldn't hear over the roar of the wind. Lucy moved closer, hoping to pull him inside before the door blew off its hinges. "What?"

"I can't," he shouted, tightening his grip on the wall.

She scowled. "Can't what?"

He slumped and would have crumpled to the ground if she hadn't wedged herself between him and the wall. His muscled weight nearly squashed her as she struggled to keep upright. "What's wrong? What happened? Are you hurt?"

"Gotta…close…the door," he rasped near her ear.

Lucy wrapped her arm around his waist and braced herself, feeling sticky warm blood on her hip. *Oh no.* Her chest constricted, and her veins tingled from excess adrenaline. None of this had gone the way she'd hoped, but she had to pull it together for Jackson.

You can do this. You're in control.

She glanced down at the long gash in his pants. The dark material made it hard to tell, but based on his weakness, she'd guess he'd lost some blood. Switching into vet mode, she began treating him like one of her animal patients and guided him toward the kitchen table. "You're going to be okay."

They barely made it before his knees buckled. Jackson fell across the table, facedown, and groaned. Lucy stumbled into one of the chairs, managing to catch herself before she tumbled to the floor. Then she scrambled back up and ran to the door, shoving hard against the fierce gusts. Once the latch clicked into place, she turned the dead bolt then raced back to the table.

"Jackson?" She grabbed a chair and turned it at an angle. He grunted. "Can you roll to your right? I'll hold the chair and you can slide into it and leave your injured leg straight in front of you."

Slowly, he did as she asked. Once he was in the chair, his head fell back, his eyes tightly shut.

She leaned over him. "Jackson?"

He opened one eye. "What happened?"

"Mitzi the gator."

"Mitzi Gaynor?" Jackson frowned. "Isn't that some lounge singer from Vegas?"

Lucy bit back a nervous laugh. Dr. Dave and his partner had named the alligator before Lucy had arrived. The fact Jackson recognized the gator's celebrity namesake made her like him a little more, against her will.

She checked his pulse to distract herself. Slow and steady. That was good.

"No. Mitzi the alligator. She lives in the pond across the compound, Normally, she stays far away from humans. I'm not sure why she charged, even with the storm. When did she get you?"

"Right after I got here. Snagged my thigh."

Lucy's thoughts flashed back to him crouching in the yard. That suddenly made more sense now. Her stomach dropped. "So, you've been running around here this whole time with a huge gash in your thigh?"

"Wasn't that bad." He opened his other eye and shifted slightly, wincing. "Superficial cut. Or at least it was, until the corner of the metal shutter caught it."

"Oh God," she gasped. "It's a miracle you made it back to the porch."

"The miracle is I got the window covered. You better secure that before the wind blows it in."

Lucy spun to see the back door shuddering on its hinges, even with the dead bolt in place and the screened-in porch as an added barrier.

She grabbed the lantern and hurried to her office, where she'd stashed the metal bars to bracket it in one of her desk drawers. Anxious bile scalded her throat, but there'd be plenty of time for that later. She grabbed the bars then rushed back to the kitchen to shove them into place. There. Secure. She took a deep breath and leaned back against the wood. The house was as protected as it was going to get.

Which left Jackson.

He shifted so his wounded leg faced the chair opposite him and started to lift it.

"No, don't!" She moved quickly to his side. "You could make the bleeding worse."

"I'm a paramedic. I know what I'm doing." He clenched his jaw and reached for his calf, batting her hands away when she tried to help, and pulled his leg up on the chair, hissing between clenched teeth.

"And you call me stubborn," she said, scowling as

she moved a third chair under his foot so the whole leg was supported. Lucy pulled the lantern closer so she could see. "Sit back."

"It's not that bad," he said, pulling at the torn fabric of his pants to inspect the wound himself. "The metal sheet jolted it, that's all. I'll be fine. Got some thread and a needle?"

"What?" She gave him an incredulous stare. "You going to suture yourself, too?"

"Maybe."

Exasperated, she threw her hands in the air. "Don't be stupid. I'm a veterinarian. I stitch up my animal patients all the time. I'm probably better at it and faster than you. And I'll be neater, too, since I can actually see what I'm doing." Grumbling, Lucy headed down to the basement for the supplies she'd stowed there earlier, taking a second to soothe her animals, then hurried back to the kitchen.

After scrubbing her hands with soap and rinsing with bottled water over the empty side of her double sink, she pulled on surgical gloves, then laid a sterile cloth on the table and quickly organized her supplies so she could reach them. "I'll need you to hold the lantern so I can see. If you feel the least bit woozy, tell me and I'll stop. Warn me if you have to move."

She knelt beside him and plucked at the ragged edges of his torn pants. The tear in the fabric was about five inches long, but she was relieved to find after peeling the fabric away that the wound was shorter by about two inches. Still, it looked deep and definitely needed cleaning. And stitching.

Lucy reached for the scissors to widen the hole in his pants, but he beat her to them.

"Tell me what you want and I'll hand it to you," he said, giving her a look.

"I *want* you to follow directions."

He snorted. "You're one to talk."

The last thing Lucy should want to do at that moment was smile. She absolutely should *not* enjoy their verbal sparring. Except she kind of did. She avoided Jackson's gaze as she deftly slit the fabric, elongating the tear.

"Be careful. This is my work uniform, you know."

"Get a new one. I have to clean this wound properly or it could get infected." She hazarded a glance up at him, then returned to her task, unable to stop her slight grin now. "And that's Dr. Lucy to you."

Jackson smiled in return. "Luis couldn't stop gushing about your program with the therapy pets when I asked him. He thinks very highly of you."

He asked his brother about me?

She focused more than was necessary on the task at hand, squashing those odd butterflies swarming inside her at his words. Lucy cleansed the wound with antiseptic, then reached for a syringe packet and vial of anesthetic and drew up the medication.

"I don't need a shot," Jackson said, his tone tense. "Don't like needles, at least when they're directed at me."

"Close your eyes. It will only sting a little." She placed a gloved hand on his muscled thigh to steady it as she gave the injection.

"Ouch! Dammit, that— Ouch!" He swore under his breath. "I think you gave me enough for a small elephant."

"I gave you the correct dose for an adult male."

She set the used syringe aside and picked up the suture packet next, waiting for the meds to take effect. "Won't be long now."

He stayed silent, staring at the far wall while she tapped the skin around his wound to make sure it was numb. The wound was small enough, thankfully, and she soon began. Tying off the first stitch and snipping it with a pair of surgical scissors, she then went in for the second. From the length of the laceration, she was thinking five should do it. "All right?"

"Fine," he murmured, still not looking down. "I've been through worse."

Lucy continued working, making small talk to distract herself and him. "Really? How?"

"Coast guard. Four years." His expression tightened. "Why'd you become a vet?"

She shrugged slightly then moved on to the third stitch. "It's my calling. I've always loved animals. I volunteered at a shelter and met Dr. Dave. He helped me get into the vet program at Clemson University before he and his partner moved to the Keys. When I decided to set up a practice of my own, Dr. Dave recommended Big Pine Key, and the rest is history."

"Is your family in South Carolina still?"

"Charleston." Lucy tried not to tense at his digging into her past and failed. The hurt of Robert's betrayal and her parents' complicity was still too fresh, too raw. She kept working. "Just a few more sutures and we're done."

Jackson took a deep breath. "How'd you end up with the gator?"

"She came with the property. Been here for a few years, according to Dr. Dave. She minds her own business and hunts away from here, returning to her nest each night. And she beats a normal security system any day of the week."

"Got that right." He shook his head, meeting her gaze at last, his smile wry. "You surprise me at every turn, Lucy."

"Same," she said, the moment drawing out between them, shimmering with possibilities.

A strange bubble of awareness swelled inside her like a balloon, filling her up, pushing all her doubts and fears aside until the wind sent something else crashing into the side of the house. Jackson flinched and looked away. Lucy steadied the needle and tied off the last knot, then bandaged his wound. Working in difficult situations was crucial in her profession, even with the adrenaline fizzing through her system.

Good thing, too, since Mathilda and the man sitting before her had officially blown her quiet, peaceful life to hell.

Finally finished, she stood to clean up the mess. Jackson watched her, her skin tingling in the wake of his perusal. It was unsettling, and she focused on wrapping up the small pile she'd made in the sterile cloth, not him. "The numbness will wear off soon. You should take some pain meds. They're in the box."

"Thanks." He found the acetaminophen, and Lucy got him a bottled water from the cooler in the basement. She did her best not to notice the sleek muscles of his throat working as he swallowed and inspected the bandaged area around his wound instead. Assured it was good, Lucy helped him lower his foot to the floor. Despite the lidocaine, he winced.

"Need to stand," Jackson said. Using her shoulders for leverage, he got himself upright, then paused.

"Okay?" she asked.

"Perfect." He reached toward her, and for a crazy moment, Lucy thought he might cup her cheek. She moved back, not liking to be touched unless it was her choice.

But he didn't touch her, just reached behind for a battery pack.

Good. Fine. She didn't want Jackson's hands on her. *Do I?*

No. She ignored the odd stab of disappointment inside her.

Their conversation lulled once more, and the howl of the wind rushed to fill the void. She finished packing the last few boxes on the counter, relieved to find he'd moved away to sit at the table again, foot propped up and his face taut as he stared down at his hands in his lap.

The glow of the lantern only highlighted how handsome he was. Not like a movie star or Robert. Jackson had a quieter sort of sexiness. One that sneaked up on you but was all the stronger for it. Not that she noticed or cared. Nope.

She turned away from the unwanted, unexpected need throbbing in her system that had as much to do with the storm as the man trapped in the house with her.

And that terrified Lucy way more than any hurricane.

CHAPTER SEVEN

"If you're hungry, we should eat before we go to the basement. Might be a while before we have a chance again." Another loud crack resounded, and she turned instinctively toward the front windows in the living room, but with the shutters in place, she couldn't see anything outside.

Frustrated, she went into the pantry and set one of the lanterns on a shelf then scanned what was left in there to put together a quick meal. A sudden chill went through her, making her cross her arms and rub them. It was more in reaction to the turmoil surrounding the house than the temperature. She hadn't thought the cacophony could get any louder, but now the whole place seemed to vibrate from the noise alone. Maybe it was just as well she couldn't see outside.

Back in Charleston, the storms she'd been through had never been this bad. Of course, they'd had a nice two-story in the suburbs, with a big yard and a swing set in the back, far from the coastline, so maybe that made a difference. Initially she hadn't minded being an only child, but then her issues, which had gone undiagnosed for years, had surfaced. Her parents had thought she was just quiet, an introvert. But as she'd gotten older and it was time to start school, they'd realized her problems went deeper. Her grades had been fine, outstanding even, but her tics had kept her from excelling socially. Around the age of nine, they'd taken her out of public school and put her with a private tutor because of the bullying. Lucy had tried to pretend it didn't matter, but that wasn't true. Living in a bubble wasn't any kind of life at all.

Then she'd met Robert through her tutor. He'd been bullied too as a kid—not because of any issues, but because he was so smart. He'd graduated high school at fifteen and gone on to college early to study psychology. He found Lucy fascinating, and they'd spend hours just talking or doing puzzles or whatever. For a girl who'd been isolated her whole life, having a friend— or even better, a man interested and attracted to her— was like a miracle. She'd fallen hard and fast for him, wanting to spend every waking minute with him, and her parents had been overjoyed. Their daughter had finally found a mate.

By the time Lucy had finished high school, Robert was nearing the end of his bachelor's degree in psychology and was ready to enter a graduate program of study, specializing in anxiety disorders. He said it would bring him and Lucy even closer together, help him understand her even more. Help him help her. But in the end it had only torn them apart.

Because the more Robert tried to understand her, the more she started to feel like she was nothing but a lab experiment to him. He'd become more controlling, more manipulative, and she'd yearned for freedom.

From him, from her parents, from all the constraints her issues brought down on her.

Her one bright spot had been volunteering at the local animal shelter.

That was where she'd first met Dr. Dave. He'd become her friend, too, but a different kind of friend than she'd had before. He never tried to "help" her, never tried to control her, never used her issues against her. He just was there for her when she needed him and listened to her when she needed to talk. When he'd mentioned she might consider a career as a vet, she'd jumped at the chance. She'd graduated with top grades in her studies and had been offered multiple scholarships at colleges in the Charleston area with the letter of recommendation Dr. Dave had written her, but she'd shocked her parents and Robert by accepting one at Clemson University in Columbia, hours away from Charleston.

She'd ended her engagement with Robert and moved out of her parents' house and never looked back. After she'd finished veterinary school she'd bought this compound, on Dr. Dave's recommendation, and forged a new life for herself.

She never wanted to be trapped again. Never wanted to be controlled and manipulated.

Never wanted to become reliant on anyone else's help, because that led to disaster.

Lucy had learned that lesson well and had no intention of repeating it ever again. That's why she'd fought so hard to stay here, why she'd fought so hard against Jackson and his damned orders and interventions.

Until today. Today the storm and fate had taken that choice away from her.

But this place was her home. A part of her. She wouldn't leave. Couldn't.

She just prayed they'd survive another twenty-four hours.

A chair scraped on the floor and jarred her out of her thoughts. Right. Dinner. She headed out of the pantry, back into the kitchen. Open and airy, it was her favorite room in the house, aside from the clinic, where she spent the most time. Jackson's back was to her, his head bent as he examined his wound. Her fingertips buzzed, remembering the feel of his warm, smooth skin, the muscles firm as marble beneath. She'd done a good job. He shouldn't even have a scar when it healed fully.

Her gaze drifted over his torso and down the length of his leg propped on her kitchen chair. Another unwanted frisson of awareness raced up her spine. She really didn't know much about him, other than he was a paramedic and adopted. She imagined him running into a crisis, saving kids and puppies and old people.

"I don't mind you checking me out, but maybe we should get a move on before Mathilda arrives."

Oh God. Busted.

Mortified heat spread from her core to her extremities, worse even than when she'd been bullied. She felt guilty and exposed and more than a little dazed and confused.

Lucy went back in the pantry, ears burning and hands shaking. The voice in her head was right. She could do this. She was in control. She'd worked way too hard for her peace of mind to let him jeopardize it now. Besides, she had no business being attracted to him. From what she had seen of Jackson so far, he was a total control freak who seemed to think he needed to rescue everyone in sight, which meant he was just like Robert. He'd only cared about her because he'd wanted to take care of her, too.

But Lucy didn't need to be taken care of. She could take care of herself.

After a deep breath to calm her nerves, she studied the shelves again. She'd already packed up most of the contents of her refrigerator in the cooler downstairs, so tortilla chips and a can of nacho dip looked like the best choice. She stood on an overturned bucket to reach the top shelf, but just as her hand closed around the can, the stupid bucket shifted and she lost her balance, nearly toppling to the floor in a painful heap—if not for the strong arms that closed around her from behind.

"What the hell are you doing now?" Jackson asked. His deep voice, rife with annoyance, rumbled through the solid chest pressed to her back.

"Getting food." She struggled against his hold. The last thing she needed was him thinking she was a klutz on top of the rest of her issues. Of course, the fact she still cared at all what he thought did little to improve her mood. She finally pulled away then gave him an irritated stare. "I told you to stay put."

His strong hands still braced her upper arms, and her skin tingled from his touch. He stood close enough she could see the hint of dark stubble on his jaw. "You sure you're okay?"

"Great." She swallowed hard, wondering when exactly it had gotten so hot in there.

He watched her a moment, frowning. "Lucy?"

She concentrated on the shelf behind him as her OCD spiked and her tics took over. There were five boxes of corn bread mix, but there should've been six.

Why weren't there six? She always bought them in even numbers and made sure to stock up often, so they stayed even. Now they were odd. She stepped past him and began to fiddle with the boxes, searching behind and around them for the missing box. The storm outside had nothing on the whirling tornado of anxiety inside her. She was getting lost again, lost in the weeds of her disorder...

Then his fingertip nudged her chin upward, and she met his eyes. Her pulse stuttered, but she couldn't look away, trapped like a deer in headlights.

Jackson narrowed his gaze, watching her more intently as he reached over and turned down the lantern, plunging the small space into shadows.

Her heart slammed harder against her rib cage, an odd mix of apprehension and anticipation crashing over her like a tsunami. "Wh—what are you doing?"

Time screeched to a halt as he pulled her against his chest, one arm around her waist, the other around her upper back, his hand in her hair, cupping the nape of her neck as he pressed her cheek against his shoulder. She stood completely still, too stunned to react, to move away, to do anything but let him hold her.

"Put your arms around me," Jackson whispered against her scalp.

Like a robot, she looped them around his lean waist. "Tighter."

She squeezed, feeling his hard body press into her soft curves. Like a life preserver in a riptide, she found herself hanging on for dear life, yet battling it every step of the way. She couldn't let him in, couldn't let him close, because if she did, she'd lose everything she'd gained. "Jackson?"

"Hmm?" His voice hummed beneath her ear.

"Let me go."

He stiffened, then released her before turning the lantern back up and moving away. She missed the heat of him immediately, crossing her arms as he hobbled back to his seat at the table. He flopped down, looking about as discombobulated as she felt. Finally, he said, "Sorry."

Me too. She left the pantry and opened the can of dip at the counter, grabbing a spoon from the drawer without looking before carrying it all over to the table, along with the chips. Taking a seat across from him she handed him a plate. "I'm sorry you came here."

"Don't be," he said, his tone defeated. "It was my choice."

She frowned. "I still don't understand why."

"You need help, and I came to provide it. That's what EMTs are supposed to do, right?" He shrugged. "Anyway, it doesn't matter now. We're stuck and need to make the best of it until the storm blows over."

"Yes." She reached for the dip at the same moment he did, their fingers tangling. She pulled away fast and mumbled, "Sorry..."

"You need to stop saying that." He winked at her then started to get up again. "Got any napkins?"

"I'll get them," she said, also rising.

"I'm not an invalid." He hobbled across the room.

She watched him go, unable to forget their brief hug. Which was stupid, because she didn't want his hugs. Didn't want him touching her and holding her and caring about her.

Do I?

They ate the rest of the food in silence.

Finally, she tucked her hair behind her ear, toying with her empty soda can. "Hope you had enough."

"Yep. It was good. Thanks." He held her gaze a moment then pulled out his phone. "Got any reception?"

She pulled out her own device and checked the bars. "Nope."

Boom! Screech!

They both stared at the ceiling as the storm intensified once more.

Wide-eyed, Lucy stared at him. "What do you think that was?"

"Roof damage, I'm guessing," Jackson said, cursing under his breath. "Don't think it's major, though, otherwise the sound would've gotten louder."

Lucy was already in the hallway heading for the stairs to the second floor. "I'm going to take a look."

"No." Jackson's chair scraped on the hardwood. "Lucy, stop!"

Her steps faltered, and she looked back at him. "You said it was probably nothing major."

"No. I said I thought the roof was still on, not that it wasn't serious." He followed her down the hall, using a mop handle from the pantry like a crutch. "We should go to the basement now."

Her mind raced, and her palms dampened. A panic attack loomed dead ahead unless she got it under control. Lucy took a deep breath and closed her eyes.

You can do this. You're in control.

Then Jackson was at her side, distracting her. "I didn't see anything comfortable to sit on when I was down there earlier. Can we take the couch cushions down with us?"

"Yes."

"Good, I'll get them."

He squeezed past her, stopping far too close for her comfort to look down at her. "Is there a bedroom on this floor?"

"What?" Her mind was still a chaotic mess of panic. She couldn't think, couldn't speak, couldn't...

"A bedroom, Lucy," he repeated, sterner this time. "Is there one down here?"

"Yes. Why?" She licked her dry lips and Jackson's gaze tracked that tiny movement, his eyes darkening. Lucy scrambled to find balance again. "I'll, uh, get the sofa cushions."

"I'll get the cushions." Jackson didn't move out of her way. "Single or double?"

She couldn't process his question. Couldn't make sense of anything but the heat of him surrounding her, making her want things she had no business wanting. All she knew was if she tried to get past him, she'd press up against him way more intimately than she'd been during their hug earlier, and that set off a whole new bunch of alarms in her head.

"Lucy," he repeated, his brusque tone slicing through the chaos inside her. "Is the bed down here single or double?"

"Queen."

"Good. Go start taking off the sheets. I'll be in to help you in a minute."

Jackson finally moved away so she could get past him, and it took most of Lucy's willpower not to break into a run. She swore she could still feel him behind her. She should be concerned about the hurricane outside, not the wild effect of Jackson on her equilibrium.

CHAPTER EIGHT

JACKSON LEANED AGAINST the wall, as much to watch her walk away as to rest his aching leg.

Once he'd tossed the sofa cushions down the stairs, he went to the bedroom to check on Lucy and stopped dead on the threshold.

The sight of her kneeling on all fours to yank the far corner of the fitted sheet off the bed shouldn't have affected him the way it did, but damn if his pulse didn't trip, and heat rose from beneath the collar of his shirt to claw up his neck. He cleared his throat and hopped into the room to grab the opposite corner.

"Let me help," he said, freeing one corner at the same moment she gave a mighty tug on the opposite side, sending her sprawling back into the center of the bed with the sheets tangled between her legs.

Well, hell.

Lucy caught him staring and gave him a dour look, then wadded up the sheet and tossed it to the floor before scrambling off the bed.

Just as well.

He sighed and bent to heave the mattress to one side. With luck, the worst of the storm would be over tomorrow and he could get back to Key West and resume his IC role. So far, cell service was still out. With luck, when it came time to explain why he had handed over command to Luis temporarily, the review board would give him a chance to defend his need to come to Big Pine Key and take into consideration his efforts to save an innocent life.

Jackson looked up again to find Lucy across from him now, her position giving him a clear view straight down the front of her white tank top. Exactly what he didn't need. He swallowed hard and glanced away fast—but not before he caught her arched brow and defiant expression.

Busted.

Dammit. He would not look again. Would not. Except his eyes drifted back to her chest, as if of their own volition. Off-kilter, in more ways than one, Jackson concentrated on moving the heavy mattress, perspiration glistening on his forehead. He felt a little woozy, too, and his pulse was erratic. Maybe he had lost more blood than he'd thought. He should probably rest, but they needed to get this thing down to the basement first.

He took a good hold on the mattress and gave a vicious tug, grunting and pulling the thing half off the bed so fast he barely had time to hop out of the way to keep it from falling on him. Once they'd maneuvered it out into the living room, Jackson motioned to Lucy to change ends with him. "You push, I'll pull."

"Explain to me why we're doing this?"

"To cover our heads and the cages. If the roof caves in, then we'll have a passing chance of not getting crushed."

"Isn't that what basements are for?" She sounded as exasperated as he felt.

Jackson dropped his forehead in the soft bedding and prayed for patience. "Yes, but this house is old, and I don't trust the structure. If the top floor goes, the whole thing could cave right in on us." He angled his head to one side so he could see her. "Okay? Good. Now push."

Lucy ducked back behind her end and together they maneuvered the heavy, bulky thing downstairs.

"I'm going to move this out of the way and you stack some of those supply boxes in the middle of the space here," Jackson said, pointing to the center of where the mattress sat on the floor. "Then we'll set a cage at each corner for support."

Now that she understood his plan, Lucy worked efficiently, arranging things on her side while Jackson did the same on his. He seemed to be moving around fine with his wound and makeshift crutch, which was good. She'd expected it to give him more trouble. And speaking of trouble, after their encounter in the pantry and again in the hall, she now couldn't seem to stop noticing him as a man, instead of just a warm body she was stuck with during the storm. Each time she looked over at Jackson, all she could see was his muscled shoulders and flexing biceps as he shoved things around, or how his taut butt looked in those black pants when he bent over. It was frustrating as hell, especially with anxiety still buzzing beneath her surface.

With a sigh, she moved King's cage into place, careful to not jar his IV bag, then stopped to waggle a playful finger at him through the bars. He remained sound asleep, though, and she stood and wiped her hands on her jeans. "What next?"

"We bring down the last of those boxes from the kitchen, then secure ourselves in for the night."

They were done in under ten minutes. Lucy stowed the lanterns and flashlights where she could reach them. Jackson shoved the cooler she'd filled earlier off to one side then went back up to bar the door at the top of the stairs. Once everything was in its place, she turned in a slow circle and surveyed the basement. The animals were oddly quiet, either sleeping or spooked.

"Right," Jackson huffed out, the mattress leaning on his shoulder. "Let's get this over our heads."

She grabbed one side, and together they propped the thing partially up onto the top of the cages. The animals were awake now, that was for sure. A chorus of meows and squawks and barks from Sam filled the air, drowning out the noise from outside. Sam kept getting underfoot, nearly tripping her, and suddenly Jackson's face was far too close to her chest for comfort.

"If it were up to me," he said into her shirt, his hot breath causing goose bumps to break out on her skin. "I'd spend the next several hours right here. But if we're going to get this done, you need to move back."

Crap.

You can do this. You're in control.

Lucy let go of the mattress and stumbled backward.

The thing slipped, its trajectory putting him on a collision course with her once again. One instant Jackson was on his side of the space. The next she was flat against the wall, his body pressing into hers. For a moment, Lucy didn't dare move, didn't dare breathe, not with the shoulder-to-belly-to-toe contact. All that power, all those muscles, all of his barely restrained...

Then he pushed back onto one elbow to look at her, and she closed eyes to hide her shame.

You can do this. You're in control.

Except she didn't feel in control, and she had serious doubts whether she could do this at all. Part of her wanted to stay right where she was forever. The other part of her wanted to run from the house and take her chances with the hurricane. Neither was an option. Not with his body holding hers in place, his warmth, his scent, his masculine presence surrounding her.

"All right?" he asked, his breath stirring the hair near her temple.

"Great," Lucy whispered past her tight throat with all the sarcasm she could muster. "You?"

"Same."

His gentle joke helped lift some of her inner tension and she relaxed a tad, staring past his shoulder. A strange intimacy crackled between them now, one that had a question popping out of her mouth before she could stop it. "Why did you hug me?"

When Jackson didn't answer, she hazarded a glance at his face, only to find him watching her.

Summoning all her courage, she kept her gaze on his, nose to nose, and persisted. "Earlier, in the pantry. Why did you turn off the lantern and hug me?"

In response, he lifted his weight from her, and she scrambled away, taking care not to bang against him as they moved the mattress into place. Her OCD wanted her to tic again, to straighten all the cages, check the knob on the basement door, walk the perimeter of the basement and count her steps, divide the number by three and hope it came out even…

"Here," Jackson said, tossing her a couch cushion.

It thumped softly against her chest, knocking her out of her anxious spiral. She took a deep breath, feeling some of the pressure inside her ease. Funny how he could do that, calm her down like that. No one had been able to do that since…

Nope. Not going there.

You can do this. You're in control.

"Thanks," she said, crawling inside their makeshift fort then arranging two cushions on her side of the space before settling down, cross legged. The cages were high enough with the boxes stacked in the middle that they could sit up straight, not hunkered over. Jackson took a seat across from her and stretched his legs out, grimacing.

Concerned, she asked, "How's your leg?"

"I'll live."

"Maybe I should take another look. Move the lantern this way a few inches." She motioned with one hand but didn't look up. He didn't reply, but the light shifted. Lucy moved the torn fabric of his pants away and peeled back part of the bandage. "It's red and there's some more bleeding, but none of the stitches popped."

"You do right good work," he said, his voice low.

"Thanks." Lucy looked up then regretted it as her simmering attraction to him notched higher toward full boil. Voice gruff, she coughed to clear her throat. "Let me get you another dose of pain meds."

She started to scoot away, but Jackson stopped her, his hand on her arm.

"Relax. I know you're worried, but don't add me to your list of things to be concerned about, okay? Maybe check on your other patients."

She looked around at King, Sam and Bubba. The kitten was asleep again, Sam was settling into his bed and Bubba was chewing on his toy.

Jackson rubbed her forearm, then his touch dropped away. "You don't like people caring about you. Why?"

He hadn't answered her questions before about the hug—no reason for her to do any differently. She didn't want him or anyone else poking into her business, taking over, thinking they knew best, no matter how well-intentioned.

Lucy slumped back onto her side of the cushions and said after a long moment, "I like being self-sufficient. Why do you like being in control?"

"Because I'm the one others depend on. I'm the hero. That's my value." Restlessness sparkled in his gaze as he turned the spotlight back on her. "There's a difference between self-sufficiency and just plain stubbornness and self-sabotage."

"And how would you know?" she said, scooting farther back until her back hit the side of Bubba's cage. The bird reached through the bars to grab a length of her hair in its beak, cleaning it. "You know what? Forget I asked."

"What if I don't want to?" Jackson countered, ignoring the imaginary Keep Out sign above her head. He wasn't comfortable with this conversation, either—or the woman he was having it with—yet he couldn't seem to let the matter drop. "Why won't you accept help, Lucy? Why won't you let anyone in?"

Why won't you let me in?

Her expression grew remote again, and he winced. Dammit. He shouldn't care. He was used to distancing himself from those he treated in order to do his job, kept his professional walls up in case things didn't go to plan. Otherwise, he couldn't live with the loss. And yes, maybe those defensive mechanisms extended to his personal life as well, but after being abandoned by his birth mother, it was amazing he'd learned to cope at all.

"Let's make a deal. If you tell me why you hugged me, then I'll tell you why I don't like to accept help and why this place is so important to me," she said, turning to give Bubba a kiss.

Jackson felt oddly jealous of that silly bird. Maybe that's why he answered, "I hugged you because I thought you needed one."

She froze, then looked back at him, her gaze dubious. "You don't strike me as a guy in touch with his emotions."

He shrugged. "Emotion had nothing to do with it."

"Pretty sure emotion has everything to do with it." Thrust into a minefield, going forward felt safer than retracing her steps. "Hugging is all about connection and feelings. That's why people do it."

His expression darkened, and he arched a brow. "Not me. No connections. That's my rule."

The excess energy bubbling through her system felt like champagne shaken to the point of exploding. She flexed her fingers to relieve some of it. At least the urge to tic had lessened. And whatever was going on between them, she wasn't about to let him get the upper hand. "Know what I think?"

"If I lie and say yes will you spare me?"

"I think you hugged me because you needed one, too."

Jackson scoffed. "Whatever."

Sensing she'd hit a bull's-eye, Lucy pressed on. "What I can't figure out is why you turned out the light. Maybe the darkness is like a mental cloak? You don't have to think, just act. Give in to instinct."

"Really?" He scowled and shifted his weight, his words emerging more as a rough purr, dangerous as a panther ready to pounce. "And what do you know about instincts, Lucy? When do you give in to yours?"

The temperature in the basement seemed to rise several degrees in the span of a second, but she refused to be deterred. "I try not to give in to instincts at all."

Jackson's lips compressed. "Then that's where we differ."

A tingle zinged through her core, and her pulse sped. "Because your instincts guide you?"

"I live by mine, but that's not what I meant."

"What did you mean, then?" That had come out far breathier than she'd wanted.

You can do this. You're in control.

"Because I think we both rely on instinct to save us. Only I don't lie to myself about it." He leaned forward, leaving only inches between them, and her breath caught. Time slowed as he ran a fingertip down the length of her nose, letting it rest on her bottom lip. "The real question is, Lucy, what do you think will happen if you let someone in, let them help you?"

The unexpected caress had her nerve endings going haywire, and she answered without thinking. "I'll get trapped again. Used. Manipulated."

He frowned. "Is that what happened before?"

"No." *Yes.* She pulled away and scooted back to her side of the small space to rummage through the cooler for a water. As she held the cool plastic to her hot cheeks, the irony smacked her right between the eyes. She might well survive the storm, only to fall prey to her own foolish reaction to Jackson.

He pulled out his phone again. "Maybe we can find out what's going on outside."

Glad to have something to think about besides him, she drank her water and waited. She'd rather listen to damage reports and the very real possibility her home might be destroyed rather than sit in this small shadowed space with Jackson and dredge up painful memories best left buried.

"Two bars," he said triumphantly, turning his phone speaker on and raising the volume so the announcer's voice echoed off the concrete basement walls.

"...heading toward Cuba, picking up speed over the open water. Mathilda's outer bands are expected to skirt right over the Keys around three tomorrow morning— just a few hours from now—and the entire area is on high alert. No matter where you are in this storm's path, there is imminent potential for loss of life, and damage to property has been estimated to reach well into the billions."

The phone went dead, and Lucy looked from it to Jackson.

"It'll be okay," he said. "We'll make it."

In the next instant, a tremendous crash reverberated through the house with enough force to rattle the cages and send the animals into a frenzy. Bubba squawked "Welcome to the Jungle" over and over. Sam curled into a quivering bundle beside Lucy's thigh, and Jackson did his best to comfort poor King. Somehow, she and Jackson had ended up side by side, too, with one of his arms around her shoulders and the other placed protectively over King's cage.

Resting on his good hip, he tucked her closer to his side, his wounded leg brushing hers. He looked down at her, then squeezed her closer.

"I think we're okay," she said.

"Me too." His hand felt strong and reassuring on her shoulder. It wasn't until he ran his fingers through her hair that she realized he was trembling, too.

"Know what I could use?" he whispered, so softly she would've missed it if she hadn't been paying attention.

"Hmm?" Her gaze held steady on his.

"I think I could use another hug."

She froze but didn't withdraw as he removed his arm from atop King's cage to lower the lantern light. Shadows surrounded them as Jackson gathered Lucy close once more and held her firm against his chest. Then, as if that wasn't close enough, he tucked her head under his chin.

Only then, in the darkness, did she feel safe letting her guard down, just a little. Maybe there was something to her theory after all. As the storm raged outside, tearing apart everything she'd worked so hard to build for the last year or so, Lucy buried her face against the base of his neck and inhaled deep, smelling soap and sweat and something uniquely Jackson. And with his heart pounding strong and steady beneath her ear, Lucy slipped her hands around his waist and hugged him back, making a final, desperate grab for the rapidly crumbling barriers around her heart. "Just so we're clear, I'm helping you out here. Not the other way around."

His arms tightened around her, and she felt him smile. "Duly noted."

CHAPTER NINE

JACKSON SAT THERE in the dark, holding Lucy, the noise of the storm raging overhead. But it was the feel of her hands at the small of his back that finally broke him. He'd tried hard to shut out the voices in his head, the ones telling him to keep his walls up, to not let anyone in, to avoid being vulnerable at any cost. The same voices he'd listened to since he'd been four years old and watched his mother drive away, never to return again.

He'd kept those barriers high and strong for two decades.

Until tonight.

Seemed all it took to crumble them down was one quiet, quirky woman with a spirit of steel and a soft spot for wounded creatures.

She'd spoken the truth earlier, about the darkness. He had acted on instinct both times he'd shut off the light—only now his motivation wasn't as simple as a hug. Nope. This time his needs were deeper, riskier. This time he wanted intimacy. Not just sex, but something more powerful. It clawed at him, leaving him raw inside, grasping for whatever was available as a defense and bringing him up short.

The very last thing he wanted—ever, ever again—was to *need* someone, to truly care for them.

And yes, he cared for his parents, for Luis, for his patients.

But this was different.

With Lucy, he wanted to keep her safe. He wanted to hold her and kiss her and swear that no one else would ever hurt her again. God. She was the last person he should be attracted to, and yet she'd brought him a sense of solace he'd never expected to feel again.

He didn't want to want her, and yet he did. He wanted so badly he burned.

"Lucy?" The word came out rougher than he'd intended.

"What?" She started to pull away, put some space between them, but he wasn't ready and tightened his arms around her, keeping her in place.

"Tell me more about Mitzi," he asked, hoping to distract them both. "From what I know, alligators are social creatures, so why does she stay here with you?"

She relaxed against him once more, her breasts brushing his chest, and Jackson struggled to steady his pulse beating under her cheek. "I'm not sure. Normally, they do spend their time with their own kind."

"What makes her different, then?" *What makes me different?*

"Her rear left leg was almost completely severed in a steel trap designed to catch small mammals. The original owners brought her to this compound because it was the closest area with a private pond. It was either bring her here or leave her to die."

"Wait. The gator that attacked me only has three legs?" He sighed. "Doesn't do much for my ego."

"Don't feel bad." Lucy laughed. "Mitzi still moves pretty darn fast, though usually it's in the other direction when humans are involved. Alligators generally prefer smaller, easily captured meals. They're cold-blooded and notorious for not expending any unnecessary energy."

"I wonder why she attacked me, then?" He frowned.

Lucy shrugged. "She's a very protective mother-to-be. The winds and impending storm probably confused her and you had the misfortune of coming between her and her nest. And you did ignore the signs, too."

"What signs?"

"The ones by the front gate. You didn't see them before when you brought King here?"

"No. I came in the back way. Plus, I was distracted because of his injuries, so…" The kitten meowed, as if realizing they were talking about him, and Jackson cooed to the little guy. "There's my brave boy. Yes, sir. Such a brave boy."

"I'm sorry you didn't know about Mitzi earlier." Lucy snuggled closer, tucking her head beneath his chin. "Most of the people on the island who visit my clinic know about her, so I guess I didn't think about it."

"It's okay." He frowned into the darkness, rubbing her back absently. "But I hope you didn't stay on her account. I'm pretty sure the rest of the wild gators in Florida ride out hurricanes on their own, nests or not. Chances are Mitzi would've been fine."

"Maybe." Lucy sighed and guilt pinched his chest. Who was he to judge someone else's choices when it came to love and devotion? Especially when his own track record there was less than stellar. He shifted on his cushion, uncomfortable in more ways than one.

"But…" Her arms tightened around him, and it took what was left of his control not to bend down and kiss her.

"Tell me," he coaxed.

She started to pull away again, but he held her tighter and whispered against her temple, "Darkness is a cloak, remember? Shut your eyes and let the words out, Lucy. Tell me why you'd willingly do something so self-destructive." His mouth grazed her skin, and he swallowed a groan. "Tell me."

"I…uh…"

Never in a million years had Lucy expected to have this conversation with him, but here she was, and if his firm embrace was any indication, she wasn't going anywhere anytime soon.

She took a deep breath and stared blankly in front of her, losing herself in the shadows. "This compound is my safe spot, my sanctuary, as much as it is for the animals I treat. No one controls me here. No one tries to use my own feelings and issues against me. I stayed here because this is where I belong, where I'm safe. When I'm here there's no games, no hidden agendas, no regrets."

Blood pounded in her ears as the silence stretched between them. She'd never told anyone the truth about what had happened with Robert. How, in the end, she'd been nothing but an experiment to him, a means to the end he wanted. A glorified lab rat. It was humiliating. It was dehumanizing. It was heartbreaking.

Yet as she sat there with Jackson, his strength braced

behind her, she wanted to tell him everything. He made her feel safe. Truly safe. Safe enough to speak her truth without fear that her words would be twisted around and used against her. Safe enough to let him help her without worrying that it made her weak.

Safe enough to connect.

Ever since Robert had betrayed her trust and her parents had been complicit in his actions, she'd successfully shut off her emotions, unwilling and unable to risk her heart. The only time she let her guard down was with her animals. She'd never once regretted her self-imposed isolation.

Until now.

Then Jackson had tried to rescue her and refused to take no for an answer. In the past, she'd rebelled against that kind of forced control. Now, she'd surrendered to Jackson. Why? Maybe because they could both be swept away with the storm. Maybe because when she looked past his charming exterior, she glimpsed a man as emotionally scarred as her. Maybe because he'd made her feel things tonight, things she'd never expected to feel again—joy, anticipation, yearning.

Against all odds and against her better judgment.

In the end, it didn't really matter, she supposed. The fact was, their lives were on the line and her nerves were rubbed raw and she wanted to open up to him, to share all her secrets, and she wanted him to confide in her as well.

After a long pause, the floodgates broke, and her inner thoughts tumbled out in a heated rush. "I let someone in. Someone I thought I could trust, but I was wrong. Not my parents, but they were part of the problem, too. This person used me. I thought they loved me, but I was mistaken."

Jackson traced his fingertips along her arm from elbow to bicep to shoulder, then paused a second before his hand drifted back down again. "You want to tell me more?"

The question sent her over some unforeseen edge, and she shattered.

She did. She really, really did. But between the storm and the anxiety roaring through her bloodstream like a runaway freight train, it was all too much. His voice, his arms. His hands, his body, his strength. The dark, the storm, the small room. Her pulse, her want had her turning in his arms and…

Oh God. What the hell am I doing?

Lucy wanted out. Had to get out. Away from Jackson, away from the way he made her feel, away from the things she wanted to say. Away from the things she wanted to do.

Light. Air. Blessed quiet. She desperately wanted them all, both outside and in her head. It was overwhelming, waiting for the moment when her OCD would turn all these perfect moments black, erasing the easiness she currently enjoyed with Jackson. Because her issues ruined everything. If she'd been normal, maybe things with Robert would've worked out. If she'd been normal, maybe she would've been married now, with kids and a white picket fence. If she'd been normal, maybe she wouldn't be alone on this island, with a man she'd barely known a week ago, preparing to possibly die soon.

Oh God.

Suffocating. She was suffocating. Unable to breathe,

unable to connect. Unable to let him in, no matter how badly her heart cried out for her to do so.

Slowly, like he was approaching a wounded animal, Jackson soothed her, his hands running up and down her back until she calmed. "Hey. Shh... It's okay. We don't have to talk. It's none of my business."

Lucy continued taking deep breaths, willing away the panic attack looming on the edges of her mind, forcing hoarse words past her constricted vocal cords. "Distract me. Tell me something about you. What were you like growing up?"

Now it was his turn to tense. "You don't really want to hear about that."

"Please. I do. I bet you were a handful."

Silence.

"If I guess will you tell me?"

His arms loosened a bit, and his pulse slowed. Better.

She smiled, the tension squeezing her chest easing. "You don't think I can, do you?"

He shrugged. "You're free to try."

She leaned back to look up at him, even though she couldn't make out much of his face in the darkness. "Promise me, no lies."

"Never." The sincerity in his tone made her believe him.

"Okay." She settled against him once more and imagined a young Jackson. "I bet you were a leader even then, always taking care of other people. You said you were adopted, so maybe you grew up too fast. Always the responsible one."

"Hmm." The sound was strained, edged with reluctant interest. "Maybe."

"I'm right, aren't I? It's why you like control so much," she said, her confidence growing now that the spotlight was off her. "Take how you showed up here earlier, determined to make me leave. Like you'd vanquish this hurricane single-handedly if you could."

Jackson snorted. "For someone who doesn't play well with others, you have excellent intuition."

"What made you like that, Jackson?"

"Maybe I was just born this way."

"Were you?"

Another long pause. "Doesn't really matter now, does it?"

Her chest pinched for the boy he'd been and whatever had made him the man he was today. "I'm sorry, Jackson."

"No need. We're both just surviving."

Except suddenly surviving didn't feel like enough for her anymore. She turned slightly, until their faces were a mere breath apart. Time seemed to slow. And then he kissed her.

Warm, firm lips covered hers, his tongue wet and hot. Not devouring, not crushing, but tasting, sampling. His mouth moved over hers slowly and thoroughly, as if trying to memorize her. Savoring her as if she were a precious treasure.

Never had Lucy been so completely seduced by a simple kiss.

Except there was nothing simple about Jackson or what he made her feel.

He moved a hand from her waist to the nape of her neck, deepening the kiss, while the other moved down to pull her hips more tightly against him. "Stop me,

Lucy," he whispered, pulling away slightly. "You won't find what you're looking for. Not with me."

"Neither will you," she panted. "But this is enough."

He tilted her head back, leaning into her so his hot breath tickled her throat. "This will never be enough."

Thunder boomed, rattling the house and shaking the foundation beneath them.

She pressed herself harder against his chest, her taut nipples grazing his warmth and making her desperate for more. "I want you, Jackson. Please."

His answer was to take her mouth again. And again. Ravaging her like Mathilda was ravaging the Keys.

Lucy gripped his shoulders, grinding against him, needing, searching, anything to take the ache away. Then his knee pushed up between her legs, and yes. Oh yes. That was what she wanted. Higher, harder. It had been so long. Too long. She clamped her thighs together to keep him there.

He growled against her neck then bucked hard.

Confused, Lucy suddenly found herself half a foot away.

Her heart raced along with her thoughts, trying to comprehend what had just happened. Jackson's harsh breaths told her where he was even though she couldn't see him in the dark. She groped for the lantern, her hand smacking against his warm, hard chest instead.

"Stay still," he hissed.

Embarrassed heat flooded her. She never threw herself at men like that. She could blame it on the storm, on her issues, on her overwhelming reaction to being cooped up in such a small, confined place, but it wouldn't wash, no matter how desperately she wished it would.

Sudden blinding light filled the space, and she shielded her eyes from the lantern's glow and Jackson's too-perceptive gaze.

"I think—" He winced and shifted his injured leg. "I'll take that painkiller now."

Oh God. She'd gotten so wrapped up in the moment she'd forgotten about his wound.

"I'm so sorry." Lucy rummaged through the box of medical supplies nearby, wishing the ground would swallow her whole as his gaze burned a hole through the side of her.

Finally, she located the bottle and held it closer to the light to check it was the right one, careful to keep her face averted. She hated being such a coward, but she'd had good reasons for keeping her distance from people, and what had happened with Jackson just now had proved her instincts were right.

"I doubt those pills cure what ails us."

So much for avoiding the subject. Lucy sighed and held out the bottle to him, without looking, glad her hand was steady. "Take two of these while I get you some water."

But instead of the bottle, he latched on to her wrist, pulling her toward him while he used his free hand to tilt up her chin. Lucy summoned all her strength not to yank out of his grasp and scurry backward like an awkward crab. But there was nothing she could do about her trembling.

"Damn, woman. You've got this retreat thing down to a science, don't you?" he asked, gaze narrowed. "I mean, I thought I was good at getting out fast, but you've got me beat."

She opened her mouth—whether to breathe or

speak, Lucy wasn't sure. Not that it mattered, since she couldn't seem to do either.

"Doesn't matter." He tugged again until she was on her hands and knees, the position putting her perilously close to his mouth again. "We've got a decision to make here, and I'm not sure either of us is thinking clearly enough to pick the right option."

She frowned, her mind whirling. "Decision?"

"About whether we're going to remember all the reasons we avoid entanglements in the first place." He leaned closer, tilting his head as if he meant to kiss her, but stopped short. "Or finish what we started a few minutes ago."

CHAPTER TEN

YESTERDAY, IF ANYONE had told Jackson his heart would override his brain, he'd have said they were crazy. Except the only crazy one here now was him. And what was even worse was he didn't care.

Not with Lucy watching him with those expressive dark eyes of hers, showing all the emotions swirling inside her, the same things he was feeling—hunger, heat, desire, doubt.

His heart rate kicked up a notch. He could've pulled her against him again and been done with it, but that wasn't how this worked. If they were going to do this, he had to be sure she wanted it as much as he did. This had to be her choice.

He just hoped she made up her mind before it killed him.

"I can't… I don't…" she said at last, pulling free to slump back against the cage behind her. The sense of loss stunned Jackson, as did the immediate urge to change her mind.

What the hell is happening to me?

In the past, he could take sex or leave it. There were always plenty of women looking for a good time with no strings attached, and when things had run their course, he moved on to the next one. But now…

He shifted back, too, putting a small but effective bit of space between them to distance himself. Mentally, anyway. His tight lower body complained, but he ignored it. Discomfort was good. The pain helped him focus.

At least, it always had in the past.

"Jackson—"

He glanced over, steeling himself against the possibility of an apology, or worse, pity. No way could he handle that. That's why he hadn't told her about his birth mother. He'd dealt with enough pity for a lifetime, and once people found out about her just leaving him behind without a word, that was the default they went to. Followed closely by morbid curiosity and wariness. So, he kept his expression aloof, relieved to see her doing the same. Or at least trying. But Lucy was just too damn easy to read.

He wondered how many times her emotions had gotten her into trouble. She'd mentioned people using her, manipulating her, controlling her. Those things made him want to punch something, namely whoever had done that to her. It made him furious to think she'd been used, hurt because her heart and issues were on display for anyone to see.

"I could use that water now," he said, his voice cold.

She grabbed another bottle from the cooler and slid it across the floor toward him. "You might not want to drink too much—"

"I know we need to conserve it."

"I wasn't thinking of that so much as…" Her voice trailed off, her cheeks pinkening.

"Oh. Right. Good point." He tossed the pills down dry instead and slid the unopened bottle back to her. "Thanks."

She returned it to the cooler then checked each of the cages and their occupants before fiddling with the box of medical supplies, arranging then rearranging them as if the fate of the universe depended on her getting them in exactly the right spot.

"Lucy."

She stilled but didn't look over at him.

"Maybe we should talk about what we might be facing in the next few hours now. Come up with plans in case…you know…things don't go smoothly."

"You mean in case we die?" She crossed her legs and shifted to face him again, blunt as usual. "I'm a vet. You're a paramedic. We're both professionals. I'm sure we can handle it."

"Yeah." He gave an unpleasant chuckle. "Funny how we can deal with life and death just fine, but not anything personal."

She shrugged then pulled a baggie of fruit out of the cooler nearby and fed an orange slice to the cockatoo through the bars of its cage. "Makes sense to me. Emotions are always harder to talk about."

That got his full attention. He didn't dare react.

"I guess they are." He fiddled with the leg of his torn pants again. "That's why I try to keep mine out of it. Not everything has to mean something, right? In fact, sometimes it's better if it doesn't, since nothing lasts forever. Better to keep things light, uncomplicated."

Jackson swallowed hard, stunned he'd said that. Admitted that.

"That's an interesting take," she said thoughtfully, giving him some serious side eye.

"Whatever." He leaned his head back and stroked King's paw through the side of his cage. "So, you're saying you've never had a fling? Just hot sex and forget the rest? No strings. All the pleasure, none of the pain? Sounds like that'd be right up your alley, a loner like you."

He did it all the time. Every time, truth be told.

Her shoulders stiffened and she gave Bubba the last slice of orange before facing Jackson again, hands clenched and knees tucked to her chest like she was trying to roll herself into a tiny ball. The ultimate defensive posture. She met his gaze directly, her stern silence making it clear she'd taken his question as a challenge. "No. I haven't."

He wanted to ask her more about that ex-fiancé of hers but never had the chance.

Another tremendous boom of thunder rocked the house, so loud it hurt his ears, followed by a more horrific tearing sound. The whole house shook as if the structure above them was being ripped in two. "Get near the middle boxes!" Jackson yelled, grabbing the edge of the mattress to anchor it above their heads, pulling the corner cages closer to the center of the space near them. Lucy did the same on her side. "Stay down, close to the floor."

The wind's screeching wail made it difficult to hear what she was saying. "Is the house collapsing?"

"Maybe." He leaned closer to her as best he could. "Part's definitely gone. The sound's louder."

Her lips brushed his earlobe, and his traitorous body

leaped in response, despite the situation—or maybe because of it.

"What do you think our chances are?" Lucy yelled.

Some people would fall apart, scream, go nuts. Not his Lucy. His already high respect for her tripled. He didn't sugarcoat reality for her. She deserved the truth. "Not good."

She stilled a second, then gathered Sam closer, scooting them both into Jackson's side so she could rest her head against his neck once again. A simple action that conveyed so much. She trusted him. And never in his life had Jackson wanted to be worthy of it more.

He kissed the top of her head and tucked her legs closer to his, the wound on his thigh the least of his concerns at that point.

"Jackson?" she said.

"Mmm?"

"Thank you."

His brows drew together, and he pulled away slightly to look down at her. "For what?"

"I know I said I could handle it, but I'm glad I'm not going through this alone. And I'm sorry you might die because of me."

Yearning ached in the center of his chest. Dammit. *She* was apologizing to *him*?

Nope. Couldn't have that.

"If I'd raised the readiness level sooner, maybe neither of us would be here. Not your fault," he said gruffly. He thought about Luis and his parents and the rest of the team back in Key West and hoped they were all faring better right now.

"I'm worried about Mitzi." The sadness in her voice pulled on his heartstrings.

"I'm sure she's all right," he said, even though he wasn't sure at all.

"She'll lose her nestlings."

"Maybe." He inhaled the sweet, clean scent of her shampoo, forcing away the terror nipping around his edges. "She can have more, right?"

"Not sure. Mitzi gets around okay on three legs, but who knows if she'll mate again."

Jackson sensed there was something more she wasn't telling him. "Was there something special about this particular nest?"

"No. Not to anyone else other than me, at least." Her slight shudder turned her words wobbly. "She's just struggled so hard to make it, and I can relate. Then she got pregnant, and I wondered if she'd live this long just so she could lay her eggs."

Jackson had never let himself think about having a family. What if something happened and he had to leave them behind? Sure, someone wonderful like the Durands might take them in, but the scars of abandonment were deep and not easily overcome.

"I helped her," Lucy said, drawing him back to the present.

"I'm sorry?" he said, frowning.

"When alligators lay their eggs, they're completely focused on the task. Normally, I wouldn't have interfered, but she was having trouble balancing and I was afraid she'd squash them as they came out. So, I helped Mitzi prop herself up so the eggs would drop into the nest."

Jackson scowled, thinking about the danger she'd risked. "You're crazy."

"Maybe. But that's why I had to stay."

"Well, you didn't have to, but—"

"This is where I'm connected, Jackson. To Mitzi, to this place. More than any person."

He lifted her chin, staring down at her. "But what about Stacy? Dr. Dave? You have connections there, too."

"They're not the same. This place is mine. I belong here. No one can hurt me here. This place is my freedom. I won't leave it behind. I can't."

Her tone had turned defensive again, but she didn't pull away, and he forced himself to be content with that.

For several long minutes they remained silent, the ominous sounds of Hurricane Mathilda raging around them. Then Lucy said, "Your turn."

He'd made it a habit never to talk about himself, and his need for self-defense kicked in full force. Still, he tried to sound casual. "What do you want to know?"

"Answer my question from earlier." Her tone had turned shy. "I won. You owe me."

It felt weird and wrong and wonderful all at the same time, the sudden odd urge to tell her whatever she wanted to know. Jackson was tempted, for the first time in forever, to share something of himself, to risk giving a piece of himself away. To Lucy.

Dangerous, that. And precisely why he avoided true intimacy, keeping things light. Physical. Primal. Never emotional. But she was right, he did owe her. And he was a man of his word.

"I was born in Miami. Not the rich part, but still nice. My dad died in the Gulf War before I was born, so it was just me and my mom." He shifted slightly to take weight off his injured thigh.

He'd done his best to keep to the facts and sound as clinical as possible, but he must've failed, because Lucy sniffled against him and squeezed him a bit tighter. "Oh, Jackson. I'm so sorry."

"It's okay." He shrugged, though it really wasn't okay at all. "And I'm sure it wasn't any harder than what you went through. Besides, if anyone's brave around here, it's you."

"I'm not—"

"You are, Lucy. The bravest woman I've ever known." He kissed her again, swallowing any further response she might've made, doing what he'd been wanting to do since the last time. And sure, he might've been avoiding all those confusing, conflicting emotions inside him, the deep wound that had reopened with the telling of his story, but what a way to do it. Lucy was sweet and sensual in ways he'd never experienced. He'd never wanted someone so much, ever. Being with her felt unique, so tantalizing he couldn't resist.

He took the kiss deeper, plunging his fingers into her hair before trailing them down to her shoulders. She trembled and gripped his arms, hanging on for dear life, arching against him, letting him know she wanted this as much as he did.

Body, mind, soul and spirit.

Their tongues dueled, and he conceded defeat willingly, allowing her what she sought, praying like hell he had it to give.

The storm forgotten, Jackson pulled her under him, rolling half on top of her in the small, cramped space. His hands slid from her shoulders to her waist, pulling her tighter against him, needing more contact between her softness and his hardness. He lifted himself enough to pull her shirt from the waistband of her jeans as her arms twined around his neck, urging him not to break the delicious contact, and he struggled to comply. Finally, he levered himself up on one arm and she groaned her disapproval, then sucked in a sharp breath when he pushed her shirt up.

"Please." Lucy's whisper was harsh with need.

He scooted down so his face was even with her torso and kissed her stomach. "Please what?"

"Please—" She gasped as he unclasped her bra to bare her breasts. "Yes!"

He palmed her breasts, circling her taut nipples with his thumbs. "So perfect."

"That feels so good."

Then he dipped his head and took one of the taut peaks into his mouth, stroking the other between his thumb and forefinger, and she dug her nails into his scalp. He teased against her skin, "I'm guessing this feels even better?"

She moaned and writhed. He nuzzled her again, reveling in the way she reacted. So responsive.

"Jackson." Her whisper was urgent, demanding. He understood.

"I know, sweetheart, I know." He shifted, kissing lightly along the center of her stomach, lingering over her navel, finding the whole experience of discovering her in the dark both frustrating and immensely erotic. He unsnapped her jeans and pulled on the zipper.

"Wait." She reached down, tugging at him. "Come here."

Everything in him urged him to continue, but not against her wishes. He sighed then shifted upward, not pulling her shirt down, but wishing like hell his was off so he could feel her bare breasts against his chest. Favoring his sore thigh, he pulled her to him. "What, sweetheart? Was I going too fast?"

"No." She ducked her head, resting her forehead on his shoulder.

"What then? You've never made love during a hurricane?" he joked, keeping his tone light, ignoring the fact he'd called what they'd been doing lovemaking and not sex, like usual.

"No. I haven't. But that's not why I wanted you to stop."

"Then what?"

"Because I'm not… That is, I didn't think you…" She buried her head again, muttering against his chest. "I'm almost thirty. I'm not a virgin. You'd think I could talk about this stuff without blushing."

A new and unexpected rush of affection flooded his system. His Lucy was strong and tough, and wonderfully adorable in ways he'd never imagined. He leaned down and gave her a hard, fast kiss. Because he thought she needed the reassurance, and because he damn well wanted to. "You should've let me continue. I guarantee you'd be feeling a whole lot less stressed than you do right now."

She smacked him lightly on the shoulder and laughed. "Pretty sure of yourself, aren't you?"

In his best Southern drawl, he said, "Why yes, ma'am, I am."

She hugged him tightly, and he hugged her right back. When he'd first gotten here, he couldn't wait for the storm to be over. Now, he never wanted it to end. Because then all this would be over, and he'd have to let her go. He realized that part was going to be more difficult than he'd ever thought possible.

"Jackson?"

"Yeah?"

"Does this mean we have to stop kissing?"

His body answered with a resounding no.

"Absolutely not." He ripped off his shirt, sending buttons flying, then quickly settled his mouth back on hers. Shifting to his back, and nudging Sam farther to the side, Jackson pulled Lucy half on top of him, groaning deeply at the feel of her breasts rubbing his chest. "Damn, you feel good."

"You too," she said, smiling down at him. "You too."

CHAPTER ELEVEN

LUCY WOKE UP SLOWLY. Awareness came in waves, like layers of sand falling into place. Memories of Jackson kissing her, of her kissing Jackson, of her heart pounding and his pulse racing under her lips when she licked his neck. Their hands on each other... Then he'd slowed things down by getting her to talk, teasing her into recounting stories both funny and sad about being a vet.

At some point along the way, she'd fallen asleep.

Her eyes flew open, not because of what was happening but because of what wasn't.

The noise. It was gone.

She couldn't see a thing, but she felt a heavy weight pressing against her chest and abdomen.

"Are we dead?" she whispered.

"God, I hope not," came a raspy reply.

Jackson shifted, the bristle of his beard scraping against her bare left breast.

Before she could react, he kissed her nipple, having no problem locating it without a bit of light.

She arched under his touch, a dozen things warring for her immediate attention. It was a toss-up which would win the battle, but then he shifted his attention to her other breast and things quickly slanted toward sensation, until she shoved at his shoulders. "Jackson, stop. The storm. Listen!"

With a deep, heartfelt sigh that made her smile, he lifted his head and paused. "It's over."

"You don't think it's just the eye passing over?" she asked, straining to hear any signs the storm still raged, but there was nothing except the rustle of the animals around them.

Sam whimpered from near her feet, most likely needing to go out and potty. King issued a cranky meow, and Bubba's cage rattled as he danced back and forth on his perch, squawking, "I can see clearly now!"

"No. Not the eye," Jackson said, his voice deep and rough with sleep. "Been too long. It's over."

"We made it?" she whispered, like Mathilda might return if she knew she'd left them behind.

"Yeah. We made it."

Lucy's thoughts instantly shifted to Mitzi, and she struggled to crawl out from under Jackson. He stopped her short, however, pinning her back down on the cushions with strong hands.

"Hold on." He slid off her. "Let me make sure the only thing on top of us is this mattress."

She pulled down her shirt while he shuffled around, trying not to think about the sudden sense of loss flooding her system. This was it. Her time with Jackson was probably over. Not that they'd done anything earth-shattering. Unless you called spending hours in the arms of the sexiest man ever important. And for her it most definitely was.

"Feels sound," he said a minute later. "I'll prop this side back up, and you feel around for the lantern."

Confused and conflicted, Lucy shoved aside her seesawing emotions and switched on the light then covered her eyes with her forearm as unnatural brightness filled the small space.

When she'd adjusted, she opened an eye and peered at Jackson, who was squinting back at her.

"I feel like a mole," he said.

"Same." She smiled, then checked on each animal and gave them each food and water before taking her own meds. "Is it day or night?"

"Uh…" Jackson glanced at his smart watch. "Morning. A bit past seven, if this thing is still right."

"Good. The sun should be up, so at least we'll be able to see the damage outside." She pulled out her phone. "Any bars yet?"

"Lucy—"

Nope. No service yet. Whether that was because of the basement or the storm damage, she wasn't sure. All the more reason to get out of here. She started to scoot out from under the mattress, grateful for things to do besides sit there and think about Jackson, and about losing him soon. There was so much to do, so much to clean up, so much to deal with. One big goodbye to come…

Her fingers tapped the cold concrete floor.

One, two, three. One, two, three.

"I need to check on Mitzi," she said. "Make sure she's okay."

"Lucy, stop." He gave her a pleading look. "You need to—"

"I know, I know. I should prepare myself for the worst, just in case. I'm fine. I'll be fine. Really." It was a lie, of course. Usually when a person said everything was fine, it most certainly wasn't. But that didn't stop her from trying. Besides, there was no way Jackson could possibly know what she was going through at that moment. He wouldn't understand her emotional limbo because of him. Even if they drew this thing out between them past this day, this moment, maybe a week or two, her anxiety would catch up to her. It always did. And other people never dealt well with her issues.

Always wanting to help her. Or control her. Or, in Jackson's case, protect her.

But there wasn't anything to protect her from, because the monster lived inside her.

She was the monster.

Still, Lucy put on a brave face, because that's what she did. "I remember after Irma hit the coast of the Carolinas. The devastation. It'll be different now, though, since it's…my home…that's rubble."

"Hey," he said, reaching out to tuck her hair behind her ear. "We're alive, Lucy. That's the most important thing."

Their gazes locked. He looked good and strong and reassuring, the same as he'd been through the long, dark hours of the night.

"Yes, you're right. Thank you, Jackson."

"Don't thank me, thank Mathilda."

Mathilda didn't hold me last night.

"If you hadn't been here, though," she said, clearing her throat, "I'd have lost it a long time ago."

His expression was unreadable, and she got the distinct impression he was distancing himself from her, memorizing her, storing his time with her away.

"You wouldn't have fallen apart," he said at last. "You're strong. You do what has to be done."

Lucy looked away, determined to let him go without embarrassing either one of them. She'd known this odd thing between them was temporary going into last night, so it was good they pulled back now. Like ripping off a bandage. Besides, she'd need all her strength and concentration to deal with whatever chaos waited on the other side of the basement door.

They'd weathered a crisis together, where the line between life and death thinned to invisible proportions. That was all. And she wasn't stupid enough to think what they'd shared in the darkness would survive in the light.

"Well, the fact remains you *were* here, and I'll always be grateful for that." Without waiting for his response, she crawled out from under the mattress, then looked back at Jackson, careful to keep her demeanor and tone businesslike. "What's the best way out of here? I don't want to move the wrong thing or open the door up there and have the remainder of the house cave in on our heads."

"Let's start by getting this mattress out of the way. Scoot next to me and help me shove this half off the cages."

Lucy did so but paid a price for being close to him again. His scent and heat made her heart flutter, and she ducked to hide what had to be written all over her face. She still wanted him. Wanted to finish what she hadn't really let him start last night. She ached with the wanting.

Once they'd made short work of the mattress, she stood and massaged the pins and needles from her legs as blood flow returned to the nerve endings. From the corner of her eye, she caught Jackson wince and hop before catching his balance with a hand on the wall.

"How's your leg this morning? You should let me look at it before we go up."

"It's fine. Don't worry. I just pulled it a bit when I stood." He brushed past her and hobbled up the stairs, taking the lantern with him. "I'll check the door frame for cracks or stress fractures."

She told herself he was a grown man and could look after himself. That was easier than admitting if she touched him again, she might not let go.

"This looks sound." Jackson angled the light downward slightly then twisted the doorknob, opening the door a crack. Nothing crashed down or caved in. He turned back to her. "Ready?"

"As I'll ever be." Lucy took a deep breath and climbed up beside him.

"Hey." His voice was low, husky. Private. Without the background noise of the storm, it sounded almost… *intimate*.

But that couldn't be. He didn't want to get close to anyone. He'd made that clear. The sooner she remembered that, the better. She bowed her head for a brief moment, then looked up at him. "I'm okay. Really."

He nodded then moved away.

Shoulders squared and mind carefully blank, Lucy stepped past him into the hallway and…

Oh. My. God.

She covered her mouth and stared, barely registering the reassuring weight of Jackson's hands on her shoulders or how he pulled her stiffened body back against his. Sam scrabbled out the basement door beside her, whining and panting.

The kitchen still stood, but her office was rubble. Squashed, like some giant had stepped on it. Down the hall toward the front door, the living room looked fine. Except for the unnatural amount of light streaming down the staircase.

Holy—

Lucy took two steps in that direction, but Jackson grabbed her arm.

"Let me go first." He moved in front of her before she could stop him.

She waited in the basement doorway, one hand buried in Sam's fur to keep him where he was and safe, the other pressed to her chest, where her heart felt like it would slam out of her chest.

Rubble from what remained of the upper level of the house scattered the stairs and heaped in piles at the bottom. For the first time, the enormity of the danger they'd been in swamped her. Staying here had always been a risk. She knew that. Or thought she had.

But this…this…ripping apart one piece of her life, then sparing another, was too much.

Jackson returned and guided her toward the kitchen, hooking his fingers through Sam's collar to lead him alongside them. "Can't check it right now, too much debris. Let's get out of here. Until we see the extent of the damage from the outside, we don't know if the structure's safe, anyway."

Lucy took one last glimpse at the stairs. Hunks of roof and insulation and drywall clogged the area. Hard to tell how much of the roof had caved in, just that some if it definitely had—given the amount of light streaming in.

"Come on." He urged her forward with a tug on her hand. "Let's check on Mitzi."

Zombie-like, she took two steps, then buried her

head on his shoulder. His arm came around her immediately, holding her tight to his side while Sam barked then licked her leg.

Her eyes burned, but no tears came. Maybe she was in shock. She concentrated on Jackson's solid warmth beside her and took deep, even breaths. *In, out. In, out.*

"Why does it feel like my life's ending anyway?" Whoops. She hadn't meant to ask that out loud.

"It'll be okay, Lucy," he whispered, nuzzling her ear. "Maybe not today or tomorrow, but soon. I promise."

To have done this much damage, the sheer magnitude of the storm must have been…

Mitzi.

Her head shot up. "I've got to check on her."

A sudden burst of anxiety had her pushing away from Jackson, thoughts racing. "Can you do a perimeter check while I go find out how she is?"

"No, I'll go with you," he said, his tone determined.

"I've got this," she rushed on, turning toward the kitchen. "I'll be—"

"Sam, stay." His commanding tone had her dog sitting obediently in a small clearing of the floor.

Jackson took her hand and helped her over the rubble pile that had blown into the kitchen from what had once been her office. "Watch your step."

Lucy stepped over a chunk of debris, then froze. Her stained-glass lamp from her office. The shade was cracked, and the bulb fixture was mangled, but otherwise, it was still intact.

Her world slowly rocked back to center, filtering out some of the anxiety and OCD screaming around her edges. Her attention zeroed to the here and now. There'd be plenty of time later to sort out her feelings about everything that had happened. She set the lamp on the untouched kitchen table and tightened her hold on Jackson's hand. He felt like a lifeline, one she could use.

"Help me get the bars off the door?" he asked, his tone quiet and calm.

She was grateful for the task. Even the smallest chore meant progress, that the worst was over and every step, no matter how tiny, was a step away from this…this…

Jackson shuddered and she frowned, dropping his hand. "Do you want the mop for a crutch again?"

"Nah. It feels better this morning." At her dubious look, he grinned. "Really. I guess last night's enforced rest was good for something after all."

She didn't want to think about last night right now. Not if she wanted to keep it together.

He was still limping a little, favoring his wounded thigh, but he could walk. She turned her attention to the door and what lay beyond. Or rather, who.

"Let me push, then you pull," he directed. "It's warped a bit."

Five minutes later the bars were removed, and the door swung open, revealing the vacant spot where her screened-in porch had once been.

Her mind registered the incredible amount of debris, both natural and man-made, littering the compound, but most of her attention was focused on the pond.

Lucy searched for a safe path through the rubble while Jackson went back inside, scooped up all sixty pounds of whining Sam in his arms and carried him out into the backyard with them, setting him down before motioning for her to follow.

After waiting for Sam to do his business, she left him with Jackson while she continued on toward the pond.

"At least there's no flooding," she called over her shoulder. Downed trees and limbs and more chunks of her roof blocked her path. She headed in what appeared to be the most direct route around it all.

A bark sounded behind her, and she stopped again to look back at Jackson and Sam.

"Seagull," he yelled. "Go on, we'll catch up."

Lucy nodded, deliberately not looking past him to her house. Not now. Mitzi first, then the rest. The house wasn't going anywhere. At least what was left of it.

The egg mound. If it was waterlogged, the hatchlings would die. The sky was still overcast, but the rain and wind had stopped. Still, it could flood. Big Pine Key was small, and a storm of Mathilda's ferocity had likely wreaked havoc on the tides, too. "Please," she prayed. "No more."

Lucy rounded a twisted piece of what had once been her storage shed and finally got her first good look at the pond. Swollen past its banks, the water had stopped several feet shy of infiltrating the egg mound. Mitzi was nowhere to be seen.

She broke into a run and didn't stop running until she was halfway around the pond. A dark shadow floated in the shallows. Lucy positioned herself to get the best view without antagonizing the gator. Having her binoculars would've helped, but they'd been in her office, which was gone. The sense of loss blindsided her again, stealing her breath for a long, painful moment.

Then, as if summoned from her fervent wishes, large, warm hands covered her shoulders again.

"Breathe," Jackson said from behind her. She hadn't even heard him come up. "Is Mitzi okay?"

"I haven't seen her move yet, but she's near the mound, and it doesn't look damaged or flooded, from what I can tell."

"How will you know for sure?"

She tore her gaze away from Mitzi and faced Jackson. Her heart skipped. She liked looking at him, looking *to* him. "Mostly observation. I'll have to get closer if she seems to be suffering. As for the nestlings, they're due to hatch in about two weeks. We'll know for certain then." She glanced around. "Where's Sam?"

"I found a leash in the clinic—which is fine, by the way," he said, watching her closely. "I cleared an area for him and left him tethered near the porch."

"Okay," she said finally, for lack of anything better to say, unable to handle his scrutiny with her control so thinly stretched. "What?"

"You." He ran a finger down her cheek.

"What about me?" *Dumb question.*

"I've never met anyone like you. Strong, tough, courageous."

"You're an EMT. You work with strong, tough, courageous people every day."

"Not like you." His mouth tipped up into a crooked smile and his eyes lit up, banishing all the darkness. She couldn't help smiling back, despite the circumstances. "You're different."

"In a good way, I hope." *Stop it. You don't need his attention. You don't need anyone.*

Then he was kissing her again, and there was no time to breathe, no time to think, no time to worry. Passion pushed her, drove her, tested her. And she wanted more, *needed* so much more.

Lucy stood in his arms, helpless against the yearning.

Helpless.

Something deep inside her clicked. Or maybe it snapped. And the whirling maelstrom of emotions she'd kept locked away for so long crashed past her barriers. Violent, powerful, the force flowing through her, energizing her. Revitalizing her.

She moved against him, pulled at him, kissed him back, arched against him. She didn't think, she didn't wonder, she just acted.

Jackson gave as good as he got, each of them fighting for control.

Now she didn't feel helpless, didn't feel broken.

Now she felt like the woman he'd described. Strong. Tough. Courageous.

Then, as swiftly as it had swept over them, the storm receded. Their kisses gentled, slowed, until they stood looking at each other.

"Thank you," she whispered past the constriction in her throat.

His gaze betrayed him. His walls, his defenses were gone. At last she saw behind them. Saw his pain, sadness, wariness. But there was also fierce strength, honor and faith.

And a banked fire that had nothing to do with protection. Her knees buckled.

Jackson's arms tightened around her, and the flickering heat in his eyes threatened to erupt into an inferno. Intimacy. Not just physical, but in far more dangerous ways—mental, emotional.

The imaginary thread they'd forged between them the night before flared brighter. Irreversible as any physical bond. Maybe more so. She couldn't have felt any more open or vulnerable if he'd stripped her naked, pulled her down and driven himself into her right on the hard, wet ground.

Jackson cupped her cheeks and rested his forehead against hers. "Don't thank me. It's not me, Lucy. It's you. It's always been you."

He was wrong. It wasn't her. It wasn't him, either. It was them.

He kissed her, sweet and short, then stepped back and held out his hand, his weight shifting unevenly on his wounded leg. "Ready?"

"Yes." She cast a swift glance at Mitzi. Then did a double take. "She's at the egg mound!"

"Good." Jackson grinned. "Let's go check out your clinic. I think it's okay, but you should check."

"Right. I need to know what resources I have available. Maybe I'll finally have some luck and Mitzi won't need my help." She didn't let herself think about the nestlings. There was nothing she could do for them at this point anyway except wait. "Once we make sure the clinic's okay, we can bring the rest of the animals up from the basement."

Lucy unhooked Sam's leash from the porch then walked with Jackson to the clinic with him. He took her hand again and fell into step beside her like he belonged there. And it seemed the most natural thing in the world to shorten her stride to accommodate his limp.

CHAPTER TWELVE

SEVERAL HOURS HAD passed by the time she and Jackson had moved Bubba and King from the basement to the clinic, then finished a rough categorization of the damage. It hadn't been easy. Several times, usually just when she thought she was handling things pretty well, she'd find something—a broken chunk of equipment or a twisted piece of furniture—and the overwhelming depth of her predicament would threaten to consume her. And each time Jackson was there. Sometimes with a steady look, sometimes with a touch, and sometimes with a quick, tight hug.

She might have been able to handle all this without him, but it would've been so much worse. And she didn't beat herself up over taking the solace he offered. He'd be gone soon enough anyway, then she'd have plenty of time to shoulder the burden alone.

In the meantime, she absorbed as much of his strength as he was willing to give, storing it up for later. For all the times he wouldn't be there, for all the times when she might wish he was.

"I think this is the last of it." Jackson entered the main treatment room, which they'd turned into a sort of inventory center. He had a small box under one arm and a large green trash bag in the other hand. "I was able to get service out on the edge of the compound. Talked to Luis on the phone. Key West came through the hurricane okay—some damage and flooding there, too. He'll send help for us as soon as he can, but it could be a while."

She nodded and went back to her work, cataloging supplies. Fortunately, Jackson had been right. Her clinic had been relatively untouched, only a few roof shingles swept away. The chain-link pens outside and a good portion of the fence surrounding the property had been twisted or destroyed, but replacing them was the least of her concerns.

Lucy hadn't missed the strain on Jackson's face, either, or how pronounced his limp had become again. He'd taken more pain meds earlier and even let her check the stitches. There was some redness, but it actually looked okay. His endurance was admirable, but there was a limit, even for him.

"I think we've done enough," she said, putting a dish of wet food into King's cage then shutting the door, doing her best to keep her voice casual to gain his compliance. "Why don't you take a break and lie down on the cot in the back room?"

"You stay out here some nights?" he asked, ignoring her suggestion. She'd thought after last night and their kiss by the pond maybe they'd gotten past his superhero complex, but apparently not.

She shrugged. "Some animals need regular attention, so it makes sense for me to stay close by."

"Hmm." He hefted the bag onto the long counter then folded his arms atop of it. "You give so much to your work, Lucy. Is there any left for yourself?"

"I love what I do." She picked up her clipboard, not meeting his gaze. "Go on. Lie down for a bit. Take some weight off that leg. Doctor's orders. I can inventory the rest of this stuff by myself."

Instead of doing as she asked, however, he grabbed a stool and took a seat, propping his leg on a box on the floor in front of him. "Satisfied?"

More than she ever thought possible. She liked his company, liked having him nearby, where she could see him whenever she wanted.

When she didn't answer, he continued. "I never asked, but it must be tough financing an operation like this. How do you do it? Grants? Private funding? Donations?"

"I manage," she said, hoping he'd let the topic drop. The last thing she wanted to do was discuss her financial situation, mainly because that would lead to more talk of her past, and she didn't want to get into all that again when everything was going so well now.

"Do you ever travel to help animals?" he asked, thankfully changing subjects. "Luis used to go on mission trips, helping underprivileged kids and adults by giving them life-saving medical care. I've heard of vets doing free spay and neuter surgeries and stuff, too."

"Sometimes," Lucy said, doing her best to concentrate on the crate of supplies she was counting, and failing. "But I don't travel. I have the patients that need my help flown in here free of charge so I can give them treatment here at the compound. Your brother, Luis, sounds like a good man."

"He is." He nodded, his crooked smile emerging again. "Though he can be difficult, too, like you."

She shot him a look. "I'm not difficult."

"Sweetheart, you're like herding cats at a rodeo." At her scowl, he chuckled. "But in the best way."

Lucy blushed as his laugh deepened.

"I meant it as a compliment," he said, taking her hand again. "You're complex. I like that."

Robert had always claimed Lucy was complex, too. But in all the wrong ways. Ways he felt compelled to fix whether she wanted him to or not. Her hackles rose. No, the last thing she needed was another man trying to take over her life, thinking he knew best. And while she cared about Jackson, more than she ever had about anyone, she'd fought too hard to let him steal her freedom, no matter how adorable he might be.

Jackson saw her close him out as effectively as the basement had shut out Hurricane Mathilda.

"Listen," Lucy said, the edge in her words telling him things were most definitely not fine at all. "About last night. And about what happened at the pond earlier. I think we should forget it. All of it."

"And if I don't want to?" he shot back. He cared, for reasons he didn't want to contemplate too deeply at the moment. Usually he never had to deal with the morning-after awkwardness because he always made sure he was long gone by then. They hadn't even had sex, not really. Just fooled around. They'd both liked it. He'd thought maybe they'd continue down that path earlier, but it seemed he'd been wrong. Again.

"Why not?" She set her clipboard aside and crossed her arms. "I'd think you'd be overjoyed. No strings, just like you wanted. So, why are fighting this?"

"I'm not." *Liar.* He gestured toward the rest of the room. "I just figured we'd enjoy each other's company a little longer until help arrives. Get to know each other better."

"I know enough about you already."

His hackles rose at that. What the hell? She'd been fine last night, having him close, holding her, touching her, kissing her. Now she wanted him gone. He leaned forward, jaw tight. "Really? Because I don't feel like I know you at all, Lucy. One minute you're cowering against me, holding on for dear life, the next you can't push me away fast enough. Sorry, but I don't go hot and cold that fast. And while we're at it, where in the hell did you get this idea that you have to do everything yourself and accepting any help or advice makes you weak? This is one battle you don't have to fight alone."

"What do you know about my battles, Jackson?" She turned away, and in the past, Jackson would've let her go, but today he couldn't. Wouldn't. He knew more about fighting demons and pain and being alone than she'd learn in two lifetimes. He didn't give an inch.

"I know you've been hurt. I know someone probably thought they were helping, and instead they nearly broke you, but you're still here. You're a survivor." Unexpected anger constricted his throat, but he forced the words out, anyway. "I am, too. But we all need help, Lucy."

"Not me. And you're one to talk," she said, her tone defensive. "You don't let others do for you, either. You didn't even want me to take care of a simple thigh wound last night." Lucy snorted and shook her head. "You're an EMT, Jackson. You know better than anyone how quickly a cut like that can get infected. But instead of worrying about yourself, you're acting like rescuing me is a personal crusade or something. You came onto my property and tried to take over. Don't tell me—"

One second he was sitting on the stool, the next it crashed to the tile floor as he took her in his arms, his face inches from hers. "Stop trying to figure me out, Lucy. You won't get it right. But you were correct about one thing. Being here *is* a crusade for me. I save people. It's what I do. Who I am. And I take that responsibility seriously." He drew her closer until barely a whisper separated them. "The reason I asked about your money situation is because I've got contacts in the area. They might be willing to help you get back on your feet. Not because I think you can't do it for yourself. I know you can." He narrowed his gaze. "So, why don't you tell me why you're really shoving me away?"

She struggled against his hold. "Because when people try to help, they end up taking over, and I can't afford to lose control of my life again. I won't. That's why I don't need your help or anyone else's."

"So that's it? You close yourself off and only open up around your animals?"

"They respect my boundaries, which is more than I can say for everyone else I've ever—"

"Loved?" he broke in, sensing he was getting close to her truth.

She opened her mouth, closed it, then opened it again.

"Tell me."

"Why?" she shouted. "It's over with. Done. I've been hurt and I won't let it happen again, Jackson. I've had my emotions, my issues, used to control me, all under the guise of help. So, no. I don't want it and I don't need it. Not from you or anyone else. Understand?" An angry sob broke through. "I won't let you in. I won't let you that close again. I can't."

He pulled her into a tight embrace, tucking her head against his chest and resting his cheek atop of her head, running his other hand up and down her back. Her pain and fear broke his soul.

"Shh. I shouldn't have pushed like that." He kissed her hair, then pressed another to her temple. "I know what it's like to love so much it hurts, then be betrayed by those who were supposed to care for you." He tilted her face upward, forcing her to look at him then placed a soft kiss on her lips. "And I'm a bastard for badgering you. It's none of my business."

"No, it's not." She sniffled, a tear trickling down her cheek. He traced it away with his thumb. "I like my life now just the way it is, Jackson. I have my work. I have my animals. Simple. Steady. Safe. I'd think you of all people would get that. Simple. Safe. Steady. But now…with you…"

He cursed under his breath, then held her gaze. "I want to help you, Lucy, not change you. No strings, no payback. Nothing. I just want to help. Please let me."

She trembled, and his chest squeezed with an odd mix of desire and dread. Desire to hold her, protect her, care for her. Dread because he knew she might not let him. Not now, not ever.

Forty-eight hours ago, he wouldn't have cared. Now he did.

More than he wanted to admit, and it rocked him to his core. As much as she feared letting him in, the thought of opening his heart to her terrified him even more. Because the one thing he wanted more than anything in the world now—true closeness, true intimacy, with Lucy—was probably the very last thing she'd give him.

"I can't, Jackson," she said at last, her voice still thick with unshed tears.

"Can't or won't?"

Frustrated, Jackson hobbled back to the counter, righted his stool, then took a seat again. The last thing he wanted to do with her today was fight, so he tried a different tack. "What about the money?"

"I don't need money. I could buy and sell this place five times over."

He blinked at her a moment. That was news. "I didn't realize being a vet paid that well."

"It doesn't. It's family money."

"You're loaded then, huh?" He'd meant it as a joke, but she didn't smile.

Honestly, he didn't care if she owned the entire state of Florida. Money didn't impress him. Never had. But if it made her more secure and happy, he was all for it.

"My grandmother married well. She left me a sizable amount in a trust fund." She stared at the center of his chest, burning a hole through it. "I only use it for the clinic and facilities. There's plenty to fix this place, even expand if I wanted, but..."

The unspoken reason made him rock back slightly on the legs of his stool. "But then you'd have to hire staff, maybe take on a partner. And you don't want to do that."

From the way her pretty face blanched, he knew he'd hit a bull's-eye.

She bit her lip. "Don't judge me."

"I wasn't."

Lucy frowned. "Why did you really become a paramedic, Jackson? Why not a doctor, like Luis?" He opened his mouth to respond, but she talked over him. "I think it's because as an EMT you get to take control and assess the situation, then turn the patients over to someone else without ever getting too close. You leave them before they can leave you." At his stunned silence, she nodded. "That's it, isn't it?"

He did his best to shut down his reaction, to choke the burning bile in his gut. She'd hit far too close to the mark for his comfort. Rather than confirm her suspicions, however, he snorted and looked away. "What a pair we are."

Her shoulders slumped. "Sorry?"

He exhaled slowly, then walked over and pulled her to him again. She went easily, sliding her arms around his waist and resting her cheek over his heart. Jackson spoke into her hair, "Yes, we are. Both of us. Sorry to the core."

"When I turned eighteen, I was supposed to get access to the money in my trust fund," she said against his skin. "But my parents didn't think I could handle it, because of my OCD and anxiety. For a long time, I bought into their idea that I was helpless. Of course, it didn't help that my ex supported that theory, too. Robert always treated me like a live grenade about to go off. I think the only reason he wanted to marry me was the money. Well, that and to use me for his graduate study work."

Tension knotted the muscles between his shoulder blades. The thought of anyone abusing Lucy's trust like that made his blood boil. Still, she needed to get this out, and he needed to listen. "Go on."

She inhaled deep. "Robert and I dated for six months

and were engaged twice as long. At first it was nice, his constant pampering and protection. But as time went on, it became suffocating. Like it had been growing up with my parents, only a million times worse. Then, one day I walked in on him discussing my case with the dean of his department—anonymously, of course—like I was some lab rat and not his beloved fiancée. He was asking for advice on how to handle me going forward, so our marriage didn't contaminate his research. That was the last straw.

"I decided then and there to leave. I'd been volunteering at a local shelter for a while by that point, and when Dr. Dave offered to help me get into vet school, I jumped at the chance. He wrote me letters of recommendation and even helped me get a couple of scholarships, since I still couldn't access my trust fund at that point. After I graduated, I got lawyers and sued to access my money. Once I won the lawsuit, I bought this place and never looked back. It's taken me a long time to find my freedom. I don't ever want to lose it again. Now do you understand why this place is so important to me and why I had to stay?"

"I do." He gently lifted her chin with his finger, his stomach sinking. "You're happy here, alone?"

"I am." She raised her head, her dark gaze determined. "Here, I have control over my own destiny. I've put my past behind me and moved forward. I won't leave that behind. Even for a hurricane."

Jackson understood. Deep in his bones, he got it. It was both a blessing and a curse, because her triumph was his defeat.

He had no right to expect more from her, because last night had been nothing but two lost, lonely souls holding on for dear life during an emergency. Just affirming life during a disaster. Nothing more, nothing less. He needed to let it go, let her go and move on.

Because that's what he did.

"You know what I think?" he asked, forcing a smile he didn't feel. "I think it's their loss. I think if they couldn't see all the wonderful potential in you, then screw them."

Lucy chuckled. "And are you talking from personal experience?"

His jaw clenched, a muscle ticking in his cheek. He could tell her about himself, about being abandoned by his own mother, by the one person who should've never left, about being unworthy of love, but what would be the point? It was water under the bridge. Literally. So, he gave her a half-truth instead. "I have some experience with being disappointed by the people you love, yeah." An image of the photo he'd found in her office the day before flashed in his head, and he let her go to rummage in the trash bag to find it. "Hey, I found something of yours yesterday, before we went down to the basement."

"What?" Her dark brows drew together.

"A photo, from your office. Since you didn't have it out, I wasn't sure whether it was something you'd want to save—"

He handed it to Lucy, and her expression shifted from happy to sad to resigned in ten seconds flat. The same emotions he experienced whenever he saw a rare picture of himself with his birth mom. There weren't many reminders left from those days before the Durands had taken him in, but the ones that had made it packed a hell of a wallop.

"Oh God," she whispered. Then she was back in his arms, hugging him tight. When she pulled away, he recognized the same vulnerability in her that he'd fought against his whole life. "This is Robert."

Jackson nodded, keeping his expression blank while his breath lodged painfully in his lungs, the pain of loneliness, abandonment, threatening to overtake him if he wasn't careful. He let her go, then shoved his hands in his pockets to hide their tremble. "I'm sorry."

Tears burned in her eyes once more. "It's okay."

The defeat in her tone hurt his heart, but he couldn't respond. Couldn't tell her what he was feeling, because he didn't understand it himself. If he did, he'd be forced to let her in, and if that happened, it would break him down, and he might never be able to build his walls up again. So, instead, he kissed her, his mouth fierce as his heart shattered inside him.

Then he was holding her again, touching her, because he needed to, needed her more than he needed his next breath. His hands cupped her cheeks then trailed down her arms, her skin hot and soft under his searching fingertips. She dropped the photo to clutch at the open edges of his shirt, pulling it off his body. Jackson let it fall, along with the rest of the tattered barriers around his heart, and claimed her mouth again, his desire for her evident in every touch and caress. Needing, wanting, more and more. He explored every inch of her, first with fingers, then with lips and tongue, desperate and worshipful, knowing this first time might be their last.

He nuzzled the side of her neck, breathing her name against her ear. "Sweet Lucy."

She opened her eyes, then leaned in and kissed his

nipple. He bucked beneath her, couldn't help it, his deep groan vibrating beneath her mouth. She stopped and looked up at him, questioning.

"No," he rasped. "Feels…wonderful."

She smiled, and a bit more of his control slipped away. It was so easy for her to distract him, disarm him, and damn if he could bring himself to care. The sudden lifting of the burden he'd carried for so long too heady to resist. She kissed her way across his chest to his other nipple and teased him again. His hips rose against hers, leaving little doubt how badly he wanted this, wanted her. His body felt on fire, his blood singing in his veins and his erection so hard it hurt. He had more experience than a man should, but it had never, ever been like this before. Like he'd die if he couldn't satisfy this hunger, this craving, this need for Lucy that pushed him, drove him, controlled him.

Then, suddenly, his hands were on her, tugging at her shirt. Humid Florida air moved across his bare skin, electrifying it. The feel of her breasts in his palms was wild, erotic. He wanted to make her feel good, feel precious. When her shirt was gone, he wanted more. Wanted his hands all over her. His mouth and tongue, too.

She seemed to feel the same urgency as she touched him right back, seeking her own pleasure.

He groaned, and her hands stilled. She tried to cover herself, but he stopped her.

"Don't. Please. You're so beautiful." Her dark eyes still glimmered with a hint of insecurity, and Jackson reassured her. "Please, Lucy. Let me see you. Let me be with you."

She did, and his wanting burned brighter, hotter. He hadn't thought it possible, but he'd been wrong.

"Perfect. That's what you are, Lucy." His hands moved lower, and her breath turned shallow. He stopped at the button on the waistband of her jeans, same as he'd done the night before, praying she wouldn't stop him this time. "Okay?"

She bit her lip, then gave a shy nod. "Yes. Please."

Jackson undid the button then lowered her zip one notch at a time. "No need to beg, sweetheart. Unless you want to…"

CHAPTER THIRTEEN

LUCY LIFTED HER hips to help him remove her jeans
and panties, then waited as he took off his own. They
were both naked now, and he leaned back against the
wall again, his casual pose saying he was completely
comfortable in his own skin. She wondered what that
was like.

"Come here," he beckoned, his voice rough with desire. "Touch me, Lucy. Wherever you want. I'm yours."

She reached out tentatively and grasped his hard
length. Hot, satiny, rigid, the skin so soft. He jerked in
her hand, and her core clenched in response. If she got
on her knees, she could take him in her mouth and…

Her intentions must've shown on her face, because
he said, "Please."

So, she did, her world reduced to this man, this moment, the feel and taste of him on her tongue. No worries, no anxiety, no regrets.

As she tightened her lips around his shaft, he slipped
his fingers through her hair, not forcing but guiding her
gently to show what he liked. Never in her life had
she felt this free, brought to such a simple common de-
nominator. One thing. Only one, that she wanted more
than her next breath.

Lucy slid her mouth slowly off him and felt his shaking groan in the depths of her soul. It echoed inside her, matching her own passion. Her gaze traveled up his taut abdomen, across his chest, to his clenched jaw, his beautiful compressed mouth, then finally to his eyes.

And there she found everything she'd ever wanted.

She had no idea what to say. She didn't have to say anything.

"There's a condom in my wallet, back pocket of my pants." His words were rough, uncivilized. And exactly what she wanted to hear.

Without looking away from him, she fumbled beside her for his balled-up pants and pulled out the tiny foil packet. Her fingers fumbled to open it then smooth it onto his hard length. Damn if it wasn't erotic as hell.

Then Jackson leaned forward and lifted her. She wrapped her arms around his neck and her legs around his hips until she straddled him. Lucy did her best not to knock against his injured leg, but any concerns she had about that disappeared as she slowly sank down onto him inch by delicious inch. His gaze stayed locked on hers until he filled her completely, so deep she wasn't sure where he started and she ended. It was wondrous, magnificent. A bit uncomfortable at first, then her body adjusted and…

"Stop thinking." He turned them so her upper back was against the cool wall of the clinic, his arms supporting her, then he leaned forward to nuzzle her neck, not moving yet. His hot breath fanned her face as he whispered, "Relax."

He massaged her hips until she did so, then cupped her breasts.

Lucy gasped and rocked forward. The motion made

her moan. Jackson bucked, then stilled almost immediately. "Sorry. Did I hurt you?"

"No." He slid a bit farther into her, and she whimpered, not from pain but from pleasure. Lucy clung to him, digging her nails into his shoulders as he nipped her earlobe.

Then they moved together, the tightly coiled need inside her unwinding. Her body took over with a single-minded intensity that sent any thought but completion spiraling away.

Jackson controlled the rhythm. She moved, he followed. Her movements became wild, frenzied, exulting in his sleek, powerful body that matched her thrust for thrust.

Then she was there. On the brink of orgasm.

He stroked her most sensitive flesh, sending her flying over the edge. The world exploded into shards of light behind her closed eyelids, like tiny firecrackers going off in every nerve ending in her body. And in the center of it all, Jackson shouted her name and found his own release.

Afterward, Lucy collapsed against him, chest heaving, skin damp, pulse pounding. For the first time in forever, she couldn't think. Didn't want to think. Hadn't gotten over feeling yet. Feeling freer than she'd ever been before, all because she'd allowed this man to take control.

Somewhere in the back of her mind, a warning bell sounded, but she was far too blissed out to care at that moment.

Jackson smoothed the tangled hair away from her face, his fingers still shaking from the force of his own climax. Then he kissed her. He'd meant it to be gentle, short, sweet. But he couldn't stop. He kept his lips on hers as their breathing slowed and their hearts returned to normal rhythms.

Sleepiness lurked around his edges, but he resisted. He wanted to stay here, connected to her like this, forever.

And then it hit him. A force as violent as the hurricane that had ripped apart her house.

He'd let her in. Past his walls and barriers and safeguards. And he *never* did that.

Until today.

He closed his eyes and rested his forehead against the base of her neck. He shouldn't still be here. No. He should get up, get dressed, get gone like he always did after sex. Sleeping with someone meant the end of the affair, not the beginning of something more.

Then his lips touched her pulse point and another, more startling realization struck.

He wasn't leaving...because he didn't want to.

Holy hell.

His eyes flew open, and Lucy shifted away. "Jackson, this... I feel... We need..."

She tried to pull away, but his arms tightened around her.

"No. Don't. Not yet. We'll have to talk about this, but not now, okay? Let me be here."

"Jackson—" She frowned, going still.

"Please." He couldn't explain it to her, because he didn't understand it himself yet. "Just let me...stay here with you...for a little while longer."

A small eternity passed before she relaxed again, and a fierce, unexpected contentment filled him. He gazed down at her, never imagining he'd hold a woman like Lucy. Didn't want to think about what would happen later…

Then the unmistakable sound of a helicopter cut into his thoughts.

Dammit.

Seemed later was closer than he'd thought. And getting closer by the second.

Sam woke up from where he'd been sleeping by the door and started barking. King meowed, and Bubba danced back and forth on his perch, squawking, "Wanted dead or alive."

Lucy lifted her head from his chest, her dark brows knitting together. "Is that the help that was on the way?"

"Probably," Jackson muttered, for once damning his brother's hyperefficiency.

He let her go reluctantly, then dragged his pants on and located his buttonless shirt while Lucy dressed as well. Awkward silence fell between them, and before he could break it, she was out the door calling to him over her shoulder, "I'm going to check on Mitzi again."

Not exactly how he'd wanted their interlude to end.

She'd finally let him in, let him close, and now it was like she couldn't get away from him fast enough. Old doubts and fears clawed awake inside him, but he shoved them aside. No, that wasn't what was happening here. They'd both needed to be ready when help arrived, that's all. He was reading too much into it. His feelings were still too new, too raw, too confusing. Jackson paused in the doorway, watching as a medevac chopper moved toward the front corner of the compound diagonally across from the pond, the only place with enough free space to land among the debris.

Limping, he headed across the littered grounds, doing his best to convince himself that this was good. Instead of being disappointed about this sudden turn of events, he should be delighted. Help was in that helicopter. He and Lucy could get things straightened out here, then he could go back to Key West. They'd talk again later. Sort it all out. Decide where to go from here.

It was all good. He didn't have to fear connection. Things wouldn't turn out like they had before.

He wouldn't be abandoned again.

Except as the helicopter swooped in, wind from the rotors whipping Lucy's hair around her face and rippling the hem of her tank top, this all seemed like more of a dream. A fever dream.

But would reality break the fever?

He stopped several feet behind Lucy, not certain she knew he was there.

His old doubts and fears dug their claws into him, growing in his gut with each beat of his heart until it felt like they might strangle him. He'd been through a lot in his life, more than most, but it felt like nothing had prepared him for this. Not his rescues in the coast guard. Not all the life-and-death situations he faced on a daily basis. Not losing his birth mom all those years ago.

As Lucy continued to shut him out, he knew nothing had prepared him for the very real possibility that he might well lose her in the next couple of minutes. And the worst part was, there wasn't a damned thing he could do about it.

Because he'd gone into it knowing how much she valued her freedom and how hard she'd fight to keep it. Just as hard as he'd had to battle to let her in. And in that kind of war, could there be a winner?

The chopper's huge rotors slowed, and the wind died down. Finally, the small hatch door opened, and the pilot climbed out and ran up to them. "Dr. Lucy Miller?"

"Yes, that's me," she said, shaking his hand. "Thanks for coming."

"It's my duty, ma'am," the pilot said, turning to Jackson next. "Got here as soon as I could."

After getting a rundown on the conditions in Key West and the surrounding area, he gave the pilot a quick tour of the compound while Lucy checked on Mitzi. Jackson had thought he'd feel worse about surrendering the IC spot, but honestly, he didn't care at the moment. Maybe because of the ordeal they'd been through. Maybe because of their brush with death. Or maybe because of the weird pressure in his chest urging him to head straight back to Lucy's side and stay there forever, consequences be damned.

But he couldn't do that. Lucy didn't want that. He didn't want that, either.

Do I?

Hands fisted at his sides, Jackson flashed the pilot a hard smile he hoped passed as normal and listened to what he was saying.

"Most of the problems in Key West came from flooding. The governor has declared a state of emergency, at least, so we can start getting federal aid in to help in the cleanup efforts." The guy took off his sunglasses and rubbed his eyes, dark shadows beneath them from lack of sleep. Jackson hadn't looked in a mirror yet that day, but he figured he probably looked much the same. "Looks like you guys were hit hard here, too. Hopefully, this will all work out and we get the funding we need to start repairs sooner rather than later, but with FEMA you never know…"

Lucy walked up to them then, distracting Jackson again. Her expression was remote again, unreadable, and he wished to hell he knew how to crack her code, because the less he knew about how this was going to go, the more his inner control freak went wild. What if she didn't want him to stay? What if instead of bringing them closer together, making love earlier had only proved to her that he wasn't the man for her? Sure, it had been great. Universe-altering, at least for him. But Lucy was a closed book now, one he desperately wished he could decipher.

"I'm sure you need to get back to work," she said, jarring him out of his thoughts.

The pilot checked his watch. "Yep, I do. I've got room for one cage onboard and one adult, whoever's ready to go."

"You should take King back with you," Lucy said, turning away. "He's healing well and is ready to foster."

He frowned. "I'm sorry?"

She headed back into the clinic. "When you go back to Key West, take King with you."

"I'm not going back." He shook his head and followed her into the clinic, not wanting to discuss things in front of the pilot. "Not yet. We've got things to talk about, Lucy. Things feel different now."

"Different how?"

His chest itched as the emotional demons inside him

tried harder to claw their way out. He rubbed the area over his heart, more than aware of the pilot waiting outside the door. Now wasn't the time and this wasn't the place. He needed space to figure all this out so he didn't do something stupid like fall to his knees and beg her to let him stay, let him help, let him into her heart and her life.

A muscle ticked in his tense cheek, and he looked away from her, old pain and new fears blotting out the light from their earlier lovemaking. *No. Not lovemaking. Don't call it that. Don't put too much meaning into it. Don't start thinking you're worthy of more than just sex.*

She was not going to keep him. A black pit of despair swirled inside him, swallowing up everything, including his patience. He waved her off and turned away before she caught the devastation lurking just beneath his surface. This. This was exactly why he kept his distance, kept his guard up.

Things didn't change. Because he didn't deserve them to change.

"Forget it. It doesn't matter." He turned away and walked over to King's cage, staring in at the tiny kitten and feeling the same embarrassment and grief and loss he'd felt when he'd watched his birth mother's taillights disappear from view for the last time. King meowed and crawled over to the front of the cage as if to offer his support. "You're right. I should head home. Lots of important things to get done," he said quietly, doing his best to rebuild his shattered defenses before it was too late. "And I'll take the kitten with me, like you wanted."

* * *

"Great." She paused, ignoring the darkening scowl on Jackson's face, because if she didn't, she'd end up getting swallowed up by the memories of them together earlier, and she couldn't handle that. Not right now. Those moments with him had been incredible, some of the most intense in her life. And while she probably should regret them, she couldn't. Never would, honestly, given how miserable the coming days ahead would be without him. She swallowed hard against the sudden constriction in her throat. "Get back to your team. Your life in Key West. I've got plenty to do here to keep me busy. Goodbye, Jackson."

She was getting her freedom back, just like she'd wanted.

Lucy thought she'd feel better about that than she did.

Rather than stand there and wallow in her sadness, she walked outside again and headed for the pond, then stopped and looked back at the pilot, eyes burning. She blinked hard. She would not cry now. No. "Jackson will be riding with you, along with a kitten. Thanks again for coming."

Near the pond, she watched as the pilot and Jackson got King's cage and IV apparatus loaded into the back of the helicopter, then looked away again as Jackson hobbled over to her.

"You sure you're okay here alone?" Jackson asked, taking her arm gently.

She pulled free, not looking up at him. Hard enough having him near now without him touching her, too. No. If this was the end, then it was best to get on with it. Like ripping off a bandage. Sam whined from where he stayed glued to her ankle. "No. But I will be."

She'd be great, as soon as she got back inside, got back on her schedule. Whenever life went south, her routines got her through. Waking up at the same time every morning, counting her steps, arranging the shirts in her closet and remotes on her coffee table. Arranging all the things in our house "just so." Working with Sam every day. Avoiding cracks in the sidewalk. Turning knobs. Walking to the beat of the ticking clock in her living room.

Except her house was gone. There were no more knobs, no more clocks, no more Jackson.

She swallowed hard, anxiety gouging away at what little peace she had left from their lovemaking. When she'd been with him, last night and this morning, all those tics and troubles had disappeared. Now that he was leaving again, though, they rushed back like a tsunami, despite her meds.

That was bad. Very bad indeed.

She needed to get inside, get away from all this stress, get herself and her life back on track again.

You can do this. You're in control.

The pilot yelled from the cockpit door. "Sir. I'm happy to fly you back, but I've got other runs, so we'll need to leave now."

Jackson kept his attention riveted on her. "Lucy?"

His voice roughened, almost like he regretted leaving. She hazarded a glance at him, searching his face for clues to how he felt but found none. In the end, she couldn't ask him to stay. They'd both said they wanted no strings, no promises, no complications. She wouldn't go back on that now, even if getting her freedom back meant her heart would be tied to Jackson forever.

How ironic.

"Go. Don't worry about me," she croaked. "I have enough supplies to last me for a while. I'll be just fine by myself. The way I like it."

Jackson's expression remained inscrutable. Then, after a long moment, he seemed to come to a decision, signaling to the pilot, who started the rotors up again.

Right. Okay. This was it. Jackson was leaving. She'd likely never spend time with him like this again. He could easily have a vet in Key West do checkups on the kitten and probably would. Less messy that way. Best make this as easy as possible. No tears or long, uncomfortable goodbyes. After all, they'd only met a few days prior. And they'd had sex not thirty minutes prior. Her chest ached.

Lucy trembled under his continued scrutiny. If he didn't leave soon, this wasn't going to be clean. Her emotions were too close to the surface, too choppy, like the still churning waters of the Gulf offshore.

God, please let me end this without humiliating myself.

Then she was in his arms, and he was kissing her. No. Not a kiss. A claiming, a branding with his taste, his textures, his touch. And at the exact moment she felt her knees wobble, he let her go.

"I know you want me gone," Jackson said roughly. "I'm sorry I wasn't what you needed. I'm sorry I wasn't better for you."

Before she could respond and tell him no, that wasn't true, he was everything she'd ever wanted and more, it was her that was wrong, her that was the problem, Jackson traced a finger across her lower lip, silencing her.

"Goodbye, Lucy," Jackson said, then turned and hobbled to the waiting helicopter.

CHAPTER FOURTEEN

JACKSON WALKED INTO the ER at Key West General and headed over to where his brother stood at the nurses' station going through patient files.

It had been two weeks since Hurricane Mathilda had roared through the Keys, and they were still picking up the pieces. The team had done a fantastic job, following the outlined plans he'd given them before heading north, and the area was recovering nicely.

As far as his own property went, his houseboat had survived the storm pretty much unscathed, except for a few minor dings and some flooding. His truck hadn't fared as well, sustaining major damage from a downed tree at the compound, but his insurance company was handling that and had towed the vehicle away without him having to make another trip to Big Pine Key.

Which was good, because he still had no idea what the hell to do about Lucy. He knew from the cleaning crew he'd sent to help her that she was alive and well and rebuilding like the rest of the residents in the area. What he didn't know, however, was if she regretted how they'd ended things as much as he did and if she'd ever give him another chance to prove himself.

I'm sorry I wasn't what you needed. I'm sorry I wasn't better for you...

"Feeling better?" Luis asked without looking up at him. "Mr. Regional Director."

"Yeah." *Nah.* Jackson shrugged, a vain attempt to relieve some of the tension that had become a permanent part of his shoulders and neck these days. Along with the headache, bad attitude and piss-poor outlook on life. Unfortunately, the fact the review board had given him the promotion hadn't filled the hole inside him like he'd thought it would. Yes, it was more pay, more responsibility, and it gave him the ability to live anywhere in the Keys he liked, but it wasn't enough. It wasn't Lucy.

He leaned his elbow on the counter. "I guess."

"Problems with the leg laceration?" Luis arched a brow but didn't look up from the chart he was documenting in.

"Nope. Lucy did a good job fixing me up."

"Well, I'm glad someone finally did."

His brother's snark didn't improve Jackson's mood, but it wasn't Luis's fault the last place he wanted to be at that moment was work. Truthfully, he wanted to head straight back to Lucy's place and hold her until all the confusion and hurt and uncertainty inside him went away. Funny, but when he'd been with her, really with her, none of those demons had haunted him. When he was with her, all he felt was peace and serenity, completion, *worthiness.*

And that scared the bejesus out of him. "Uh, can we talk?"

Luis stared at him for a moment, then handed his chart to the nurse behind the desk before gesturing for Jackson to follow him down the hall to his office. "Have a seat."

He started toward the chairs in front of his brother's desk, the limp barely noticeable anymore. His thigh was mostly healed, and the stitches had come out several days ago. Barely even ached at all. Jackson didn't allow himself to think about why that depressed him.

He started to sit when Luis gestured him away.

"Other one."

He barely stopped himself in time, then straightened and looked behind him, biting off a curse. A tiny creature blinked up at him. "Why's there a baby turtle in your office?"

His brother's tanned cheeks darkened a shade. Besides himself, the only other person he'd seen who could make his brother react like a schoolboy caught passing notes in study hall was Stacy Williams. They'd been spending a lot of time together lately, he'd noticed. Apparently, something big had happened between them during the storm, but Jackson hadn't quite worked it all out yet and he and his brother had both been too busy to sit down and discuss what they'd both been through like they needed to. Still, Jackson wouldn't usually miss a chance to razz his brother about it, but now he remained silent, feeling envious of his brother for the first time. It irritated the hell out of him.

"His owner's in the hospital, so I'm looking out for him until they recover," Luis said, pointing at the turtle. "Figured it might be good practice if we…"

The telltale signs of crickets chirping echoed through the office. Jackson would've noticed that right off if his mind hadn't been distracted…again.

He looked at Luis. "If we what?"

Luis shrugged and smiled slowly. "Stacy and I…"

Jackson still wasn't sure exactly what was going on, but based on the anticipation on his brother's face, it was something good. There was a time he'd feared Luis would let his work take over his life and never find the love he sought. Then Stacy had reappeared in his brother's life, and everything had changed. Sometimes joy came from the most unlikely of places.

That had certainly been true in Jackson's case, as Lucy's face filled his mind once more.

And he wondered—for the millionth time over the last two weeks—how she was doing, whether Mitzi's eggs had hatched, how the renovations were going. For his part, King was coping well with his amputation. The IV was gone and the kitten was moving around well, playing with his toys and eating his food, manipulating the hell out of Jackson for cuddles and treats at every opportunity. Now, if Jackson could just stop lying awake at night, aching for Lucy, they'd both sleep a lot better.

Luis sat back in his chair, staring at his brother with a narrowed gaze. "You haven't been the same since you came back from Big Pine Key. Something else happened during the hurricane."

It wasn't a question.

Jackson trusted Luis completely, and the feeling was mutual. His brother had never pushed him about what had happened during those twenty-four hours he and Lucy had been trapped together, same as Jackson hadn't pushed Luis about his history with Stacy. It was a code. An unspoken understanding. If they wanted to talk about it, they would. Eventually. But what Jackson really needed was advice on the rest of it. How to make a relationship work, how to even try to be that open, that vulnerable to someone, how to love a person when there was no guarantee they'd love you back or stay…

He stared at Luis for a long moment, then looked down at his toes. "Maybe."

"I thought so." Luis laughed. "So, what are you going to do about her?"

That was the question of the century. Part of him knew exactly what he wanted to do about Lucy. Jackson wanted to hug her and kiss her and apologize for making such a muck of things and beg her to take him back and let him try again. But the other part of him was still that scared little boy, watching his mother walk away from him forever and never wanting his heart ripped out like that again.

But in the end, his battered, scarred soul was done for anyway, when it came to Lucy. Somehow, some way, she'd smashed through all his walls and claimed him the moment she'd asked for directions that day in the ER. Now, all he could think about was her cute smile and the cute way she counted things and the not-so-cute anxiety attacks she had when things got too overwhelming, and he wanted to be there for them all. Wanted to support her, in whatever way she needed him to, wanted to stand by her side and love her and grow old with her.

But she didn't need him, didn't want him there. Unless…

Jackson stared at his brother a moment, then turned to the baby turtle. It had worked once before. Did he dare hope it might work again? "You care if I take this little guy off your hands for a bit?"

"Why?"

"I think a vet should take a look at him."

Luis gave a lopsided smile then came around the desk to hand him the crate. "Take good care of him, brother. He belongs to my patient."

"Will do." Jackson peered inside the front of the cage, walked to the door, then turned back. "My shift's over, so I might be gone for a few—"

"Take whatever you need. My patient won't be released until tomorrow, at least."

Jackson nodded. "Thanks, brother. I owe you one."

"Yes, you do." He chuckled, following Jackson out into the hall.

An hour and a half later, he thanked the captain of the boat he'd hired to take him from Key West and headed toward her compound on foot, the turtle cage in one hand and King under his other arm. He wasn't surprised to see things hadn't improved much in the two weeks since he'd left Lucy's compound on Big Pine Key. Mathilda had only brushed the coast before heading back out into the Gulf toward Texas, and most of the damage was outside the Keys. But Lucy had been lucky. Some of the smaller spits of coastal land had been flattened.

The first thing he noticed when he reached her place was that she'd moved most of the smaller bits of wreckage into rubbish piles near the perimeter of the compound, but most of the work still lay ahead. As he entered the grounds through a downed section of fence, he wondered if he'd be lucky enough to stay and help her with it. But luck had never been his claim to fame.

His grip tightened on the small crate he carried, and he looked down at King. "Well, guys, here goes nothing."

He was halfway to the house when he spied Lucy standing near the side of the pond, a pair of binoculars perched on her nose, Sam by her side.

His heart rate doubled, then tripled. Man, he was nervous. Maybe he was imagining all this. Imagining he'd found the one woman who made him feel whole, who knew him better than he knew himself, who saw his secrets and loved him, anyway. She whirled around when he was less than ten feet away, and he saw the reflection of the maelstrom inside him in her lovely dark eyes.

Nope. No imagining that.

"Jackson." As quickly as she'd said his name, that mask of hers fell back into place again. But that one unguarded moment was all he needed. Her expression might be closed now, distanced, but he vowed one way or another, that wouldn't last long. Sam, of course, had no such reservations, rushing over to him, yipping and twirling around, demanding attention.

"What are you doing here?" Lucy asked, her gaze flickering to the squirming kitten under his arm. "Something wrong with King?"

"No." He set the turtle cage down then bent to scratch Sam behind the ears before straightening again and meeting her eyes.

Her gaze faltered for a split second, then held his firmly once more. "Oh. What then?"

Something heavy and hot in his heart shifted. "I needed to see you again."

"You did?" Her eyes widened slightly, then her shoulders squared, and her chin lifted. "Why?"

He pointed at the crate in his hand. "Luis and Stacy are caring for this little guy while the owner recovers, and they can't get him to eat. Thought maybe you could help." Then King meowed loudly, as if outraged to have been ignored so long. "And this little guy missed you and wanted to say hi."

"Oh."

Happy as Jackson would have been to watch his kitten running around the yard, playing with Sam like nothing had ever happened to him, the sheer disappointment in that one word from Lucy made him want to forget his plans and hug her tight right then, but he had to play this right. If he didn't, he could lose it all, and he wouldn't let that happen.

Not again.

Jackson wasn't certain of much at the moment, but the one thing he knew for sure was he wasn't going anywhere. Not now. Not yet. Maybe not ever, if he had his way.

"What's wrong with the turtle?" Lucy asked, shifting her attention to the small crate.

"Not sure. Maybe he needed to get out in the wild again."

"Then why bring him to me?" The hurt and uncertainty in her dark eyes was his undoing.

These two weeks apart had been torture, and Jackson was tired of dancing around the truth. "Because there is no one else, Lucy. There never will be. Not for me."

She stilled, looking at him, her expression…blank. Except for her gaze. Those deep, dark eyes.

Please let me in. Please believe in me.

Lucy turned her back then, and the hurt searing Jackson's chest nearly floored him.

Memories of his mother driving away for the last time flooded his mind, only to be quickly replaced by the joy he'd felt becoming a part of the Durand family. How he'd found new connections with them and Luis. How he wanted to start a new future with Lucy now. She wouldn't make this easy. Nothing about her was. That's why he loved her.

He stepped closer, keeping his hands at his sides, even though he wanted to touch her so much he ached. She'd lifted those damned binoculars of hers again and was staring across the pond, seemingly ignoring what he'd said.

After a few tense seconds, Jackson asked, "What are you looking at?"

"Mitzi's nestlings are hatching."

"They're okay?"

"Not sure if they'll all survive. Typically, they don't, but there aren't any natural predators around here, so their chances are dramatically improved."

"So the chances are—"

"Shh." She waved her hand to silence him. "Listen. Hear those tiny little gulping sounds?" Lucy turned to him, imitating the sound. "Like that."

His pulse pounded and his blood burned, but he kept his gaze on hers and strained his ears. "Yeah, I hear it."

"That's the nestlings. And if we can hear them from here, that means there's a bunch of them. Which means they made it, Jackson. They made it!"

He almost pulled her into his arms right then and

there but stopped himself. *Patience, man.* He didn't want to give her any reason to run away from him again.

"Can we, uh, go to the clinic?" he asked, his voice rough with need and emotion. "To talk?"

She nodded. After one last look across the pond, Lucy slipped her binoculars from around her neck, jotted some notes in the notebook she'd been carrying, then stuffed it all in the pocket of her baggy cargo shorts.

"I'm living in there for the time being," she said as they headed in that direction.

Once inside, he placed the turtle's crate on one of the long, shiny exam tables while she put away her stuff. King and Sam were playing with each other, chasing each other around in circles on the clinic floor. Jackson reached down to scratch King behind the ears when he hobbled over to him, then grinned at the kitten's loud purr.

"Looks like he's doing well," Lucy said, watching them. Jackson turned to find her across the room, leaning her hips against the edge of the sink, crossing her arms. "That's wonderful."

"Yeah. He's good."

Silence fell and his adrenaline spiked, igniting his blood. He swallowed hard. This was it. The big moment. But where to start?

The beginning. He needed to tell her everything. About his past. About why he'd acted the way he did that day at the helicopter.

"After my dad died in the war, life got hard, Lucy." The words emerged in a short burst, then he drew a long, shaky breath. "My mom had a hard time finding work because she had to take care of me, and we ended up on welfare. Eventually, we lost everything. Our house, our friends. We lived on the streets for a few months. She did the best she could, but I knew she wasn't happy. She cried a lot. I tried to help, but I was only four. Then one day, I guess she'd had enough. She got me dressed that morning, fed me my favorite cereal for breakfast, then walked me out to the car. I remember thinking it was weird that she'd packed my suitcase when we weren't going anywhere, but when I asked her about it, she wouldn't say why. Then we pulled up in front of a big brick building, and she got me out of the car. It was cold that day. So cold I could see my breath. She told me to sit on the steps and wait there until an adult came and got me. She told me to not forget my suitcase. She was crying."

His throat constricted and his eyes burned, but he kept going.

"She hugged me tight then. Tighter than she'd ever hugged me before. Then she got in the car and drove away. I watched those red taillights until I couldn't see them anymore, and then I started crying, too."

He sniffed and stared down at his toes.

"She left me. Abandoned me. I was so scared, but I still wanted to be with her. Even after all that, I thought if I was just better, she'd come back. If I just did enough, if I tried a little bit harder to be a good boy, to do the right thing. But she never did. Even after the Durands adopted me, and I got older, I never forgot her or what it felt like to not be enough. To not be worthy of love from the one person who should love you unconditionally. To be left behind by the one person who should never walk away. I used to dream of her at night sometimes as a kid, that she returned. That we had our old life back and we were a family again. But it didn't happen. I never heard a word from her again. She just disappeared from my life. I blamed myself."

"What…why?" Her voice shook with sadness. "Oh, Jackson. I'm so sorry."

"I was her son. I should have been enough, been there for her, but I couldn't." He scrubbed his hand over his short dark hair, gave an unpleasant laugh. "You were right. I think that's why I save people for a living. Make them all better. Because it made me feel worthy. Made me feel like I was something, like I mattered." He shook his head and dug the toe of his boot into the floor. "What hurts the most, though, is knowing she's out there somewhere, and that she wants nothing to do with me."

"Oh, Jackson."

He knew—*knew*—she understood, from the ache in her voice, the pain. But he had to get it out.

"So, yeah. I've spent my whole life trying to make myself worthy. By protecting those who needed my help, whether they wanted it or not. I joined the coast guard, became an EMT. Volunteered for the local Boys and Girls Club. Whatever I can do to prove I am good enough, worthy enough for people to stick around and love. But it doesn't work. Because at the end of the day, I'm still the same old me."

"That's not true, Jackson. You are one of the best, most honorable men I know. You don't have to prove your worth. You're worthy of love just by being alive. And what she did was never your fault. Never," Lucy whispered, her tone edged with anguish. "You were only a child."

"Maybe." He shrugged. "I don't have any memories

of my father, but I always thought he would want me to stand up for those who couldn't stand up for themselves." He looked up at her then. "And I did the best damn job I could. I gave it everything I had. But it didn't make a difference."

"Yes, it did, Jackson. It does make a difference. You're still helping people."

"But it's not enough. Because at the end of the day, I'm still alone. I thought by closing my heart, avoiding any kind of intimacy, I could keep from ever feeling that kind of anguish and abandonment again." He closed the distance between them and took her by the shoulders. "That I could avoid the pain of losing the people I loved. But it doesn't work. It never worked. The day I first came here, when I found King, I was on my way back from Miami. I mentioned it that day, but I didn't tell you why I'd gone up there. It was to get results from my DNA testing. I thought I'd try finding her one more time, maybe hire someone to track her down like they do on those TV shows or something. But then I met you, and suddenly it didn't seem to matter so much anymore. I finally feel like I'm ready to let that go, release the past and start fresh. With you. Do you understand, Lucy?"

"I think so." She nodded, her gaze guarded. "But you told me you don't want any messy ties. You want things to be neat. Fun. Clean. No complications." Her voice rose, shaking now. "So, where does that leave us?"

"I don't know." He lowered his head, putting his face close to hers. "Being with you during the storm changed me somehow. It's like there's this…emotional hole…inside me, Lucy. And crazy as it sounds, I *know* you're the only one who can fill it."

She tried to pull free, but he held fast. "What happens when things get tough or someone else comes along? Someone easier, someone normal? You just walk away? You have another fling? Because I can't do that. I can't let you do that to me."

"I won't walk away, Lucy." He clenched his jaw so tight his ears popped. "I can't walk away, Lucy. Don't you see? I tried, these past two weeks, but I can't. I think about you constantly, worry about you. Want to be with you so badly it hurts. The hurricane made me realize that there are no guarantees in life, Lucy. The world isn't perfect. But locking myself in a box or a bubble thinking it made me safe only made me alone and miserable." When she didn't respond, a new doubt stabbed him in the chest. "Or don't you want me?"

Her eyes widened. "Yes, I want you! More than I've ever let myself want anything. When I turned around and saw you behind me out there, I knew I'd take whatever you had to give me, but…"

"But what?"

"I'm not sure I'll be enough for you."

"What?" Jackson said, clearly confused. "You're so brave and strong and confident. You are, Lucy."

Her resolve to stay distant crumpled in the face of his certainty, leaving her hollow and yearning inside. "If I let you in, give you my heart, and what you want turns out not to be me, it would kill me when you walked away, Jackson."

He cupped her face, his hold unbearably gentle. "Then I'll never do that, Lucy. I swear. Even when times get tough. Even when you tic like crazy and you count every step from here to Miami and back." She laughed, and he chuckled. "You are enough for me, Lucy. More than enough. The reason I said I didn't want anything more than sex was because I was terrified. Terrified of what you made me feel. Terrified because you filled that emptiness inside me. The one I'd tried for years to fill myself with meaningless flings and control and my need to protect others and avoid failure. But none of that worked. I kept you at a distance because I didn't let myself believe I could have you. Part of me still knows I don't deserve you. But when I looked into your eyes and saw myself, saw the other part of me, I knew."

Finally, he opened up and let his barriers all the way down, allowed her to see him, really see him—the vulnerability, the pain, the damage and flaws for the first time. "I knew you were the one for me. The only one for me. Lucy, I've never been so sure of anything in my entire life as I am of you."

His words scared her to death. They were complete opposites. And yet she loved him anyway, completely, unconditionally. The way she'd always wanted to *be* loved.

The longer she'd stayed at the compound alone, the more she realized everything had gone gray. Like she'd been cast into a barren wasteland. And the truth struck her like a death blow. Her knees buckled. Pinpoints of light flickered in the periphery of her vision, but Jackson was there, his warm, strong arms around her, holding her, supporting her, and she knew. Knew that if she didn't take this chance, with him, she'd regret it until the moment she drew her last breath.

Shoving her anxiety aside, she whispered hoarsely, "Jackson..."

He stared down at her, concern lining his handsome face. "What?"

"You really meant it, didn't you?"

"Of course. I've never lied to you."

Panic clawed at her throat, her need for control nearly overwhelming. So much rode on her response. Everything. Her whole life. Her future. A future with him. It could all be hers, if only she had the courage.

"I want you, too," she blurted, forcing the words out on a choked whisper. "More than I've ever wanted anything. But I'm scared."

"And you think I'm not?" He scowled.

"I don't know. You're braver than anyone I've ever known."

"You're brave, too, Lucy."

The way he said her name, like a prayer, a benediction, made her heart slam against her rib cage.

"I thought Robert loved me, but he didn't. Not really. He just wanted to use me for research."

"I love you, Lucy." He held her tighter. "Real love. And screw Robert. If I ever meet him face-to-face, I'll punch him."

"I'd like to see that." She lowered her gaze. "But it's also about me not trusting myself. That's why I moved here. To prove to myself that I was strong and capable and not broken. That I could go it alone. But when I was with you during the storm, I realized those same needs to prove myself had crippled me, Jackson. They made me afraid to ever risk again. You were right about me, too. I thought if I never opened my heart to anyone again, if I stayed alone, I was guaranteed not to lose. I could have true freedom, but at what cost?"

"What are you telling me, Lucy?"

Now or never. She took that final step and met his gaze. "I'm telling you I'm sorry I hurt you. It's the very last thing I ever wanted to do. I'm sorry that I sent you away after the storm. I never meant to make you feel unworthy. You're the worthiest person I know."

Lucy pulled his face down to hers and kissed him hard. Put her heart, her life, her soul, everything she could say into it. He tensed, then accepted the fierce pressure of her mouth on his, but he didn't respond.

Dammit. She was losing him. Tears gathered in her eyes as she pulled away. "I'm sorry. I don't know what else to say. How else to apologize." Tears trickled down her cheeks. "Being scared was no excuse. I was wrong. I don't want you to go. I never wanted you to go."

It took a second, then his expression shifted to wariness. "What exactly are you saying?"

"I'm saying I love you, Jackson Durand. Don't leave. Don't walk away. And I swear I will never, ever, walk away, either."

"You'll never lose me, Lucy." This time he kissed her, hard. "Never."

"Thank God," she said, her sniffles turning to great gulping sobs. "I'm sorry… I can't seem…to stop…" She took a shuddering breath. "It's just I'm so—"

Jackson held her and tilted her face up to his. "I know, Lucy. I know."

She laughed and cried and hugged him again. "What a pair we are, huh?"

From his cage, Bubba squawked and danced across his perch, screeching, "Crazy in love."

"Lucy?" Jackson's voice was sweetly hoarse now.

"Mmm?" She nuzzled more deeply into his embrace, sighing happily when his arms tightened around her.

"Tell me again." He pressed his lips to her ear. "I need to hear you tell me again."

She smiled and gazed up at him once more. "I love you, Jackson Durand. For better, for worse. For always."

"I love you, too, Lucy Miller," he said, rubbing her arms. "It's scary, believing that I'm worthy of you, but I do. You make me believe it. And I promise to never let you down. I feel connected to you in a way I don't even understand yet. And I don't care. You're part of me, too. Always."

* * * * *

HER ONE-NIGHT
SECRET

TRACI DOUGLASS

MILLS & BOON

CHAPTER ONE

FIRE CAPTAIN STACY WILLIAMS climbed out of the back of the fire truck just as soon as it halted beneath the ambulance bay of Key West General Hospital, along with most of the rescue crew. They'd only left a skeleton staff back at the firehouse in case of other emergency calls coming in, as per protocol. Everyone else was here because one of their own was on a stretcher today.

She trailed behind the EMTs wheeling in Assistant Chief Reed Parker, unable to look away from Reed's too-pale face. The guy had been with the department for more than two decades, dedicating his life to protecting the good people of Key West, but today the father of three was the one who needed saving.

"What's the rundown?" one of the ER docs said as they lowered the gurney from the back of the ambulance. Stacy's focus remained steady on Reed, not looking up or budging as noise from the controlled chaos of the busy trauma department inside leaked out each time the automatic doors whooshed open then closed.

"Forty-one-year-old firefighter with Key West FD," one of the EMTs, Jackson Durand, said. "Riding his motorcycle and thrown from the bike, no loss of consciousness on scene. Obvious open left femur fracture."

Reed moaned loudly then and tried to get up, but Jackson held him in place with a hand on his chest. Stacy's heart went out to the guy. Reed prized his bike and rode to escape the stress of the job. To have this happen doing something he loved was devastating. They all clambered inside then down a corridor to the left toward one of the open treatment bays.

"Sir," the ER doc said, leaning over Reed as he stepped in beside Jackson, his back to Stacy. "Can you tell me your name?"

They transferred Reed from the gurney to the hospital bed, and one of the nurses lifted the sheet covering his lower body to look at the wound. "What's wrong with my leg?" he groaned, and Stacy's heart thudded hard in her chest. "It hurts so bad."

"Your leg is broken, sir," the doctor said, placing his stethoscope on the man's chest and listening before continuing. "Pretty badly, I'm afraid. But we're going to take good care of you." He nodded to Jackson, then took over the EMT's position at the patient's bedside. "Okay, we've got a good airway here. Good breath sounds bilaterally. Sir, can you open your eyes again for me? Looks like you're getting drowsy. Reed, can you wiggle your left toes for me?"

Reed screamed, writhing on the bed. "Argh! It hurts, it hurts. I can't. I can't. My leg hurts so bad."

"Blood pressure?" the doctor asked the nurse across the gurney.

"Seventy over forty, Doc."

Stacy stood with the rest of her crew in the hallway outside the treatment bay, close enough to hear what was being done and said but out of the way of the important staff. As the assessment of Reed's condition continued, her gut knotted tighter in empathy for her coworker. An open compound fracture of the femur would hurt like hell, yet the hospital wouldn't be able to give him anything for the pain because of his low blood pressure. It could lead to even more issues, maybe even kill him if Reed stopped breathing all together.

Not good. Not good at all.

"Right," the doctor said, his slight accent snagging something in Stacy's memory before she waved it off. Key West was a true melting pot of people, between the locals and the vacationers and the refugees who came here for a better life. Just because that deep voice reminded her of a long-ago night on the beach, when a handsome Cuban stranger had wooed her into one night of passion that led to her son, Miguel, didn't mean it was the same guy. Couldn't be. The man she'd known was halfway around the world by now, location unknown…

"Let's give him six units of blood, stat!" the doctor said from the treatment bay, jarring Stacy out of the past and back to the high-stakes reality. "Heart rate's high but blood pressure's low. Get ortho on the phone, stat, please. This man needs to be in an operating room now. I don't know if that leg is salvageable, but right now the primary concern is stopping the bleeding and saving his life."

Stacy stepped back, head lowered, as the curtain swished open and the doctor walked out. She caught a hint of alcohol from the hand sanitizer he used as he passed by her, his rubber soles squeaking on the shiny tile floor as he headed to the nurses' station down the hall. He was tall, maybe six inches above her own five-foot-six height, with broad shoulders that filled out his green scrubs nicely. She still had no idea what he looked like, though, since she hadn't seen his face. She and the rest of the crew knew most of the docs around here, as they often assisted the ambulance crews on emergency runs since they were cross-trained as EMTs. Most times, fire arrived before the ambulance when 911 was called.

One of the nurses she knew, Jenny, walked out of the treatment bay, and Stacy plied her for information about Reed while Jenny typed into a computer against the wall. "How is he?"

"Not good," Jenny said. "He's not responding to the blood we're giving him. Doc's sending him up to surgery to see what's happening internally. We'll know more after that."

Jenny took off again, and Stacy and the rest of her crew wandered back down the corridor toward the waiting area, passing by the doc on the phone as they went. She did her best not to eavesdrop, but given it was a friend of hers whose life was in peril, that was pretty much impossible. Stacy wasn't sure whom he was talking to, but she was able to glean a few more details as she passed by.

"...yes. Fireman thrown from his motorcycle. Known femur fracture, suspected pelvic fracture. No. I'm not sure, but he's not responding to transfusions. That's my worry, too. Maybe an undiagnosed solid organ injury. Liver or spleen. Or perhaps internal bleeding from the pelvic fracture. We can't be certain until you get in there. Saving the leg is the least of our worries..."

Oh boy. Stacy sat in one of the hard plastic chairs and stared down at her hands.

Please, God. Please let Reed be okay. Please.

She couldn't imagine having that conversation with his wife, his kids. Telling them their father had died. Images from her own childhood, the day her mother had told Stacy that her dad was gone, flashed in her head.

Her dad hadn't died. He'd just walked out on them, but still.

She'd never seen the man again either way, so it didn't much matter.

The doctor hung up, and Stacy pushed to her feet. Enough. She needed to find out what was happening before Reed's family showed up demanding answers. As captain and the ranking officer on scene, it would be her duty to keep the family and her team informed.

Before she could reach the doc, whose long legs carried him surprisingly fast toward the stairwell, the automatic doors swished open once more and Reed's wife, Annette, ran in with their three teenaged kids.

"What's happened? Where's my husband?" Annette said in a panicked rush. "Is he okay? I told him not to ride that damned bike of his so fast around the curves. I told him he was going to kill himself one day if he…" Her words caught on a sob, and she collapsed into Stacy's arms. "Oh God. I didn't mean it. I swear I didn't. If anything happens to my Reed, I don't know what I'll do."

Stacy led the crying woman and the kids to a more private area down the hall, near the elevators, to tell her what she knew, which was precious little at the moment until she talked to the doctor in charge. She looked up and spotted him still near the nurses' station, talking to Jackson. Good. Maybe if she hurried she could still catch him before he went up to surgery, or wherever he was going.

"Hang on, Annie," Stacy said, gripping the near-hysterical woman by the shoulders. "Let me see if I can catch the doctor real quick and find out what's happening."

She looked up again and froze.

Not because the doctor was gone, but because she finally got a look at his face. A face she'd never thought she'd see again. She blinked, stared, the phantom smells of sand and surf surrounding her. The sounds of the ER morphed into the crash of waves. They'd been young and drunk and stupid in lust with each other, both looking for a good time, nothing more.

She'd ended up with more, though. A life-altering more that had given her more joy and sorrow and unexpected gifts that she'd ever imagined. A son she'd never expected. A son his father knew nothing about.

Oh no.

Her breath seized, and her chest ached. Time slowed as her eyes locked with his hazel ones, the same caramel color she remembered from that long-ago night on the beach.

It was him.

Luis.

Then, as quickly as the spell had fallen, it shattered, and things sped up. He pushed through the stairwell door and was gone, looking as shell-shocked as she felt. Stacy was left staring at Jackson, who gave her an inquiring look before going back to his paperwork.

Snap out of it, she scolded herself. *Breathe.*

She couldn't afford this right now. Not with Reed fighting for his life and an Emergency Response Team meeting on her agenda in a little over an hour's time.

Dammit. She was supposed to meet her friend Lucy Miller and take her to the meeting. It was Lucy's first time and she was anxious as it was, and Stacy didn't want to make that worse.

"Come on," she said to Annette, ushering her and the kids into a private consult room nearby. "You guys sit here for a little while until we find out more, okay?" She hugged Annie, then excused herself. "I'll be back. I need to take care of something." Stacy headed out the door then turned back to her crew, who were sitting with the Parkers. "Watch over them. Text me if anything changes."

Then she was out the door and heading for the waiting area where she was supposed to meet Lucy, but nope. No sign of her friend. Dammit. Stacy checked everywhere, even went up to the children's ward but found no Lucy or her service dog, Sam.

She went back to the nurses' station, thinking she'd ask Jackson, but he was gone now, too.

Great. Her day was going from bad to worse.

It can't be. And yet...it was.

He knew that as surely as he knew the patient he was watching through the glass of the observation room upstairs in the OR would still have a long way to go before he was out of the woods. The surgery could stop the bleeding and stabilize his condition. That was the good news. The bad news was afterward they'd still need to evaluate that leg, wash out the wound to get rid of all the gravel and denim and bits of bone that had been broken off and were embedded with it. Then the ortho surgeon would apply a fixation device to stabilize his broken femur. Unfortunately, when Luis had checked in the ER, there was no pulse in the patient's left foot, and from what he could hear through the intercom system from the surgical suite, there still wasn't now, even after an hour on the table. Which could signify two bigger injuries—compromised blood supply to the leg or possible nerve damage to the area.

Yes, the man's life was much more secure at that point, but at what cost?

It was a question that plagued Luis as he went back downstairs for the ERT meeting. He was already running late, which was nothing new. Schedules had to be flexible when you packed as much into them as Luis did. He liked to stay busy, stay productive, stay focused on his goals.

After all, people had died to make his life today possible. People like his birth parents.

He owed it to them to accomplish as much as possible for as many people as possible in the time he had. It was a philosophy that Luis lived by and the idea that kept him circling back to that original question, usually late at night, when he lay awake in his bed, alone.

At what cost?

Luis wasn't a man who sat around feeling sorry for himself. Nope. He was blessed, and he knew it.

He pushed out into the ER on the first floor and checked in at the nurses' station before grabbing his lab coat and heading down the hall to the conference room where the meeting was being held. He nodded greetings to several colleagues along the way before easing his way into the crowded space, where the speakers had already begun.

Truthfully, he was proud as hell of his adopted brother, Jackson, for taking on the incident commander position for this latest hurricane. His brother was the hardest-working EMT in the area, and the promotion and recognition that came with it had been a long time coming for Jackson. He hoped everything went to plan and his brother got the new job he wanted. No one deserved it more than Jackson, but then, life didn't always give us what we deserved.

Silently, he moved in beside his brother now and leaned back against the wall, grateful for the dimmed lights in the room as he stared up at the podium and the presenter.

Stacy Williams.

The name suited her—steady, sure, sensible, sexy as hell yet completely unassuming.

It was that last one that had his throat constricting with adrenaline as long-ago memories assailed him. Still hushed, still shadowed. But then they'd been on the beach, just the two of them beneath the moonlight, huddled on a blanket, entwined in each other's arms, the stars the only witness as they'd made love on the sand dune and his world had been rocked forever.

That had been the night before he'd left to go to Myanmar. The night when the future had seemed so uncertain and the only tangible thing he'd had to hold on to had been her. If he closed his eyes, he could still remember the feel of her silky skin against him, hear her soft cries as she came undone in his arms, taste the sweetness of her kisses on his lips...

"Everything okay?" Jackson asked, giving him some serious side-eye.

"Fine," Luis said, shaking off the unwanted warmth inside him. It had been one night, a drunken fling. It didn't mean anything at all. Even if it kind of felt like it did, at least to him. He wasn't really a one-night-stand kind of man. Wasn't a relationship guy at all, honestly. He didn't have the time.

Too busy taking care of others. Always putting others' wants and needs ahead of his own.

He was a doctor. That's what he did. Who he was.

"And now I'll turn things back over to IC Jackson Durand," Stacy said before heading back to her seat, her gaze briefly meeting Luis's before flickering away again.

Luis's gut clenched. She recognized him. She *knew*.

They'd never spoken after that night. He'd left the US early the next morning on his flight, and she'd gone back to Miami, he'd assumed. They'd both gotten on with their lives, obviously. But in that brief meeting of their eyes, he'd seen her blue ones widen slightly and Luis knew she'd been remembering that night, too. Before he caught himself, he was moving across the room to stand closer to where she was sitting. He had no intention of rekindling old flames, but he did want to talk to her, to dispel the awkward tension between them, especially since he'd seen her earlier with the injured firefighter and chances were they might run into each other again.

After all, they were both on the ERT team and Luis was coordinating the ER to handle any casualties the storm might cause. A good working relationship with the fire department was key to any response plan. He was just doing his job.

And perhaps, if he told himself that enough times, he might actually believe it.

First, though, Luis needed to get through this damned meeting.

Which seemed to drag on and on and on.

He got up and gave his presentation about the hospital's contingency plans and triage protocols during disasters. With Key West and the surrounding islands in the hot zone for hurricanes, it wasn't uncommon for them to experience several each season. This year had been worse, though, with more named storms than any on record so far, and it didn't appear that it would let up anytime soon.

When he was done, Luis made his way back over to where Stacy sat with another woman, Lucy Miller. Luis recognized her and her therapy dog from the days they made their rounds upstairs in the children's ward. He had to admit he was a bit shocked to see Lucy here, given her anxiety disorders, but then, he of all people should know that being neurodivergent didn't preclude one from doing whatever one put one's mind to. In fact, for him at least, his mild case of Asperger's syndrome actually benefited his work as a doctor, made him more focused, better able to retain and use information about his patients. And yes, sometimes the social aspects were still a struggle for him, even after years of adapting, but people loved to talk about themselves, so as long as he kept that spotlight pointed away from himself and firmly on them, he was fine.

"All right, folks," Jackson said from the podium. "That's it for today. Please keep one eye on the weather reports, and if predictions change, I'll let everyone know and we'll meet again. Thank you."

People began to file out of the room, and Stacy whispered something to Lucy before standing, pushing her chair in then heading for the door. It was now or never, and Luis's pulse kicked up a notch.

He was hardly some fumbling schoolboy, unsure and untested around women, but for some reason the thought of talking to this woman made him nervous as hell. Maybe because he'd relived that night five years ago in his head so many times during the lonely days in between that he'd built it into something completely magical and fantastic. Maybe reality would never equal the dream. Maybe this was all a horrible mistake.

Before he could stop himself, Luis touched her arm just as she reached the door and she turned, the end of her long blond ponytail brushing the back of his hand and sending a slight shiver through him. Her blue eyes widened, just as pretty and deep azure as he remembered, and just like that, Luis felt like he was drowning. He choked out words past his tight vocal cords. "It is you."

CHAPTER TWO

HER FIRST IMPULSE was to feign ignorance, but from the way he'd been watching her this whole time, it was clear he'd recognized her, so what was the point? Besides, the last thing Stacy wanted to do was draw more attention to her past indiscretions, so she hiked her chin toward the other members of her fire crew to go on out into the hall, then waited until they were gone before turning back to face Luis.

"It is." She forced a smile she didn't feel and looked him over. Man, he was still gorgeous as ever. At first, when she'd looked back on that night, she'd figured she'd been imagining that thick, curly dark hair, those velvety caramel-colored eyes, the impossibly long eyelashes that most women would kill for. Of course, then, as luck would have it, her own son was born with those same features nine months later, so...

Stacy swallowed hard and did her best to cover her nervousness with chatter. "Didn't think I'd see you again. How are you? You look well."

Luis blinked at her a moment, a slight frown lining the smooth skin between his dark brows. "I wondered what happened to you after that night, if you were okay."

That slight accent of his sent a sudden shiver of unwanted awareness through her, taking her right back to that night on the beach, the stars twinkling above, his strong arms around her, sweet endearments on his lips as he'd moved over her, in her, so careful, so tender, so...

"I'm fine. Great, actually." She needed air, and space. The walls of the room seemed to be closing in on her with him that close, his warmth and scent surrounding her—soap and sandalwood. Stacy turned fast and pushed out into the hallway, grateful for the bright lights and noise of the other meeting members to distract her. She pointed at her badge and headed down the corridor toward the entrance to the ER. "Captain now."

"I see that," Luis said, keeping pace beside her, adjusting his long-legged stride to accommodate her shorter one. Funny how that worked. She was a good six inches shorter than him, but that night they'd fit perfectly together.

Stop thinking about that night. Stop it.

"Are you living in Key West now?" he asked as they passed her fire crew, who were giving her curious looks.

"I am," she said, leaving it at that. She and Miguel had moved into a nice apartment at a local complex the previous year when she'd taken the captain's job here after leaving her department in Miami. "And you? Are you still traveling the world on your mission trips?"

"No. Not anymore," he said, tapping the square metal handicapped button on the wall with his elbow so the automatic doors swung open ahead of them. "I've taken the position as head of the emergency department here at Key West General, so I'm staying put now."

"Good to know." Actually, it wasn't good. Not at all. Because if they were both staying here in Key West, that meant she needed to tell him about Miguel. Honestly, Stacy had never meant to keep it a secret from Luis for this long. It was just that once she'd found out she was pregnant, he was long gone, and she'd had no way to get a hold of him. Then she'd had the baby and had to fend for herself, and she'd been too busy working and surviving to consider another trip back down to Key West to search for Luis. Being accepted into the fire academy training program had been a godsend—good pay, good benefits, good exercise and a new, extended family she'd always wanted but never dreamed she'd have. The guys in the Miami-Dade County Fire and Rescue Department had embraced Stacy and Miguel as their own, giving her son all the attention and positive male role models he could ever want or need.

Still, having a father—*his* father—in his life was important for her son, at least to Stacy. So, no matter how awkward, she would tell Luis. Just maybe when the time and place were more appropriate.

"You work with Reed?" Luis asked as they stopped near the nurses' station in the bustling ER. "The injured firefighter?"

"I do. He's on a different crew than mine, but we're all in the same battalion." She swallowed hard against the lingering constriction in her throat. "It's like a big family."

"That's nice," Luis said, turning his attention to a chart the nurse behind the desk handed him. "Your colleague is in for a tough battle."

"Is there any word on how the surgery went?" she asked, glad for a topic of discussion.

"I can't discuss the specifics because of privacy laws, but suffice it to say that when I left the OR upstairs, he was holding his own. With luck they got the bleeding under control and we can move on to evaluating his leg injury."

"Will he walk again?"

"I can't give you a prognosis on that at the moment, I'm afraid." Luis continued jotting notes in the chart he was working on. "It will be a long recovery either way. Given the extent of the initial injury, there will be nerve and tissue damage that will take time to heal. Physical therapy and bed rest are definitely in his future whether he keeps that leg or not. It will just depend on what the focus is—restoring strength and mobility or retraining him to use a prosthetic."

"Will he be able to return to active duty as a firefighter?" Stacy asked, her heart aching for his family and what they were going through. "He'll have his pension, but I know Reed, and he'd hate sitting behind a desk all day."

"We won't know until after the surgery and the ortho consult." He glanced over at her. "But if everything works out well, I don't see why not. They've made huge strides in technology and many people with prosthetics can do just as well, and in some cases better, than their counterparts without disabilities. That would be up to your department, however, and what the physical therapists have to say once they work with and evaluate him. We're getting way ahead of ourselves here, though."

Now that Stacy had a chance to really study him as

he worked, she could see tiny lines near the corners of his eyes that hadn't been there before, and a hint of dark stubble just beneath the surface of his strong jaw. She wondered how long his shift had been, if he had someone waiting at home for him once he was done…

Not that it was any of her business. Nope. She was not looking for a relationship. She had plenty enough on her plate as it was with work and Miguel and now the hurricane heading in their general direction. It was just that if he was involved with someone else, that would add another dimension to him finding out he had a son from a previous liaison. She needed to tread carefully, since the last thing Miguel needed right now was more upset to his schedule. With his mild Asperger's, routine was the glue that held their little world together. And most of all, she didn't want her son hurt.

As someone who knew the pain of being an only child, raised by a single mother, Stacy knew all too well the pain of letting someone in, only to have them walk away or disappoint you. She remembered when her own father had walked out on them. At first, she'd cried and cried, running to the window each time a car drove by their house, thinking it might be him. Then, after a while, she'd turned the pain and hurt inward, thinking it was her fault he was gone. That it must've been something she'd done, or if she'd only been better, somehow, her father wouldn't have left them. Eventually she'd internalized that feeling of never being enough and translated it into constantly pushing herself to do more, be more, hoping someday it might be enough to keep those she loved from leaving.

Stacy refused to have her son experience that same trauma by exposing Miguel to a man who might just as likely disappear from their lives as quickly as he'd arrived. She'd never really explained to Miguel about where his father was, and luckily he hadn't asked. It had always just been the two of them. Now, though, as he was getting older, she feared the questions would come and, with them, the knowledge that he'd been a surprise baby. But in the best possible way. Stacy couldn't image her life without her son. He was her reason for being, her reason for getting up every day, her reason for everything.

There wasn't anything she wouldn't do for Miguel, including telling Luis the truth.

Soon. Just not yet.

They stood there a moment, neither knowing what to say, until finally Stacy spotted Reed's wife and daughter in the hall and seized on her opportunity to escape. "Uh, I should get back to my crew and Reed's family. Excuse me. It was nice seeing you again."

"I'd like to have dinner," Luis said as she was walking away, halting her in her tracks. "To discuss coordination of our protocols for the hurricane."

Her heart thudded harder against her rib cage. The hurricane. Right. "Uh, I…"

"Stacy," he said, handing the chart back to the nurse then stepping toward her, a hint of his tanned chest visible through the vee of his light green scrub shirt. She concentrated there and not on his eyes, those too-perceptive eyes that sent tingles of heat through her like fireworks and always saw way more than she wanted to reveal. Like how nervous she was around him. Like how he still affected her, even after all these years. Like how almost five years later and a lifetime of changes apart, her attraction to him burned bright as the sun. "Just dinner. That's all. How about tonight? Say, 8:00 p.m., after my shift? Unless you have other plans already."

There it was. Her out. She seized on it with both hands, even as she cursed herself a coward. "Actually, I do have other plans tonight. Sorry." Namely, mac and cheese and homework with Miguel. "Maybe another time."

She took off before he could ask any more questions, the weight of his stare prickling the back of her neck all the way down the corridor.

Luis went back to work, seeing patients and finishing his shift in the ER before going upstairs to check on Reed's progress before going home for the night. The man's family had moved upstairs to the private waiting area near the ICU. Luis peeked in as he passed by and spotted the orthopedic surgeon in with them, giving them a post-op update. Stacy was there, too, glancing up to meet Luis's gaze before quickly refocusing her attention back on the doctor.

He didn't want to intrude, but from where he stood, Luis could overhear part of what his colleague was saying to them.

"So the good news is, we were able to reestablish blood flow to his leg, okay," the orthopedic surgeon said. "The bad news is, his leg was without blood flow for a significant period of time."

A quiet murmur passed through the family before the wife asked, "What are your biggest concerns then, for tonight?"

"Well, I won't lie," the surgeon said, sighing. "There are a lot of hurdles to get over before we can save his leg."

It was as Luis had thought. He turned away then to go back downstairs, this time using the elevators, because damn, he was tired. He pushed the button and waited, staring up at the digital numbers above the shiny metal doors. Having a conversation like that with the family was tough. One of the toughest parts of the job, frankly, regardless of what area of medicine you practiced. Human nature made you want to offer as much hope as possible to them, but conscience and scientific fact meant you also needed to be very realistic about the possible outcomes and set realistic expectations for everyone involved. It was a tightrope he walked daily in the ER, especially with the more severe trauma cases such as Reed's.

In truth, those conversations were the ones that kept him up at night, worrying about the patient's future. And even though Luis wasn't in charge of the man's case any longer, releasing that responsibility was not so easy to do. Regardless of his exhaustion, Luis was pretty certain he'd lose plenty of sleep worrying about whether Reed would be able to return to his career as a firefighter.

It was just part of who he was, to worry, to overanalyze, to think things to death.

Like his conversation with Stacy earlier.

That night five years ago, he'd had no idea that she'd wanted to be a firefighter. Not that they'd discussed their future plans or talked about anything at all much beyond that moment, but she'd not struck him as an adrenaline junkie or a risk taker. In fact, back then she'd seemed the epitome of the South Florida party girl, a wild, reckless, devil-may-care woman on spring break looking to have a good time and leave her cares and concerns behind. She'd told him she was twenty-two that night, but there'd been a maturity in her eyes and in her heart that went well beyond her age. Of course, once he'd looked into those wide blue eyes of hers he'd been lost anyway, and fighting his attraction to her had gone right out the window. Jackson and some of his buddies from his residency program had taken Luis out as a farewell party before his flight to Bangkok the next morning to begin his mission trip. And what a send-off it was. They'd taken over his parents' pub and partied until well after midnight. Needing a break from the noise and revelry, Luis had excused himself to take a walk on the beach and he'd found Stacy outside as well, staring up at the starry sky.

Their chemistry had been instant, as had the fiery passion between them.

She'd taken his hand as they'd strolled across the moonlit sand. Then, once they'd left the thumping music and raucous cheers of the pub behind, he'd kissed her. Neither of them was completely sober, but they both had surrendered willingly to the desire shimmering between them. Being with her had been both a revelation and a curse. Stacy had been like no one else he'd ever been with before—so soft and sweet and exquisitely responsive to his every touch and kiss and nuzzle. But that same uniqueness had also been a curse, because he'd never forgotten her, or that night. Not in nearly five long years. And now, seeing her again so unexpectedly today had shaken him to his core, and...

"Seems we can't avoid each other today."

Ding!

Stacy stood a few feet away, looking anywhere but

at him. "I can, uh…" She pointed toward the stairwell door across the corridor. "I'll just take the steps."

"Don't be silly," Luis said, tired of playing the avoidance game. He held the elevators doors open for her. "We're both adults. I think we can handle this."

She stood there a moment, her expression uncertain, then seemed to reach a decision and boarded the elevator beside him with a decisive nod. "True."

Luis pushed the buttons for the first floor then stepped back and clasped his hands in front of him as the doors swished closed. He stared down at his toes while Stacy stared straight ahead, his stomach lurching as the car jolted then began to descend.

"So," he said after a moment, unable to tolerate the choking silence any longer. "Reed came through his surgery okay."

"Yes," Stacy said. "The prognosis for his leg is still uncertain, though. Just like you mentioned earlier."

"Yes." The elevator stopped on the second floor and a little old lady who looked like someone's grandmother got on. She smiled and nodded to Luis then Stacy, then turned and faced the doors, her large tote bag with knitting needles sticking out the top nearly poking him in the leg. Luis stepped back and cleared his throat. "My thoughts are with his family during this difficult time."

"Mine, too." Stacy took a deep breath. "Look, Luis. I'm sorry about earlier, if I seemed abrupt. I was just surprised to see you and I've been busy and have a lot on my plate at the moment and—"

Ding!

The doors opened on the first floor and Luis sidled around the woman and her knitting needles to stick his arms against the door to hold it so Stacy could get out then followed her into the corridor. He waited until the elevator closed again before taking Stacy's arm and leading her down the hall to a quieter area for privacy.

"No need to apologize. I think we were both thrown before. But my offer still stands." He checked his watch then put his hands on his hips and looked at her. "My shift is done. I'm heading home. We can still grab dinner if you'd like."

"Oh, I can't tonight. Sorry." She pulled out her phone. "I've got things at the apartment to handle."

"Okay. Fair enough. How about tomorrow night, then?" He pulled up his schedule on his smart watch. "I'm off the whole day, but I have plans until later in the afternoon. How about dinner after that? Say, seven at the pub?"

"Durand's Duck Bill Pub?" She glanced up at him, her expression surprised. "I haven't been there in years."

"All the more reason to go, then." He smiled. He'd been planning to help out his adopted parents tomorrow anyway, doing odd jobs for them around the bar, same as he'd done since joining their family at the age of six. "I doubt the place has changed that much since the last time you saw it. More flags, probably. And T-shirts."

"Oh, I remember those." She grinned, and his night suddenly brightened. Her smile faltered, though, as her phone buzzed with a new message. Stacy frowned at the screen, then swallowed hard, putting the device back in her pocket then taking a deep breath, as if her decision was a difficult one. "Okay. Fine. Yes. Dinner tomorrow night sounds good. We have a lot to talk about."

Luis nodded, adding the event to his calendar. He wasn't sure what exactly they needed to discuss, but he was glad for the chance to get reacquainted with her and see if his memories did her justice or if he'd somehow turned her into some kind of fantasy in his mind. "Great. Tomorrow night at seven, then. I'll probably be behind the bar when you get there, in case you can't find me."

She gave him a quizzical look. "You work there, too?"

"No." He chuckled. "Well, not on the official payroll, anyway. But you help out family when you can."

"Oh, right. I forgot." A brief shadow flickered across her pretty face, so fast he would've missed it if he hadn't been watching her so closely. "Well, then. I guess I'll see you there."

"You will." He stood in the hall as she backed away from him, neither of them looking away until finally the automatic doors of the ER swished open behind her and she disappeared into the darkness outside. Luis sighed and shook his head, then turned on his heel to head to the staff locker room to change, an odd mix of apprehension and anticipation simmering inside him. He shouldn't get excited about their dinner tomorrow. It was nothing more than two strangers meeting for a meal.

Two strangers who'd had sex. On the beach. Beneath the stars and moon, her skin glowing and her eyes bright with passion. If he closed his eyes, Luis swore he could still hear his name on her lips as she climaxed around him, could still feel the heat of her tight against his skin, could still taste her sweetness on his tongue.

God, he was getting sentimental and silly with fatigue. That had to be it. Fantasy indeed.

He was a man who lived by logic. He prized truth and facts and science above all else. He didn't deal with emotions and intuition, because those things only ever got you in trouble. Those things could cost you everything, if you weren't careful. Take his birth parents. They'd ignored the obvious danger of crossing the strong currents and shark-infested waters of the Straits of Florida at night, plus the weather reports at that time heralding the impending arrival of a tropical storm, in order to give young Luis and themselves a chance at a better life. That effort had cost them their lives and left Luis an orphan. Luckily, the Durands had taken him in shortly after he'd entered foster care, and they'd given him a good life, the life his birth parents would've wanted for him. But still…

No. Luis was a man with a purpose. One he took seriously, without his emotions getting in the way.

Except for that one night almost five years ago with Stacy. That had been all about his feelings…

He changed into his street clothes and headed home to his secluded, lush beachfront property on the north side of the island of Key West, unable to shake the odd sense of inevitability that there was more happening between him and Stacy than just the past. Luis pulled into his driveway and cut the engine on his Mercedes then sat there staring at the white facade of his modern two-story luxury home. He'd worked hard for his good life and enjoyed the perks it bought him, but he also gave generously of both his time and money to local charities to help the underprivileged and refugees, having been both himself once upon a time.

Yep. There was definitely a reason fate had brought the two of them together again. And tomorrow night, Luis intended to find out exactly what that reason was.

CHAPTER THREE

STACY HEARD THE music pouring out of the open doors of the bar on the corner of Duval and Greene Streets before she ever reached the entrance of the Duck Bill Pub. A blend of calypso and pop, the song had a catchy beat and an island vibe that had her toes tapping in her strappy sandals.

With each step she took, it felt like the past five years slipped away a bit more. She'd not been back here since moving to Key West the prior year because there were just too many memories, too much water under the proverbial bridge, but now...

Well, now she had important business to take care of. Namely telling Luis about the son he didn't know he had. She owed that to him, and she owed it to Miguel.

If only she could get the nervous butterflies in her stomach to settle down, she'd be all set.

A small crowd had already gathered near the entrance, waiting to get in. Duval Street was famous with the tourists anyway, and Durand's Duck Bill Pub was practically a legend in these parts. It was why she and her friends had come that first night, to see the place where Hemingway used to hang out with his buddies and maybe pick up a T-shirt and a hangover as souvenirs.

What she'd ended up with after spending the night on the beach with Luis, however, had changed her life forever.

As she crossed the street at the light and approached the bouncer outside, the band ended their song to thunderous applause. She stopped near the door and leaned closer to the bulky guard to say, "I'm supposed to be meeting Luis Durand at the bar?"

The guy nodded and pointed. "Go on in. He's waiting for you."

"Thanks." She wove through the people milling about and the tables packed with patrons toward the large curved bar in the back corner of the place. It didn't look much different in there than the last time—shiny tile floors, paneled walls covered with local memorabilia and photos of the owners with visiting celebrities, and those flags hanging from the exposed beams in the ceiling. Each time a visitor from a new country arrived at the Duck Bill, they hung the person's native flag from the rafters. According to the tally sign on the wall, the pub was up to 178. Impressive, given there were only 195 total in the world. Seemed it really was the Crossroads of the Keys, as the pub's slogan proclaimed.

And speaking of crossroads...

Stacy finally reached the bar and squeezed between two sets of patrons to ask the bartender about Luis, except when she opened her mouth, no words came out, because the bartender *was* Luis.

He glanced up at her then went back to mixing the cocktail he was working on before doing a double take and grinning. "Hello."

"Hello." She watched him assemble two complicated-looking beverages with a mix of alcohols and fizzy water and fruit then deliver them to a server waiting farther down the bar before returning to her. He looked different tonight, out of his scrubs and wearing one the Duck Bill Pub's logo T-shirts like the rest of the staff. Honestly, he looked younger in his casual jeans. Younger and most definitely sexier.

She swallowed hard against the sudden, unwanted lump of awareness in her throat.

"Working a side hustle?" she asked as he slung a dish towel over one muscled shoulder, those warm caramel-colored eyes of his watching her far too closely for her comfort. Humor and snark were always her fall-backs when she was nervous, and she hoped they'd help her out of her awkwardness now. "Maybe they need to pay you more at the hospital."

"They pay me just fine," he said, leaning one hand on the bar, his teeth even and white against his tanned skin. "Can I get you something to drink?"

"Oh, uh…" She hadn't even bothered to look at the menu, hadn't noticed anything but him since she'd arrived at the bar. Stacy shook her head and glanced over at what the other bartender was making. Something tall and frothy and bright pink with what looked like a flamingo head sticking out of it. "I'll take one of those, if it's not too much trouble."

"No trouble at all," he said, his gaze narrowing for a fraction of a second, as if he was trying to figure out something about her and then did, before he cocked his head. "One Hot Pink Barbie coming up."

While he made her drink, she studied him more closely. He was muscled but not bulky, more sinewy and lithe, moving with a grace that most dancers would envy. That was one thing she remembered about Luis from that night. Well…one of the things. Every move he made seemed purposeful, like he wanted to get everything done as efficiently as possible. She saw the same grace in Miguel.

Her son, too, shared his father's dark curly hair and easy smile. Sometimes, at night, when she closed her eyes, she swore she could still feel the silky strands between her fingers, feel the scrape of his stubbled jaw on her neck as he nuzzled her throat, feel the warm strength of his arms around her as he'd called out her name as he climaxed inside her beneath the stars. The moment they'd made Miguel. The moment her future had swerved onto an entirely new and unexpected path…

The moment that connected them even now.

Tell him.

Luis returned with her drink, and she took a sip for courage. Fruity with a hint of rum and mint for balance. Delicious. She tucked her hair behind her ear then glanced around the busy place. "Any chance we can find a quiet spot to talk in here?"

"Of course." He came around from behind the bar and placed his hand at the small of her back, deftly guiding her through the crowd to a smaller room near the back of the place. There were fewer people in here, and Luis led her to a table for two in the corner with a Reserved sign on it. "I set it aside for us earlier."

"Great."

They took their seats and he removed the towel from his shoulder, twisting it in his hands atop the table. It hadn't occurred to her that he might be nervous, too, but based on his body language, they were both on pins and needles here.

"So," she said, fiddling with the flamingo straw in her glass to distract herself from the enormity of what she had to tell him. "Uh, your parents are doing well?"

"Yes, fine." He smiled, still staring down at his hands. "They are up in Miami right now, and I told them to stay up there until after the storm passes, just to be on the safe side. The staff here can handle things until they get back."

"Is that why you were bartending tonight?"

"What?" He frowned slightly then shook his head. "No. We had someone call in sick at the last minute and I was here waiting for you, so I filled in until the replacement arrived, that's all."

"Ah." She sipped a little more of her drink, careful not to have too much alcohol on her empty stomach. She knew all too well where that could lead. "Right. Well, um." *Just tell him already.* "There's something I, uh, wanted to talk to you about tonight…"

"Are you hungry?" Luis asked, glancing up at her. "We have a full menu now. Sandwiches, steaks, seafood, salads, whatever you like. My treat."

"Oh." She blinked at him a moment. "Uh, okay. I didn't eat lunch today, so I'm starved."

"Excellent." He stood and grinned down at her again, the smile that made her toes curl in her sandals. "Allow me to choose for you? Do you have any allergies? Any foods you dislike?"

"No allergies," she said. "And nothing too spicy, please."

"Got it." He held up a finger then walked over to talk to the man behind a second, smaller bar. The guy nodded as Luis spoke then turned to type an order into the computer behind him while Luis returned to their table. "Done. Our appetizers should be out soon. Now, please. Tell me what you wanted to discuss. We know so little about each other, really."

True enough.

She'd been thinking that same thing earlier on her way here. Weird how you could share such intimacy with a person and yet not know their middle name, or their birthday, or even their favorite color or food. Then again, that was kind of the point of one-night stands. No ties, no strings, no messy details to clean up later.

Oh God.

In her mind, Stacy had imagined a million times how this moment would go, how she'd tell Miguel's father about him, but this was nothing like what she'd pictured in her head. Where they sat in the shadowed corner gave them a modicum of privacy, but you could still hear the raucous cheers from the crowd in the main bar, the twang and percussion of the steel drum band, smell the scent of the fried food and the hint of booze in the air.

So very much like the night they'd met five years ago, and yet so different.

Growing up the only child of a single mom in a poor neighborhood in Miami, Stacy had learned early on how to take care of herself and how to handle difficult situations—head-on, direct, deal with it and be done. It was one of the things that made her so good at her job as a firefighter. But now, those skills failed her. She had no clue how to broach the subject with him in a way that wouldn't smack of secrets and lies.

No. Not lies. She'd never lied to him about Miguel.

She'd just omitted telling Luis about him. And it wasn't for lack of wanting to. He'd been out of the country. Unreachable. She'd had to get on with things for her own survival. And then time had passed, and life moved on. Now that they were both here, she was doing the responsible thing and letting him know. How he chose to deal with the news was his business. She didn't expect anything from him, hadn't even mentioned anything to Miguel, in case things didn't go well tonight. The last thing she wanted was for her son to be hurt by any of this.

Miguel had never asked about his father up until now, but at four, that was bound to change soon.

Right.

She took a deep breath and exhaled slowly, nervous heat prickling her cheeks. "Do you remember our night together years ago?"

Luis met her gaze then, warmth and wariness burning in them. "Yes." The word emerged gruffly. "One does not forget so easily."

Her chest squeezed. That was accurate enough. She'd lost count of how many times she'd relived that night on the beach, the pleasure she'd found in his arms, the hollow ache that persisted inside her. She'd never been a fling sort of girl, her only one being with him, and Luis had left an impression on her, in more ways than one.

"No." Her mouth dried and her mind whirled, but she forced herself to keep going. "Um, there's something you need to know about that night. Something that happened…"

"Oh God," he said, sitting back on his seat to rake a hand through his hair, rocking back on the rear legs of his chair. "I didn't hurt you, did I? I was pretty far gone that night, and parts are a bit murky."

"No, no. You didn't hurt me," she said. *Not in the way you think.* "It's more…um…" *God, just say it.* "I got pregnant. That night. We didn't use anything, and…"

His eyes widened slightly, and his mouth opened, closed, then opened again. The chair plunked down flatly. "I'm sorry. I don't—what?"

"I got pregnant that night, Luis. I had a baby. A son. Our son. Miguel."

Time seemed to slow around Luis, and the room tunneled as he took that in. A million words raced through his head at once, but all he managed to say was "I have a son?"

"Yes."

She sat back as the server brought a large platter filled with all sorts of beer-battered, deep-fried goodies. Too bad Luis's appetite had vanished.

"His name is Miguel, after my father. He's four," she said once they were alone again, fiddling with her napkin, her fingers trembling slightly. "He's smart and sensitive and quiet. He was diagnosed with a mild case of Asperger's syndrome, which is on the—"

"Autism scale. I know." Luis couldn't quite get his brain working properly. He scrubbed a hand over his face, hoping to wipe away some of the shock. A son. A family he knew nothing about. There were so many questions in his mind.

Before he could ask any of them, though, Stacy held up a hand to stop him. "I'm not telling you any of this because I want anything from you. I just felt you should know. Miguel and I have done fine on our own, and nothing will change that."

That brought Luis up short, finally jarring him from his daze. "Wait. Are you saying you don't want me to meet him?"

"No. He's your son and I don't intend to deny you your parental rights, but I want you to think long and hard about it before you decide. He's a very special boy and he means the world to me. I don't want to see him hurt. So, if you don't intend to stick around and become a meaningful part of his life going forward, it might be best for you to not start anything with him at all."

He opened his mouth, then closed it. He could hardly believe this was really happening, but it was. He'd always wanted children of his own someday, once he got settled, got his life in order, got past the lingering fears from his childhood that he might not be around to take care of his own family.

Oh God.

His son had been living without him for the last four years and done just fine, apparently. So much time lost, so many things he'd missed. So few chances to get any of it back or get it right now. He sat there, watching Stacy from across the table, his gut twisted in knots. There was no doubt in his mind she was telling him the truth. The fact his son had inherited his Asperger's just clinched it.

Welcome to fatherhood.

"I, uh… Wow," he said at last, shaking his head, sitting forward to clasp his hands atop the table. "I have no idea what I'm doing here. And you're right. I don't want to see the boy hurt, either. If I'm not planning on maintaining a relationship with him, then I should steer clear. But what if I do want to be a part of his life?"

Stacy halted midbite as she nibbled on a piece of calamari and stared at him, eyes wide. "Oh, well…" She swallowed hard and set the food back on her plate, wiping her fingers on her napkin. "Then I guess we should talk about that, then." She exhaled slowly then sat forward, too, looking as discombobulated as he felt. "Sorry. I honestly wasn't sure what to expect when I came here tonight. It's a lot. I know. Trust me, I know. And I want you to know that I would have told you sooner, but when I tried to contact you after I first found out, they told me you were gone and they weren't sure when you were coming back to the States and I needed to find a job to support myself and figure out what to do about the baby and…"

He frowned. "No, no. I understand. I do." Luis raked a hand through his hair. "I don't blame you. I just… did you not think to try to find me sooner? I mean yes, you tried when you were first pregnant, but what about after that?" He cursed and shook his head. "Sorry. That didn't come out right. We were both responsible for what happened that night on the beach. I shouldn't put it all on you. I could have checked on you, too, once I was back in the States."

"True." She looked up at him. "I guess we both should have tried harder."

Luis gave a curt nod then watched her as she picked up her calamari again. "Did you go back to Miami?"

"I did. Lived with my mother for a while as I went through the fire academy, then once I graduated and was hired onto the force, I got my own place for myself and Miguel. It wasn't anything fancy, but it did all right for us."

"That must've been hard, working full-time with a baby at home." His chest constricted with guilt and worry. If only he'd known, he'd have helped her, supported her. Then again, he'd been busy himself, establishing his practice at the hospital and working his way up in the department. Who's to say that he would've reacted honorably? He liked to think he would, but given his own issues and anxieties, he might also have handled things badly.

Or worse than he already was.

"It was tough, not going to lie. More so after my mom got sick with breast cancer." She finished her food then pushed her plate away, not looking at him, her voice cracking. "She used to watch Miguel for me sometimes, but then she got so sick from the chemo. Thankfully she beat it in the end, and we all moved back to Key West after to start over again."

"Oh God. I'm so sorry, Stacy." And now he felt like an even bigger ass, if that were possible. "If I'd known this was going on, I would have been there for you, for both of you." He reached over and took her hand without thinking. "I'm really sorry."

"It's okay. You didn't know." She shrugged, pulled away. "And I don't need your pity. He doesn't know about you," she said, her cheeks pinkening. "Miguel. He's never really asked about his father, and I haven't told him anything. So, if you want out, tell me. We can both continue on as we have been."

Regret dug sharp claws into his belly. He'd only been two years older than his son was now when he'd lost his parents, and Luis would give anything to have them back, to have just one more day with them. Now that he knew about Miguel, no way could he abandon him. And yes, his schedule was busy, impossibly so. But he'd find a way to be there for his son, if that's what he chose to do, because it was important.

"What if I want in?" he asked. "What if I want to be a part of his life going forward?"

"Then we need to—" Before she could finish her sentence, her phone buzzed in her purse and she pulled it out. "I'm sorry. It's the department. I really need to take this. Excuse me for a second."

Luis sat back as she got up and wandered out a nearby door to the patio outside.

He had a son. A son named Miguel who he'd had no idea existed. If the ground beneath his feet had opened and swallowed him whole, Luis couldn't have been more stunned than he was right then. But he needed to pull it together and find a way through this. He was someone whom everyone else depended on, the person who got things done. Continuing on as they had been wouldn't work for him, not anymore. Not with his child's future on the line.

Many times over the years he'd wondered what must've driven his parents to take that fateful journey across the treacherous straits in the middle of the night in a rickety boat, to risk everything on an uncertain outcome.

Now, as he sat there staring through the glass at Stacy pacing back and forth on the patio as she talked on her phone, he finally knew the answer.

Some things were worth the risk.

Miguel was worth the risk to him. Even if it cost him everything.

And as Stacy looked up and caught his eye, he realized it just might.

CHAPTER FOUR

THE NEXT TWO days were crazy busy, and Stacy was glad because they kept her mind off Luis and focused on her work. She gripped the edge of her seat in the back of the fire truck as they rounded a corner, lights and sirens blazing.

They were on their way to an accident scene, having received a report of a car in a ditch with victims trapped inside. Fire rescue would need to use the Jaws of Life to cut them out. As they sped toward the disaster, Stacy couldn't help wishing there was an equivalent tool she could use to get her out of the mess she'd made of things last night.

She couldn't seem to get the expression on his face when she'd told him about Miguel out of her head. Stunned, then scared, then stoic. And while he'd said he wanted to be involved in their son's life, well, didn't all fathers say that? Her own dad certainly had, then he'd just left one day and never come back. Stacy had waited all night on the porch for him, refusing to leave, until finally she'd had to admit to herself that she'd never see him again.

No way in hell Stacy would ever put Miguel through that. She'd rather him never know his father then grow up hurting because Luis changed his mind at some point.

"We're here!" Rob, the firefighter driving the truck, shouted to the crew in the back. He eased the large vehicle in between several parked squad cars and an ambulance. "Pretty overgrown. Looks like it's going to be tough getting them out."

Stacy and the rest of her crew climbed out of the back and came face-to-face with a thick wall of foliage. At first she saw nothing but trees and bushes, with the occasional fallen log that could've been mistaken for something else. But then one of the police officers on scene pointed to a barely visible curve of black jutting out from the bottom of the steep embankment.

"There's definitely someone trapped in the car," the officer said above the roar of the fire truck's engine, the reflection in his sunglasses alternating red and blue from the lights. "Condensation on the inside of the windows from their breath. Looks like whoever was driving hit a tree there." He pointed to a massive oak a few feet away with a large gouge where the bark had been sheared off. "The impact crumpled the front of the vehicle. Airbags deployed."

"Right." Stacy made her way carefully down the embankment, her boots slipping on the loose soil, until she reached the vehicle along with two other members of the crew. Phil made his way around to the passenger side of the vehicle while she took the driver's side, heart racing and blood pounding in her ears. She yanked on the handle of the dented door on her side, but it didn't budge. Phil tried his side, too, with no luck, either. The ground down here was muddier and slippery, and they both struggled to stay upright as they tried each of the rear doors as well with no luck. "John, go get the cutters."

"Will do, boss," the younger guy said, trekking back up the hill to return a few minutes later with the hydraulic blades they called the Jaws of Life. He and another firefighter made short work of the driver's side door, careful not to further injure the victim inside, then stepped back so Stacy could assess her patient.

As she stepped near the wrecked vehicle again, a pained groan issued from the person inside, and her chest constricted. The noise was actually a good sign. Noise meant the victim was still alive. Stacy leaned inside the car to check the pulse of the woman behind the wheel. Maybe midtwenties, dressed in shorts and flip-flops, the hint of a bikini top beneath her T-shirt and the distinct smell of alcohol on her breath. Unfortunately, drunk driving was an all-too-common occurrence down in the Keys. As she counted the woman's heart rate, she checked her respirations as well. Both normal. That was good, at least.

"Ma'am?" she said, patting the groggy woman's cheek. "My name is Stacy Williams. I'm with the Key West Fire Department. We're going to get you out of here, okay?"

The woman squinted open one eye at her words, then her dark eyes widened like saucers with instant panic. "What happened?"

"Looks like you went off the road, hit a tree," Stacy said, seeing the woman's slight nod. "You're very lucky to be alive," she said looking at Phil over the roof of the car.

After palpating the woman's arms, shoulders and chest for injuries, she checked her pupils, then glanced down toward her legs. Not good. The collision had caused the dashboard to collapse, pinning both of the victim's legs in place.

Phil ducked his head in through the passenger side while Stacy bent to retrieve the woman's purse from where it was wedged in the foot well and riffled through it to find ID. The woman's name was Alicia. Meanwhile, the EMTs made their way down the embankment as well to check the victim's blood pressure, made more difficult by the fact they couldn't move her out of her seat.

"Alicia, stay with us, okay?" Stacy said.

The woman grunted and opened her eyes again.

"Can you tell me where you're hurting?" one of the EMTs asked. "Any pain around your neck or shoulders?"

Alicia shook her head slightly, then groaned and pointed to her legs. Stacy glanced over at the EMTs. "It's difficult to tell what's happening down there because of the dashboard in the way."

The other EMT snapped on a pair of gloves and moved in beside Stacy to slip his hands beneath the dashboard to feel around. When he pulled it back out again, his glove was covered in blood.

"Broken tibia at least. Maybe fibula, too." He took off the soiled glove then dug in the med pack at his feet. "We'll give her something for the pain. Alicia, what have you had to drink?"

She mumbled something about just a few beers, and the EMT and Stacy exchanged a look.

"I'll radio it in," the first EMT said, heading back up the hill. "And I'll have the Air Vac ready just in case."

Stacy edged farther into the car so she could figure out how to get the victim out of there safely as the EMT packed gauze pads beneath the dashboard around Alicia's legs to help stem the bleeding. If they knew for certain the woman had no spinal injuries, they could feel safer examining her more thoroughly. But until they got a cervical collar on her and spinal boards down here, no way was Stacy going to risk paralyzing the woman.

A moan issued from Alicia, and Stacy glanced back at her face. Her lips looked slightly bluer than before. Never a good sign. She signaled for the EMT to check her breath sounds again.

"Definitely decreased," the guy said a moment later. "Especially on the right-hand side. Punctured lung, maybe, due to a broken rib from the steering wheel."

Trouble was they had no idea of Alicia's medical history, and the victim was in no proper state to tell them. Alicia started wheezing and gasping for breath, more than Stacy would have expected from a collapsed lung alone. Scowling, she eased out of the car and picked up the woman's purse again to find an inhaler. Yep, Alicia was asthmatic. She managed to get the inhaler into Alicia's mouth and administer the medication. "That's it. I'm going to give you a few puffs. I know it's hard to breathe when your chest hurts, but try to get as much air as you can, okay? That's it. You're doing great, Alicia. That should help a bit until we can get you out of there."

An hour later they'd managed to get the spinal board down to the crumpled vehicle, and between six cops, three firefighters and two EMTs, they eased the dashboard off Alicia's legs and got both her and the passenger out of the vehicle and safely back up the hill to the ambulance.

Stacy rode in the back of the rig to the hospital with her, mainly because Alicia refused to let go of Stacy's hand the entire way. When they got to Key West General, the ER was swarming with people, as usual.

Luis met them at the door, looking about as haggard as Stacy felt after their dinner together two nights ago. "What have we got?"

She stayed by the gurney as the EMTs ran down the case and they wheeled Alicia down the corridor to an open trauma bay. Stacy kept her focus on the patient, even as she could feel Luis's stare burning a hole through the side of her.

"Patient's name is Alicia Myers. Twenty-seven. MVA near Higgs Beach. Jaws of Life used to cut her from the car. Cause of accident unknown at this point, but alcohol may have been a factor. Suspected fractured left tibia, possibly fibula as well. We gave her ten of morphine at the scene around an hour ago. Patient is also asthmatic and may have a right-sided pneumothorax. Her color has improved with omalizumab, but she's been struggling with her breathing since we came on scene."

Luis took over from there. "Let's get her set up in trauma bay three. We'll need a portable chest X-ray and a chest tube tray, please." He turned and locked gazes with Stacy for a long moment, then followed his nurses and staff into the trauma bay and closed the curtain. "Let's go, people. Time is life."

By the time Luis got his patient stabilized and headed off to the OR with an orthopedic surgeon, several hours had passed. Alicia was expected to make it. She was a lucky woman.

And speaking of lucky, Luis headed upstairs to check in on Reed, the firefighter with the bad fracture. It had been four days since his accident. Normally, when he passed patients on to other physicians, that was the end of his involvement. But Reed's case had stuck with him, in no small part because of Stacy.

Speaking of Stacy, he'd been unable to get her or her son out of his mind, despite the busy day. Correction. *Their* son. What did he look like? Was he smart, funny, tenacious like his mother? The only thing he knew for certain was that the boy had inherited his father's autism. He wanted to meet Miguel, see for himself, but he didn't want to push Stacy too far too soon. He didn't blame her for not telling him before; he just wished he hadn't missed so much time in his son's life.

Luis pushed out onto the ICU floor where Reed's room was then walked down the brightly lit corridor to the last door on the right. He knocked softly then stuck his head in to make sure he wasn't disturbing anything. Reed's wife spotted him and waved him inside, her smile kind and inviting.

"Dr. Durand, how nice to see you," she said, resuming her seat at her husband's bedside. "We weren't expecting you. Is everything okay?"

"Fine," he said, taking a chance to glance at Reed's file on the computer in the corner. "I'm on shift in the ER and there was a lull in cases, so I thought I'd pop up and see how things were going."

From what he could see in the file, the surgeon had been able to reestablish blood flow to Reed's leg. That was good news. The bad news was that leg had been without proper circulation for a significant period of time after the accident, which meant possible nerve and muscle damage that would only become evident as the days progressed.

"We're hanging in there, Doc," Reed said, taking his wife's hand. "Eager to get out of here and get back to work. When do you think that will be?"

Luis took a deep breath and faced the family. It was a tough conversation to have and not really his place. That was up to the ortho surgeon. But he could offer his opinion and hopefully set some realistic expectations. "Well, first off, considering your condition the last time I saw you, I'd say you're doing well. The fact you're up and talking with your family and laughing and smiling is good."

"But what about my leg, Doc?" Reed asked, his gaze pointed. "Give it to me straight. The ortho doc dances around the subject, but I want to know the truth."

"Right." Luis checked the file again then nodded. "This isn't my case anymore, but I'd say you have reason to be cautiously optimistic at this point. Once they get you started on physical therapy and up and around on that leg again, they'll be in a better position to give you a prognosis. It's important to keep in mind the severity of the injury and the amount of blood lost. Depending on how quickly you heal and how hard you work at regaining your mobility, there's a chance you can return to the fire department in some capacity."

"But not as a firefighter." Reed's voice held an edge of sadness. "I'm not sure I can sit behind a desk all day. I love being out in the thick of the danger, you know?"

Luis nodded. That adrenaline rush was what had gotten the man into trouble to begin with, but he wasn't going to mention that now. "As I said, the orthopedic surgeon will have a better idea of prognosis. Be sure to bring up your concerns to him when he stops by next time to check on you."

"He's right, honey," Reed's wife said, kissing his fingers. "I'm just glad you're still here with me."

"Yeah." Reed frowned down at the sheets. "I just wish everything wasn't so up in the air."

"How are you feeling?" Luis asked, changing the subject.

"Like crap."

"But you're alive," his wife countered. "Do you remember any more about the accident?"

Reed sighed, sagging back into his pillows. "I remember everything."

Before Luis could ask him more about that, a couple of teens walked into the room, sidling past Luis to their dad's beside. A girl and boy who looked maybe fifteen and sixteen, respectively. No sign of the third kid yet. The girl was crying as she leaned carefully over the bed to cuddle into her dad's uninjured side.

"Dad, I missed you so much," the girl said, sniffling.

"I missed you, too, baby," Reed said, kissing the top of her head then looking over at Luis. "You got kids, Doc?"

He'd been about to answer no but stopped himself. That wasn't true. Not anymore. His pulse kicked up a notch as he gave a curt nod, saying for the first time, "Yes, a son. His name is Miguel."

"Aw, that's great." Reed's wife stood to move toward him. "Got any pics?"

"What?" He didn't have any pictures of Miguel. Not yet. Someday, though, he vowed to fill his entire memory with images of his son. Until then, he fudged a bit. "No. New phone. Haven't transferred them yet."

"Next time." Reed's wife went back to her seat, while their son slouched against the wall to check his phone. "They can be a handful, that's for sure. But so worth it. Right, honey?"

"Totally." Reed grinned, hugging his daughter tighter. "And because of them, I've promised never to ride another motorcycle again. Life's too precious to take those kinds of risks."

Luis chatted with them a bit more before heading back down to the ER. He liked to stay busy when things were slower, so he did busy work, like charting or inventory. Perhaps he'd do some of that tonight, since he'd already prepped the staff for the upcoming tropical storm. They'd just gotten a shipment of supplies in today, in fact, so maybe he'd help the orderlies put that away. It had been a long time since he'd done that kind of thing, but physical labor always helped clear his head, and Lord knew he could use some of that tonight with everything else going on.

He pushed out of the stairwell door, intending to head toward the supply closet at the end of the hall when he found his path blocked by the very woman who'd been foremost in his thoughts all day.

Stacy looked flushed and tense, and the hairs on the back of his neck rose at the fear in her eyes.

"What's wrong?" Luis asked, concerned. "What's happened?"

"It's Miguel—he's hurt," she said, the tiny catch in her voice tearing at his heart. "They've got him in trauma bay one."

They rushed toward the nurses' station and around

the circular desk to the treatment area closest to the door. Luis didn't hesitate at all, just swished aside the curtain and rushed into the exam room with Stacy by his side. He had no idea what to expect. Blood, gore, some horrific disfigurement.

What he saw was a small boy with dark hair and wide brown eyes clutching a stuffed bear in his right arm while a nurse carefully treated his left one. Tears shone on the little boy's cheeks beneath the bright overhead lights. From the bruising and swelling on his left forearm, Luis quickly surmised he'd broken it. He turned to Stacy. "What happened?"

"I took him to the park near our apartment after I got off work today. It was nice out, and I thought it would be good to get some fresh air. My mom usually watches him, but she's up in Miami now visiting a sick friend before the storm hits. Anyway, Miguel was climbing the play set when I called hello to a friend from the complex, and his foot slipped and he fell."

She closed her eyes. "It's my fault. If I'd just waited until he was done before calling out..." Stacy sighed and shook her head. "I know it's not serious, but when I saw him lying on the ground, screaming and crying, holding his arm, it felt like my own heart was ripped out of my chest."

"Dr. Durand," the resident handling Miguel's case said as he sidled past Luis. "You want to handle this one?"

He did, very much. But that would be a conflict of interest, so he couldn't. He fisted his hands at his sides, feeling none too steady himself at the moment. "No. You go ahead."

"Okay." The resident smiled down at little Miguel

as he took a seat on his stool and wheeled into position near the side of the bed. "All right, buddy, I'm going to examine your arm now. It might be uncomfortable, but I promise it will be over quickly. Okay?"

Miguel gave a tiny nod, his little chin quivering. Luis wanted to rush over and gather the child in his arms, but that was impossible under the circumstances, so he stayed put, stomach churning and throat tight.

"He's very brave." Luis bent closer to whisper to Stacy, inhaling her sweet, floral scent and finding it calmed his nerves a bit. "Poor guy."

For a moment, she just stared at her son. Then, finally, she glanced up at him. "He's the best little boy in the world."

Luis believed her. Then Miguel whimpered slightly as the resident pressed a sore spot, and Luis's chest imploded. Pulse thudding, he turned away to check the boy's chart, needing something to occupy himself so he didn't act foolish and do something crazy like tell the boy who he was right then and there. He needed to speak with Stacy again, discuss how and when they'd let Miguel know about him. He wanted to be a part of this.

Needed to be a part of this.

A nurse stuck her head in to say, "Radiology is ready for him upstairs, Doc."

"Thanks," the resident said over his shoulder. "Okay, folks. We need to take him up to the third floor for some scans so we can set this bone properly. They're usually running a little behind, so it could take up to an hour." He reached down and ruffled Miguel's hair, and Luis felt a stab of jealousy.

"I'll stay with him the whole time," the nurse promised.

Stacy started to object, but Luis took her arm. Given their crazy schedules and the coming storm, this could be the last chance they had to discuss their son. "Let them handle it. We need to talk."

She looked like she wanted to argue with him, but then she exhaled slowly and glanced at the nurse. "Fine." Then she walked over to kiss the top of Miguel's head. "This nice lady is going to go upstairs with you okay, honey? Mommy will be waiting right here for you when you're done."

Miguel nodded, retuning his attention to what the nurse was doing beside him, seemingly fascinated by the details of her prepping the tray for the doctor to put on his cast.

The techs arrived a few minutes later, and they stepped out of the room. While they maneuvered Miguel's bed from the trauma bay, Luis whispered, "This wasn't how I expected to meet my son for the first time."

"No." Stacy tucked her hair behind her ear, then crossed her arms. "I still haven't said anything to him yet. Not until we know what we're going to do going forward."

"He's going to find out about me sooner or later." Luis frowned. "He has a right to know. I have a right to get to know my son. I don't want to fight over this, but…"

"I know." She held up a hand to forestall him. "I know. I just… It's hard for me."

"And you think it's not for me?" He did his best to keep the rising tension curdling inside him from his voice. Took a deep breath and started again. The last thing he wanted right now was to get into a fight with

Stacy. They were both under a lot of pressure, and that could make you say or do things you'd regret later. Luis had enough regret for a lifetime already. They needed time to cool off and space to think clearly. "Look, this is important, and we need to plan out what we're going to say. Together. He'll be gone for a while for his scans. Perhaps we can grab a coffee in the cafeteria while they do that?"

Stacy hesitated then nodded, her stiff shoulders slumping. "Fine. Yes. Let me stay with him until they go upstairs. I don't want Miguel to be alone right now."

"Agreed." The boy had seemed okay earlier, but that could change fast depending on his condition and how he handled the discomfort of the casting process. Luis's chest constricted as they stepped out of the waiting room and back into the trauma bay. Miguel's eyes were red and Luis felt an unexpected urge to hug the boy and protect him, tell him everything would be all right. Those emotions were quickly followed by a bone-deep fear that his son could've been hurt even worse and how in the world would Luis ever keep him safe? Working in the ER, he'd dealt with his fair share of worried, distraught parents, but he'd never truly understood what they were going through until now. The feeling of helplessness, the overwhelming desire to do whatever was in his power to protect his son no matter what. He'd known the boy was his for barely forty-eight hours, and already the bond he felt to his son was strong.

Finally, the techs got the bed out into the hall and headed toward the elevators. Stacy was at Miguel's side, holding his right hand and whispering things to him to make him smile. His heart pinched with joy when Miguel smiled at him and held out his bear to Luis.

"His name is Dozer," the boy said, his expression serious. "They said I can't take him to the scans, so I want you to look after him until I get back. Don't let anything happen to him, Dr. Durand."

"Never," Luis vowed, taking the bear and grinning. The boy's hair was dark and curly, like his own. "And since we're friends, why don't you call me Luis?"

"Friends?" Miguel asked, brown eyes wide. "Are we?"

"I'm guarding Dozer. If that's not a friend, I don't know what is. Right, Mom?"

Stacy watched him closely for a second, then stepped back to allow one of the techs to get past her to steer their son's bed onto the elevator. "Right. Are you sure you don't want me to go with you, honey?"

"No. I'm a big boy now." Miguel shook his head and pointed at the tech. "And she said she'll give me a treat when I'm done."

The tech grinned. "Sure thing."

They rolled Miguel away and Luis waited until the elevator doors closed and he and Stacy were alone again. He tucked Dozer safely in the pocket of his lab coat, then said, "Let's grab that coffee."

CHAPTER FIVE

"I WANT TO tell Miguel," Luis said, once they were sitting across a small table from one another in the cafeteria's glass atrium. "Today, before you leave the hospital."

"I thought we were going to talk about this first. Decide how it should be done." She was still trying to get her thoughts in order about him reappearing in their lives, let alone becoming a father to Miguel. Her mouth dried and her heart thudded hard against her rib cage. "I don't want to overwhelm him…"

"I know." Luis shook his head. "And I won't. I just want to get to know him a little, tell him who I am. With the storm coming and everything else going on, I believe we need to do this now. I want to tell my parents, too."

Stacy held up a hand and exhaled slowly. "Wait a second. This is all moving very fast."

"Yes. And I'm sorry for that, but that's the situation we're in, Stacy, so we need to go with it. If anything happens to any of us during the storm…" He shook his head and stared down at the table. "Well, I don't want to take that chance and leave things unsaid."

The hint of sadness in his voice intrigued her far

more than was wise. They still had so much to learn about each other, about their pasts. His pained expression told her now was not a good time to ask, though. Besides, she was too antsy, checking her watch frequently to make sure she didn't miss her son returning to his room in the ER. This was the first time she wasn't there by his bedside, and it felt wrong. She shook that off and concentrated on the conversation at hand, needing reassurance. "What are you going to say to him? His autism makes things a bit different. Maybe I can help you choose your words. Or I could be there when you tell him."

"I don't know." Luis toyed with his barely touched paper coffee cup. "But I think we should decide ahead of time. And when I do tell him, you should stay close, in case I get in trouble."

Oh, she'd stay close all right. Stacy watched him a moment then sat back, doing her best to quell the rising tide of dread inside her and failing. Luis was a good man. She knew that from what she'd seen of him and from what she remembered of their long-ago night together. He was hardworking, decent, kind, fair and true. But he was also an unknown factor here, and Stacy very much needed all her ducks in a row. "Look, Luis. Tell me honestly. Are you going to tell Miguel you're his father then disappear on him? Because if that's your plan, I'll need to do some damage control with Miguel. I don't want him getting attached only to be devastated later."

Luis looked at her, his dark eyes so similar to her son's it made her heart hurt. God, he was handsome, even after hours on a shift that had left him a bit rough and ruffled. He seemed so raw and vulnerable now that it made her feel like she'd kicked a puppy or something. But she'd lived through the pain of loving a dad so much only to have him walk away and never return, the pain of growing up without a father. She'd do anything in the world to keep her son from experiencing that. She'd taken a risk telling Luis about Miguel, and yes, he had a right to know. But if he betrayed the trust she'd put in him now, then…

Breath held, she waited for his response.

Finally, he said, "No. I'm not going anywhere. My traveling days are done. My plan is to begin a relationship with Miguel that will last a lifetime. But I need you to be patient with me. I've never done this and have no clue how to go about it. For a guy who is a stickler for rules and details, this is scary and maddening for me, but I'm doing the best I can here. You said Miguel knows nothing about me?"

The pressure in her chest easing a bit, Stacy took a deep breath then nodded. "No, not really. I mean, he's asked some questions. But more in a general sense than anything else. He noticed all his friends had dads around from time to time, even the ones with divorced parents. He wanted to know where his daddy was. I said you were helping people around the world, in far-off countries. So, not a total lie." She gave a small smile. "Anyway, one lesson you need to learn is to tell kids only what they want to know. Miguel never asked who you were, just where. That was a few months ago. Then I saw you in the ER that day, and now here we are."

"Hmm." He sipped his coffee then winced. "I wish you'd found me earlier."

"I tried, like I said. But working in Miami made

it harder to make it down to Key West all that often. When I took the job here last year, I started asking around again, but things were busy at the department and with my mom moving down here with us, I was getting her stuff transferred and settled, too, and I just expected I'd have more time to work it all out."

"Is that all?"

"Yes." Defensiveness prickled up her skin, hot and uncomfortable. "I never intended to keep Miguel from you. Honest. You were gone when I first asked and things got so busy, and maybe I didn't want to face it at first, with what I'd been through in my past. And the longer it went on, the angrier I figured you'd be and the more confused Miguel would get and—" She threw her hands up in exasperation. "Things were complicated enough as it was. And if I told you and you didn't accept it, didn't want to acknowledge him as yours then—"

"Not acknowledge him?" Luis repeated, clearly confused.

Her spine stiffened, and she sat up straighter in her seat. "We had a one-night stand, Luis. It was hardly a committed relationship. And I didn't want you to think I was trapping you, that I wanted anything from you. It wouldn't have been completely out of left field for you to say you didn't want him or say he wasn't yours. Happens way more often than you think."

"No." Luis took her wrist, his hold gentle but firm. Tingles of awareness spread like wildfire through her system from his touch despite her wishes. He sat forward, closing the distance between them, close enough that she could see the hint of dark stubble just below the surface of his firm jaw, could feel the warmth of his breath on her skin, could smell his scent—soap and sandalwood. "It might have been just one night, but it meant something to me. I keep remembering that night between us…" His voice trailed off, and he shook his head at her inquiring look.

He thinks about me? About that night?

Lord knew she'd thought about that night, too, over the past five years, his tender touch, his heated words, his kisses and moans and the way he'd felt against her, within her…

No. This wasn't about that. This was about Miguel. Period. Amen.

She shifted slightly in her seat and crossed her legs away from him. "Go on."

"I believed you from the moment you told me about our son. And now that I've seen him, there's no denying he's mine. None. Miguel is my son." His hold on her wrist loosened, and he sat back a little. "Stacy, there are many things we still have to work out between us, about the past, but that doesn't have anything to do with what I need to work out with Miguel. If we can keep the two things in separate corners for now, it will make things much easier. I don't want to hurt Miguel because of things between us. That wouldn't be fair."

She swallowed hard against the unwanted lump of need in her throat and resisted the urge to rub her wrist. The old attraction to him still simmered inside her, even after all these years, but she forced it onto the back burner. "No," she said after a few tense seconds. "I suppose it wouldn't."

"So, I'll talk to him after he gets back from radiology." Luis looked up at her, his dark gaze unreadable. "Is that all right? Or should we do it together?"

Stacy gave a small nod. "I think that would be best."

Luis seemed to consider that a moment then shrugged. "Okay. Maybe you can tell him you were surprised to see me, which is true. Then I'll tell him that from now on, I'll always be around and he'll always know where I am. Sound good?"

"I guess." Her words sounded uncertain to her own ears, but she couldn't help it.

"Hey." He reached across the table again, this time taking her hand in his. His fingers felt strong and sturdy intertwined with hers. It felt right, which only made her nerves flare higher. He rubbed small circles on her palm with his thumb, his tone soft and soothing. "I know this is hard, but we can do this."

Her gaze met his and she wanted to believe him—boy, did she want to. "Okay."

"Okay." His phone vibrated in his pocket and he pulled it out with his free hand to frown down at the screen. "Looks like Miguel's done in radiology. We should get back up to the ER."

Luis stood in the doorway of the trauma bay while the resident finished up with Miguel's cast. The nurse who was assisting stood nearby with a tray of tools, chatting with the boy about what they were all for. Miguel seemed completely engrossed with it all. That was the Asperger's. Luis had had the same focus on details growing up. Still did.

Miguel looked a bit perkier now that they'd given him some meds for the pain and his arm was set. Still, in his shorts and brightly colored striped T-shirt, he looked very small in the large hospital bed. His dark hair was hopelessly rumpled and his cheeks were flushed, but he wasn't crying anymore, which was good.

The resident finished and stood, wheeling his stool back into the corner, and the nurse cleared out with the tray of instruments, leaving just Luis and Miguel and Stacy in the room. He took out the boy's teddy bear and handed him back safely to his owner.

"Safe and sound," Luis said, smiling.

"Thanks, Dr. Durand," Miguel said, hugging the beloved toy close. "I missed Dozer."

"He's a very good bear." Luis stood beside the bed.

"He helps me sleep."

"I bet he does." Luis couldn't hold back a grin even though his heart was lodged in his throat. "Do you mind if I sit down for a while?" he asked, pulling over the hard plastic chair near the wall and catching Stacy's eye. She gave him a tiny nod. It was time. "I'd like to ask you a couple questions, if that's okay."

Miguel blinked at him, dark eyes huge and serious in his small face. "Okay."

Blood racing, Luis took a deep breath. He'd had difficult conversations with patients' families that were easier than this. It felt like his entire future hung in the balance. He needed to get this right. "Um, I wanted to talk to you about your daddy."

The little boy scowled at Dozer, straightening the bear's bow tie. "My daddy is across the world."

"Is that what Mommy said?"

"Yes." Miguel nodded, his brows knit as he glanced up at Stacy. "He helps people. He's a good daddy."

Luis's chest constricted. "What if I told you your daddy was here, now?"

The boy shrugged in response.

"Miguel." All the oxygen seemed to evaporate from the room, and time slowed. "I'm your daddy."

His son looked over at him then up at Stacy, not appearing incredibly impressed, and Luis's gut sank. "Where are your people?"

"The people I help?" Luis asked, connecting the dots of their odd talk. "Here, in this hospital. I help the people here in Key West now instead of traveling the world. I run this ER."

"Oh." That seemed to resonate a bit more with Miguel. "Can you get me another sucker?"

Stacy chuckled then bit her lip at his look. "Sorry."

Luis hid a smile of his own. "I'll see about having one sent over from the gift shop. What's your favorite flavor?"

"Raspberry."

"Mine, too," Luis said. "I'll tell the nurses as soon as we're done."

Miguel nodded then went back to fiddling with his bear. His purple and white cast stood out sharply against his tanned skin. "Do you want to sign this?"

It took Luis a second to realize he was talking about the cast. "Of course. Does it hurt?"

"Not really. Feels weird, though." The little boy frowned again then met Luis's gaze. "Do you have a dog?"

"No." Luis didn't have time for pets. He barely spent any time at all at his house. Which was a shame, since he'd had it built specifically to his designs the year prior, and it was lovely. Lots of glass and steel and lush landscaping. Even a pool. He imagined his son there now and suddenly couldn't wait to invite him and Stacy over. "I don't have a dog. Do you?"

"Not yet. Mommy's working to get me one, though, from her friend Lucy. She's a trainer."

"Nice. You must be excited."

"I am," Miguel said, his tone flat. "Do you have a grandma?"

Luis's gut tumbled a bit at that reminder of his past. He'd taken that fateful boat ride with his birth parents at six, but he could still vaguely remember his Cuban grandparents. Both sets of parents of his adopted parents had passed away before Luis had become part of their family. He swallowed hard. Now wasn't the time to get into all that yet, so instead he said, "I used to. When I was your age, I had a grandma and a grandpa. *Abuela y abuelo.*"

He braced himself for more hard questions, but they never came.

Instead, Miguel switched subjects entirely. "Did you know there is a hurricane on the way?"

"Yes." The knots between Luis's shoulder blades eased. "Hurricane Mathilda. Your uncle, Jackson, is actually running the team to handle the recovery efforts."

"Mommy's on that team, too. A typical hurricane can dump six inches to a foot of rain across a region. The most violent winds and heaviest rains take place in the eye wall, the ring of clouds and thunderstorms closely surrounding the eye. Every second, a large hurricane releases the energy of ten atomic bombs. Hurricanes can also produce tornadoes."

"That's very impressive," Luis said, pride over his son's memory swelling inside him like a balloon. Luis himself had a near-eidetic memory. It was both a blessing and a curse. "Did you know the word 'hurricane' comes from the Taino Native American word *huru-*

cane, meaning evil spirit of the wind? The first time anyone flew into a hurricane happened in 1943 in the middle of World War II. And a tropical storm is classified as a hurricane once winds go up to seventy-four miles per hour or higher."

Miguel narrowed his gaze on his father. "Is that true?"

"Of course. I would never lie to you, *mijito*." That last word sent a warm rush through Luis he'd never experienced before. *My son.* They continued chatting for a while about storms and bears and even the Florida Keys. Luis lost track of time as the last of his tension drained away. It had gone well. He was still glad to know Stacy was right there and thought he was getting along pretty well for a man new to all this.

Then Miguel yawned and asked Luis to read him a story. They kept some children's books at the nurses' station, so Stacy went out and got one, letting the staff know that the room would be occupied a little longer. Thankfully, they weren't that busy at the moment, so it wasn't a problem.

Stacy returned and closed the door behind her then handed the book to Luis. He started to settle back in his chair, but Miguel insisted he sit beside him on the bed because that's how his mommy always did it.

Right. Luis wrestled with the bedrails and got them lowered, then stretched out beside his son's smaller form while Stacy took a seat in his vacated chair. The boy snuggled into his side, warm and wonderful, and rested his head on Luis's chest, his bear tucked beneath his cast. If Luis died right then and there, he'd be a happy man.

The longer he read about dogs in race cars and mermaids on buses, the more Luis realized he was tired. Exhausted, really. He hadn't slept well since reconnecting with Stacy, filled with stress and recriminations and what-ifs. Miguel fell asleep halfway through the second book, and Luis wasn't far behind.

"Luis," a voice said, followed by a shake of his shoulder.

He awoke slowly and it took a second for him to remember where he was. The hospital. Miguel's room. His son's room. Luis yawned and stared up at Stacy. So lovely. He smiled. Looked down at Miguel's dark head still snuggled on his chest then bent and kissed it. "How long was I asleep?"

His voice sounded groggy to his own ears.

"About half an hour," she said, helping him extricate himself from the bed without waking Miguel. "They need us to clear out so they can use the room for incoming cases."

"Oh, right." He yawned and stretched, then straightened his lab coat while she stacked the books he'd read and set them on the counter. At least things between them didn't seem quite so strained anymore, which was good.

Luis straightened his hair and clothes in the mirror over the sink in the room.

Stacy caught his gaze in the reflection. "I should wake Miguel so we can go."

Before he could stop himself, Luis turned to face her. "Have dinner with me. Just the two of us. There's still so much we need to talk about, and I'd like us to be friends." At her cautious look, he added, "For Miguel."

Stacy looked from him to their son, then back again. "I don't know. I'm super busy with the response team

and then we've got a new recruit class getting ready
to graduate at the fire station, and I teach a couple of
classes on Monday and Thursday for the corps and I've
got my captain's paperwork to catch up on in the after-
noons. And that doesn't include my regular shifts with
the fire crew. And I'll need to check with my neighbor since my mom's in Miami right now, and I'm just
so busy and I—"

"Please. Come on. You have to eat, right? And we
need to plan some things."

She winced and shook her head. "I don't know. I'm
not sure that's such a good idea after what happened
between us."

He frowned. "What? When?" Then it dawned on
him. "You can't mean that night on the beach. I'm not
going to seduce you again. It's just dinner."

Of course, now that he'd brought it up, seducing her
seemed to be the only thing he could think about, but
no. That was wrong. They had a son now, important
matters to talk about. He needed to concentrate on that,
no matter what his body might want.

Stacy was quiet a moment, staring down at her toes.
Then she met his gaze, her blue eyes large and soft,
full of conflicting emotions—anger, anticipation, anxiety, wary hope. "Look, Luis. I really need you to hear
what I'm about to say. You've been back in my life less
than a week, and you've known about Miguel for even
less than that. I'm glad you two have connected, but
our situation doesn't change just because we made a
child together."

"Miguel deserves a mother and a father," he said,
keeping his voice low so as not to wake the boy.

"And he has them," she answered. "No matter what

happens with us, we are his parents. But let's not rush ahead and make mistakes we might both regret later."

Frustrated, he raked a hand through his hair, disheveling it again, but he couldn't care less at the moment. "So, what the hell are we supposed to do, then? I thought planning out custody and finances and all that was what I should be doing."

"It is, but..." Stacy shook her head and pulled him into the corner farthest from the bed. "You still don't get it, do you? I don't want you in Miguel's life because you're doing what you think you should. I want you in his life because you love him and want to be there. He's your son, I won't get in the way of that, but I want you to consider what I've said carefully."

"Consider it? Hell, it's all I've thought about since that night at the pub." Luis stood there a second, staring at her, until finally he said, "Look, I'm not going anywhere. I don't know what I need to do to convince you of that, Stacy, but whatever it is, I'm determined to try. I know your father hurt you deeply when he left, but please don't punish me for his mistakes. Please. I'd like to come over tomorrow after you get off work and spend some time with Miguel, if that's acceptable. Will you trust me enough to do that?"

Without thinking Luis reached over and put his hand on the back of her neck, running his thumb from her earlobe to the base of her throat, remembering she'd liked that before and hoping it soothed away some of the tension from her beautiful face. Then he leaned in and kissed her. Light, sweet, fast.

They both blinked. She looked as stunned as he felt.

Heat prickled his cheeks and he let her go. "I... uh... I..."

"Mommy?" a small voice said from the bed. "What are you doing?"

Stacy blushed and looked past him to their son. "Daddy and I were just talking. Are you ready to go home?"

While she went over to collect him, Luis leaned a hand against the wall, scrubbing the other over his face. *What the hell am I doing?* Kissing Stacy was not going to help the situation, but that seemed like all he wanted to do at the moment. He was a man ruled by science, facts, details, service to others.

But at the moment, the emotions roiling inside him felt every bit as dangerous and disturbing as the hurricane headed their direction.

CHAPTER SIX

THE NEXT DAY, the only thing that surprised Luis more than how easy it had been to fall into a routine with Miguel was how readily the boy had seemed to take to him. It shocked him to realize how much he looked forward to spending time with his son.

In fact, as soon as his shift was over, he headed for Stacy's apartment, as promised. According to his watch, she should have just arrived home after her shift as well. She answered the door wearing a loose, comfy-looking sweat suit, her hair still damp from the shower.

"Hey," he said. "Looks like I'm right on time. Okay if I come in?"

She stepped aside to let him in. "Yes."

"Tough day?"

"I expected it to be slower at the station, but nope." She closed the door then brushed past him, the sweet scent of her shampoo surrounding him as she passed. "One run after another all day long. I'm exhausted, honestly."

"Then rest. Why don't you take a nap?" He smiled. "I can take Miguel to the park and with me while I run some errands while you sleep. Would that be acceptable?"

"Oh. I…" She frowned then yawned, dark circles

marring the delicate skin beneath her eyes. "I don't know. You've not been alone with him yet. Not for any length of time, and he can be a handful and—"

"Please?" Luis stepped closer and took her hand. "I'm an ER doc. I deal with difficult patients every day. I think I can handle one four-year-old boy. I promise I'll take good care of him, and I'll call you if any issues arise." He placed his other hand over his heart as a sign of sincerity. "Please trust me?"

She seemed to consider that a second then glanced at the clock. "Two hours. That's it. Then I want you both back here. And don't let him talk you into buying him a bunch of junk food. I'm making dinner. Mom's still in Miami, so it's just us."

"Sounds good. And thank you. I'll take good care of our son, I swear." He grinned, more relieved than he could say. "Now, where's Miguel?"

"Daddy!" The boy called from down the hall then came running out to throw his arm around Luis's legs. The move made it a tad awkward to keep his balance, but he wouldn't change it for the world.

Stacy and Luis both looked at each other, shocked. Twenty-four hours after they'd just met for the first time and now he was Daddy. A small frisson of pleasure jolted through Luis from that title, and from Stacy's expression he saw some chasm between them had been crossed. Now there was no going back. Everyone had their assigned roles, and you didn't shirk a responsibility like that.

It was both the most complicated and simplest transition Luis had ever experienced. But the problem remained that he and Stacy still had not negotiated their relationship. They were still dancing around it and hadn't even mentioned their brief kiss in the trauma bay. Essentially, they were still two strangers, navigating these murky waters. And now there was one more person to consider. And that person was currently squeezing his leg like his life depended on it. Luis reached down and ruffled Miguel's hair like he'd wanted to do the day before, loving the silky feel of the kid's hair on his fingers.

"Hey, *mijito*. How are you?" he said, grinning down at the boy. "Want to go to the park with me?"

"Yes, please," Miguel said, stepping back to gaze up at him. "I'm ready."

"You need shoes first, mister," Stacy said, shooing him back toward his bedroom. "And socks."

Miguel grumbled but did as he was told.

Alone again, Luis turned back to Stacy. "Need anything at the store while we're out? Any advice?"

"No, nothing from the store. And advicewise, use his car seat even though he complains, wear seat belts, make frequent bathroom stops, never let him out of your sight. And come home safe. Both of you."

"Got it." He grinned.

"Good. And don't forget to call me with any problems. I'm a light sleeper, especially when I nap."

"Will do." He nodded, his expression serious now, thinking about all the things they had to discuss. If they'd had more time, or better weather on the horizon, it would've been easier to spread this stuff out. But with the storm strengthening each day and changing trajectory by the hour, everything seemed up in the air. And once an emergency declaration was made for the Keys, all their attention would need to be focused on the rescue and recovery efforts, and who knew where they'd stand after that, if they'd even be standing at all.

His phone buzzed in his pocket, and he pulled it out to check the screen.

"Anything important?" Stacy asked.

"No. Just a calendar reminder for the team meeting day after next."

"Right."

Miguel ran back down the hall, shoes and socks in place and Dozer tucked under his arm. "Ready!"

"Okay." Luis took his son's hand then walked to the door, speaking to Stacy over his shoulder. "Get some rest, Mommy. We'll see you later."

"See you," Stacy said, waving to them then walking down the hall to her own bedroom and shutting the door.

"All right, *mijito*," Luis said to his son. "How about we hit the park first then do some errands?"

"Okay, Daddy," Miguel said, tugging on his hand. "Ready."

Luis let them out of the apartment and locked the door behind them. He hadn't lied to Stacy about his experience dealing with difficult patients, but honestly, they were mostly of the adult variety. And while he was sure those skills would translate to the younger generation, the fact was he'd never spent much time alone with kids as an adult. When he'd been on his mission trips, it was always busy and hectic and there wasn't much time for socializing outside work. And most of his free time now was taken up with hospital functions and working at the pub, so not many kids there, either. On the few occasions where he'd been with friends who had children, he'd fit in fine, tossing a ball around or making faces and playing dolls or whatever. But this was the first time he was solely responsible for a child's well-being—and that child belonged to him.

While they were at the park, Luis learned something he'd never encountered before. Apparently, a man with a child held some extreme fascination and attraction to women. He never really paid much attention to his looks, though his brother, Jackson, was always teasing him about being a "chick magnet." Now, though, strange women came up to him at the park, remarking on how cute Miguel was and making small talk. They kept asking him if he was having a father-son day or if he lived in the area and if they could set up a play-date for their kids sometime.

He refused them all, saying the first thing that came to mind, feeling extremely uncomfortable under the added scrutiny. "Thanks, but I have to get going. My wife is waiting."

Miguel tugged on his hand and asked, "Who's your wife, Daddy?"

The pregnant woman he was talking to gave Luis a look and he chuckled awkwardly, hurrying them out of there fast. On the way back to his car he said to Miguel, "We need to get our story straight, *mijito.*"

They got in the car and started into town. Luis was feeling better about things until Miguel said out of nowhere, "Daddy? How do babies get in a mommy's tummy?"

Oh, Lord.

Guessing this had been brought on by the last conversation at the park, he slowed for a red light then turned to his son, hoping to change the subject. "How about if we stop and get some ice cream for dessert to-night after dinner?"

"Yes!" Miguel squealed. "Ice cream."

"What kind should we get?" he asked, glad for the reprieve. "Chocolate or vanilla?"

"Chocolate!"

Later that night, after dinner and chocolate ice cream, Miguel played in his room while Luis and Stacy did the dishes together in the kitchen.

"How'd it go today?" she asked, reaching up to put a plate on an upper shelf, the motion revealing a tempt-ing swath of creamy skin at her lower back. Luis swal-lowed hard and looked away fast.

"Uh… Good. We went to the park then into town for a while." He laughed. "It was weird, because all these women kept coming up to me to chat. They even asked me for my phone number."

She stopped midway through putting away another plate and looked back at him over her shoulder. "Are you serious? They were propositioning you right there with my son standing by?"

"What?" Luis's face flamed hot, the flames licking down his neck to the open vee of his dress shirt. "No. They weren't propositioning me. They wanted to set up playdates."

"Uh-huh." Stacy lowered from tiptoe to flat foot, smirking. "I'm sure they wanted to play, all right."

He frowned, flustered. It hadn't been like that, had it? It didn't mean anything. He wasn't looking for that. Not with Miguel in his life now. And Stacy. If he wanted to become intimate with anyone again, it was her. Except he shouldn't be thinking like that. They'd had a nice dinner. Later, they'd have a nice chat. That was all tonight was about.

Isn't it?

The sound of blocks tumbling down echoed from the hall, followed by Miguel singing an off-key tune from one of his favorite children's shows on TV. Stacy tossed her towel aside. "I should check on him. Be right back."

After she returned, Luis told her about Miguel's question in the car. Stacy laughed so hard she had to lean against the counter as she doubled over.

"It wasn't funny," he said, perplexed. "What should I have said?"

"I have a special book all about that for him," Stacy said, wiping her eyes with her towel. "I guess it's about time we start reading that together. I'd put it off, thinking he wasn't ready yet, but apparently I was wrong."

He scrunched his nose. "They have books for kids his age about *that*?"

"No. Not about *that*, per se." She smiled at him. "It talks about the differences between mommy and daddy bodies. It's all very sweet and nonthreatening." She nudged him with her shoulder. "If you're good, maybe I'll read it to you later, too."

Relaxing a bit, he flirted right along with her. "Yeah? Well, maybe if you're very good, I'll give you a live demonstration."

Pretty pink flushed her cheeks, and she turned away to put away the rest of the dishes. "I remember how it goes, thanks so much."

So do I.

He bit back those words and took a deep breath, instead asking something that had been on his mind for a while now. "How did it happen in our case?" He waved a hand between them. "I mean, I know the mechanics of it, and we'd both had a lot to drink, which is probably why I didn't use a condom that night. That part's all a bit fuzzy, to tell you the truth."

She took a deep breath. "It's kind of fuzzy for me, too. But I do remember I'd messed up my pills a week or so before that night, so that didn't help, I'm sure. Things happen."

Silence descended for a short time. Then Luis couldn't resist and leaned forward to kiss her forehead. "Well, I'm not sorry about it. Miguel is awesome. Big accident, huge reward."

Stacy smiled then gave him a quick hug. Apparently, he'd managed to say the right thing for once since this whole thing started, and relief warmed him. "You've had a good time with Miguel, haven't you?"

"He's amazing. Seriously." He squeezed her back then stepped away. "But once we get him to bed, I do think we really need to talk about all this."

"You're right." Her expression shifted from joy to resignation. "I'll go get him changed into his pj's. He's probably finished building his skyscraper anyway."

Once Miguel was tucked in for the night and the lights were out, the apartment was still. Luis and Stacy sat on the sofa in her living room, two glasses of wine on the coffee table before them. They chatted quietly about their pasts, their families, their hopes and dreams and fears. All the things most people knew about each other before they hopped into bed together. For them, it was a revelation.

"That must have been terrible," she said, her voice

rough with unshed tears as she pictured a little Luis alone in a strange, new country, orphaned, left to fend for himself. It helped her understand him so much better. Why he worked so hard, why he went to such great lengths to help others, why he was so driven.

"They sacrificed everything to give me a better life," he said, staring down at his hands in his lap. "The least I can do is live my life in a way that makes them proud."

She couldn't resist reaching over and placing her hand over his. "I'm sure they're proud of you, Luis. Look at everything you've accomplished. They must be looking down on you from heaven and beaming with joy."

"I hope so." He took a deep breath then looked up at her. "What about you? What about your family? What happened to your father?"

Stacy flinched slightly then sat back, pulling her hand away from his. Luis frowned, but didn't reach for her. She picked up her wineglass then tucked her legs beneath her. "He left us when I was eight. Just packed up his stuff and walked out the door without so much as a goodbye. I haven't seen him since."

"I'm sorry."

"Why?" She snorted. "Wasn't your fault."

"No. But that must have hurt you very much."

"It's fine." She tried to shrug it off, as she always did. But with Luis watching her so closely, those deep, dark eyes of his filled with caring and concern, she felt an unexpected, nearly overwhelming need to let down her walls, to let him in, show him the wound inside her from her father's abandonment that hadn't healed, might never heal. Even all these years later, it felt like a great, gaping hole in her soul. But putting that into words, laying herself bare like that, terrified her. "I've had a good life despite it."

This time, Luis reached for her, twining his fingers with hers, so strong, so warm, so tempting. "You've worked very hard. You're very brave."

Stacy blinked hard, sipping her wine to swallow the lump of emotion in her throat. She had worked hard. Harder than most folks knew. "After he left, Mom and I had to move into government housing in Miami because we couldn't afford the house anymore. She worked three jobs just to make ends meet. As soon as I was old enough, I went to work, too. Saved enough money to put myself through college, determined to prove that I didn't need a father to be successful. To prove I was good enough." She squeezed her eyes shut, concentrating on his silent, supportive presence beside her. "Prove I was worthy."

Luis scooted a bit closer, bringing her hand to his lips to kiss the back of it. "*Mi sirenita*, you have nothing to prove. You are good enough. You are worthy."

My mermaid?

The nickname he'd given her fit, she had to admit, given how they'd found each other on a moonlit beach that long-ago night. The sweetness of it fractured the barriers around her heart a little more and made her smile. She leaned forward to set her wineglass on the table, untucking her leg from beneath her. "Well, that's nice of you to say. Harder to believe, though. I always feel like I'm fighting battles. At work, in the world in general, just to be taken seriously. Just to be treated as an equal."

Luis sighed, keeping hold of her hand, rubbing his

thumb softly, soothingly over her knuckles. "I've never experienced what you're going through, so I can't say I truly understand, but please know I'm there to support you and Miguel any way I can. In fact, I plan to set up a special bank account tomorrow for Miguel with you as the trustee, to cover educational expenses for him, plus anything else that he might need as he grows. I want you to use the funds as well, as you need, to be comfortable."

Stacy listened quietly, mind swirling with this new information. She'd known he ran the emergency medicine department at Key West General and expected him to be wealthy because of it, but his generosity was beyond her imaginings. After their long-ago night together, she'd sometimes imagined what he'd be like in everyday life. Back then, she'd pictured him as some kind of millionaire playboy superhero, roaming the world saving puppies and old people. But the reality of Luis Durand was so much better than anything she'd ever expected. Kind, loyal, smart, strong, sexy as hell.

She swallowed hard. Nope. Not going there. No matter how easy it would be at this moment. She didn't want to go back there again with him, because having Miguel changed everything. Made it more real, more important, more meaningful. And she didn't want to need Luis like that.

Do I?

She hung her head and pulled away from him, wary and uncertain. Old habits died hard. "I don't know about all this. I've built a good life here. We have this apartment and Miguel is settled. I like my job at the fire department. It's hard work, but it keeps me in shape and sharp. And my mother visits frequently, too, and watches Miguel for me while I'm at work. Changing all that now…"

"I know," he said softly.

"For as long as I can remember, it's always been just Mom and me. And now Miguel. She's my best friend. And she and Miguel are very close, too."

"I know that, too. When Miguel asked me about my grandparents…" He gave a sad little laugh, and she sat back, moving closer to him so their shoulders touched, needing his support and wanting to return it to him as well. "I'm not trying to rush anything. I just wanted to help take the pressure off you. I know it's only been a few days, but I thought things were going well so far."

Tears stung her eyes, and she looked over at him. "They have been going well. Very well."

Their gazes locked, and slowly, they leaned toward each other. Stacy held her breath, her eyes flickering down to his firm, full lips, remembering how they'd felt against hers, how he'd tasted that night on the beach— booze and pure, sinful decadence. Luis stopped a millimeter away, his breath fast like hers, giving her a choice, waiting for her consent.

In the end, there was no choice for Stacy. Want clawed inside her, demanding this kiss, this moment, this night with him. She desired him more than she'd thought possible, and tonight, she'd have him.

Stacy closed the tiny gap between them, kissing him softly at first, then harder as she licked his lips and he gasped. All at once, he took charge, one hand at the back of her head and the other at her waist, pulling her across his lap and holding her against him. When he pulled away at last, they were both breathless.

"Is this what they mean by coparenting?" he asked,

his forehead resting against hers before he trailed his lips up her neck to her ear.

She giggled, sinking her fingers into his thick, dark hair. "Pretty sure that's a no. But we're a bit more than coparents anyway."

He pulled back slightly to flash a sly smile. "Are we? *Si.* I think we are, *mi sirenita.*"

They kissed and touched and cuddled on the sofa until their clothes got in the way, then by mutual consent they moved to her bedroom at the end of the hall, careful not to make any noise to wake Miguel.

Luis was the same considerate, caring, expert lover she remembered from their night together. She'd never been more grateful for his attention to detail than she was now. He started at her ankles and worked his way up, nuzzling and licking then making love to her with his lips and tongue and fingers. When she came apart in his arms, he kissed his way up her body then covered her mouth with his to swallow her cries of pleasure. He pulled a condom from his pants pocket and smoothed it on, then he was inside her once more, filling her, completing her in a way she'd only ever experienced with Luis.

He set up a rhythm, rocking slowly and gently, gradually building to an easy pace that had them both on the edge of ecstasy again all too soon. Stacy tried to hurry him, digging her heels into his buttocks, nails biting into his shoulders, into his hair, arching beneath him. She needed more, deeper, faster.

She whimpered. "Please, Luis. Please…"

Luis chuckled low, whispering Spanish endearments in her ear as his thrusts grew deep and powerful, hitting the right spot within her, and that was all it took.

Stacy's world shattered into a million fireworks of pleasure. He whispered into her ear, *"El mar y el cielo se ven igual de azules y en la distancia parece que se unen,"* then let himself go with a low moan of pleasure.

For a long time after, they just lay there, holding each other as they slowly floated back down to earth. Finally, as he lay partially atop her, his head resting between her breasts and her fingers toying with his hair, she asked, "What did that mean?"

"Hmm," Luis said lazily, raising up to meet her gaze. He looked tired and tousled and totally adorable. Her heat squeezed at the picture they made.

You couldn't live in Miami without picking up some Spanish, but she'd been a bit preoccupied and hadn't caught every word he'd said at that crucial moment. "What did you whisper right before...you know?"

His soft laugh ghosted across her skin, raising goose bumps in its wake. He kissed the side of her breast then smiled against her skin. "It's a line from a song. I remember my mother singing it to me on our way from Cuba. 'The sea and the sky look the same blue, and in the distance, it looks like they join.'"

Stacy blinked up at the ceiling, stunned. Touched more deeply than she wanted to say at the moment, she just lay there, stroking Luis's scalp until he fell asleep. Did he see this as a step toward something more? Did she?

She wasn't sure. She'd meant what she said before about being in a good place in her life. She was glad he and Miguel were getting along so well and wanted them to have a connection in the future, but was she willing to upend everything she'd worked so hard to build to start over again with Luis?

Maybe she was reading too much into it, like she usually did. He'd not mentioned anything about getting together with her, beyond taking care of Miguel. Maybe he didn't want a relationship, just the occasional hookup. Maybe he'd decide to go off to the other side of the planet again and leave them behind.

That last thought scared her most of all, and it took a long while, surrounded by shadows, before Stacy followed Luis into sleep.

CHAPTER SEVEN

STACY HAD THE next day off from the fire department but went in for a few hours that morning anyway to take care of some paperwork, leaving Miguel with Luis at her house. Her mother was still in Miami until the weekend, and Luis didn't have another shift in the ER until that night.

When Stacy walked into her apartment that afternoon, she encountered one of the biggest messes she'd ever seen. Newspapers spread over the island in the kitchen were covered in craft supplies. There were scraps of paper on the floor and glitter literally everywhere. In the center of it all sat a black backpack covered in hand-painted designs and bright sparkling handprints.

"Hey," Luis said, coming out of the bathroom down the hall, drying his hands on a towel. "You're home early. We were just getting Miguel's school supplies ready for September."

"Mommy!" Miguel shouted excitedly, running up to her from down the hall. "Look what Daddy and I made!"

"It was a bit awkward with him only having one hand and I think there's as much glitter on his cast as there is on the backpack, but..." Luis said, ruffling his son's hair with a wink.

"And on the floor," Stacy noted. "Please tell me you're planning on cleaning this up, too?"

"Of course." Luis leaned in and kissed her cheek. "Why don't you change and relax until I get this under control."

"Or I can change then come help. Glitter is notoriously hard to get rid of." She went to her bedroom and returned two seconds later. "There's a duffel bag in my bedroom."

"Uh, yeah," Luis said, looking up at her from where he was stooped over, dustpan in hand, grinning. "I thought I might stay the rest of the week. Until your mother returns."

She stared at him, speechless.

He set his broom and dustpan aside and walked over to her, taking her arms gently, his expression serious. "Look, I'm sorry I didn't ask, but after last night, I thought..." He looked away then shook his head. "I'm sorry. I should have run it by you first, but I thought it might be more convenient for both of us if I'm here. With the storm coming soon and me over here all the time as it is, I can take babysitting shifts when you're at work to fill in for your mother, and I promise I'm neat and won't get in the way. Can I stay?"

Her heart thudded hard against her rib cage and she wanted to say yes, but that small niggle of doubt was still there in the background. "Uh, we've never really done this before." She gestured between them. "Living together."

Luis's dark gaze turned tender, and her knees tingled. "First time for everything."

True. And it wasn't like this was long term or anything. No need to get too flustered about it. It was a couple of days at most. And he was right. It would be easier with them all together through the storm. They had another team meeting tomorrow, and with her mom gone, she did need to arrange care for Miguel when she wasn't home, so...

"Okay," she said at last.

He gave her a quick kiss then returned to his sweeping while she went back to the bedroom to change. By the time she came back out, Luis had the kitchen cleaned and he was starting dinner. Thick pork chops in a marinade. He looked back at her over his shoulder as he worked near the stove. "Better?"

"Yes, thanks. Where's Miguel?"

"In his room, playing with his new backpack."

She walked to his side and hugged him around the waist. "Thanks for that."

"No problem." He put an arm around her and pulled her into his side, whispering in her ear, "Hope you don't mind if we eat a little earlier, since my shift at the hospital starts at eight."

"Fine with me," she said, kissing his neck then stepping away. "What can I do to help?"

It all felt very domestic and normal and safe.

Stacy found herself liking it. A lot. Way more than she should.

They had a nice dinner as a family, then Luis excused himself to get ready for work while Stacy and Miguel did the dishes. Okay, Stacy did the dishes and Miguel mainly played in the bubbles, but still. After they were done, they sat in the living room together, watching a movie.

"Okay. I'm on for twenty-four, so I won't see you again until the meeting tomorrow." Luis stopped by the sofa on his way to the door, kissing her on the cheek and Miguel on the top of the head. "Be good. Both of you. And call me if you need anything."

As she watched her son's cartoons on TV, Stacy ran through everything that had happened in the last few days. It was a lot. Too much, really, to process in such a short time. Miguel seemed to be dealing with it better than her, but his worldview and experiences of life were much simpler. Hers, on the other hand, were complicated with a capital *C*.

Part of her said Luis was great and she was lucky to have him. The other part of her, though, wasn't so sure. Honestly, the truth was, she wasn't good at asking for help or taking it when it was offered. Probably because she'd always been the helper. First with her single mother growing up, and now in her job and as a single mother herself. Her whole life, she'd always experienced that imbalance, more give than take, so her first instinct was always to handle things herself, to figure it out on her own. Self-reliance was her go-to mode.

Giving that up was hard, even when something that could be wonderful was at stake.

Restless, she got up and puttered around the apartment while Miguel finished his show. She took out the trash, looked through her emails, gave Miguel his bath, then put him to bed, reading with him until he fell asleep, his little mouth open like a tiny bird's. Even now, each time Stacy watched her son, she couldn't help thinking *He's mine!* It still filled her with wonder, with awe. Miguel was the miracle she didn't deserve.

About nine o'clock that night, she got a pint of ice cream out of the freezer and took a seat on the sofa again, clicking on the TV without really watching it as she checked her phone for text messages. Surprisingly, there was one from Luis already.

Did you find your surprise?

She chuckled and patted the pint of her favorite flavor of ice cream then texted back.

I did. Thank you. I think this live-in situation is working out just fine for now.

Right? Only took us five years to get here.

Her stomach knotted and she swallowed hard against the sudden constriction in her throat. She didn't believe Luis would run out on her and Miguel, but it had only been a few days. What would happen when things got tough? Miguel would start school next month, and even with him being in a special needs class, it was bound to be tough on him. Then there was the hurricane. If the weather reports were any indication, it was getting stronger, which meant increased chances of widespread flooding and damage. Both she and Luis would be on the front lines of search and rescue and recovery for the people of Key West. Could this, whatever this was between them now, survive the coming storm?

She wasn't so sure. There were still a lot of things

to work out between them. Her phone buzzed again, and a new text popped up from Luis.

Still there? Something I said?

Torn and twisted, Stacy typed back a quick response then shut her phone off and stared at the TV without really paying much attention.

Sorry. Tired. Going to bed. Talk to you tomorrow.

Luis worked through the night, and luckily it was busy, keeping him from dwelling too much on Stacy's odd response to his text. The cases ranged from the usual cuts and broken bones to an allergic reaction to shellfish that had quickly escalated to anaphylaxis with the patient unable to breathe. He'd had to perform an emergency tracheostomy to clear an airway for the man, who was now recovering nicely in an overnight room after they'd pumped him full of Benadryl and epinephrine.

But as dawn drew closer, the new arrivals dwindled and Luis found himself thinking about Stacy and how well the last few days had gone. He wasn't a man prone to wild bouts of emotion—another side effect of his mild Asperger's—but when he did go off the deep end, he fell hard and fast.

He worried now that perhaps he'd become too invested in his relationship with Stacy too fast and scared her off. That was the last thing he'd wanted to do, but man. Miguel had definitely thrown him for a loop. Such a great kid. So much like Luis, but also with Stacy's fierce independent spirit.

Independence. Something he knew was very important to Stacy. And he would never want to infringe on that. He just wanted to be a part of their lives, if she'd let him.

That was a big *if* at this point, though.

Not that Luis could blame her.

In those moments when he could take a step back and look at the situation objectively, he knew things were moving fast. Maybe too fast. But then he also knew how quickly things could spin out of control and be snatched away from you. He never wanted to lose something precious to him again because he'd failed.

It was confusing and confounding and had him completely tied in stressful knots inside.

He took a break and went down to the cafeteria, forced down some tasteless eggs and toast, drank some much-needed coffee, then went upstairs to check on the firefighter, Reed. The guy was still in the hospital but had been moved from the ICU to a regular ward. He took the stairs up to the fifth floor and pushed out into the brightly lit corridor. The halls were bustling with carts of breakfast orders for patients in rooms, and the air smelled of bacon and oatmeal. Luis nodded to a few nurses and doctors he passed along the way then knocked on Reed's door at the end of the hall before entering.

It was a bit before 8:00 a.m., but patients were up early at Key West General, what with their vitals being checked and physicians making rounds before going to their offices for appointments. Luis found Reed sitting up this morning in the chair by his bed, a tray of food on the table before him and a walker in the corner, near where his wife sat reading the paper.

"Good morning," Luis said, raising a hand in greeting. "Just thought I'd stop in again to see how you're doing."

"Morning, Doc," Reed said with a nod. "Doing well, thanks."

He hiked his chin toward the walker. "Looks like they've got you up and moving now?"

"They do." Reed chugged some orange juice then wiped his mouth with a napkin. "Surgeon said he did everything he could for my leg. Now it's up to me to finish what he started. After the accident, I didn't know how bad I was hurt. I mean, I knew it was bad, but not like this." He vaguely gestured to his lower half. "Anyway, at least I didn't lose my leg. The surgeon didn't think I'd walk again, but I'm not giving up until I try."

Luis admired the man's determination and grit. Seemed that was a prerequisite in their department, at least based on what he knew from Stacy. He'd meant what he'd told her before. She was one of the bravest people he'd ever met.

"Well," Luis said, "I'm sure with that attitude, you'll get much farther. Outlook is everything is some cases."

"Agreed." Reed bit off half a piece of bacon and chewed, grinning over at his wife. "People told me no way would I be using a walker yet, so I had to prove them wrong, didn't I, honey?"

His wife nodded from behind her paper, not looking up.

"They tell me I can't do something, that's the best way ever to make damn sure I do." He winked. "Most of us hose haulers are that way."

Luis bit back a laugh. "Excuse me? Hose haulers?"

Reed waved him off. "Nickname the cops had for

us in the last blood drive. Friendly rivalry and all. I won't tell you what we called them." He winked again. "Anyway, like I said, I like being told I can't do something. Always been outgoing, crazy, up for anything, doing anything." With a sigh, his shoulders slumped. "But I'll tell you something. When I woke up after the surgery on my leg, found out the extent of what had happened, saw what I put my wife and my kids and my crew through, I'm done. I won't ever deliberately put them through that again."

"Sounds like a wise choice," Luis said, leaning back against the wall behind him. "Looks like you're recovering well."

"I'm doing good, Doc." Reed nodded. "But my goal isn't just to walk. I want to get back to work again, too. I know I've got a ways to go, but I need that in my life. The job's dangerous, I know that, but I help a lot of people and that's what I enjoy most. Know what I mean?"

"I do." His phone buzzed with a text from the ER requesting him back downstairs. Luis smiled at Reed and his wife. "Need to get back downstairs. I'll try to stop in again before you're released to say goodbye."

"Goodbye?" Reed's wife glanced up at him over the top of her paper. "From what I heard, we might start seeing a lot more of you around the fire department."

Luis froze in place, eyes wide. He and Stacy hadn't told anyone about what was happening with them, since it was so new. They'd not really had a formal arrangement about that, though. Had she said something to her crew when she'd gone into work earlier? "Uh…"

Reed's wife grinned at his obvious discomfort. "I'm just teasing you. I've seen you and Captain Williams spending time together around the hospital, that's all.

You're both single, so if something did spark between you then…"

"Leave the doc alone, Annette," Reed chided his wife. "Poor guy's busy. Let him get on with it."

Luis left quickly, feeling oddly like he'd just escaped a firing squad, and headed back down to the ER, glad for the cool air in the stairwell on his heated face.

The rest of the morning passed quickly, and before he knew it, it was time for the Emergency Response Team meeting. He was looking over the new films of Reed's leg postsurgery at the nurses' station when his brother, Jackson, walked in.

"Those for the motorcycle accident victim we brought in last week?" Jackson asked, checking out the scans of a badly fractured leg.

"Yes." Luis scrolled through several more images then clicked off the computer. "He's doing much better, according to the last report I got from the ortho surgeon. Took hours of surgery to repair all the damage. They're going to evaluate his leg today."

"That's tough, man. I know when we picked him up from the scene, there was a lot of gravel and denim and bits of bone we had to debride from the wound. I hope they can save it."

They walked out of the ER together and down the hall toward the conference room. From what Luis had seen from the weather reports on the TVs in the cafeteria earlier, Hurricane Mathilda had changed course yet again and Luis wondered if they'd be raising the readiness level in the area since the storm seemed to be on a trajectory to at least cause some damage in the area. From the tense look on his brother's face, Luis guessed that answer was yes.

They discussed Reed's case a bit more as he held the door for Jackson then followed him inside the large room, immediately searching out Stacy and spotting her seated at the table near several other firefighters. There was one seat still open near her, and he made his way over to it as Jackson headed for the podium at the front of the room.

"Hi," Luis said, as he slipped into his seat then frowned at Stacy's distant expression. Not cold, exactly, but not warm, either. Given her odd response to his text, he could only guess there was something wrong, but he had no idea what. Now wasn't really the time he could ask, either, with the meeting starting. Meanwhile his mind raced with horrible scenarios. Was it Miguel? Had something happened to his son? Or was it something he'd done that had offended Stacy? Had he overstepped the mark by moving himself into her apartment like that and she'd just not wanted to tell him earlier?

He was hardly an expert on relationships, and sometimes his issues made him not the best judge of social norms. Dammit. He scowled up at his brother as the meeting got underway.

"Right. Let's get started, then," Jackson said. He was two years younger than Luis and adopted as well, but they were closer than blood. "Thanks, everyone, for coming in. We've got a lot of new information to cover today, so best get to it."

Jackson waited for the hushed murmurs to die down then jumped right in. "Unfortunately, the news I have today isn't good. Based on the latest forecast models from the National Weather Service, Mathilda is expected to strengthen to a category four storm by tomorrow morning, and though it won't make direct landfall in the Keys, we are expecting the outer bands to cause significant storm surge and wind damages throughout the area as it passes by. Therefore, I'm raising our readiness level to one, effective midnight tonight. You all know how this goes and should have been expecting it."

"Tomorrow morning?" Luis shook his head in disbelief. There was still much left to do in the ER. "That's much sooner than originally expected. I thought it wouldn't hit until tomorrow evening at the soonest."

"Like I said, things have changed fast." Jackson took a deep breath. "And given the hurricane's current speed and trajectory, once it hits the Gulf of Mexico and the warmer waters there, it's going to be a monster. So I've already put out bulletins to the local media, per our ERT protocol. Everyone on the team quarantines in Key West until after Mathilda passes. All top-level protocols are now in place and emergency services mobilized. We are warning residents in the Keys to evacuate to the mainland now or find lodging within Key West proper for the duration of the event. Any questions?"

Stacy cursed under her breath. "This is bad. My crew needs to double up on prep to be ready by that time. And I tried to call my friend Lucy before I came here. You met her last week, but she's not answering her phone. I texted her and offered to drive up and bring her, but she said no. She told me once before that if a storm like this happened, she'd stay at her place and ride it out, but this is going to be worse than anything we've seen in a while."

Luis swiveled to face Stacy. He wanted very much

to take her in his arms and hold her but didn't dare in the crowded room of their colleagues. Not until he knew where they stood. "Please don't worry. I'm sure everything's fine. Lucy's a veterinarian. Maybe she had an emergency case come up or something. She'll call you later, I'm sure." He took a deep breath and plunged ahead, knowing he needed to find out, but dreading it all the same. "*Mi sirenita*, I can tell something is bothering you. Please talk to me, tell me what's wrong so we can—"

Jackson made his way over to them. "Everything okay?"

"Not really." Stacy rubbed her crossed arms. "Lucy isn't here today. I offered to pick her up and drive her in, but she refuses to leave her compound."

Jackson looked a bit sick at that. "I'll call her and talk to her about it."

"I don't think it will do any good," Stacy said, her expression concerned. "She's determined to stay there and ride this thing out, but I think this one's going to be bad, Jackson. She's tough, but not that tough."

"No. You're right. She can't stay there by herself." Jackson scowled. "It's too dangerous."

"Well, good luck getting her to budge, brother," Luis said, scrubbing a hand over his face. He thought of the conversation he'd just had with Reed and his wife. "All she has to do is not answer her phone. People do what they want and what they think is best, no matter the danger or who they hurt in the process, even themselves."

Beside him, Stacy gave a pained gasp, and he realized too late that she must have interpreted his words to be about her. He wanted to tell her the opposite was true, but she'd already turned away to talk to one of her fire crew members and Jackson was still there, and… Dammit it all to hell and back.

Jackson's phone buzzed, and his brother's dour expression lit with hope for a second before dying away. Luis wasn't sure exactly what was happening there between his brother and Lucy Miller, but it was quite apparent to him that something definitely was. His brother tapped Stacy on the shoulder and told her to go ahead and brief her departments and that he'd handle Lucy. After she left, Jackson turned to Luis again. "Can you take over IC for me tonight after my shift ends?"

"What? Why?" Luis frowned, warning bells clanging in his head. "You aren't going to do anything reckless, are you?"

"No."

Luis had heard that tone many times before from his brother and knew it meant exactly the opposite was true. His pulse thundered as adrenaline flooded his system.

"I can't leave Lucy out there by herself." He rubbed his hand over the top of his short hair as they made their way back toward the ER and the ambulance bay. "Look, the level one doesn't go into effect until midnight. If I drive out to Big Pine Key after my shift at nine, I'm sure I can get her and get back to Key West in plenty of time."

Yep. Reckless as hell. Luis gave him a look. "That's cutting it awfully close. No. I don't like it, Jackson."

"Well, good thing it's not up to you, then." Jackson dug in his heels. The brothers rarely fought, but when they did, it was usually over a matter of principle. "Look, I'm the one taking the risk here, okay? And I'm fine doing it." Luis gave his brother a dubious stare, and Jackson's expression hardened with anger. "Stop glaring at me like that. Really, it's fine. And this has nothing to do with sex, if that's what you're thinking. Lucy barely tolerates me. But as IC I can't just leave her out there to die, can I? Besides, she's disobeying my orders already by not being at the meeting. If I let her continue to do that I won't be seen as an effective leader, will I? So yeah. I'm going out there to get her."

"So, this is about the promotion then?" Luis asked, thoroughly unconvinced.

"Of course it is," Jackson said, throwing up his hands. "What else would it be about?"

Luis stared at him a moment, then sighed. Who was he to judge someone else's rocky relationship? He said as much for Jackson as himself, "I just hope you know what you're doing, brother."

Jackson exhaled slow, then nodded. "Keep an eye on your phone tonight. I'll text you if there are any problems."

By the time Luis turned back to Stacy, she was gone, which was probably just as well. They both had a lot to get done now in a very short amount of time.

CHAPTER EIGHT

THAT NIGHT, FOLLOWING an exhausting, frenetic afternoon getting all the final prep done in her department for the upcoming storm and bolstering outreach to the community to make sure everyone was prepared for the hurricane making landfall on the Keys later that night, Stacy and her crew were helping the Key West General maintenance guys get the final storm shutters in place over the windows in the ER waiting area.

The wind had picked up significantly since that morning, with the storm's rapid approach, and even the enormous palm trees lining the parking lot outside were starting to bend like drinking straws. Her nerves were thrumming with purpose and a pointed need to get down to the basement where Miguel was staying with one of the nurses until Stacy finished up here.

Luckily, under Luis's excellent guidance, the hospital had been well prepared and it was only a matter of kicking their evacuation plans into high gear today. They had released as many patients as they could safely to hunker down at home, and the more critically ill or not-yet-ready-for-release patients had been moved to an emergency triage unit set up in the basement cafeteria, which had been cleared and prepped as a small hospital in itself, with the corridors and other rooms down there acting as overflow space.

A loud crash sounded against the wall outside, jarring her from her thoughts as they fit the last metal storm shutter into place over the windows. It was a public trash can, the heavy kind made of cement with a steel liner. The last huge gust had picked it up and rolled it into the building like it was nothing more than an empty soda can.

"There goes the Luigi's awning," one of the other firefighters said, pointing across the street toward a local Italian restaurant. Sure enough, the huge red-and-white-striped expanse of fabric billowed through the air like a huge kite before disappearing around the corner.

Right. If that wasn't a signal to get downstairs, Stacy didn't know what was. Pulse racing, she wiped her hands on the legs of her uniform pants then hiked her thumb toward the stairwell door. "Basement. Now. I'm going to make one more sweep up here then I'll join you."

"Want me to go with you, Captain?" Jeffrey, one of the youngest members of her crew, asked.

"No. I got it. Pretty sure everyone's downstairs now. This is just a precaution." She watched them all leave then headed through the automatic doors into the trauma bay area. She'd never seen it so eerily quiet. Even in here, you could still hear the low howl of the wind outside, like an approaching banshee. The lights flickered then came back on. The hospital had generators, thank goodness, so no worries about losing power tonight. As she walked around the circular layout of the department, checking for any stragglers, she came across one last charge nurse, filling up a supply bag with syringe packs, bandages, gauze and other necessities, in case reinforcements were needed downstairs.

Stacy walked over to help, grateful for something to do other than worry. "Anyone else in the department?"

"No. I sent them all downstairs half an hour ago," the nurse said. Her name was Ethel, and Stacy knew her in passing from her EMS runs here. Ethel's eyes kept darting toward the clock on the wall, her expression pinched with concern. "Any update on the hurricane's arrival time?"

"Not that I've heard," Stacy said, shoving handfuls of alcohol swabs and Q-tips into a pocket of the supply bag the nurse was holding. "It's a little after nine now, so another couple of hours yet before the eye wall passes. The winds are bad enough now, but they'll get worse. Rain, too. With the storm surge, we're expecting lots of flooding tomorrow. Let's hope people took the warning seriously and stayed inside."

"My little girl's at home with my husband," Ethel said, blinking hard then frowning. "I tried to call them earlier, but the lines were jammed. Sent a text, too, but haven't gotten a response yet. I hope they're okay."

Stacy felt for her. She really did. She was still praying that Jackson had made Lucy see some sense and convinced her to get off that island compound of hers, but there wasn't a thing she could do about it now. Thankfully, her mother had decided to ride out the storm on the mainland in Miami, which hopefully would avoid the brunt of Mathilda's wrath. And Stacy had Miguel here with her. And Luis. Much as she didn't want to depend on him too much, he'd become a safe harbor for her these past few days, a source of silent strength that she needed tonight more than ever. She reached over and placed her hand on Ethel's shoulder. "I'm sure they're okay. Did you have an emergency plan in place?"

"Of course." Ethel looked up then, her eyes bright with tears. "I've lived in the Keys my whole life. You always have an emergency plan ready."

"Good. Then I'm sure they've followed it and are doing exactly what they need to do." Stacy helped the nurse zip up the heavy bag then took it from her to carry out into the hall. "The best thing you can do for them right now is take care of yourself. And Ethel, I promise when all this is over, I'll go check on them personally and let you know they're okay."

Ethel gave her a watery smile. "Thank you."

"What's taking so long up here?" an irritated male voice said from the other end of the hallway, followed by a string of Spanish curses.

Luis.

Stacy sent Ethel on her way down to the basement then walked over to join him near the automatic doors. "Just finishing up a final sweep of the ER to make sure everyone's out."

"They are," he said, taking the supply bag from her and slinging it over his shoulder like it weighed nothing. "I've checked the rest of the floor, and the other units have already checked in with me in the basement. It's done. All we've left to do is ride this out."

"Let's go," she said, following him through the silent waiting area, the ominous creaks and groans from the storm shutters the only noise echoing through the empty hospital now. Her natural instinct was to take over, but Luis was in charge here. And if she'd doubted that for a second, the look on his face now convinced her. He looked tough, alpha, ready and willing to do what had to be done. But within his dark eyes flickered something else, so fast she couldn't quite identify it. Based on what he'd said at the meeting earlier, though, it made her stomach clench.

People do what they want and what they think is best, no matter the danger or who they hurt in the process, even themselves...

If those hurtful words weren't directed at her, then who else were they for? She and Luis had spent a lot of time together over the last few days. She'd let him into her home, into her bed again. If she was honest, she'd even let him into her heart, but maybe that wasn't enough.

Lord knew it hadn't been enough for her father. She'd never been good enough for him. That's why he'd left. If she'd just been a better student, a better daughter, a better person, maybe he would have stayed.

No. Her skin prickled, and her spine stiffened. Now wasn't the time to go there. And Luis wasn't her father. He'd been nothing but kind and supportive of her during their time together.

But what if he goes, too?

They pushed out the stairwell door into the basement and a scene of controlled pandemonium. All the sounds that were missing upstairs were concentrated down here—the chatter of staff and patients, the beep and buzz of monitors, the clinking of instruments and the squeaking of rubber-soled shoes and wheels on the shiny linoleum floors—creating a cacophony of busyness.

As she and Luis wove through the crowded hallways

heading toward the cafeteria, they passed by patient beds pushed up against the walls, nurses and doctors attending to them as best they could under the circumstances. Portable ventilators wheezed and oxygen cylinders were attached to sides of beds, along with IV bags hung from steel trolleys. One of the residents rushed up to Luis's side with an update.

"We've sectioned the floor off, Doc, as you outlined. Surgical recovery and ICU is down that corridor." The resident pointed to a hall they passed on their right. "The geriatric patients are on the other side of the cafeteria there, and pediatrics is back on the other side of the elevators."

The lights flickered again then clicked back on, steady.

"Good work," Luis told the resident then sent him on his way.

They passed Ethel in the hall, fiddling with some cables for a patient's heart monitor, and they passed the bag of supplies back over to her for handling. As Stacy followed Luis down the corridor, she couldn't shake the feeling like she was walking through a scene from a disaster movie. She'd lived in South Florida her whole life. She'd been through plenty of storms, and as a firefighter, she worked in unpleasant or strange environments a lot, but she'd never experienced anything quite like this. It felt like the monster was outside, stalking them, waiting to get in, and it was up to her and her crew and Luis and his staff to keep the monster out. It felt almost like a war. One she was determined to win.

"Where's Miguel?" she asked, needing to see her son to reassure herself he was safe.

"He's with the nurses in the pediatric unit for now.

Right before I came up to get you, I checked on him, and he was playing with Dozer, happy as a clam."

They'd stopped in front of the nonfunctioning elevators and Stacy started to respond, but before she could, the lights flickered again. Except this time they went out completely, plunging the basement into darkness. A collective gasp rippled through the corridors before the sound of machines churning on cut through the tension and suddenly there was illumination again as the generators took over. The light was different now, a sort of dull amber instead of the bright white of before, but it was better than nothing.

"C'mon," Luis said, taking her hand and tugging her toward the end of the hall where the pediatric unit was. "Let's get Miguel."

For a moment, she couldn't move, couldn't breathe, the gravity of the situation rooting her in place. Then Luis was there, turning back to her, leaning closer, to whisper in her ear, "Don't worry. You've got this. We've got this. Together." He rested his forehead against hers, his dark eyes locked on hers, genuine and steady, and for once, she didn't care what people would think. She compressed her lips and inhaled deep through her nose, seeking to calm the riot of thoughts in her head. Concentrated on the feel of his palm against hers, the warmth of his breath on her cheeks, the rise and fall of his chest.

She could do this. She would do this. Now wasn't the time to doubt or fall apart.

Stacy had spent her whole life feeling like she wasn't good enough, like she had to prove herself. Constantly trying to earn the approval of a man who'd walked out on them and never looked back. Luis seemed to accept her for who she was without judgment or reserve. He seemed pretty amazing, actually, but they'd only known each other in more than a biblical sense for a few days. It wasn't possible to love someone after that short a time.

Or was it?

Her inner turmoil ratcheted higher. Give her a fire to fight, a disaster to clear, an accident scene, and she could take care of it like nobody's business. Put her own heart, her own future at risk, and she felt completely overwhelmed and incompetent.

But she couldn't fall apart now. Nope. People were depending on her. She needed to pull it together fast. Put her emotions and her personal issues aside and get moving. She had a focus here. She had a purpose. She was a captain for the Key West Fire Department, and she had a job to do.

After another deep breath, Stacy stepped back and nodded. "Let's go."

They continued on down the hall, her heart pounding in time with her footsteps on the floor. This wasn't safe. Her heart wasn't safe with Luis anywhere around her. It was all happening so fast, yet it seemed like it had been coming for five years, ever since that night on the beach.

And despite the hurricane on their doorstep, Stacy was far more scared of her feelings for Luis.

Luis still felt as confused about what was happening with Stacy as he had earlier. Usually work centered him, cleared his head and helped him focus. But not now. As they made their way toward the small private waiting room where he'd left his son with a nurse to play with his bear and a few other toys, he kept running through his time with Stacy in his head. He'd been with several women in his life, but he'd never let anyone close to him like he had Stacy.

He wanted to pull her close and hug her, assure her that everything would be all right, even if he had no clue whether it would or not. He'd been in more than enough war zones and disaster scenes on his mission trips to know nothing was a given.

Still, he felt better with her at his side. That had to mean something.

And even if he had no idea what he was doing with regard to her and Miguel, he refused to walk away. Not yet. Maybe not ever.

They reached Miguel and he left Stacy in the room with him while he went to check on the other units before grabbing a weather radio from the makeshift command center he'd set up in the cafeteria kitchen and going back to hunker down with them for the next few hours.

Without windows or doors, they had no clue what raged outside, and the cell reception was poor down here even on the best of days. Tonight, it was dismal. One lonely bar showed on his phone screen, but he kept checking anyway, worried for his brother as much for himself and his family.

The staff were taking turns checking on patients and his wasn't for a few more hours yet, so he sat in a chair against the wall and did his best not to worry. It would be fine. Because it had to be fine. He would make it fine. That's what he did. Ride in to the rescue and save the day.

It was his purpose in life, who he was. The vow he'd made to his poor deceased parents.

I'll make you proud, I promise.

Luis wasn't so sure they'd be proud of him now, as he watched Stacy and Miguel on the floor, playing with some blocks, sharing their own little private jokes, in their own little world.

Dammit. What a mess he'd made of this.

Maybe he was wrong to try to insert himself into their lives the way he was. Stacy had told him she'd been fine, happy, before he'd returned. Was that the reason she seemed to be shutting him out now? Did they truly not need him? Were they better off without him?

He loved his son more than his own life, would do anything for the boy. Even walk out of his life again if that was truly the best thing for him.

And Stacy… Well, she'd rocked his world, in more ways than one.

He'd never imagined on that long-ago night on that moonlit beach that she'd be so perfect for him in all the ways that mattered. Not just sexually, either. She was smart and funny and sweet and strong. She was everything he wanted in a mate.

Except emotionally available.

Every time he thought about her father leaving her behind, making her feel less than, he wanted to hit something. Mainly the man who'd turned his back on his family. He'd lost his own parents during a treacherous crossing of the Florida Straits, but that had been different. His parents had loved him so much that they'd given up their lives to try to give him a better future. Her father had turned his back on Stacy and her mother, forcing them into a life of struggle and poverty.

Hands fisted, Luis clenched his teeth, a muscle ticking near his tense jaw.

Luis wanted to make up for that loss, wanted to show Stacy that she was good enough, that she was enough. Period. Amen. But each time he got closer, she shut him out.

"Mommy, why are we down here?" Miguel asked, cutting through Luis's turbulent thoughts.

"Because it's storming outside, honey," she said, handing him another block. "We need to stay down here to be safe until it's over."

"Where's Grandma?" the boy asked.

"She's in Miami with her friend." At her son's concerned look, she smoothed his hair with her fingers. "Grandma will be fine. I talked to her earlier today and she'll be back with us just as soon as she can be, I promise."

Miguel gave a small nod, frowning. "Daddy's here."

"Yes, he is." Stacy glanced his way, holding his gaze a moment before looking away again, her deep blue eyes unreadable.

Luis wanted to shout that he'd always be there, come hell or high water or anything Mother Nature might throw their way. He'd be there for as long as they'd have him, but given Stacy's reaction to his proclamations earlier, he didn't think that was wise. So, instead, he got up to pace away some of the pent-up energy inside him threatening to burst out of his skin. Finally, he couldn't take it anymore. Feeling claustrophobic and conflicted, he headed for the door. "Stay here with him. I'm going to see if they need help out there."

Thankfully, they did. As he'd predicted, several new injuries had arrived along with the storm's gales. The EMTs had been directed to bring any patients that weren't hunkered down to the basement, and now there were several. Mainly people who'd waited until the last minute to board up and had gotten caught in the storm and lashed by flying debris.

He treated a man with a nasty gash on his forehead and a woman with a broken wrist from a fall, then headed to the crisis triage center in the cafeteria kitchen to help field radio calls. Other members of the Emergency Response Team were there also, including members of the police and fire departments.

He'd done work like this on several of his previous mission trips, so it came as second nature to him. There were already plenty of reports that had come in as the first bands lashed the Keys, mainly building damage. No casualty reports yet, though, thank goodness. He dealt with a call from a home health agency about several elderly clients they hadn't had time to check on before Mathilda hit but reassured the caller that most likely they were safe. If they'd been living down here for any length of time, they'd know about hurricanes. Just in case, though, he passed those notes on to law enforcement so they could add the residents to their list of people to check on once the storm had passed.

Meanwhile, the weather radios crackled on in the background with reports of black skies and hammering winds. Cars were being flipped and roofs were being peeled off like tin cans. Scary stuff indeed.

Luis pulled out his phone to check for a message from Jackson. His brother had told him he'd text him tonight to let him know he'd made it safely to Lucy's place. Based on the intel now, if he'd gotten there, Jackson would likely be stuck out on Big Pine Key for the duration of the storm. No way could anyone drive on the Overseas Highway in this. He prayed Jackson wouldn't try something reckless like he usually did. His brother was one of the bravest men Luis had ever known. One of the best, too. But he let his heart rule too often over his head.

Not something Luis had ever been accused of. Until now.

The buzzing of his phone in his hand made Luis jump.

He looked down to see a short text shining on his screen.

At Big Pine Key. Won't make it back.

Luis was happy his brother was safe. Less so that he would have to continue to be interim incident commander. He knew how much that position had meant to Jackson and how hard it must've been for him to give it up, even temporarily. Lucy must be very special to his brother indeed.

There was no time to dwell on that, however, as the storm raged on, radio calls continued to come in and there were patients to treat and a community to keep together during a hurricane.

After an hour or so, Luis needed a break and turned his position over to another team member who was fresh off break. He wandered back down the corridors, checking patients as he went. According to his smart watch, it was close to eleven now and things had quieted a bit in the basement even as conditions worsened outside. He passed by a gurney where a man with a cut on his arm was telling the nurse who was treating him about what he'd seen on his way into the ER.

"Rain coming down in sheets. You couldn't see two feet in front of you," the guy said, eyes wide. "Stuff flying through the air, smashing into windows. I've been down here through three hurricanes, but ain't never seen anything like this one. She's a doozy!"

Finally, he turned the corner and headed back down the hall toward the room where Stacy and Miguel were. He took a deep breath. The angsty knot in his stomach that had been there all day was still present, he'd just learned to ignore it. His back and neck ached and the thought of lying down for a bit to rest his eyes, especially with Stacy, sounded wonderful.

He stopped by a vending machine and bought them some waters and snacks then opened the door to the room with his elbow and went in. Stacy was sitting against the wall in the chair he'd vacated earlier, and she motioned for him to be quiet before pointing down at a sleeping Miguel on the floor. She'd managed to find some extra blankets and pillows, it looked like, and had made a bed for their son in one corner of the small room. In the opposite corner sat a stack of linens for them to use.

There was only one lamp in the room and the bulb looked like it was on its last legs, given the weak light it was putting out. Still, it was better than nothing, so he took a seat in the other chair beside Stacy and handed her a water and bag of chips. "The best I could do for dinner."

She laughed and took her food. "Thanks. I got Miguel something from the vending machines, too, before he fell asleep. Poor guy."

"How's he holding up?" Luis asked around a mouthful of pretzels. "He seemed okay earlier."

"He's good. A bit agitated, but I think sleep will help with that. Usually does." She glanced at him. "How are things out there?"

"Hectic." He filled her in on everything he'd seen and heard while they ate, including the text from Jackson. "If he's there with Lucy, she'll be fine. My brother was in the coast guard and there's no one I'd want at my back in a dangerous situation more than Jackson. They'll be okay."

"I hope so." She finished her chips then tossed their bags into the trash. "Lucy's special."

"Hmm. She seemed very intent on her job when I met her at the last ERT meeting. You two are good friends?"

"We are. I met her after she moved here last year. She's going to help me get a service dog for Miguel."

"Oh. That's wonderful." He stretched then winced as his right shoulder ached from sitting in one position too long taking those radio calls. "Ouch."

"Stiff?" Stacy asked walking back over to sit beside him again.

"A little. Nothing I can't handle."

Stacy smiled. "Well, Jackson picked the right man to be interim IC."

"Thanks. Though there isn't much for me to do. My brother had it all set up before he left." He shifted slightly to look at her. "And you did a fine job with the fire department, getting everything done today on such short notice."

"Thanks," she said, though her tone sounded a bit flat.

Curious, he shifted slightly to face her better. "What?"

"Nothing."

"Stacy?" he prodded. Maybe it wasn't a good thing to do with the stress between them, but they were trapped here with each other for hours. Why not put it to good use talking some of this out? "Tell me."

At first, he thought she'd shut him out again, but then she sighed and rested her head back against the wall. "I know I'm good at my job. I wouldn't be a captain if I wasn't. But I always wonder if I'm good enough. Not as a firefighter, but as a person."

The urge to punch her errant father returned full force, and Luis shoved his hands in the pockets of his lab coat so she couldn't see his fists. The rawness in her voice, the intensity in those words, made his heart pinch for her. "You're a good person, Stacy."

She blinked, the dim light in the room catching the moisture in her eyes, and his breath caught. He forced himself to relax and took her hand. "I mean it. You're a wonderful woman. An excellent firefighter. And the best mom ever to Miguel. I don't think a person could ask for anything more."

"You only see the good in me." Stacy smiled and leaned closer to rest her head on his shoulder.

This close, the sweet floral scent of her shampoo surrounded him, the warmth of her cheek pressed against the side of his throat. The need to touch her, to hold her, to make her see all the incredible things he did when he saw her, jolted through him like electricity. But still he held back, conscious of their son sleeping a short distance away and wary of ruining this moment between them.

"True," he whispered at last. "But man, is it glorious."

Stacy raised her head then to look at him, her beautiful blue eyes and long eyelashes highlighted by the dim glow of the lamp. Even though they were still in the busy basement of the hospital, this felt so private, and he was grateful for their tiny spot to be alone.

She reached up and traced his profile with her finger, then smiled, banishing his shadows. "Thank you."

He kissed the tip of her finger then settled back, closing his eyes as he gathered her closer into his side. Luckily these chairs were padded and had no arms, which made for better snuggling. At first Stacy didn't move. Then she wrapped her arms around his middle, like a hug. It felt good. It felt right.

He'd spent the last few years always working, always running, always trying to be whatever he thought he needed to be to fulfill his vow to his deceased birth parents. And none of that had included letting anyone close to his heart. So now, sitting here, with Stacy, the sensations sizzling through him almost hurt. Still, Stacy didn't let go. And finally, after what felt like a small eternity, the tension knotted inside him drained away. The same thing had happened their first night together years ago, he realized, but at the time, he'd put it down to the alcohol and the passion of the moment.

Now, though, he knew it to be something more. Something real. Something bigger than he'd ever experienced before, and he was scared. His chest ached. Not from exertion, but from emotion. Yearning, need, desire, affection. All of them swirled into a riotous blend of color and sound and sensation.

Impossible as it seemed to his logical mind, his one-night stand had actually brought the perfect woman for him into his life. He hadn't seen it at the time, and he was still trying to understand it.

He traced the backs of his fingers down her cheeks, pulling back from her embrace just enough to tilt her chin up and kiss her. He was hesitant at first, not wanting to push where he wasn't wanted, but then he deepened the kiss as her hand slid into his hair and she responded beneath him. Just as she started to move across his lap to straddle him, Miguel murmured in his sleep behind them, and they both froze.

This time, it was Stacy who rested her forehead against his and smiled. "Guess we should stop."

Luis laughed. "Guess we should."

Stacy climbed off him just as something bumped into the other side of the door. Luis straightened and raked a hand through his hair. He needed a shave and probably a shower as well, but both of those would have to wait.

"I should go see what's going on," he said, getting up. "You okay here with Miguel?"

"Yep," she said, yawning. "I'll probably take a nap myself before my next shift."

"Good idea." He opened the door then looked back at her. "Sleep well. See you later."

"See you."

Luis closed the door and headed back toward the cafeteria command center, unable to wipe the silly smile from his face, even as the storm raged around them.

CHAPTER NINE

STACY DID SLEEP, more exhausted than she thought after the day's craziness, and when she woke it took her a moment to realize where she was. Through the dim light of the room, she spotted Miguel still asleep across from her, his thumb in his mouth and his bear, Dozer, tucked at his side beneath his cast.

She went to shift slightly from where she was lying on the floor, having pushed the chairs back to the corner to make room to stretch out, and found a warm, heavy weight draped over her waist, pinning her in place. Next came the awareness of the solid warm body pressed behind hers.

Slowly, she turned her head slightly to see Luis asleep behind her, his handsome features relaxed and so open it made her heart ache. He'd called her a good person. He treated her as an equal. He seemed too good to be true.

But is he?

Her hip hurt from staying in one spot too long, and eventually, she had to move. She sat up carefully, trying to avoid waking the two guys in her life, and failed when Miguel stirred then awoke with a start.

"Mommy?" he wailed, reaching for her, his little face scrunched. "I had a bad dream!"

She rushed to him and held him close as Luis jolted up, rumpled and groggy and far too gorgeous than a man had a right to be. Stacy bit back a grin at his obvious disorientation and hugged her son closer, kissing the top of his dark little head. "It's okay, honey. It was just a dream. You're okay."

"What happened?" Luis asked, squinting over at her. "What time is it?"

"It's…" She checked her watch. "About 2:00 a.m., and your son had a nightmare."

Following another kiss and a squeeze, she set Miguel away from her and scooted back. He seemed fine now, as he did after most of his bad dreams, forgetting them promptly as new adventures took hold. The little boy climbed out from beneath his covers and itched his arm above his cast.

"I need to potty, Mommy," Miguel said, rubbing his eyes with his free hand.

"Me, too," Stacy said, climbing to her feet as well. "And then we need to eat before Mommy needs to work for a bit."

Luis yawned and stood as well. "The cafeteria is serving cold meals for staff and patients. How about we all freshen up then meet again in the hallway?"

"Sounds good." Stacy got her son squared away and then herself while Luis headed to the staff locker rooms for a quick shower and shave. By the time they met up again, he looked fresh and alert while she still felt a bit musty without her coffee.

They went into the cafeteria and stood in line with other members of the staff to get food. Everyone was looking a little worse for wear as the hurricane continued to rage on outside. From here, they were a bit insulated from the chaos, but from the conversations she heard around her, things were pretty bad outside. Power was out for most of the Keys, and they were saying it could be days before it was restored. The local emergency shelters that had been set up were close to capacity as well, and the worst of the flooding was yet to come.

She picked up Miguel and held him in her arms as they moved closer in the food line. The room was noisy and Miguel tucked his head against her neck, not liking the clamor of voices all trying to talk over one another. Luis pushed two trays, one for himself and one for her and Miguel, stocking them each with water and food as they made their way through the line. Finally, they found seats at the end of a crowded table of cops and firefighters and Stacy sat Miguel on her lap as she handed him a fork to eat with.

One of the guys from her crew, Harley, was sitting down the bench from her, so while her son ate, Stacy asked him for a rundown on the conditions outside.

"The eye wall's passing over now," Harley said. "It's weird. The rain's stopped and you can see the stars. It'll pick up again soon, though, Captain."

No doubt about that. The winds were usually strongest around the eye wall, too, so they were far from out of danger yet. Luis stayed silent eating his food like he feared someone would take it away from him. Miguel did the same. One more similarity between father and son. She smiled again. Luis had shaved, too, she noticed. His still-damp hair shined beneath the amber emergency lights overhead.

"I'll have one of the nurses watch Miguel for me while I check in with my crew and see what needs to be done next," Stacy said. "What about you?"

"I've got some patients to check on and some other logistics to handle."

"Any more texts from Jackson?" she asked, thinking again of her friend Lucy.

"No, not yet." Luis frowned and pushed away his empty cereal bowl. "But since the storm is heading north, they're probably still getting the brunt of it. Hopefully, we'll all be in the clear by morning and they can get out and assess the damage."

They finished their meal in silence, the voices dying down around them to a dull roar.

Miguel wanted down, and she let him slip off her lap with a warning not to go far. Luis tracked their son's movement, his expression unreadable. She'd never felt such a deep, instant connection to someone like she did to Luis, and it was unsettling. It didn't matter that they'd only known each other—really known each other—for such a short time. It was what it was. And what it was, was exhilarating. Exhilarating and excruciating and enormously terrifying, all rolled into one.

Luis transferred his gaze from their son to her, and the look in his dark eyes made the hairs on the back of her neck stand at attention. "Are we friends, Stacy?"

"Uh…" She frowned, not sure how to categorize what they were to each other at that point. "I don't know. Why?"

He reached over and took her hand, gaze steady on hers. "What if I want to be more?"

Stunned, she sat there blinking at him. Seriously? He was going to do this here? "Uh…"

That seemed the only word she was capable of at the moment.

Lacing his fingers with hers, Luis continued. "I realize my timing isn't the best here, but I need to say this. Stacy, I—"

"Dr. Durand?" a nurse called over the din in the room. "We need you right away, please!"

Stacy cursed internally. Seemed fate was forever interfering in their story. Luis scrubbed a hand over his face and flashed an apologetic smile. "Duty calls."

"Apparently." She raised an annoyed brow at him then stood to throw away their trash and open up the seats for someone else. "Go on. I'll get Miguel and get him to his nurse babysitter. I'll see you later after my shift."

She watched him walk away, feeling like they'd lost something precious in that moment.

The next few hours passed in a blur of cases and damage reports and orders for rescue teams to deploy to different areas of Key West as Hurricane Mathilda slowly made her way northward, leaving behind a path of destruction for the Emergency Response Team to clean up.

For his part, Luis was glad for the distraction. A strange restlessness buzzed inside him following their interrupted conversation this morning, and he felt like he had to keep moving, keep pushing forward or something bad would happen.

Up until Stacy had reappeared in his life, he'd felt safe and secure on his path. It had always served him well, putting the needs of others before his own. But now, he saw a future he wanted for himself, the rest of the world's thoughts and concerns about it be damned. A future with Stacy and Miguel by his side, and all he had to do was reach for it. Well, reach for it and convince her that it would work and that he wasn't going anywhere.

He couldn't say exactly when the switch had flipped for him from coparent to friend to lover to...*more*. But flip it had, and now the deep sense of yearning in his chest, the near-constant ache for more that had dogged him since the loss of his parents way back when had transformed into certainty. Over the past few days, spending time with Stacy, getting to know her, and their son through her, had changed his feelings from like to love. And it wasn't just physical, either, though that was definitely there. No. He loved her heart, and her intelligence. Her drive and her desire to help others. Even her stubbornness was sexy as hell, when it wasn't directed at him, of course.

With Stacy, he'd found what he was looking for. An equal. A partner. A soul mate.

He'd spotted her a few times throughout the predawn hours, meeting with her crew and coordinating rescue efforts with the local ambulance authority. She was impressive, no doubt about it, and it made him love her even more. There was nothing sexier than competence for him, and his Stacy had that in spades.

She was excellent at her job and an excellent mother and would make an excellent wife, too, one day, he had no doubt, if and when they got to that point. Together, they'd save the world and raise their son.

Now he just needed to convince her of that, too.

By late morning, the storm had passed completely and they'd gotten the first floor opened up again. He went outside with the cops to assess the damage and was pleased to see that the hospital hadn't fared too badly overall. There were some broken windows and lots of downed trees and power lines, but the generators were holding up well and now that conditions were improving, weatherwise, restoration crews could start moving in to get life back to normal again. Jackson's early planning had meant that all of it was running smoothly. Luis was sure his brother would get the promotion he'd worked so hard for, even if he'd temporarily turned over command to Luis.

And speaking of Jackson, shortly after noon Luis finally spoke to his brother. Cell service was still spotty but getting better.

"How did you fare on Big Pine Key?" Luis asked as he stood outside the hospital, glad for some fresh air after hours locked down in the basement.

"It's been..." Jackson hesitated, then sighed. "It's been interesting. We're okay up here. Lucy's house took on quite a bit of damage, though, and from what I can see there's a lot of cleanup to do around here. The highway's completely blocked, so I'm not sure when I'll get back. How about Key West?"

"About the same, brother." He told Jackson about the wind damage and the reports of several cars off the road and a couple of older residents trapped in their homes by floodwaters. "I'll let the flight crew know about your situation and see if they can send someone down to pick you up today. Any casualties?"

"No. I got attacked by a gator when I first arrived, but that's about it."

"I'm sorry?" Luis scowled. "You what?"

Jackson laughed. "Long story. I'll tell you about

it later. I'm glad to hear things are going well down there. I should get back to Lucy. My battery's about dead anyway. Take care, brother."

"You, too," Luis said. "I'll send that helicopter soon."

The call ended, and Luis headed back inside. A glance at his smart watch showed that Stacy's shift was almost done, and a fresh wave of doctors and staff were slowly making their way in to relieve those who'd been on duty all night, including Luis. Signs of recovery and goodwill were popping up all around them, including several people who'd set up grills around the parking lot and were cooking food for staff and anyone else who needed a hot meal after the storm.

He wanted to stand under a hot shower for days, then fall into bed and sleep for a few more. But first, he had something else to do and a newly formed plan in his mind of how to go about it.

CHAPTER TEN

STACY HAD JUST finished up dispatching her last crew to an accident on the edge of town when she turned to find Luis in the doorway of the cafeteria kitchen, smiling at her. He'd changed out of his scrubs and lab coat and had on the jeans and T-shirt he'd left her apartment in the day before.

"You look beat," he said.

"I feel beat." She stretched then rubbed her sore neck. "Have you been outside yet?"

"I have." He moved into the room to stand before her. "It's messy, but not horrible. The cleanup is already underway. Why don't you go clean up in the staff locker room? I checked on Miguel and he's doing fine with the nurse, and I even found you a spare set of scrubs to change into when you're done. Meet me back here. I've got a surprise for you."

She was a bit taken aback but in no fit state to argue. For once, Stacy was too tired anyway, so she did as he asked, taking a shower and brushing her teeth using one of the disposable kits in the locker room. She changed into the pink scrubs he'd set on the bench in the locker room for her, then stared down at her black work boots. They'd look pretty silly with the scrubs, but they were all she had here with her. She hadn't thought to bring a change of clothes from her apartment, what with everything else on her mind.

Once that was done, she grabbed her phone from the charger in the locker room and checked in with her mother via text. She was doing fine in Miami, though the storm was still a bit stronger there. No word from Lucy yet, but if anything had happened to her and Jackson, Stacy was sure Luis would've mentioned it.

Finally, she checked her appearance in the mirror. She'd smoothed her wet hair back into a low ponytail at the base of her neck and scrubbed her face clean. Her cheeks were pink, but she wished she'd had some makeup to put on.

Oh, well. Nothing for it now. Besides, considering what they'd been through last night, makeup should be the least of her concerns. She headed out of the locker room and back to the cafeteria to find Luis waiting for her in the hall. In his hand was a tray covered with aluminum foil. Even from where she stood, the smell of barbecue wafted around her, and her stomach growled. In his other hand was a bag she hoped held utensils to eat the food.

"Where did you get that?" she asked, walking up to him.

"It's a surprise." He winked then checked out her outfit. "Nice look."

She nudged him with her shoulder and chuckled. "Are you sure Miguel's okay?"

"Yep." Luis pushed open the stairwell door with his shoulder then held it for her. "When I looked in on him right before you got here, he had a stack of books and a willing nurse to help him read them. Our son's in heaven."

"Sounds like it." Stacy took the bag from him and headed upstairs, Luis behind her. "So where are we going?"

"I thought we'd get out of here for a bit. When I was out earlier, I took a glance at the beach nearby. Looks safe enough."

"Sounds good." They pushed out into the lobby, and she squinted into the hazy sunlight streaming in through the windows. They'd started removing some of the storm shutters, and she got her first look at the damage. Shards of glass sparkled on the tiled floor from some of the shattered windows, along with palm fronds and assorted trash. Outside, the air still felt humid on her skin, but the oppressive heat of earlier was gone. In its wake a steady breeze blew, nothing like the onslaught of the night before. People were out wandering around, snapping pictures or gawking over missing roofs and caved-in buildings. Overall, it wasn't as bad as she'd expected, though this was only a small part of their community. There'd been other places, closer to the water, where the damage had been much worse, she knew from her crews out and about in the city.

Luis took her hand and led her across the empty street and down the path to the beach. There were more palm fronds down here and scattered debris, but they managed to find a clear spot to sit.

"There's a towel in the bag for us to sit on," he said.

She pulled it out and spread it on the wet, firm sand. The ocean was quiet now, dark and steady. They settled down and Luis pulled the foil off the tray to reveal a platter of barbecued meats, most likely from one of

the vendors she'd spotted in the parking lot on their
way here. It was so thoughtful, it made Stacy's chest
squeeze. "Thank you."

"My pleasure," Luis said, shrugging like it wasn't
a big deal. He dug in the bag again and came out with
two paper plates and plastic flatware. Then he pulled
out two bottled waters and handed her one. "Nothing fancy, but we both deserve a good meal after last
night."

"Agreed."

They dug into the food like starving people, chatting around mouthfuls, just enjoying the fresh air and
freedom after hours in captivity.

"So," Stacy said at last, full and sated. She gave Luis
a side glance, still uncertain where things stood with
him after their interrupted conversation earlier that
day. When she'd thought he'd been about to suggest
they take things to the next level, she'd been frozen.
There was no other way to describe it. She liked Luis.
Loved him, even. But were they ready for a committed relationship?

She'd seen how that had turned out for her parents,
and she never wanted Miguel to go through something
like that. Not that Luis was anything like her father, but
still. She wasn't ready. They weren't ready.

Were they?

Luis wrapped up their trash in the tinfoil then leaned
back on one elbow, watching her. "So."

He turned to stare out at the ocean, giving her a
glimpse of his perfect profile, his dark hair ruffled by
the breeze, the scents of sand and sea around them.
From somewhere above a plaintive seagull cried, and

she got the uneasy feeling that this was an important moment, though she wasn't sure why.

Finally, Luis looked over at her and said, "I think we should try to make this work between us. As a couple. For Miguel's sake."

Blood rushed in her ears, and she forced herself to breathe. "Isn't that what we're doing?"

"I mean more formally." Luis sat up and reached for her hand, and Stacy pulled away before she could stop herself. The hurt look on his face nearly gutted her. He bit his lip and stared down at the towel for a moment before saying, "I don't mean marriage. Neither of us is ready for that yet, I don't think."

The air in her lungs whooshed out in a great, relieved rush before she could stop it. "Oh, thank God."

At his startled look, she amended, "I just mean... Well..."

"I know what you meant." He shook his head and gave a small, sad snort. "I just don't want to go backward from where we are now, Stacy. Do you understand?"

She took that in a minute then nodded. "I think I do."

"Good." Luis reached for her hand again, and this time she let him take it. The slow skim of his thumb over her knuckles was hypnotic. "What happens next then, Stacy?"

She licked her lips, not sure exactly what he wanted her to say, so she went with the truth. "I'm not sure. The last few days have been...odd."

"Odd?"

"Yes." She shrugged. "I mean, challenging. Maybe

that's a better word. In a lot of ways. With work and life, and…us."

"Agreed." He exhaled slowly. "I didn't expect to feel so close to you and Miguel so quickly."

"But you do?"

"*Sí.* I do." He kissed her fingers, his dark eyes warm. "I feel like I've known you my whole life. Like when I'm with you, I'm home."

Her breath caught and her chest squeezed, and if she hadn't been sitting down, she feared she might have melted into a puddle of goo at his feet at the sweetness of that. And she wasn't the melting-goo sort of girl usually. But Luis brought that out in her. That was what was so great about him. And what was so scary.

Stacy turned slightly to face him and slid her arms around his neck, tipping her head to the side. "I'm comfortable with you, too. But this is very new to me. After what I told you about my father and my past, you know it's hard for me to let people in, to depend on other people. But I'm willing to try, with you."

"That's all I can ask," he said, leaning in to close the gap between them and kiss her.

The ease with which they seemed to fall into a comfortable routine over the next seven days lulled Luis into a sense of security he'd never expected to find. There was much work to be done, both at the hospital and out on the streets of Key West, and between himself and Stacy, they were pulling extra shifts right and left just to cover it all.

There'd been an influx of patients to the ER following the storm, everything from minor scrapes and bruises to more serious broken bones and concussions from falling debris, and even one poor guy who'd required a partial amputation of his leg due to an infection that had set in after wading through polluted floodwater to rescue his neighbors. Still, it felt good to be busy and useful, and Luis was in his element. He'd even gone down to one of the emergency shelters near Key West General on his breaks several times to help them feed the hungry and displaced. It helped satisfy his niggling conscience, the tiny voice whispering in his head that he wasn't doing enough to be of service, that he should be traveling more, that there were other, harder-hit places that were much worse off than the Keys and much poorer to boot.

He managed to shove that voice aside, knowing he was where he needed to be right now.

Personally, things were moving along at a good clip, too. He'd been spending pretty much every night at Stacy's, giving them even more privacy to explore their relationship and figure out what the next step should be. After their talk on the beach, they'd begun taking turns watching Miguel while the other one worked. Luckily, their shifts weren't on the same schedule, so when one was away, the other was available. Miguel loved spending more time with his daddy and was getting to the point where he refused to go to sleep until both Mommy and Daddy had read him a story.

Luis had even taken Stacy and Miguel to his house for dinner one night. He'd been so proud to show them around the place and let them see what his hard work and dedication had allowed him to build. Miguel loved all the windows overlooking the gardens outside and the pool, too. Plus, there was a large room upstairs Luis planned to turn into a playroom for his son and fill with toys and books, just as soon as he had the free time to do it. Stacy had clearly been impressed, too, if a bit quieter about it. At first, Luis had been concerned that she didn't like it, but she'd assured him that wasn't it at all. She was just awed by it all, she said.

One day, he hoped to move them both in there and become a real family. There was even a separate guest house where her mother could stay when she visited.

Jackson had made it back fine from Big Pine Key, too. His leg was healing nicely, though he'd yet to fully explain to Luis what had happened. His brother was cranky as all get-out, too, moody and miserable, though they'd had precious little time to talk, what with Jackson overseeing the disaster relief and Luis busy with Miguel and Stacy. Someday soon, though, they needed to sit down and hash it all out, if for no other reason than to try to lift Jackson out of his surly mood.

Speaking of icy exteriors, he scrolled through his tablet to bring up the chart on the new patient in trauma bay two before knocking on the door and walking in to introduce himself.

"Hello, I'm Dr. Luis Durand. What seems to be the problem today?" he asked, professional smile firmly in place. He glanced down at his tablet again. "Mr. Rojas."

"My chest hurts," the older man said. According to his file he was seventy-one. "Thought I should have it checked out."

"Good thinking." Luis set his tablet aside to check the man's vitals. "I've looked over your chart, and there's no family history of heart disease."

"No, sir," the man said, wincing slightly when Luis pressed his stethoscope to his chest below his sternum. "Ow."

"That hurts?" Luis frowned. "Any injury to the area? Were you struck by anything there, or walk into anything?"

"Not that I can recall. It was fine this morning." Mr. Rojas took a deep breath when Luis prompted him to. He seemed a bit groggy, and his blood pressure was a tad low, but nothing too far out of the ideal range. "I was on my way to the gas station to fill up for the generator when the pain started. It scared me, so I came right over here. But I need to let my wife know where I am so she won't worry."

"We'll take care of letting your wife know, Mr. Rojas." Luis straightened and went over to check the EKG results that the nurse had running. All normal. Blood work, too.

"Right." Luis picked up his tablet and entered his orders. "I'm going to get an X-ray so I can see what's happening inside there, since everything seems normal so far. We can do that right down here, so it shouldn't take long." He went to the door to wave the nurse in. "I'll be back once I've seen those results."

Fifteen minutes later, Luis stood staring at the images on the computer screen at the nurses' station. At first glance, it all seemed normal, but then Luis squinted and leaned in farther. The aorta seemed wider than it should have been, which was concerning. The placement of the suspected enlargement coincided with where Mr. Rojas was experiencing his pain, too. He sat down and searched the hospital's records to see if the man had been treated at Key West General before and had any previous chest X-rays done. Sure enough, there was one from two years prior, when he'd been treated for flu and possible pneumonia. Pulling those films up onscreen, Luis compared them side by side and discovered that, yes, there was definitely enlargement there. Enough to make Luis suspect a possible rupture. It would explain all Mr. Rojas's symptoms and would require immediate surgery to repair. He contacted the cardiothoracic surgeon on call and explained the case to him before heading back in the patient's room.

The nurse was there, checking the monitors. "I called his wife. She's on her way."

"Good." Luis took a seat on the wheeled stool in the corner and moved to the patient's bedside. "Mr. Rojas, I've got good news and bad news for you. Which would you like first?"

The man grimaced. "Give me the bad. Considering what we've been through the last couple weeks, I want to get it over with."

"Okay. I looked at your X-ray results and compared them with the films you had done here at the hospital a few years ago, and it appears that you've ruptured your aorta."

"My what?"

"Aorta. It's the major blood vessel that runs from your heart through your torso." He pulled up a diagram on his tablet to show the man, pointing to the spot where the trouble was.

"How did that happen?" Mr. Rojas frowned. "I haven't done anything to that area, like I said. And I've been working to clean up the damage around my property, but nothing too strenuous."

"It's hard to say." Luis lowered the tablet to his lap again. "Most likely there was a congenital weakness in that area that has been present from birth. Without this rupture, we might never have known it was there.

Now that it's burst, however, we need to get it fixed. And fast, so you don't lose too much blood."

"Fixed?" Mr. Rojas's eyes widened. "You mean surgery?"

"Yes. I've contacted the specialist, and he's on his way to consult. He'll be able to give you more information about the procedure, but it's a good thing you came in today. It probably saved your life."

Ms. Rojas arrived a short time later, followed by the cardiothoracic surgeon, who took over the case from Luis with a hearty thank-you.

"Good work, Dr. Durand," the surgeon said. "Spotting a rupture like that on films is difficult. Lots of doctors miss it."

"I've had lots of practice discerning issues in less-than-optimal conditions," Luis said, stepping aside as the staff wheeled Mr. Rojas, with his wife by his side, out of the trauma bay and into the elevator to whisk him up to the OR. "Good luck with the surgery."

After that, things slowed down a bit, and Luis took the opportunity to catch up on all the paperwork he'd put off since before the hurricane. He had a small office on the first floor, near the ER, and he holed himself up in there with his stacks of paper to get some of it off his desk.

Unfortunately, he only got about an hour in before his phone buzzed in his pocket, interrupting his workflow. Luis pulled it out and answered without checking the caller ID. "Dr. Durand."

"Luis?" a voice said through the line. One he hadn't heard in over a year.

"Xavier." Luis dropped his pen on the desk and sat back, smiling. "How are you? Where are you?"

"I'm good. Busy as hell, but good. We just arrived in Honduras. They got hit hard by a storm down here, too, you know."

He did know. Luis had kept an eye on the news reports out of Central America more out of habit than anything. Docs on Duty, the charity group he had been a part of for his mission trips, spent a lot of time in that area helping the poor and underprivileged get the supplies and medical care they needed. He'd been eyeing the tropical storm that had formed right on Mathilda's heels and had cringed to hear that it had not only strengthened into a hurricane itself, but one even stronger than Mathilda had been. The people of Honduras and the surrounding countries hadn't stood a chance.

"How bad is it?" Luis asked, scrubbing a hand over his face. He'd gone to Haiti after Hurricane Matthew, a category five storm, and had seen the devastation firsthand—two hundred thousand homes destroyed, over five hundred people dead, $2.8 billion of destruction. The small island nation was still recovering. It was times like that his near-eidetic memory was more curse than blessing. For years, each time he closed his eyes, he'd see the faces of the survivors, hear their cries for help, feel the anguish of those who'd lost everything. The memories from that time replayed over and over his head, spurring him onward to do more, be of more service. Even now, he felt the pull to rush to action, despite all the things tethering him to his new life in Key West.

"Worse than you can imagine. The damage from the storm was bad enough, but now we've got landslides on top of it." Xavier took a deep breath then said the thing Luis had been dreading since he'd answered the call. "Look, buddy. I know you left this behind and you've settled down in Florida, but we could really use your help here."

The tug on Luis's soul was strong, almost as strong as the one keeping him here for Stacy and Miguel. He bit his lip and sighed. "I can't. I'm head of emergency medicine at Key West General now. I've got commitments and constraints." He tapped his fingers on the desk to expel some of the adrenaline burning through his bloodstream. He couldn't walk away from his life here, not now. His community needed him. Stacy needed him. Miguel needed him. "Sorry, but I just can't. Perhaps I can pass the word around to my colleagues, though, see if anyone else is interested."

"Thanks. I appreciate it, but we need people with experience in these conditions." Xavier murmured something to someone off the line then got back on with Luis. "Listen, we'd work with you on the logistics and the scheduling. I know you've got other stuff going on right now and I wouldn't ask if I wasn't desperate, but we really need help here, Luis. Please at least think about it. One last time? Even if it's only for a month or a few weeks."

One last time.

After the call ended, Luis sat there at his desk, staring down at his paperwork without really seeing it, torn and twisted inside. When he'd left the charity the previous year, it was with the assurance that they had more than enough adequate doctors to take over his position with the team. But the past twelve months had been beyond rough on a global scale, and it seemed their resources had been depleted faster than the charity could recoup them. If the call had come six months earlier— hell, even last month—he'd have put in for an extended leave and gone without a second thought, but now...

Well, now he had more than himself to consider. He had Stacy and Miguel. He'd made a commitment to them, too. Had promised to be there for them and try to work things out. And given Stacy's past, she would not take his leaving again well, no matter the reason.

He felt stuck between a rock and a hard place with no easy solution. He needed to talk to Stacy. Thankfully they were both off tonight, for once. He'd planned to have a romantic evening at his house. Cook dinner, relax, let Miguel play with his toys while he and Stacy enjoyed each other's company.

Tension knotted tight within him. The call to service was one he felt obligated to answer, but Stacy needed him now, too. They were just starting out on this new path together and he didn't want to do anything to risk their relationship or the one with his son by leaving again. And given Stacy's past, there was the possibility she'd see it as a betrayal. But he wanted things to be open and honest between them, so he'd tell her. They'd discuss it and then they'd decide. Maybe it wouldn't be as bad as he imagined.

The dread knotting in his gut said otherwise.

CHAPTER ELEVEN

"LISTEN, SWEETHEART," STACY'S mother said over the phone line as Stacy finished up in her office at the fire station. "I'm thinking of staying up here in Miami awhile longer, if that's all right with you."

"You're an adult, Mom. You don't need my permission." Stacy switched her cell phone to her other ear as she tidied her desk. "Is everything okay with your friend?"

"Oh yes. He's doing much better now. In fact, we're thinking about taking a short trip to Bermuda to celebrate his recovery, once they get all this storm damage resolved."

"Oh." Stacy paused for a second. Maybe this thing between her mom and her mom's new friend went beyond platonic. If so, it would be the first time in Stacy's memory. She hoped for her mother's sake it was good. Her mom deserved it. She'd worked so hard raising Stacy on her own. She deserved love and happiness. She just wished she'd gotten to meet the mysterious man first. Concerned on her mother's behalf, she said, "What's his name again?"

"Ted, dear," her mother chided. "And you knew that." Stacy couldn't help grinning. She'd been doing that a lot lately since Luis had reappeared in her life. "You're right, I did. Well, that's fine. I'll need to shuffle Miguel's schedule, but it shouldn't be too much of an issue."

"I should hope not. Isn't Luis helping you these days?" her mother asked.

"Yes, he is. And *you* knew that." Stacy turned the words back against her mom. They both laughed.

"He's a good man," her mother said.

Surprised, Stacy stopped and leaned a hip against her desk. "Really? You think so?"

"I do. I'll admit when you first told me you'd found him again, I was skeptical," her mother said. "And after what I went through with your father, I think I had every right to be. But from the happiness in your voice and what you've told me about how close he and Miguel are, I think he's proved himself."

Her mom was right. Luis did make her happy. And he'd been nothing but kind and loyal and trustworthy the past few weeks. He had proven himself many times over.

The last of the barriers around Stacy's heart crumbled to dust, and in their place blossomed love. Deep, abiding, undeniable love. She'd been so scared, put it off for so long, waiting, watching.

But finally, she admitted to herself that yes. She loved Luis Durand.

And if he asked her again to be with him, she would.

Nervous butterflies took flight in her stomach. Was that what tonight was about?

He'd been a bit evasive when he'd invited her the other day, only telling her to dress nicely and to bring Miguel's favorite toys along.

"Sweetheart?" her mother said. "Are you still there?"

"Uh, yeah." Stacy straightened and finished clearing the clutter from her desk. "I'm sorry."

"I said I'd keep that Luis around. At least until I get back to Key West, then I'll want my grandson to myself for a while." Her mom chuckled.

"Right. Sure," she said, fiddling with her ponytail with her free hand, distracted.

She'd nearly conquered that niggle of doubt inside her that warned disaster was just around the corner and Luis would walk away again, run to some far-off land and leave her and Miguel behind, just like her father had. Most days, she didn't even think about it anymore, staying busy with work on her shifts and Miguel during her time off. Then there were the hours in bed with Luis, when she let go completely and just savored her time with him, touching, kissing, holding one another, talking about anything and everything. Those were the times when she imagined a future with them together, raising their son, having more babies, living a good life in Key West. Even if that house of his made her feel like a country church mouse at a high-society wedding.

The fire station alarm went off, signaling another emergency run. Damn. "I need to go, Mom. I'll talk to you tomorrow. Love you!"

"Love you, too, honey. Good luck tonight. Kiss Miguel for me."

"I will." Stacy ended the call then rushed out to the equipment room to suit up with the rest of her crew. "What do we have?"

"Ambulance call. MVA. Mother and baby inside with injuries," one of her crew called while she finished grabbing her gear. "Aren't you about done, Captain?"

"Last run for this shift," she said, sliding into the truck just before they pulled out of the station, lights and sirens blazing.

The ride to the scene was short, as it was only about a mile away, and Stacy surveyed the wreck while the rest of her crew got out. Police were already on scene directing traffic, but the EMTs hadn't arrived yet. Not uncommon and why fire responded, too. Most fire-fighters cross-trained as paramedics so they could re-spond in emergencies. The extra boost in pay didn't hurt, either.

Stacy climbed out of the rig last and walked over to the SUV that was resting on its side. From what she could see, the other car had T-boned it, tipping the SUV over and sending it skidding into the opposite lane of traffic. The windows had shattered on impact, and the airbags had deployed. One of her crew was talking to the female crash victim in the front seat now, who seemed alert, if understandably panicked. In the back-ground, the tiny, high-pitched wail of an infant could be heard from the rear of the vehicle, and Stacy's heart squeezed in response.

"What's the situation?" she asked, walking over to get a better look inside the wreckage. She stooped down to peer through the spiderweb of cracked glass and spotted the car seat, still strapped in tight, holding the squalling baby safely within its padded confines. The tension inside her eased slightly. She carefully knocked on the glass and cooed to the infant inside. "It's okay, little one. We're going to get you out of there, I promise."

"Is my baby okay?" the woman called from the front of the car, the seat belt cutting painfully across her clavicle, from what Stacy could tell. "Please, help my baby."

"Your baby looks fine," Stacy said, straightening and moving to the mother. The woman looked young, maybe twenty-two, twenty-three, with dark hair and light blue eyes. There was a cut on her forehead that was bleeding profusely and most likely a broken collarbone from that seat belt, but otherwise she seemed all right. They'd transport them both to the nearest hospital to be on the safe side, regardless. "We're just waiting on the ambulance to get here before we get you both out of there." In the distance more sirens wailed, and Stacy patted the woman's hand. "Sounds like that's them coming now."

"Oh, thank God," the woman said, and sure enough, minutes later, the EMTs and fire crew had both mom and baby out of the vehicle and onto stretchers with neck braces in place for transport to Key West General.

Stacy and her crew left the accident scene and headed back to the station house. It was going on 5:00 p.m. now, and she needed to get home to change then pick up Miguel from her neighbor, who was watching him this afternoon, since both she and Luis had had to work. Luis was sending a car to get them at seven for dinner at his place.

Fresh adrenaline fizzed in her blood at the thought. They'd been together for a few weeks now, and things were going well. He was everything she'd ever wanted in a man—smart, strong, kind, supportive—and he was wonderful with Miguel. The boy loved his father already, and each day they spent together only tightened the bond they shared.

It was both amazing and terrifying.

As a little girl, Stacy had thought her father hung the moon and stars. She could still remember the nights he'd sit with her and read to her or tell her stories about princesses and knights in shining armor. She'd thought her daddy would always be there. She'd been wrong.

"He's a good man. He's proved himself."

Her mother's words rang through her mind again as Stacy stared at her reflection in the mirror a short while later. She'd chosen a dark green sheath dress to wear tonight, with matching flats. It was dressy without being too fancy and she hoped it was enough for Luis. He always looked perfect, no matter what he wore, with his handsome face and fit body. Sometimes she felt a bit dumpy, with her sensible clothes and curvy shape.

And his house…

Lord, it made her little apartment look like a shoebox. Three stories, all glass and steel and modern luxury. He even had a second house outside for guests. She'd been afraid to touch anything the first time they'd been there in case she broke something. But Luis had been so proud, and so she tried to make herself comfortable there for his sake. But Stacy had grown up lower middle class, and she never forgot her roots.

"Mommy," Miguel called from down the hall. "Do I look okay?"

She walked into his room to find him dressed like a little clone of Luis, in dark pants and a white button-down shirt. Like father, like son. She stood behind him at the full-length mirror and adjusted his collar then bent to kiss the top of his head. "You look very handsome, honey."

Miguel blushed and squirmed under her hands on his shoulders. "Mom…"

"Fine." She chuckled and ruffled his dark curls. "You look like Daddy. How about that?"

"Okay." He grinned up at her. "Is it time to go?"

Stacy checked her watch then nodded. "Just about. Let me grab my purse and then we can go downstairs to wait for the car."

The ride to Luis's house, in the exclusive community of Casa Marina on Flagler Drive, was short. They entered the property through the front gate in the white-washed walls surrounding the compound and drove up the drive to stop beneath a portico. The style of architecture was midcentury modern, Luis had told her the first time she'd been here, and he'd designed it himself. His pride in the work was evident in his sparkling dark eyes. The driver got out and opened the door for her and Miguel, and they climbed from the back seat and walked to the door, where Luis was waiting for them, looking breathtakingly gorgeous in a suit and tie. He smiled widely at her and bent to pick up Miguel, kissing the top of the little boy's head before putting him down to let him scamper into the house and run wild.

"Hey," Luis said, bending to kiss her. This close, she could see the faint lines of stress at the corners of his eyes and around his mouth, and for a moment that tiny niggle of worry burrowed into her gut before she could stop it. Then she pushed it aside. Her mother was right. Luis was a good man. He'd more than proved himself. He wasn't like her father. He would be here for her and Miguel. Given how hard they'd both been working the past week or so, Luis was probably just tired. Still, when she pulled back, she whispered, "Everything okay?"

He smiled and ushered her inside, his hand at the

small of her back sending a warm tingle of awareness through her. "Come, let me get you some wine. Dinner is almost ready."

The interior of the house was just as stunning as she remembered, all open spaces and lots of windows. The inlaid marble floors were two-tone, white around the edges with darker gray in the middle, and the furniture was all oversize and comfy-looking, in shades of ivory and taupe with brighter green and turquoise accents. Luis had mentioned his home had even been featured in *Architectural Digest* earlier in the year, and she could see why.

It was stunning, just like him.

"Please, have a seat," he said, settling her on a large sofa in the living room before going to check on Miguel in the next room, where he'd already spread out his blocks and was busy building something. Stacy could see him through the door, and the picture of father and son together, heads bent as they worked together, warmed her heart.

A few minutes later, Luis returned with a glass of chardonnay for her and a deep ruby-red cabernet for himself. They chatted for a while about their days and about Miguel, then Stacy said, "Oh, and I talked to my mom this afternoon before I left work."

"Hmm." He watched her over the rim of his wineglass, seeming a bit distracted. "How is she doing?"

"Good. In fact, she's planning on staying up in Miami for a while longer with her friend."

Luis nodded, frowning down into his wineglass. "The friend is recovering well, I hope?"

"Yes. So well, in fact, he and my mother are planning a trip to Bermuda together soon." Stacy chuckled, her pulse pounding. "Guess love finds you when you least expect it."

"Yes, it does." Luis looked up at her then, his expression serious. "Listen, *mi sirenita*. There is something we need to discuss tonight and—"

"Mommy!" Miguel ran in to climb up on the sofa onto her lap. Luckily, Stacy moved her hand out of the way fast to avoid spilling her wine. "I'm hungry. When are we going to eat?"

She looked over at Luis, stomach nosediving to her toes. He wanted to talk. About what? Was her intuition correct for once? Was he going to ask her to take the next step with him in their relationship? "Uh, I don't know. Daddy?"

"How about now?" Luis said, setting his empty glass on the coffee table, not meeting her gaze. He stood and headed over to the open kitchen, from where the delicious scents of roasted vegetables and chicken drifted. "Just give me a moment to get everything ready to serve."

"Here." Stacy set Miguel on the seat beside hers and stood, carrying both their wineglasses to the kitchen and setting them gently in the sink. "Let me help you."

"Thanks," Luis said to her over his shoulder as he pulled a pan out of the oven. "If you could set the table, that would be great. Everything is on the island there."

"Sure." Stacy did as he asked, keeping one eye on Miguel as she did so. He'd become fascinated with the various sculptures around the living room, staring up at them like they were aliens or something. If she and Miguel did end up moving in here, those statues would have to go or risk becoming casualties of an overactive four-year-old boy. She finished setting out the plates and silverware and napkins then returned to the kitchen. Standing shoulder to shoulder with Luis at the granite island, she whispered, "What did you want to talk to me about?"

"Not now," he said, dishing up yummy-looking roasted chicken and veggies into a serving dish. "Let's have a nice meal first."

Her gut twisted a little at that. If the talk was indeed about them moving in together, then that would be a happy thing and would endanger their "nice" meal, would it? Unless he was worried about her saying no again. Maybe that was it. Frowning, she carried the serving dish into the dining room area and set it atop the long, thick glass table. It reminded her of the fancy dinners she'd seen on the telenovelas her mom used to watch on TV. Fancy people eating fancy food in fancy clothes. Considering what she and Luis were wearing, maybe they were getting posh all of a sudden.

Chuckling, she corralled her son into the dining room and got him set up in one of the chairs, then pulled it closer to her own at the end of the table so she could keep an eye on him while Luis finished bringing the salad and bread to the table. They both sat down and he poured her more wine and then they were eating. The food tasted every bit as good as it looked, and even picky eater Miguel cleaned his plate. Then he was off to play with his blocks again while she and Luis finished their wine at the table.

"So, that was very good. I didn't know you were such a good cook," Stacy said, hoping to ease that stress in his face that had only seemed to worsen through dinner. "Where did you learn to make such wonderful things?"

"During my mission trips," he said, wiping his mouth with his napkin. "On my days off, I always tried to experience the local culture as much as I could, and what better way to do that then through their food? I leaned to make dishes directly from the people in the villages I was there to help. A good exchange, I think."

"Agreed."

Awkward silence descended as she stared down at her empty plate and Luis looked anywhere but at her. Finally, he reached over and covered her hand with his. "Stacy, I got a phone call today while I was at the ER."

All the elation that had been swelling inside her like a balloon over the possibility of this being it—the moment he proclaimed his love and asked her to be his—deflated like a pricked balloon.

"Oh," she managed to say around her constricted throat, swallowing more wine to dislodge the lump now present there. "From who?"

"An old friend, Xavier Lewis. He runs the charity I used to work with, Docs on Duty."

And that lump became a boulder, crashing down into her stomach and leaving a gaping hole of shadows behind it. No. No, no, no. This could not be happening. She wanted to plug her ears with her fingers and make noise so she couldn't hear him, wanted to get up and run away. But she sat, silent and stony as he continued talking.

"I don't know if you've had a chance to watch much of the news this week, but Central America, and Honduras in particular, was hard hit with a category five hurricane a few days ago. Xavier and his team are there now, and it's bad, *mi sirenita*." He rubbed his thumb over her skin absently, his gaze far off and cloudy as he seemed to be remembering other times, other disasters. Deep down, she knew what was coming, and yet it still broke her when he said it. "He called because he needs my help. Desperately. I told him I would need to talk to you first before I agreed."

Stacy swallowed hard, her mouth dry and her eyes stinging. Of course he would run off to the rescue, because that's what Luis did. He was a good man. The best. Except where did that leave her and Miguel? Right back where they started. "I see," she croaked out, slipping her hand from beneath his. "How long will you be gone?"

Luis scowled, closing his eyes a moment. "I haven't said I'd go yet, but if I do, it would probably be for at least a month, maybe longer, depending on the conditions. Xavier said that in addition to the storm damage and flooding, they've got a serious risk of landslides from additional rains sweeping through the area."

Oh God.

Bile rose in her throat, and she gulped more wine to keep her dinner down. So, not only would she lose Luis, the man she'd fallen in love with against her better judgment and let into both her heart and her son's life, but there was a good possibility Luis could die as well.

She closed her eyes and inhaled deep through her nose. Stupid Stacy. So, so stupid. She knew better than to believe that fairy tales came true and life worked out happily ever after. She didn't begrudge Luis his charity work—in fact, she admired it. She just wished it didn't cost her everything she'd ever wanted. A home, stability, the security of knowing that someone would be there for her and Miguel no matter what at the end of the day.

"*Mi sirenita,*" Luis said, reaching over to cup her cheek. "Please. Stacy. Please say something. Talk to me. I won't go if you don't want me to. I just—"

"Just what?" She turned to him, shaking off his touch, hurt and anger pushing her to her feet, the anger mainly directed at herself for becoming so dependent on Luis. "Look, go if you want to. I need to get home because I need to figure out childcare for Miguel since you'll be gone. If you can let me know your itinerary once you get it, so I can schedule appropriately around it, I'd appreciate it." She put her napkin down and started toward the next room where her son was playing. "Come on, Miguel. Time to go home."

"Stacy, wait." Luis stood as well, following after her and taking her arm. "Please, let's discuss this. It doesn't have to change anything between us. I'll be gone a few weeks, a month at most, then we can pick up where we left off here."

"Can we?" She whirled to face him, tears welling in her eyes against her wishes. "And what about the next time, Luis? And the time after that? Because there's always going to be some dangerous disaster somewhere in the world that you're going to want to race off to. And what—Miguel and I are just supposed to sit at home and wait for you to come back? We're supposed to put our lives on hold while you keep doing things for everyone but yourself?"

She shook her head and pulled away, forcing a smile for Miguel, who was watching them closely now. "I'm sorry, but I can't do that. I know what it's like not to be enough. Hell, I've lived that my whole life, and I will not put my son through that. I won't. We won't be second best to your need to save the world. If that's what you want, fine. Go. Be a superhero. But we won't be waiting for you when you get back. I just can't do that. I'm sorry."

She walked over and helped Miguel put his blocks back into the carry case, then took his hand and headed for the front door, where the car and driver were still waiting beneath the portico. Apparently, the guy had nothing better to do in life. Good for him. Good for her, too. She charged outside, Miguel by her side, and helped her son into the back seat as the driver held the door for them.

"Stacy, please." Luis rushed outside to stand behind her. "*Mi sirenita*, don't do this. I thought we were building something strong between us. Don't tear that all down over one more mission trip."

Cheeks damp and broken heart thudding painfully against her rib cage, Stacy said, "It's not just one more, though, is it Luis? There'll always be another. And another. And what if you die over there, huh? What am I supposed to do then? How do I tell Miguel that the father he loves and just found is gone again and he's never coming back?"

Stacy lost it then, tears flowing freely now. "I'm sorry, Luis. I can't. I just can't. I already lost one man I loved. I won't sit by and do it again. Goodbye. You can say goodbye to Miguel tomorrow at my apartment when you come by to watch him."

With that, she climbed into the car beside her son and closed the door, leaving Luis behind in the drive to watch them go, his face growing smaller and smaller in the rear window until they turned the corner and he disappeared completely.

"Mommy?" Miguel asked from beside her as she did her best to keep her sobs inside. "Are you okay?"

"No, honey, I'm not." She pulled Miguel into her side and put her head back against the seat as he hugged her tight. "But I will be tomorrow. We'll be fine."

Somehow, some way, she had to keep going. Alone. Even if her battered heart might never heal again.

That had gone worse than Luis had expected. And it was all his fault.

He stood in the drive, watching the woman he loved leave his life, until the red taillights of the car disappeared from sight, then he went back inside. Cleaned up dinner to keep himself busy, then took off his suit coat and loosened his tie before slumping down on the sofa with another glass of wine in his hand. He wasn't on call, so no need to worry about staying sober.

If only the alcohol could ease the pain in his heart.

God, what a mess he'd made of things tonight. He'd hoped to explain it to her gently, get her to see that it wasn't a big deal. They'd both been working so much that they hadn't seen each other a lot over the last week or so anyway. Him going to Honduras would just be like an extended period of that for a few extra weeks, and then they'd be back to normal again.

He would come back. He'd always come back to her and Miguel. Always.

And what if you die over there?

Her question returned to haunt him, and he drained his glass in one long swallow before pouring more. It was a good cabernet. Dark and deep, just like the hole he'd dug for himself.

Honestly, he'd never really considered that part of things before. He'd just gone, driven to fulfill the vow he'd made to his parents so long ago. Determined to make his life count, to honor the sacrifices they'd made so he could be here today.

But when would it be enough? When would he be allowed to rest and have a life of his own choosing? When would he have repaid his debt?

He drank his second glass of wine and poured a third, staring across the living room and out through the windows to the lush tropical gardens beyond. He was tired, exhausted, after years of giving, giving, giving. And there was still so much more to be done.

Luis conceded, reluctantly, that Stacy was right. It wouldn't be just this mission if he went back. Because there would always be more storms, more earthquakes, more impoverished areas that needed help. He could do what he could, but it would never, ever be enough.

Sinking back into the plush sofa cushions, he stared up at the ceiling, Stacy's tearstained face flashing before his eyes like a tragic movie. He hadn't even gotten to say goodbye to Miguel.

Miguel. My son. *Mijito.*

If he lost his relationship with his son because of some damned fool trip halfway around the world, that would be a tragedy indeed. He'd only known Miguel a few weeks, but he loved the boy more than his own life. He'd do anything for his son. Would do anything for Stacy, too.

Mi sirenita. My mermaid. He'd thought of her that way since their first night together on the beach.

He loved Stacy, too, more than any other woman ever. His beautiful, strong, stubborn siren.

But can I stay?

Chest aching, he shook his head and stood again, restless and weary. There were no easy answers.

He felt stretched in two different directions and near to snapping. Usually, Luis was the person everyone else came to with their problems, and he solved them. But now he needed help, and there wasn't anyone to turn to. Jackson had his own problems going on, though he'd yet to share them with Luis. His brother was driving himself into the ground, constantly working and taking extra shifts as if the devil himself was on his tail.

Luis knew the feeling.

Maybe he'd head down to the Duck Bill Pub soon and talk to his father about things. His dad always seemed to know best, and Lord knew Luis needed some good advice.

CHAPTER TWELVE

"IT'S OVER, MOM," Stacy said on the phone. "Done. He's going off to Honduras, and Miguel and I are getting on with our lives."

"Oh, honey," her mother said. "I'm so sorry."

"Me, too." It had been six days since the dinner at Luis's house, and each time Stacy thought about that night, she really thought she ought to feel better about her actions than she did. In truth, she felt horrid. She hadn't slept more than a few hours all week, despite pulling extra shifts to cover several guys who were off sick. Yet each time she lay down and closed her eyes, all she could see was Luis's face as he'd pleaded with her to understand, the sadness in his eyes, the empty, hollow feeling where her heart used to be. She'd figured she'd cried herself out by now, but damn if fresh tears didn't sting her eyes now. "I love him, Mom. And he's gone. Just like Daddy."

"No, sweetie. Oh God. Is that what this is all about?" Her mother shushed her and murmured soothing words until Stacy got a grip on herself again. Her poor mom was always good at cheering other people up, but Stacy doubted now if she'd ever find her joy again. Silence echoed for a few moments on the phone line before her mother continued, after a huge sigh. "Well, I guess maybe that is what you got from that business with your father. But you should know, honey, that him leaving was the best thing that ever happened to us."

"What?" Surprise jolted Stacy straight out of sadness into astonishment. "How can you say that, Mom? After he left you had to work your tail off to keep a roof over our heads."

"True. But without him constantly nagging and putting me down, I got my self-esteem back. And hard work never hurt anyone." Her mother's tone turned defensive. "We always had enough, didn't we?"

"Yes, barely."

"Enough is enough. No need for more. And being on my own, with you to take care of, made me work harder."

Stacy's chest constricted at the long, horrible pause that followed. "He just left us. Walked out and never returned. I never want Miguel to have to go through that. I have to protect him. This isn't just about me."

"This is everything to do with you," her mother countered, her tone exasperated. "Listen to me, honey. You were very little when your father left, but we were both so young when we had you. Neither of us knew what we were doing, and yes, we married for all the wrong reasons. I'm sorry that him leaving and us fighting beforehand is all you remember, honey, but there were good times, too. And yes, I cried, but…"

Her mother's voice turned rough with emotion, and Stacy sat up from where she'd been lying on her sofa, devouring yet another pint of ice cream, same as she'd done each night after putting Miguel to bed since the breakup with Luis. She should buy stock in the dairy company that made these. She'd be a rich woman soon. She set her food and spoon aside and tucked her knees beneath her chin, sensing this was important. "What about the tears, Mom?"

"Not all of them are bad." Her mother sniffled and gave a little laugh. "Sometimes they can be cleansing, cathartic, too. Sometimes, they help clear away the dirt of what's been and show you a new path forward."

Stacy considered that a moment, then took a deep breath. Maybe her mother was right. Maybe she and Luis had needed to have that fight, have that pain of separation to figure out where they wanted to go from here.

"Without your dad leaving, hard as that was, I never would've put myself through school, never would've gotten my master's degree and moved up into upper management at the insurance firm. Yes, it was hard, but I wouldn't have changed it for the world." She sighed. "My only regret is that it took time away from you. And obviously left you thinking things that weren't right. My commitment to bettering our lives meant I had to work long hours and crazy shifts for a while. But after everyone told me I'd ruined my life and my chance at anything good by getting pregnant and married so young, I had to prove them wrong, honey. I wanted to show the world that I could make it on my own." Her mother chuckled. "Where do you think your stubborn-ness comes from, eh?"

"So, Daddy leaving was all…okay?" Stacy asked, confused and more than a little stunned.

"No. He should have said goodbye to you, but he had problems of his own and he needed to deal with them to be any good to anyone, let alone a child. I know that hurt you, honey, but it really was for the best. You saw my tears, heard our arguments. Those came from both of us being so tired and young and jealous and guilty. He had his own path to follow and we had ours. And I think you and I did just fine for ourselves."

Stacy was crying again by the time her mom finished. "Oh God. You're right. We did do fine. But I said some awful things to Luis and didn't even give him a chance to explain himself the other night, only thought the worst of him even though he's the best man I've ever met, Mom. Seriously. He loves Miguel and he takes care of us. He takes care of everyone. And I just turned my back on him." She dropped her head onto her forearms and sobbed. "I've ruined everything. I'm so stupid."

"You are not stupid!" Her mother's fierce words jarred Stacy out of her sorrow for a minute, and she snapped her head up once more. "And don't ever talk about yourself like that again, young lady. You are smart and talented and funny and kind. You have a good heart and a smart brain. You're the mother of my grandson, who's the most perfect child ever born. And if Luis is half the man I think he is and you say he is, he'll forgive you. It may take a little work, but the best things in life often do. Now pick yourself up off that sofa and stop stuffing your feelings down with sugar and deal with it."

Abashed, Stacy quickly hid her empty ice cream carton and spoon, the wiped the double fudge remnants off the corners of her mouth with her sweatshirt sleeve. Her messy hair was piled atop her head, and she needed a good scrub. She'd done the bare minimum this past week, taking time off from the fire department to watch Miguel and wallow in her grief over losing Luis. She hadn't answered her phone or gone outside in days.

Now, though, something inside her had changed, or shifted, or both.

For the first time since their awful fight, Stacy felt a glimmer of hope. Hope that perhaps if she got her act together and put the past in the past and groveled enough, she might just be able to win Luis back.

It would take a lot of patience and care and love, but she was willing to try.

"I lost her," Luis said, sitting at the bar of an empty Duck Bill Pub.

He'd finally made it in to see his father, though it was days later than he'd planned. Days where he'd spent nearly every waking hour at the hospital because it was easier than sitting at home in his empty house, replaying that fight with Stacy over and over again in his head. Missing Miguel, missing Stacy, missing everything he'd found during those precious weeks with them.

Family, faith, a future he wanted more than he wanted his next breath.

There'd been so many times where he'd almost charged over to her apartment and pounded on her door, demanded she see him, talk to him, let him try to work this out between them, but he'd stopped himself. Stacy wouldn't respond well to force. She deserved consideration, patience, care.

He toyed with his glass of seltzer water, frowning. He'd never been much of a drinker, since alcohol basically went straight to his head and made him sleepy.

He also didn't like the way it made him feel, out of control and reckless. Take that night on the beach five years ago. He'd been drunk then and look what happened. Or the night of the dinner with Stacy. He'd finished off that bottle of cabernet after she'd gone and woken up with hell's own hangover the next morning. And he'd then had to pull an all-nighter at work. Not good. Not good at all.

His father finished chopping up fruit for the garnishes and glanced up at him. "This the woman you were in here with a few weeks back?"

"Yeah." Luis rubbed the back of his neck. That had been the night Stacy had told him about Miguel. The night she'd changed his life forever. He wished now he could go back to then, start over again, do better. Be better.

"She's a firefighter," his dad said.

"Yep."

"I recognize her from her crew. They come in here sometimes for dinner. Good group."

Luis had thought he'd seen Stacy a few times over the past six days, and he'd perked up each time a new emergency run came in or fire truck passed, thinking he might catch a glimpse of her, but no. She'd been nowhere around, and damn. He missed her. So much it physically hurt. Missed talking to her. Missed laughing with her. Missed holding her and kissing her and sleeping with her and waking up next to her. Missed taking care of Miguel with her and even missed doing dishes with her.

He had it bad and that wasn't good, because Stacy wanted nothing more to do with him.

His phone buzzed in his pocket, but he ignored it.

Most likely it was Xavier again, and he still hadn't made up his mind about that mission. Part of him said he should just go, get out of Key West for a while and help some people along the way. And if a mountain of mud slid down and buried him, well, it couldn't be any worse than what he was going through right now.

His father kept working, quietly. Too quietly.

"I came here for advice, Dad," Luis said at last, scrubbing a hand over his face. His stubble felt rough against his palm, and he probably looked as scruffy as he felt. He hadn't even bothered to change out of his scrubs after his last shift, just headed over here to hang his head and brood. "You've always been there for me since I was six years old and you and Mom took me in. I don't know what to do." He sighed and stared down into his seltzer water like the answers he sought might be in there. "I thought I was living my life in the way I should. All I ever wanted to do was make my birth parents proud. Make you and Mom proud. But I don't feel like I'm doing anyone any favors now."

Footsteps echoed behind the bar followed by the squeak of the little door that led out into the restaurant as his dad came to sit next to him.

"Let me get this straight, son," his dad said. "You and this firefighter lady have feelings for each other, but you had a fight and now she won't see you. Is that it?"

He hadn't told them about Miguel, not yet. It still hurt too much, and he and Stacy had never gotten around to discussing exactly how they were going to break that news to everyone. So he just nodded.

"Right." One of the few patrons in the place walked over to the jukebox along the wall and slid in a few quarters. The overhead speakers crackled, and a song began. Some new country tune. His father shook his head. "Thank God it isn't 'Wind Beneath My Wings' again. Since the storm, people think that's funny to play. I've heard it so many times I think my head's going to explode."

Luis managed a little chuckle at that.

"Seriously, though. Let me start off by saying your mother and I *are* proud of you, son. Always have been, always will be. You and Jackson are the best things that ever happened to Juanita and me. And as far as your birth parents? Kid, they'd be proud of you no matter what. You could sweep streets or race cars or whatever you chose to do. As long as it made you happy. That's all they ever wanted for you. Just to be happy and have the freedom to live the life you want."

After a grunt, Luis scowled. "They died bringing me here to this country. That kind of sacrifice demands greatness."

"And you don't think saving lives in your ER is greatness?" His dad gave him a side glance. "Not sure I can think of anything more heroic, son."

"It's not enough."

"Not enough?" His father snorted. "Wait a second. Is that why you spent years racing around the globe to one hot spot after another? You were trying to repay some kind of debt to them?"

It didn't sound quite so noble when his dad put it that way, but still Luis gave a curt nod.

"I see." His father inhaled deep then let it out slow, a sure sign a lecture was coming. "Okay. Well, first off, let me tell you how ridiculous that is." Luis started to object, but his dad held up a hand to stop him. "Now before you get all upset about it, hear me out. I never met your parents, that's true. But being first-generation Cuban myself, I know from whence they came. And I can tell you that the only reason any of us escaped that repressive regime was freedom, pure and simple. And that word meant different things to everyone, but it came down to being able to do what you want, when you want, in whatever way you want. For yourself and for your family. Your parents took that dangerous trip in the middle of the night through rough waters because they wanted you to be happy, Luis. That's all. There was no debt to repay, no obligation you had to fulfill attached to it. They wanted you to make a life for yourself of your choosing, to have love and a family of your own someday. That's all they ever wanted. And if you can do that, then you will have fulfilled whatever promise you made to them."

It took a moment for those words to sink into his mind, really sink in, but when they did, Luis felt like a huge burden had been lifted off his shoulders, one he'd been carrying his whole life without realizing it. He raised his head and looked at his father. "You really think so?"

"Son, I know so," his dad said, grinning. "Is that the advice you needed?"

"I think so." Luis downed the rest of his seltzer water in one gulp, feeling more energetic and hopeful than he had in days. He knew what he needed to do nnow. All he had to figure out was how to go about it. "Thanks, Dad. I've got to go. There are some things I need to take care of."

"Sure, sure," his father said, picking up his towel again and slinging it over his shoulder. As Miguel crossed the threshold out onto sunny Duval Street, his dad called from behind him. "And if you see that brother of yours, tell Jackson to call me. Haven't heard from him in a while, either."

CHAPTER THIRTEEN

STACY TOOK A deep breath and stared at herself in the mirror on the wall of her office at the fire station. After the conversation with her mother yesterday, she knew she needed to find a way to talk to Luis again and apologize for how she'd reacted to his news, but she was still figuring out what to say.

Frankly, she was shaken. Finding out that all the things she'd thought about her parents' breakup all these years weren't true had left her reeling. If she'd been so off about that, what other things had she gotten wrong?

Luis, for one.

Yep. No way around that. She'd screwed up with him big-time. The one man she should've let into her heart and she'd stonewalled him. Well, no more. For what felt like the first time in forever, she was open. Open and raw and vulnerable, and it was scary as hell. Also exhilarating, but also frightening.

What if he couldn't forgive her? What if he decided she and Miguel were more trouble than they were worth and left Key West permanently? What if she lost him all over again when she'd only just finally found him?

All the turmoil left her throat tight and her stomach churning. Of course, it didn't help that the fire chief wanted to see her in his office, either. The last thing she was focused on at this point was work, but she needed to pull it together. If she and Miguel were going to be on their own from now on, she needed her job more than ever.

After a deep breath to steady and center herself, Stacy adjusted her white uniform shirt and smoothed a hand down her black pants, then headed out into the hall toward her boss's office. She passed several of her crew along the way, and they gave her encouraging nods or smiles. Seemed the gossip mill around here was alive and well, which was another reason why she hadn't told anyone about her and Luis. A good thing, she supposed, since it could all be over.

Her heart squeezed painfully at that, and she resisted the urge to rub her chest over the sore spot, instead raising her hand to knock on the fire chief's door.

There seemed to be fewer people around the station house today for some reason. Even the chief's secretary wasn't at her desk. But it had been slow today, and maybe people were taking time off after the storm to rest and recharge, she supposed.

"Come in, AC Williams," a low, masculine voice said. When she entered, he waved her into a chair in front of his desk while he finished up a phone call. "Yes. Fine. Thank you, Mayor. I'll get right on it."

Chief Hernandez ended the call then smiled across the desk at Stacy. "Thanks for taking time out of your busy day to speak with me."

"Of course," Stacy said, swallowing hard against the arid desert that had formed in her mouth. "What did you want to see me about, sir?"

"First off, let me commend you and your crew on a job well done during Hurricane Mathilda and the subsequent cleanup. I'm meeting with all my ACs to pass on my well wishes to the rest of the department."

Stacy gave a small nod. "I'll be sure to let them know. They'll appreciate it, I'm certain."

"Good." The chief clasped his hands atop his desk. A bulky man, he was in his midfifties, with thick salt-and-pepper hair and a handlebar moustache. "Moving on to my second order of business then. I'm sure you've heard Battalion Chief Webber is retiring next month?"

"Uh…" Stacy blinked at him. She'd vaguely heard something about it a few weeks ago, but what with the storm and all, it had fallen off her radar. "His wife was sick, I think?"

"Yes. Breast cancer. But she beat it, thank God." Hernandez raised his hands skyward for a second then zeroed his attention in on her again. "Webber understandably wants to spend more time at home, enjoy life again, reconnect with his wife, so I'm considering candidates to fill his position. You're at the top of my list, Captain Williams."

"Oh." Stunned, she just sat there a second, wide-eyed. Of all the things she thought this meeting could have been about, that wasn't it. "Um, wow. I don't know what to say, sir. Thank you for considering me."

"You check all the boxes. You're smart, ambitious, hardworking, knowledgeable, and all your crew members speak very highly of your leadership skills."

Huh. That explained the nods and smiles she'd gotten over the past few days, then.

"There's an increase in rank, of course, but also a substantial raise in pay as well," the chief continued.

"Webber's planning on retiring next month, so I'd like to get someone into the position as soon as possible to make the transition a smooth one. You'd be overseeing not just the fire stations here on Key West but throughout the other Keys as well, and you'd report directly to Assistant Chief Mercer. Sound like something you'd be interested in?"

It was what she'd worked for since she'd transferred to Key West, honestly. She'd just never expected it to happen so quickly. Then again, a lot of things in her life had happened fast—meeting Luis at that party, getting pregnant with Miguel, suddenly finding Luis again after five years apart. Overall, those quick changes had been good things. Given her situation, she'd be a fool to turn it down. But she needed to talk with Luis first. It was only fair, since he'd talked to her about the Honduras mission trip, even if she'd handled it badly.

She owed him that. Owed him so much more, truthfully.

And it was debt she hoped she'd get a chance to repay a millionfold in the future.

"I'm flattered to be your top pick, sir. Really. But could I have a few days to think it over?" she asked, hands clenched in her lap to hide their tremble. Excitement and astonishment and anxiety sizzled through her in an intoxicating mix. "There's someone I need to discuss it with first."

"Ah, of course, Captain Williams." Chief Hernandez grinned. "Absolutely. How about we meet again on Friday and you can give me your answer then?"

"Perfect." Stacy stood and shook his hand. "Again, I really appreciate your support and confidence in me, sir. I'll speak with you again in a few days."

Stacy walked out of the office and bit back a whoop of joy. Life was funny. A few weeks ago, they'd experienced the wrath of Mathilda, with all the danger and destruction the storm brought with it. A few more weeks before that, Luis had just been a brilliant memory from her past, one she'd never expected to see again. Now, all her dreams seemed to be coming true professionally, while her personal life hung in the balance.

She walked back to her office, pulling out her phone along the way to see a text from Lucy on her screen.

Service dog ready for Miguel next week. Will call later with details.

Yep, dreams coming true all around.

Her son would have his canine companion just in time for the start of school, and if Stacy's good luck held, she might have a chance to see Luis again, too. Even if he didn't take her back, hopefully they could at least reconcile enough to keep things peaceful between them for Miguel's sake.

Miguel loved his daddy.

Stacy did, too.

So much she ached.

Please, God. Please let him forgive me. Please help us find our way past this and back to good again.

She looked up just in time to avoid colliding with Harley and Jeffrey, who were loitering by her office door, looking suspicious. "What? No fires to put out today, guys?"

"Uh, we actually just got a call, Captain," Jeffrey said, following her into the room. "Waiting on you to go."

Stacy frowned. "I didn't hear the alarm go off."

"No. It's a nonemergency run, but they requested fire backup," Harley said, filling the doorway with his muscled frame, arms crossed and expression unreadable. "We're ready when you are."

"You guys go on ahead," she said, sitting down at her desk. "I've got some things to catch up on here before I go home to Miguel."

The two exchanged a look, then moved to flank her sides.

"No can do, Captain," Jeffrey said. He was in his early twenties and was still filling out his height, all gangly legs and long arms. At her pointed look, his cheeks reddened. "I mean, we really need you on this one, Captain."

"Why?" The adrenaline from her meeting earlier with the chief was quickly burning away to annoyance. "If it's nonessential, then you don't need a full crew. You and Harley grab a couple more people and go. I have things to do here."

Things like calling Luis and setting up a time to talk.

"Uh…there is no one else," Harley said. "I sent them all to lunch."

"All of them?" She gave her crew member an incredulous look then glanced at the clock. "It's almost three in the afternoon. A bit late for lunch, isn't it?"

"We were busy earlier." Harley shrugged. "So we need you to come with us to make up the numbers."

"Guys?" She called on the last threads of her rapidly fraying patience. "What is going on?"

"Just come on, Captain," Jeffrey said, his tone pleading. "Please?"

Irritated and intrigued, she finally gave up and walked out of her office and out to the truck bay with them. "This better be good," she said, pulling on her gear then climbing into the back of the truck with Jeffrey. "And it better not take too long. I need to get home to Miguel before my neighbor leaves for work."

"Won't take long, Captain," Harley said, steering the big rig out of the bay and onto the street. "And it will definitely be good. Promise."

Alarm bells went off inside Stacy's head. Something was going on, but as they headed away from the station toward downtown Key West, all she could do was sit back and enjoy the ride.

Luis had been running around all morning, from one case to the next. Busy was good, especially today. It kept him from being too nervous about what he had planned.

"Any word on those blood work results for the patient in trauma bay one?" he asked one of the nurses at the desk.

"Let me check, Doc," she said, typing on her computer. "Nope. Nothing yet. Oh." The nurse reached down under the desk and pulled out a small cage, setting it on the counter near Luis. "Your abdominal pain patient we just sent up to surgery had this in his car. Asked if you would keep an eye on it for him. I've been trying to get him to eat, but I don't think he's feeling well."

Luis sighed and peered into the cage at the small turtle there, chewing on a leaf nearly twice his size. "Great. Looks like it's you and me, buddy. Can you put him in my office for me?"

"Sure thing, Doc," she said before heading off down the hall, cage in hand.

They were a bit short staffed today, so he was helping out wherever he could at this point. Luis had just started going through a stack of patient files when his brother, Jackson, arrived. His brother looked like hell, dark circles under his eyes and lines around his mouth from stress. From his dark scowl, Luis imagined Jackson probably felt like hell, too. He wanted to know why but was smart enough not to ask at this point.

"Feeling better, Mr. Regional Director?" Luis asked, staring down at his files again.

"Yeah." From his brother's gruff tone, it sounded like the exact opposite. At Luis's arched brow, Jackson leaned his elbow on the counter. "I guess."

"Problems with the leg laceration?" Luis arched a brow as he continued jotting notes in his chart.

"Nope. Lucy did a good job fixing me up."

"Well, I'm glad someone finally did." Luis couldn't help a little snark, hoping it might cheer his brother up a bit. Didn't seem to work, however, as Jackson's dark frown stayed firmly in place.

"Uh, can we talk?" Jackson asked.

Luis stared at him for a moment, then handed his chart to the nurse behind the desk before gesturing for Jackson to follow him down the hall to his office. He had about a half an hour before his big plans got underway. Would do him good not to dwell on it, considering how nervous he was. He just hoped the fire crew got Stacy here on time or else it would all be for naught. He walked into his office and gestured toward the chairs in front of the desk without looking. "Have a seat."

Whoops. Luis turned around just in time to see the

turtle cage on the chair where the nurse had left it. He gestured his brother away. "Other chair."

Jackson barely stopped himself in time then straightened and looked behind him, biting off a curse. The tiny creature blinked up at him. "Why's there a baby turtle in your office?"

Heat climbed Luis's cheeks as he thought of Stacy and Miguel again. His son would love a pet. They'd talked about it on several occasions. He knew Stacy was getting him a service dog, but maybe a turtle would be good, too. He'd have to talk to Stacy about it later, if things went well today...

"The poor thing's not feeling well," Luis said, pointing at the turtle. "We can't get him to eat."

Jackson looked at him. "We?"

"His owner is stuck in the hospital, and there was no one to care for the poor thing, so I thought Stacy and I..."

Damn. Realizing he'd said too much, Luis shut up fast. Awkward silence fell as he hoped his brother wouldn't notice, but Jackson was too sharp for that.

Jackson blinked at him a moment, and Luis knew his anticipation was written all over his face. He couldn't help it. He loved Stacy, more than any woman he'd ever loved before. And he loved Miguel, too, more than he ever thought it was possible to love another human being. He planned to tell them that today. He also planned to tell them he wasn't going anywhere.

He'd phoned Xavier back and given him the names of three other doctors who were as experienced with search and rescue or more so than Luis himself. He was tired of traveling, tired of danger and distress. He was ready to settle down and start a family, start a future with Stacy and Miguel.

If they'd still have him.

Luis glanced at the clock then sat back in his chair, shifting his attention from the growing bubble of nervous energy inside him and toward his brother across from him. He narrowed his gaze on his brother's strained expression. "You haven't been the same since you came back from Big Pine Key. Something else happened during the hurricane."

It wasn't a question.

He and Jackson had always had a special bond, and they trusted each other completely. He'd implied what was happening between himself and Stacy and hoped his brother might confide in him as well.

After a long moment, Jackson sighed and stared down at his feet. "Maybe."

Right. His brother was a secretive person, especially about matters of the heart, so his answer spoke volumes. "I thought so." Luis gave a short laugh. "So, what are you going to do about her?"

Jackson stared at Luis a moment, as if coming to some decision, the turned to the baby turtle again. "You care if I take this little guy off your hands for a bit?"

"Why?"

"I think a vet should take a look at him."

Luis gave a lopsided smile then came around the desk to hand him the crate. "Take good care of him, brother. He belongs to my patient."

"Will do." Jackson peered inside the front of the cage, walked to the door, then turned back. "My shift's over, so I might be gone for a few—"

"Take whatever you need. My patient won't be released for a few more days."

Jackson nodded. "Thanks, brother. I owe you one."

"Yes, you do." Luis chuckled, following Jackson out into the hall then stopping to check his watch again. Five minutes. Right. He took off his lab coat and tossed it back in his office, then checked his reflection in the glass on his door as he left. His blue scrubs weren't ideal for what he planned to do, but they were who he was. Stacy knew that. He'd showered and shaved before coming in, and his curly hair was still relatively behaved. He smoothed a hand over it, then peeked into the pocket on his scrub shirt to make sure his precious cargo was still in there. Check.

"Doc, incoming," one of the nurses said from down the hall. She winked at him then left in a flurry of squeaky shoes on linoleum. "Good luck!"

Luis said a silent prayer, then headed out to the automatic doors near the ambulance bay just as a fire truck pulled up outside, horn honking and sirens wailing to announce their arrival. He walked outside into the warm day, heart pounding and blood racing. Several doctors and nurses had already gathered there, along with a couple off-duty EMTs and a good chunk of Stacy's fire crew. Even Reed and his wife were there, standing off to the side with his walker, under the shade of the portico, grinning from ear to ear.

Stacy climbed out of the back of the truck looking confused and thoroughly annoyed. She glanced around then turned back to the driver. "Harley, what the hell is going on?"

The burly guy behind the wheel walked around the truck to stand before Stacy as a second firefighter, a young guy, climbed out behind Stacy then shut the door on the rig. For a moment, Luis stood there, on the brink of everything he wanted and nothing he'd ever expected, before striding forward to Stacy.

"They brought you here for me," he said, gazing into her beautiful blue eyes. She was dressed in her gear and her hair was pulled back in a ponytail as usual, her only makeup the gloss on her lips. Luis had never seen a more gorgeous sight in his life.

She opened her mouth, then closed it, finally saying, "Hi."

"Hi," he whispered back. Part of him wanted to fall to one knee right there and beg her to be his forever, but he had some things to say first, so he swallowed hard and continued. "I asked your crew to bring you here today because I need to tell you that I love you, Stacy Williams. I've loved you since that first night on the beach, and these past few weeks with you and Miguel have been the best of my life. I've loved every minute of getting to know you and our son. I've loved making you laugh and sitting with you when you cry. I've loved getting our son ready for the day and reading to Miguel at night. But most of all, I've loved being a family with you and Miguel. Being with you both made me realize that I don't need to rush off to far-flung lands to make a difference. I can do that right here, in this hospital, in this community, with you. With Miguel. I want to do that, now and forever."

Hope and hesitation flashed in Stacy's eyes. "What about Honduras?"

"The charity is well staffed now for Honduras, or for any other disasters that might come in the foreseeable future. They don't need me anymore. I'm needed right here, with you. At least, I pray I am." He reached into the pocket of his scrubs and pulled out the small velvet box, creaking it open before kneeling on the cold cement. He took her trembling hand in his and held her teary blue gaze. "Stacy Williams, I know there is much we still need to learn about each other, but I want to be there with you every step of the way. Now, today and always. Will you marry me?"

"I..." She stared down at him, cheeks damp and pink, and he lived and died in those few seconds.

Then a voice yelled from the small crowd surrounding them, followed by a high-pitched squeal of delight. Miguel. The little boy rushed up to them, quivering with joy. "Daddy! Are you coming back? Please, Mommy! Please can Daddy come stay with us forever?"

Stacy looked from Luis to Miguel then back again. "How did you get here?"

"Ms. Abrams brought me." Miguel pointed over to the neighbor from Stacy's apartment complex who'd been babysitting him. "She said Daddy called her this morning."

Luis shrugged up at Stacy and grinned. "I thought he should have some say in the matter, too. Since he's the one who brought us back together again."

Her blue eyes widened, and then she sniffled and knelt before him, her one hand still in Luis's and her other on Miguel's back, bringing their son closer. "I'm sorry."

His heart sank. "For what?"

"For what I said the other night. I shouldn't have made you choose like that. It wasn't fair. If your passion is helping people, then that's what you should do and I should love you and want you because of that, not despite it. And I do." She sniffled and blinked hard before meeting his gaze again. "Love you, I mean. Unconditionally. Uncontrollably. Irrevocably."

"Me, too, Daddy!" Miguel chimed in. "Irre… Irre… Irrevascably!"

Miguel bungled the word completely and Luis couldn't have cared less. In fact, it was probably the most adorable and sweetest thing he'd ever heard.

"So," he said, his voice thick with emotion. "Will you marry me?"

His gaze darted from mother to son then back again.

Stacy gave him a watery smile then nodded. "Yes. I'll marry you."

Whoops and cheers and applause rose from the gathered crowd, drawing even more people out of the hospital to see what was going on. Luis let Stacy go to slide the ring on her finger, then pulled her and Miguel into a group hug, kissing them both on the cheek. When Miguel scampered off back to Ms. Abrams, and the crowds began dispersing, he pulled Stacy closer, cupping the back of her head, relishing the silky softness of her hair and how her soft curves molded perfectly to his hard edges. This was what he wanted. Just this, for the rest of his life. "Thank you."

Now, it was her turn to ask, "For what?"

"For everything."

She laughed. "Better hold that thought a second. I forgot to tell you that my boss offered me a battalion chief position today. It's more money, but it's also more responsibility, which means more work. Are you okay with me taking it?"

"I'm okay with it if you're okay." He smiled. "I just want you to be happy. As happy as you've made me."

"I'll think about it," she said. "Depends on how soon we plan to expand our family."

"Expand, eh?" His heart expanded in his chest to the point it was hard to breathe, and he just gathered her close, grinning. "Is that what we're going to do next?"

"Maybe," she said after a moment of holding him. "If you want to, I mean."

He drew in a deep lungful of her scent, then he felt a huge grin stretch his lips. "Oh, yes, *mi sirenita*. I want to. Very, very much."

CHAPTER FOURTEEN

One month later

THE WHOLE ERT team was gathered in the back room of the Duck Bill Pub on Duval Street to celebrate the return to readiness level one and the successful ongoing efforts at cleanup after Hurricane Mathilda. Life wasn't one hundred percent back to normal, but it was closer than before.

For Jackson and Lucy and Luis and Stacy, it was better than ever.

"I'd like to offer a toast," Luis said, standing at the front of the large room, a bottle of dark ale in his hand. "To my brother, Jackson Durand, for guiding us all through the crisis with a steady hand and a clear vision. The ambulance authority is lucky to have you as regional director."

"Hear, hear," the rest of the team cheered, clinking glasses and laughing.

"And to Dr. Luis Durand," Jackson said, hoisting his own bottle of craft beer high. "Who took over for me on short notice and kept things running properly in my absence. You run the best damned ER in Florida, man, and you're an asset to the Keys."

"And to Battalion Chief Stacy Williams," one of the firefighters said. "Congrats on the promotion!"

Another rousing cheer went up, followed by a new Jimmy Buffett tune piped in through the overhead sound system. Pretty soon people broke up into groups, dancing or talking or indulging in the excellent taco bar set up against one wall of the private room.

Jackson settled back down at his table with Lucy and rubbed her service dog Sam's side under the table with his foot. The dog went pretty much everywhere with them, as did King, Jackson's kitten, whose cage was on the seat beside him. Actually, the kitten was more cat now than anything, taller and leaner, moving fine on three legs.

Lucy reached across the table and took his hand, beaming with joy, and his heart squeezed with sweetness. Jackson was a lucky, lucky man, and he knew it. Life had given him a second chance in Lucy, and he refused to take it for granted, not for a second.

Luis and Stacy came over and sat in the chairs opposite them, holding hands and kissing, unable to keep their hands off each other. Jackson had never known his reserved brother to be so open with his public displays of affection before, but then he'd never seen Luis so in love before, either.

It was weird and wonderful, that they'd both found their soul mates during the hurricane. But considering how unconventional their childhoods had been, why should their love lives be any different?

"We have an announcement to make," Luis said, his arm around Stacy's shoulders.

"What?" Lucy asked, her fingers tightening on Jackson's. She didn't do well with surprises, and he brought her hand to his lips, kissing it, hoping to reassure her that whatever it was, they'd handle it together. "Something good, I hope?"

"We think so," Stacy said, glancing at Luis. "We're having a baby. I'm pregnant."

"Dude!" Jackson grinned. "Congratulations. That's awesome!"

"I'm so happy for you!" Lucy hugged her friend then took her seat once more, lacing her fingers with Jackson's again. "I'm going to be an aunt again."

"Yes, you are." Luis kissed Stacy then rested his head against hers. "And Miguel's going to be an older brother."

"Have you told him yet?" Jackson asked.

"Not yet," Stacy said. "You guys are the first to know, so don't tell anyone, please."

"Promise." Jackson took another sip of beer, aware of the lump in his jeans pocket. He had a secret himself, one he hoped would result in a happy announcement, too. But he had to ask Lucy first, and for that he needed a bit of privacy. So, after one more swig of alcohol for courage, he stood and looked down at the woman he loved. "Let's take a walk on the beach."

"Oh…uh…" She looked from him to Luis and Stacy. "What about Sam?"

"We can watch him for you for a second," Stacy said, winking. "Go on."

Luis held up his bottle. "Go for it, brother."

Jackson took a deep breath and led Lucy out of the pub and down the street toward the beach. Tourists were beginning to flock back to the area, but it was still not as crowded as usual, which was good, since he hoped to find a secluded spot for his special proposal.

They strolled along the sand, hand in hand, to a spot where a few sea-swept boulders lined the shore. He helped Lucy up to take a seat on one of them, then climbed up beside her. For a long moment, they just sat side by side, watching the sunset as the sky erupted in fiery reds and oranges and deeper purples. It felt right. It felt perfect. It felt like forever.

And speaking of forever…

"Uh… Lucy," he said, moving away slightly to pull the small velvet box from his pocket. "There's something I want to ask you."

Her dark eyes widened as she looked from his hand to his eyes. "What?"

"I know it's only been a month, and I just moved in with you at the compound, but I wanted to give you something to show how much you mean to me, how invested I am in this relationship and how I plan to be around for as long as you'll have me."

"Oh God…" She covered her mouth with a shaky hand. "What are you…?"

He opened the box to reveal a sparkling diamond engagement ring. "Lucy Miller, will you marry me?"

Tears welled in her lovely eyes, and she bit her lip. "Jackson. I…" She sniffled then nodded fast. "Yes! Yes, I'll marry you. I mean, not right now. We have lots of stuff to work out first. But someday. We'll need to pick a date. Not an odd day. An even one. I'll need to look at my calendar and find out when we…"

He kissed her, as much to distract her from her tic as just because he wanted to. "I love you, Lucy. Everything about you."

She smiled through her tears and hugged him tight. "Even with my quirks?"

"Because of your quirks," he said, squeezing her tight then pulling back. "Should we go tell the others now?"

Lucy admired her ring then nodded. "Yep. Let's go make an announcement of our own."

* * * * *

MILLS & BOON

Coming next month

HOW TO WIN THE SURGEON'S HEART
Tina Beckett

'Okay. Nate…"

Except saying his given name…out loud…made whatever she'd been about to say vanish. So she just stood there, taking in his casual clothing, that was now rumpled in a way that was somehow wonderful. The hard lines of his body were more visible now, and she was having a difficult time looking away. Her gaze trailed up his face, noting there were dark circles under his eyes, probably from the stress of the day. She imagined he put in long hours most every day. A little far removed from the lap-of-luxury living she'd pictured him in over in this corner of the island.

"Not so hard, after all, was it?"

"W-what?" Had he read her thoughts?

"Saying my name."

Her senses went on high alert as an image of her whispering his name in an entirely different way scurried through her head, only to run away when she tried to catch it and banish it. Instead, the two beds in the room behind her seemed to taunt her, to remind her of how long it had been since she'd been with anyone.

She cleared her throat. "Maybe I was being a little silly when we met. I'd just heard stories…"

"Stories?" His frown was back. "Such as?"

Um, not happening. Because the words delectable and delicious had been interjected time and time again. "Nothing bad."

That line in his face played peekaboo. "I find that rather hard to believe."

"That nothing bad was said?"

He made a sound of assent. "Are you saying *you've* never had an unkind thing to say about me?"

Ugh. She'd had lots of unkind things to say. Patty had called her on it time and time again. But then again, her friend was a newlywed, still caught up in the early stages of love.

Her lips twitched. "Maybe you'll have to work on changing my mind."

"Is that a challenge…Sasha?"

The shock of hearing her name on his tongue washed over her like the waves of the sea. Warm. Sensual. Snaking up her calves, edging over her hips and making her nipples tighten.

Some dangerous part of her brain sent the word, "Maybe" from her mouth before she could stop it.

And when his hand moved from the railing and slid up her forearm, she was powerless to stop from leaning toward him, her eyes closing.

"That's one challenge I might have to accept."

Continue reading
HOW TO WIN THE SURGEON'S HEART
Tina Beckett

Available next month
www.millsandboon.co.uk

COMING SOON!

We really hope you enjoyed reading this book.
If you're looking for more romance, be sure to
head to the shops when new books are
available on

Thursday 24th June

To see which titles are coming soon, please visit

millsandboon.co.uk/nextmonth

MILLS & BOON

THE HEART OF ROMANCE

A ROMANCE FOR EVERY READER

MODERN

Prepare to be swept off your feet by sophisticated, sexy and seductive heroes, in some of the world's most glamourous and romantic locations, where power and passion collide.

HISTORICAL

Escape with historical heroes from time gone by. Whether your passion is for wicked Regency Rakes, muscled Vikings or rugged Highlanders, awak the romance of the past.

MEDICAL

Set your pulse racing with dedicated, delectable doctors in the high-pressure world of medicine, where emotions run high and passion, comfort ar love are the best medicine.

True Love

Celebrate true love with tender stories of heartfelt romance, from the rush of falling in love to the joy a new baby can bring, and a focus on the emotional heart of a relationship.

Desire

Indulge in secrets and scandal, intense drama and plenty of sizzling hot action with powerful and passionate heroes who have it all: wealth, status, good looks…everything but the right woman.

HEROES

Experience all the excitement of a gripping thriller, with an intense romance at its heart. Resourceful, true-to-life women and strong, fearless me face danger and desire - a killer combination!

To see which titles are coming soon, please visit

millsandboon.co.uk/nextmonth